THE COUNTESS

Books by Hans Habe

Ilona
Devil's Agent
Off Limits
Our Love Affair with Germany
Black Earth
Walk in Darkness
Aftermath
Kathrine
A Thousand Shall Fall
Sixteen Days
Three Over the Frontier

THE COUNTESS

HANS HABE

Translated from the German by Catherine Hutter

Harcourt, Brace & World, Inc. / New York

c.1

First American edition 1963
First published in German under the title *Die Tarnowska*
Library of Congress Catalog Card Number: 63-17770
Printed in the United States of America

The historic events described in this book are historic facts;
in a few places, locality and time were inessentially changed.
In the interpretation of the statutes of the Dominican Order,
the author adhered as much as possible to the actual instructions. The figure of the Master General is fictitious. Since
most of the Biblical quotes appear in connection with the
Dominican friar, Andrey Antonovich Vyrubov, the Saint
Joseph New Catholic Edition of the Holy Bible has been used
for all Bible quotations.

For Licci, of course

The Search for Maria Tarnovska
A Prologue

It all began in Vienna, 1930. I counted among my friends a man named Raoul Korthy. He was a collector of photographs. Compulsive, perhaps obsessed, a lovable eccentric. His collection contained more than a million prints. He loved them as a collector of paintings loves his Degas or Renoirs. They were neither indexed nor catalogued. When he died, they became worthless.

One day I was looking through his collection and came across a picture that captured me at once. It showed a slender young woman dressed in the widow's weeds of the turn of the century. Lovely, enchanting. She was being aided up the steps of the Palace of Justice in Venice by *carabinieri* in their anachronistic Napoleonic uniforms. An inadvertent witness to some crime? Possibly the widow of some unfortunate who had met death through violence? No, Korthy explained, she was a murderess; and she was in mourning for the man she was accused of murdering. It was then that I heard the name Countess Maria Tarnovska for the first time.

That was more than thirty years ago; I was just twenty, and I began —casually at first—to trace the history of the woman's fate. Whenever I came to Venice, the image of her photograph haunted me. I searched for material. In an antique bookshop, the Countess Tarnovska's memoirs fell into my hands. It was a faded volume, a sparse document, mendacious, as yellow in content as time had made its paper. And, on page 269, the picture I had seen at Korthy's. Now I had to find out the truth.

Four years ago, my wife and I began our journey into the past. We already carried with us the records of public and secret legal proceedings, police investigations, and psychiatrists' findings; whole volumes of letters; historic documents from Tsarist Russia, the land where Maria was born. And then we were standing in the Palace of Justice in Venice; black leather armchairs, pigeons on the window sills above the vegetable market. "We don't have anything but sensational cases here," the guide told us. The last one was Italy's *Dolce Vita* case, the Montesi affair. Nothing changes, obviously. Later, at the San Michele Cemetery, we found the grave of the murdered Count Pavel. Later still, we stood in front of the house on the former Campo Santa Maria del Giglio where he had been murdered.

From Venice to Rome. My visions had taken on the substance of reality; now reality was leading to visions. Could I see the figure of the Dominican friar, Father Andrey, disappearing through the gates of the monastery of Santa Maria sopra Minerva, standing beside the tomb of Torquemada? The Dominicans answered my questions readily and fearlessly. Andrey, fearless; some parts of the huge puzzle fit together.

And then we were traveling south, the highway paralleling the railroad tracks. The sun burned down upon us. For miles not a soul; suddenly a few mules and white dust. The scent of acacias. "The looped vines," Maria had written, "like slim green dancers holding hands." Her forehead pressed against the train window—what must she have thought? Where had fate taken her, from the snowy plains of Russia?

In Trani, a parched city on the Adriatic coast of Italy, we asked for the women's penitentiary and were shown the way with indifference; no one came here unless it was to visit a prisoner. The last nun who knew Maria Tarnovska was dead, but she had told the others about their famous prisoner. The cell—unchanged. Italy.

The trip through reality was over; now the journey toward truth began.

I have had to invent a great deal; facts are not truth. I have had to omit some things; life is not always plausible. Yet, there were certain events I would scarcely have dared to write if I had not seen them documented in the files of the case—Maria's visit to the grave of the murdered man, the duel in Kossino, the years of her addiction, the vow by Tioka's life, the death of Alexis, Stahl's seduction. Most of the characters here portrayed lived. The others, I hope, could have lived. What matters is to breathe truth into reality.

In a quest so long pursued, it is inevitable that the novelist ask

viii

himself what compelled him to follow a course as strange as the life of Maria Tarnovska. The photograph, certainly, was merely a signpost. What was it?

First, perhaps, the drama of an extraordinary life, breathless in its startling events, wonderfully susceptible to a sweeping narrative. Yes, that was an undeniable lure—and why should the narrator deny it?

Then the discovery that almost all we see today—the sickness of our epoch, the coming of happy and unhappy knowledge, the impatience of our evolution, the paradoxical predominance of sex in the time of soul-searching—all this was already caught up in the life and downfall of the Countess.

And then again, other elements. The times we like to call "ours" originated in the East, some time between 1880 and 1905. Not only the sun, but darkness, too, can rise in the East. What is happening now, symbolized by *la dolce vita* on Rome's Via Vittorio Veneto, began half a century ago on the Tverskaya Boulevard in Moscow.

Between the fall of Maria Tarnovska and the day she was called to account, a new arm of science, psychoanalysis, was born. It shed light into areas until then shrouded in total darkness. But light alone does not grant men the courage to look openly into the impenetrable, nor does it convey the wisdom to understand what is seen. A world fighting pain as never before suffers more than ever.

When I first pursued the story of Maria, I thought of it as something that had happened a long time ago. Now I am not so sure. Was it, perhaps, only yesterday? Is it today? Or tomorrow? An ancient poet first suggested that truth is the daughter of time. In time, then, we may know more, not of Maria, but of ourselves.

—Hans Habe

Ascona, Switzerland
Summer, 1963

CONTENTS

CHARACTERS

Count Nikolay Vladimirovich O'Rourke, Knight Marshal of the Province of Poltava

Countess Katharina O'Rourke, née Seletzka, his wife

Maria Nikolaevna O'Rourke, Countess Tarnovska, his daughter

Olga Nikolaevna O'Rourke, Princess Katerinovich, his daughter

Count Nikolay Nikolaevich O'Rourke, his son by first marriage

Count Tioka Vassilyevich Tarnovsky, Maria's son

Count Andrey Antonovich Vyrubov, a Dominican friar

Count Vassily Vassilyevich Tarnovsky, a nobleman from Charkov

Count Peter Vassilyevich Tarnovsky, his younger brother

Sergey Ivanovich Burintzev, student and revolutionary

Baron Vladimir Mihailovich Stahl, a drug addict

Count Pavel Ergrafovich Kamarovsky, fiancé of the Countess Tarnovska

Donat Dmitrievich Prilukov, lawyer in Moscow

Nicholas Gregorievich Naumov, son of the Governor of Orel

Count Alexis Ivanovich Bozevsky, "the handsomest officer in His Imperial Majesty's Guard"

The Master General of the Dominican Order

Count Antonio Tusitano, President of the Provincial Court presiding over the Tarnovska case

Professor Enrico Ceresa, a psychiatrist

Giorgio Garzoni, Public Prosecutor

Commendatore Roberto Randi, Public Prosecutor

Cavalliere Francesco Vecchini, lawyer for the defense

Dr. Hugo Friedlieber, a journalist from Vienna

Elise Perrier, a Swiss maid

BOOK I

THE INQUIRY

Fictionized life of beautiful Russo-
Irish Countess Maria Tarnovska who is
brought to trial in Venice for persuading
one of her lovers to murder another.

CHAPTER 1

I

The men came up to Maria Tarnovska without doffing their hats. She then knew that they had come to arrest her. She was accustomed to men greeting her—those she knew and those she didn't know—obsequiously, admiringly, provocatively. These two did not.

The Countess hated the dirty familiarity of railway stations. People scattered the dirt before them, and the dirt scattered them. Right now she could think of nothing but Tioka. Her son was getting out of the sleeper. Elise Perrier was helping him. He was twelve; he still enjoyed railway stations. He paid no attention to the two men. His mother was always surrounded by men.

The Countess leaned down and gave him a quick kiss. "We'll meet at the hotel." One of the men took her arm; she didn't remonstrate. She saw her maid's face. Elise Perrier was smiling. Her smile was like the light music that in some places in the south accompanies the burial of a child.

Maria Tarnovska thought of the cocaine she was carrying in her luggage. Cocaine, love letters, obscene photographs. And the switch made of the branches she had broken off the willow tree on Vladimir Stahl's grave. They would examine her luggage. She was not ashamed, only afraid.

The locomotive let off a last puff of steam. It was the breath of a dying man. The soot-blackened man went home to his wife and children. The Countess hated and envied him for his contentment. She stepped on some apple peel. The officer steadied her. "Thank you," she said.

She should have protested, but that would have attracted Tioka's

3

attention. Recalcitrant criminals were ridiculous. The powerless protectors of the law were only protecting their absurd power.

In front of the station, the men stood still, all in black, with bowler hats—mourning relatives with a widow. They looked like twins. Proletarians who came in contact with society only when she fell at their feet, a rotten fruit.

A cab drove up, an ugly, black cubicle drawn by a lean horse. One of the twins sat beside the driver; the other beside Maria Tarnovska, his heavy cane between his knees.

The closed cab, not recognizable as a police vehicle, still looked strange among the open carriages. It was the seventh of September, 1907, an afternoon that was hurrying to catch up with the vanished summer. The sky was a restless blue. Families were returning from their vacations, gay and already oppressed. Cab drivers sat with their legs hunched over wicker luggage; fathers, mothers, children, squashed in the back seats.

At last Maria Tarnovska turned and addressed the man at her side. "What do you want of me?"

He didn't answer; he didn't look at her. He was afraid. That was nothing new to her; most men were frightened by her. But this man feared her only because duty had sent him out on a shiny parquetry.

She took a lace handkerchief out of her purse, sprinkled perfume on it, held it to her nose. Now the officer was watching her from the side.

She had traveled a day, a night, and half another day, from Kiev to Vienna. Had she expected to be arrested? She had slept during the day and lain awake at night. Day and night had merged. Dreamless the nights, the days, nightmares. Vladimir Stahl's grave; Nicholas' vow; her mother's grave; children laughing. The house in Otrada; the tinkling of a piano; the rabid dog; the French governess; the groom; Andrey in his Dominican habit; children laughing. The doctor in Alexis' hotel room; the cigarettes; the flogged man; Elise's laughter behind her tears; birth pains; Vladimir with a hypodermic needle; children laughing; morphine; the fall over the precipice. You fell, fell, into blessedness. Donat, Donat again and again; behind drapes, behind balcony doors, behind the bath house. The lamentation of train wheels. From next door, Tioka's laughter. Elise Perrier: "Is there anything else I can do for you, madame?" Stations, dirt, people. Her

4

conscience wasn't dead; it only belonged to someone else. Her life had been unbelievable, that was why she couldn't believe it had happened. They said that atonement could wash away fear. Cocaine, love letters, obscene pictures, the switch with which she had flogged Nicholas. Tioka would ask questions. Elise would laugh and cry.

Where was the telegram? Pavel's telegram, which she had received three days ago, addressed to his *dushka,* in his sickening style? The telegram alone could prove her innocence. No one would call for his murderess. There were no miracles. She had forgotten the telegram in her dressing case, as if she were driving to the Hotel Sacher with her child and her maid, while another woman was rattling through the tremulous afternoon in a black cube. She wondered, Should she say anything? But the officers hadn't said a word about the assassination of Count Kamarovsky. She would do better not to mention the name.

The shadows of the suburban barracks fell on the asphalt as if their walls wanted to sink down after them. Houses like that had stood along the tracks. Soon they would be in Venice. Pavel would come to meet her. Their gondola would rock gently across the Canale Grande. "I am glad you came, *dushka.*" Passing under the Bridge of Sighs. Liveried pages would open the door of the Hotel Danieli for them. . . .

"Get out!" said the man in black.

2

In the police station on the Rossauer Laende, the policemen were at home; they weren't on a shiny parquetry any longer. They were joined by other uniformed proletarians. One of them took the Countess' handbag from her. Keys, earrings, a comb, a gold cigarette case, a locket with two miniatures were emptied out onto a table. One of the men barked at her: "We don't steal around here," and handed her a receipt. "Cigarette case, gold, one . . ." They told her to take off her hat. They stood around her, staring at her as if she were undressing. Her dark blond hair was untidy; the light streaks in it looked white. She picked up her comb from the table. One of the officers made a note of the hatpins. "Pearl. Not real. Three."

She roused herself out of her lethargy when she was told to remove her shoelaces. She had on high, two-tone shoes; only the tips showed under her dress. She refused to comply. A young man, cheeks like an unripe plum, kneeled down, touched the hem of her skirt. The toe of her shoe hit him in the stomach. He rolled back. The others laughed.

An old man with a gold collar appeared. She had to rise. Standing, she gave her particulars. Countess Maria Nikolaevna Tarnovska, born Countess O'Rourke. Thirty years old. Born in Otrada, near Kiev, province of Poltava, June 9, 1877. Married to Count Vassily Tarnovsky. Marriage annulled. Two children. Citizenship, Russian. The man with the gold collar ordered her to be led away.

The corridors were empty. Although the windows were open, there was a smell of urine, odor of schools and prisons. She could hear the singing of a hurdy-gurdy man. She was astonished that she could feel nothing. Once Alexis had told her, "Grief devours itself; pain is the best narcotic." Alexis had been permitted to die under an anesthetic of grief and pain. She thought of Tioka. For his sake she could not let herself fall into merciful oblivion.

Abruptly, she stopped. At the end of a dimly lit corridor, a glass door opened. Between two guards, a man emerged whom she had thought in safety. Donat Dmitrievich Prilukov was handcuffed, but he had on a light, elegant summer suit, and a *borsellino,* as if he were coming out of a restaurant, or from the races. He came forward, staggering like a drunkard. His hat sat lopsided on his head; he laughed and rattled his chains like a tipsy tambourine player. As he was led past her, he stopped, raised his chained hands to his head, shoved his hat off his forehead. He bowed ceremoniously, made a formal scrape with his right leg, repeated the word *"Molci!"* twice, and did not protest when one of the guards rammed his hat back on his head. Finally he withdrew with grotesque dignity. Now the Countess knew that he was neither drunk nor insane. He had behaved foolishly so that the police might take the command "Be silent!" for a Russian salutation.

A plaque with the inscription "Hofrat Dr. Emil Stuckart" passed by her. She recalled Donat's first letter. "Wherever you go, I shall go. Wherever you are, I shall be there. Only death shall part us, because then devils will tear me from your side for fear I might mistake hell for heaven." They were both in hell, but not dead. *"Molci!"* She would be silent, not because Donat had ordered it, but because with every word one became more confused. Blessed were the mute. And the deaf. And the blind. Not to speak, to hear, to see!

When they left her alone with Hofrat Stuckart, tiredness fell from her. She was afraid only of plebeians, and the Hofrat was not a plebeian. She smoothed her hair and sat down. "They took my hat," she said.

"Because of the hatpins, Countess." She appreciated the fact that he addressed her as "Countess," without the plebeian "Frau."

Hofrat Stuckart sat down at his desk. Striped trousers, gray hair, well groomed, he looked like a hotel receptionist inquiring as to the wishes of an honored guest who had arrived for a prolonged stay. He spoke the lullaby Viennese of the higher officials—soothing, half asleep, yet in intricate language and stilted terms.

"Your apprehension," he began, "occurred at the instigation of the Italian authorities—the Venetian police, to be specific. What I now have to state may not necessarily be unfamiliar to you, but I am compelled to confront you with it—those are the rules of law. On the morning of September 3, therefore, the twenty-four-year-old student Nicholas Naumov, son of the governor of Orel, a translator of Baudelaire, and of considerable reputation, well known to you, just arrived in Venice from Kiev, forcibly entered the apartment of your fiancé, Count Pavel Ergrafovich Kamarovsky, on the Campo Santa Maria del Giglio, and with four shots from a revolver wounded the Count grievously. Naumov succeeded in escaping to Verona. He offered no resistance, however, when an alert police officer, Commissar Caruss, detained him in a train compartment just as he was about to buy flowers for a lady. At first Naumov declared he was Belgian, called himself Henri Duran from Brussels, but he soon revealed his true identity and made, remorsefully, it seems, a complete confession. Like quite a few of your people, Countess, young Naumov is inclined to be theatrical—so, when he was signing the statement, he continually looked at his hand, murmuring, 'This is the hand that has killed a man'; kissed a small gold crucifix ecstatically, which, I am sure, sooner or later you will recognize as yours; finally insisted that the Count's last words, which were addressed to him—'My dear young man, why? What harm have I ever done you?'—be entered into the record. In the same confession Naumov declared that he had not acted on his own initiative: on the contrary, you, Countess, had incited him to murder the Count, possibly on the advice of the former attorney, Donat Dmitrievich Prilukov. You had gone so far as to make Naumov swear on the grave of a friend, Captain Baron Vladimir Stahl, not to rest until he had killed your fiancé. He had assured you that he would kill himself rather than betray you, but the weapon he used against himself hadn't worked—this possibly true—so, as unto many a sinner before, instead of death, nothing was left to him but remorse."

After these acrobatics of memory—he hadn't consulted his papers once—Hofrat Stuckart looked at the Countess with interest, without, however, inviting her to make a declaration.

She arranged her clothes, a Paris traveling suit that fitted tightly across her perfectly formed breasts, around her waist, which you could enfold with two hands, down to the narrow wrists of her soft white hands. *Molci, molci,* she thought, as she passed a hand across her taut blouse and wide skirt, as if wanting to convince herself of her own presence. *Molci, molci!*

It wasn't easy. As a child she had gone to confession of her own free will, sometimes in secret. She had invented all sorts of sins, the more terrible, the better. At first she hadn't known what excited her more—her confession, or the horror of her confessor. A sensual excitement it had always been, like at sinful games. In Moscow she had looked upon her confessor as a holy man, until she had heard that he was a hypocrite, a woman chaser who visited bordellos. Her delight ceased. It couldn't be painful for him to hear her sins; for her it was no longer a pleasure to confess them. Later she recognized the wantonness of her behavior and the drive of her audacity; still, for a long time she experienced ecstasy more readily in the confessional than in the beds of her lovers.

The Countess was tempted to confess more to this chief investigator than he expected to hear. That she had promised Nicholas Naumov to lead him on a leash, naked, behind her sled; that Alexis Bozevsky had died while Vladimir Stahl was making love to her in the next room; that she had lain hidden in the grass to see Vassily's blood flow. Carnival night in the Eremitage, and the drive from the cemetery, and the temptation of the Dominican. Now the urge was gone. No horror, and of course no pain on the features of the highly experienced official. She sat up straight.

"You speak of murder, Herr Hofrat," she said. "My fiancé is not dead, thank God. Or are you insinuating that the telegram he sent

8

me from the Saints Giovanni e Paolo Hospital in Venice is a forgery?"

"Not at all, not at all," Hofrat Stuckart protested. "Count Kamarovsky did not succumb to his wounds until yesterday."

Should she put on a show of grief and cry? Fear and relief—she couldn't keep the two feelings apart. The fear that if Pavel was dead the police would not rest until they had found out everything; the relief that comes with clarity. She had been on her way to Pavel in answer to his telegram, with no idea of whether she wanted to live with him or not. After all, she had wished him dead. Now he was dead. "But his telegram?" she stammered.

Hofrat Stuckart leaned back and embarked on a lecture. "Inconclusive, Countess. It falls clearly into the pattern of human nature, you see, that one doesn't know who shall be his murderer. If we were to raise every murdered man from the dead, it wouldn't resolve the matter one iota. Most of those murdered wouldn't believe us when we told them who had killed them; they would make trouble for us, as champions of their own murderers; and they would die a second time in their disappointment. Concerning the question of evidence, I confess, things might have appeared better for you if Donat Prilukov had departed this life as well, but that doesn't happen to be the case, and since he is a man who has chosen to discard a conventional way of life, yet at the same time, as often happens, has clung to conventional habits, we have found telegrams at his lodgings, carefully preserved, that are highly incriminating as far as you are concerned. I shall merely mention the names Bertha and Adele. I don't believe I need explain what they mean. Should you, then, feel inclined to relieve your conscience, I am at your disposal, although I assure you I am devoid of the slightest intention of persuading you into any such action; a confession made lightly may always be revoked, and the right to reflect quietly is not denied to you in any respect. The Italian request to extradite you is adequately supported by your complicity in the murder of Count Pavel Kamarovsky, and your arrest remains entirely valid."

"It is a terrible mistake."

"Let us hope so, Countess."

Hofrat Stuckart opened the window. Night was falling. They could hear the hurdy-gurdy, but the man was no longer singing.

"I live here," said the Hofrat. "You may call a guard, not only during the day but at any hour of the night. I shall always be ready to listen to you."

"I want a lawyer."

"Of course. Anyone in particular?"

"No. But at once."

"It is late, Countess. I'm afraid you will have to wait until to-morrow."

"Tioka . . . What is going to happen to Tioka?"

"He is at the hotel. I presume your maid has informed your family. He doesn't know the truth yet. In the end I suppose it can't be kept from him."

Maria Tarnovska jumped to her feet. "Let me go to my child," she screamed. "Let me see Tioka." That was all she screamed, but year-old scars broke open in her and began to bleed. They accused Vassily Tarnovsky, who had swept Tania into the safety of his miserable existence but had left her Tioka; they accused her father, who had stood by while she did what he had forbidden; they accused Nicholas, who had broken his vow. She screamed, "Tioka, Tioka!," fists clenched, over and over again.

"The best thing for you is a good night's rest," said the solicitous receptionist of the hotel on the Rossauer Laende.

4

When they took Maria Tarnovska to her cell, it was almost dark. Not until she sat down did she notice that a woman was sitting on another cot. She looked as bodiless as a damp spot on the wall.

For a while they sat facing each other, wordlessly. Then the woman said, "Did you kill anybody?"

The Countess laughed, an irritated laugh. "Why should I have murdered anyone?"

"You're a lady. Ladies don't go in for petty crimes."

"No, I haven't murdered anyone."

"Are you a foreigner?"

"Russian."

"You're right. Deny everything. I'm sorry I confessed. Those who pass judgment are insatiable. The more you give them, the more they demand."

"You are a cultured woman."

"Semicultured. I was a teacher."

"Why are you here?"

"Crime against burgeoning life."

"Are you married?"

A laugh came from the wall. "He was the first man in my life. I'm forty. He deserted me."

The shock Maria Tarnovska had felt at sight of her cellmate was gone. "I envy you," she said. "You have dragged no one into your misery."

"Do you have children?"

"Two. But I haven't seen my daughter for a long time."

"You're beautiful. I guess you're rich."

Beautiful and rich, the Countess thought. In a week, at most, Elise wouldn't be able to pay the hotel bill. Pavel wouldn't pay it because he was dead. Donat wouldn't pay it because he was in jail. And if they arrested Elise? Tioka alone? Not that, not that. He who had nothing left should also be relieved of fear. But fear remained even in nothingness. Beauty? "Now you look like a murderess," Mademoiselle Larue had said. She had been sixteen at the time, and the young men had admired her mature figure, her soft blond hair, her blue eyes, her mouth with the slightly protruding lower lip, offering itself. "My angel face, my chaste bride," Pavel had called her. She herself, at least, should know what she looked like, but mirrors were like passports with the pictures torn out. The description was there; the picture was missing. And now she didn't even have a mirror.

"I was beautiful and rich once," she said.

"That's good. There's always a chance of again becoming what you once were. You know you can only become what you once were. I never was anything."

"Don't tell me we're envying each other, Miss . . ."

"The name doesn't matter. Tomorrow they'll take me away, to a house of detention. There'll be only women there. Women hate women."

"How did it happen?"

"How does anything happen? You make a mistake. You want to rectify it, so you make another. One should never try to rectify anything. In prison you can't, fortunately. Everybody should be locked up once. I'm glad we're not staying together. We'd talk and talk until we knew everything about each other and nothing about ourselves. I'm going to ask for solitary confinement. One can do that, you know."

Her body separated from the wall—small, slight, with smoothed-down hair of a nondescript shade. She began to undress. Her breasts were meager.

"If you have to go," she said, "there's a pail. They try to humiliate you." She sat down on the pail, shamelessly, her legs spread. "Are you religious?"

"I don't know."

"You should ask for solitary confinement too. Something is wrong with Hell. If God were just, everyone would have his own hell. There is no such thing as sins that are alike, yet all punishment is the same." She got up. "Get undressed. Try to sleep. You have no idea how much suffering one can bear."

The Countess was determined not to undress. She yearned for morphine, as in the days of her addiction. Sins were not alike. Once Andrey had said something to the same effect. If only Andrey were here! The woman had known one man and he had abandoned her. She had known many men, but they had only gone from her in death. Peter and Alexis and Vladimir and Pavel—all of them were dead, and one of them she had murdered. Or all of them? She couldn't murder Andrey. She thought of Elise, who always knew what she was thinking. If only she could send Elise a message, through the prison walls, across the city . . . *Call Andrey! Call Andrey!*

It had grown dark in the cell, as if darkness could grow still darker. The light of a gas lamp fell through a crack in the window onto the teacher standing beside the Countess' cot. She had on a long prison nightgown; she held a second one in her hand.

"You're lucky," she said. "I spent my first night with a whore who reviled me. She didn't know why. Tomorrow morning you'll scream, because the worst thing is to wake up to misery."

Gently she laid the gown at the Countess' feet.

CHAPTER 2

I

The newspaper, telling of the arrest of the Countess Maria Nikolaevna Tarnovska, lay on the wooden seat beside the Dominican friar. He knew the telegram, which had reached him in Cracow, by heart. It had come from Elise Perrier, her maid.

Father Andrey, or Count Andrey Antonovich Vyrubov, as he was once called, pressed his forehead against the window pane of the compartment. The September rain was falling. The face in the glass was as if bathed in sweat.

Andrey hadn't looked at himself in a mirror for many years. He didn't like the face he saw now. The face of a Roman senator—a high straight forehead, a bony nose with no bridge, stern eyes, the full lips almost rectangular. His white habit, scapular, and cowl stressed the masculinity they were supposed to hide. Nature had endowed him with masculine beauty, as she stamped others as unworthy and weaklings; justly, perhaps, in the sense that one's physiognomy expressed one's nature, yet unjustly in that nature blindly ignored the will— which was after all part of nature, too—with which the creature thus marked should be justified in disassociating himself from his face. Andrey Vyrubov had been wishing for another face for a long time.

He had known Maria Tarnovska since the day she was born; in fact, her birth was one of the first events he thought he could remember, as happened with events that became important later. His father had taken him, at the age of six, to the baptism of Count O'Rourke's second daughter, in Otrada. Thirty years had passed since then, but to Andrey it seemed as if Maria Tarnovska's life was spanned like a bridge across his. Her maid's telegram had startled but not surprised him. What had disquieted him was the inexorable, and therefore devilish, logic with which the life of the only woman he had ever loved had grown toward disaster. He didn't speculate at great length whether Maria had had anything to do with the murder in Venice. He considered her capable of committing murder, but who was not? Sometimes he wondered if God didn't include the Devil in His limitless patience. Love on this earth was infinite, but it was as vague as infinity; it shaped nothing; it only filled the empty spaces that had been stamped by evil. There was no such thing as devil or angel in human form; man was a hollow in which the Devil spread himself like a mirror in its frame.

Maria Tarnovska. When one looks at the picture of someone who has died, one sometimes thinks he is seeing death behind smiling eyes. It is so easy to prophesy the past. His mother had died in childbirth; he had had no brothers or sisters. His playmates had come only rarely to see him in the palace in Lipki, the linden city of Kiev. Rigid routine, parsimony, and quiet decorum had prevailed there. In Otrada there had been three children, later five. Nearly always you could hear the tinkle of finger exercises through the open windows, from the kitchen the rumpus of the servants—yet it seemed to Andrey that even then the shadows of unrest had hovered over Otrada. When Maria had become the wife of Count Tarnovsky; when she had called him to her sickbed and cursed him; when he had heard her confession and resisted the temptation of her—that was when he should have looked out of his becalmed ship up at the bridge that rose and fell above him and ran out into confusion.

The train approached Vienna. The rain drummed against the window pane; the wheels turned faster, as if the train wanted to escape the downpour. Andrey asked himself why he had answered her maid's call. He had been in Cracow with Prior Johannes Redlich, helping him to establish a school for preachers. It had not been difficult to obtain the Prior's permission to go to Vienna, for his missions often took him back and forth between many countries. Then too, he had frankly stated the purpose of his trip, and besides, he inspired confidence in his fellow men, just as naturally as the advantages of his appearance seemed naturally his own. "I have been journeying after the Devil for quite a few years, Father Prior. I don't recognize him often, but I recognize him in Maria Tarnovska." That was what he had said, and the Prior had answered with Paul's Epistle to the Philippians: "Have this mind in you, which was also in Christ Jesus."

But was he really journeying after the Devil?

2

Two or three travelers were standing at the desk. Andrey waited until it was his turn. Then he spoke quickly, before the desk clerk could offer him alms. "I would like to see Countess Tarnovska's son. I am a friend of the Countess." He could have said that he was a friend of the family, but that would have been a false identification.

"The police are up there. Suite 104. If you want to go up . . ."

Andrey crossed the hall, passed festively dressed people. It was nearly seven. He was accustomed to people whispering behind his back. The founders of the Order should not have dressed humility in such a conspicuous uniform, he sometimes thought; and now he was angry as he thought so again. "Lustful eyes are an abomination to the Lord." But probably Saint Augustine had had only the eyes of his brethren in mind.

When he opened the door, Tioka ran toward him. "Andrey! Andrey!" and clung to his habit, sobbing.

The salon was in shameless disorder. The contents of Maria Tarnovska's trunks had been vomited over carpets, tables, chairs. A police officer was bending over a suitcase like a burglar in a hurry. Andrey could hear Elise Perrier's voice in the next room, but all he could see was the broad back of a police officer who was standing in front of the disheveled bed on which Maria's maid was sitting, deathly pale, looking up at her inquisitor.

After Andrey had explained his presence, the man was willing to give an explanation, too. "She's hidden important evidence. She's in this with the Countess."

On the bed, beside hypodermic needles, phials, letters, and telegrams, lay a row of photographs of naked men and women; beside them, drawings of flagellants and women copulating with dogs and horses. Andrey covered the boy's face with his scapular.

"We're going to take her with us," said the officer, pocketing the pictures. "Can you stay with the boy?"

Tioka tore away from Andrey and flung his arms around the

15

maid. The little woman smiled across the boy's shoulder like someone who started to smile long ago and, since then, couldn't remember anything.

When they were alone, Andrey drew the boy to him.

"You're twelve now, Tioka, aren't you? Almost a man." It didn't sound right. Whenever adults had done something incomprehensible, they appealed to a child's comprehension. "You and I know that it is a mistake."

"Will you stay with me?"

"Of course. And now let us make order here, so that Mama will be pleased when she comes home."

As he walked up and down, the boy at his heels, he had to admit to himself that he wasn't trying only to distract the boy. This hectic sense of order was second nature to him, for he was convinced that external order could become inner order, and that he himself had found peace only through the discipline forced upon him. Science believed that the brain ordered the motion of one's hands, but he wasn't so sure. It was quite possible that strength also flowed from hands to the brain, or to the heart, or from the heart to the brain, or that perhaps all strength came from outside. In the beginning only hands folded in prayer had exhorted him to pray.

The trunks he dragged into position himself, leaving everything else for the boy to arrange. His eyes fell on Maria's silk underwear, but when he secretly crossed himself, it was because he had haughtily felt himself to be above all temptation. Once you had lost contact with the Devil, dearth, renunciation, and discipline lost their sacrificial meaning.

When they had re-established order, Tioka began to speak about his mother again. How could they make such a mistake? Uncle Pavel had been murdered in Venice while his mother had been with him in Kiev. He is offering himself as a witness for the defense, the monk thought. The child was coming forward with circumstantial evidence. But the faith of their children was an alibi only for the innocent.

He answered the boy's questions, then offered to play a game with him. To his surprise Tioka was agreeable to this, and chose a horse race from a heap of toys. His orders forbade Andrey to play games of any kind, yet he sat down beside Tioka on the floor to throw dice with him. Tioka was lying on his stomach, his head between his hands, his chin pressed against his lower lip, so that his little head seemed even smaller than it was. Although his features were finely drawn, as if only indicated, Andrey was reminded of Tolstoy's peasant lads, for a subtle guilelessness emanated from the straw-blond youth, as in the case of those who have to remain children to endure life. Tioka was well built, although small for his age, but he carried his right shoulder higher than the left, and he had a way of leaning his head to one side as if he wanted to cover his eyes with his arm. Andrey reproached himself for having felt sometimes that Tioka was not quite sincere, even sly, but this child couldn't very well do anything else but hold his arm up to his eyes. Had he seen the obscene pictures? With any other child it would have been easy to tell, but Tioka's whole nature was attuned to keeping secrets, those he had grasped, and those he could only sense. Now, as he threw the dice, moved the little horses, laughed, fell silent, it seemed to Andrey that the boy was playing only to please him, in the bitter habitude of not wanting to be a burden to anyone, since life had become such a burden to him. Not until the game was over and Andrey told the boy that it was time to go to bed, did he begin to cry again. He wasn't crying for his mother; he was crying because he was afraid Andrey might leave him. He had had to be alone often but had never grown accustomed to it, because being alone, instead of becoming a habit, becomes increasingly difficult.

"I will stay," said Andrey. "I promise," he added, and was astonished to find that his word, commanding confidence as always, did not fail him now.

Tioka fell asleep. Andrey remained at his bedside. He looked at the boy, whose face was calm, as if he no longer needed his arm. Sleep had protected his eyes.

3

Hofrat Stuckart received Father Andrey with oily amiability. "Your presence in Vienna is a great comfort to me," he said. "The Russian Embassy has duly informed me about your venerable person."

Andrey shook his head.

"The Countess continues to deny everything," Hofrat Stuckart went on. "She has retreated to a safe line of defense, which, of course, she'll soon have to abandon in a less orderly fashion. Nicholas

Naumov, she alleges, killed the Count out of a consuming jealousy; the thought of her engagement to Kamarovsky was more than the young man could bear. She has a deft answer, too, for Prilukov's part in the whole affair. Him she sent to Venice to stop Naumov, after the young man had threatened to murder Kamarovsky, but Prilukov came too late; and to inform her of this, he followed her to Vienna. This contradicts not only Prilukov's defense, which is just as sly, yet totally different, but it also fails to explain the exchange of letters and telegrams between the Countess and her lover—I mean Prilukov, this time."

"And the motive, Herr Hofrat?"

"Count Kamarovsky carried insurance, naming the Countess as beneficiary, for half a million francs with the Vienna Anker Company. In consideration of the lady's extremely depleted financial situation, quite a sum. On the other hand—and this is what the defense will contend—with her marriage to the Count, Frau von Tarnovska would have become one of the wealthiest women in Russia. I readily admit my respect for the persuasiveness of a strong hypothetical defense, but I don't believe for a moment that these purely financial factors weaken the proof we have against the Countess; they merely admonish us to search for other motives than material ones. You have known all the persons involved, Father. Could you perhaps give me a clue that—even if it cannot eliminate the crime—would at least explain its meaning?"

"As long as the Countess denies everything, I don't want to come forward as defendant or prosecutor."

"But you have asked for permission to visit her?"

Andrey nodded.

"You could do both justice and the Countess a service," said Hofrat Stuckart.

"I want to console Frau von Tarnovska, not question her."

"I take it you are in touch with her family?"

"I didn't receive an answer to my telegram from Count O'Rourke. I have been trying to find the Countess' sister."

"And the boy's father?"

"Vassily Tarnovsky has given up all rights to his son."

"The court may not see it that way. Very well, what do you intend to do?"

"Tioka and I have found refuge in a hostel of my Order, for the time being."

"We shall extradite the Countess to Venice. That action is temporarily deferred because of 'Doctor' Prilukov, who is wanted here in Vienna on some other counts. Prilukov is the enigmatic factor, the question being, did he seduce Frau von Tarnovska, or vice versa? Whenever a crime is committed, the curtains open upon the lives of men, but they do not always open all the way, nor do they reveal everyone concerned; guilt remains offstage, and innocence is paraded bare; you don't see what you want to see, but you get a full view of what should have remained hidden. In order to grasp, even remotely, what is commonly termed the motive, you have first to discover the way to the sources, very often alien sources, I remind you, since what we do doesn't necessarily always evolve from our own character. And as if that were not enough, information out of the past is perplexing to us because just those circumstances and experiences that make a criminal of one man serve the next person—you will pardon me for putting it like this—as the raw material for sainthood." He rose. "However much we appreciate it that you have taken the boy under your care, I can't spare you the unpleasant fact that you are wasting your anxiety for the Countess on one who does not deserve it. In the Middle Ages they would have burned her. I always considered the burning of witches barbaric. Now I am beginning to wonder if we shouldn't look upon the witch-hunters with more indulgence."

"Am I to understand that permission to visit her has been denied?" asked Andrey.

"It is too early to offer the Countess religious consolation," Hofrat Stuckart replied.

Andrey walked through the September afternoon. The sky was a glassy gray. Leaves were falling from the trees, slowly, singly, as if they were afraid to settle on the ground. Wasted anxiety, the priest thought. As if there were such a thing. As if such waste didn't serve to clear the air. He who loved breathed out; he alone did not rob the air of oxygen; the air was full of the oxygen of love. The others, who didn't love, inhaled it. Systole and diastole. Had love led him here, or his quest for the Devil? One should never cease mistrusting oneself. Had he come to see Maria in her mortification? Had the desire to see others suffer, of which she had spoken to him not so long ago, in this city, filtered into his pure love for her? "Save me!" she had implored him, and perhaps he could have saved her, if he had offered the Devil his soul in exchange for hers. It would have been a good bargain; too good a bargain for the Devil. Arrogance? Pavel Kamarovsky would still be alive; Nicholas Naumov free. But Count Andrey Vyrubov and the Countess Tarnovska would be wandering from country to country, from city to city; wretched and damned, they would be breathing the oxygen of the innocent. Diastole instead of systole. It would not have been the way to save Maria's soul.

Andrey looked up at the towers of the Votive Church. He entered.

CHAPTER 3

I

When Maria Tarnovska stepped into Hofrat Stuckart's office, Donat Prilukov was standing against the wall between two policemen. His hands were free. She tried to recall his face but found it more difficult than when he had not been present. The face she knew moved in front of the face that was unknown to her, disappeared behind it, became one with it, and this third face was like neither of the other two.

This time Hofrat Stuckart did not get up. "Countess Tarnovska," he said. "Herr Prilukov has made a confession, and I would like to stress the fact that he has also confessed to having told you in the corridor to deny everything. I think it is high time that you answered my questions truthfully, if you can see your way to doing so. Were you in Venice this spring?"

"Yes."

"With Prilukov and Count Kamarovsky?"

"Herr Prilukov happened to be there."

20

"Did the two men know about each other?"

"No."

"You had a relationship with both of them?"

"I broke off my relationship with Herr Prilukov long ago."

"But when you traveled home, from Venice to Vienna, he was on the same train?"

"Yes."

"On the train you ordered Prilukov to kill your fiancé."

"That is a lie."

"You gave him a revolver."

Should she tell that Donat had threatened to commit suicide— a threat as empty as his promises?

"If I had told him to do so, he would have killed Pavel."

Hofrat Stuckart gave the stenographer a sign. "So Prilukov was your helpless tool," he said.

The Countess did not reply.

"Do you deny," Hofrat Stuckart went on, "that you changed your plans later when you found a more malleable tool in Naumov?"

"That is absurd!"

"You ordered Naumov to come to Vienna. In Vienna, Prilukov and Naumov planned the murder together."

"Then why did Naumov go to Kiev, when the 'victim' was in Vienna?"

"Naumov wasn't ready yet."

Hofrat Stuckart handed her a telegram. It read, "Your Naumov is no good. I regret my good intentions. And you are no better. Kamarovsky."

Yes, she told him, she knew the telegram.

"This telegram," the Hofrat said, "was sent by Prilukov in Kamarovsky's name, without his knowledge or permission, so that you could more easily persuade Naumov to the murder."

"I had no reason to doubt the validity of the telegram. Kamarovsky was jealous. . . ."

Again Hofrat Stuckart pushed a telegram in front of her. It was her own, sent from Kiev. "Telegram has had its effect on Bertha."

"Bertha is the code name for Naumov," said the Hofrat.

"But it has nothing to do with Pavel's telegram."

Prilukov stepped forward. He spoke Russian. He held his folded hands up to the Countess, as if he were praying to her or praying for her. "For the sake of our love," he said, "tell the truth. They will torture you until you tell the truth. I don't want them to torture you, Mura." Tears and sweat ran down his cheeks.

She turned her back on him. He grew silent, murmured something to himself; the stenographer translated what had been said.

All Maria Tarnovska could feel was disgust. Now that she was turned from him, she could recall his face. A giant of a man, thick eyebrows shading his eyes, big teeth in a gentle mouth. Made of clay like the Golem, the servant without a first letter to his name, Maeth. In the bedroom, a different face, not ugly any more. A body that knew no weariness, ready for love, three times, four times; in the morning, in the evening, in the afternoon; capable of quick fulfillment and endless restraint; his bald head a phallic symbol. In the courtroom, another face. Lawyer for the defense. Nothing counted— not the object in question, not the human being, not justice—only she, watching. The face that promised security. Maeth became Aemaeth. One obeyed. Then, again, the monkey behind the drapes, pursued, malicious, and sly. The face of a forger. And now—a destroyed face, flaccid, impotent, in his eyes the murderous lust of the eunuch.

"I think you would do well to stop all these legal tricks, Herr Hofrat," she said. "Herr Prilukov was jealous of Kamarovsky. Why should I betray a man like Kamarovsky, who could give me the most wonderful life, for a sick youth and a degenerate lawyer?"

She thought she was putting up a good defense. If only Prilukov could be present at all the hearings. His humiliation had delighted her; now her courage grew out of his humiliation.

"'A degenerate lawyer,'" the Hofrat repeated. "Are you referring to his embezzlements?"

"I know nothing about them."

"Sixty-five thousand rubles, lavished on you."

"I have my own fortune."

"Your maid couldn't pay your hotel bill."

"My maid doesn't have access to my money."

"You have eighty rubles in your account." The Hofrat handed Prilukov a letter. "Did you write this letter? We found it on the Countess." Prilukov nodded.

The Hofrat read, "'I couldn't bear it that you should belong to this man. I saw you in his arms. I shot him.' What have you to say to this letter, Countess Tarnovska?"

"Herr Prilukov did not shoot Kamarovsky," she replied.

Prilukov said, "I wrote the letter when I intended to kill him. You were to prove your innocence with it."

The interpreter translated.

Maria Tarnovska addressed the Hofrat. "The outgrowth of a sick imagination. Why shouldn't I rather have persuaded Naumov to write such a letter?"

She should have forced Donat to kill Kamarovsky. A famous lawyer, a friend of the revolutionaries, a family man. Then his embezzlements: "What do I care for wife and child?" Their orgies, their trips, his false name, the general's money. "Let me worry about it, Mura." The envelope with no banknotes in it. But he had never sunk low enough. "You couldn't love a murderer, Mura." Her fatal compassion. And now no greater ambition was left to him than to be an obedient convict. When had she loved him last? Yesterday? Inconceivable! A ruin. But a few walls were still standing, a bastion here, a tower there—why hadn't she burned the remains?

The Hofrat had the prisoner led away and turned to address her. "I have bad news for you. Don't you want to spare yourself a confrontation with your maid?"

"Is Elise here?"

"She has been arrested."

"Where is Tioka?"

"He is safe."

"With whom?"

The Hofrat removed a wisp of straw from his Virginia cigar. "Don't forget that you are a mother, Countess."

So they were not going to tell her where Tioka was. Had her father come? Or Olga? Or Vassily Tarnovsky? Would Vassily triumph? Prisoners were fed like Hansel and Gretel by the witch, until the confession was fat, until the slaughter could begin. For Tioka she had sacrificed Tania, laid Alexis' ghost, endured Granya's moods. For Tioka she had become engaged to Kamarovsky. She had no more pity for herself, only for her child. She had always felt compassion for him—because he was with her, or because he was not; because he had playmates, or none; because he saved kopeks or squandered rubles; because he boasted, or went around with his shoulders sagging; because he clung to her, or was heartless. This unfathomable compassion, this sense of his innocence, which magnified her guilt; this anxiety for her own victim. Compassion, endlessly. Tioka was still attached to her umbilical cord. Only by confession would she become a murderess.

She looked at the door through which Donat Prilukov had disappeared. There was no door. The wall had swallowed him up, as it had done in Kiev, Nice, Venice.

The wall opened up again, and Elise Perrier entered.

2

It was the morning of the twenty-sixth of October. Rain was falling like soot, fine and dirty. People crept along the walls, heads bowed, like cows rubbing their noses against a barnyard wall when it rained. The city seemed to grow because people were lonely.

They had taken Maria Tarnovska to the station. A few days before, one suitcase had been delivered to her. She wore a long dark green dress, with a wide collar, a silk vestee, and a loose coat. Her little traveling hat was covered and held down by a veil, which was tied loosely under her chin. The wind blew into the shawl as if it wanted to comb her hair. She didn't have to worry about being taken for a prisoner, because the guard walked behind her and a second man carried her bag. He was a Hungarian called Fenyvesi, a fraudulent-marriage swindler of international renown who was being extradited to Rome. He was about fifty, small and nimble; his hair was dyed; on his chin, a dab of a goatee. Herr Fenyvesi in his short brown coat was dressed so neatly, he might have been taken for the lady's footman.

The two didn't attract any attention until they took their seats in a third-class compartment, the delinquents at the window, the guard at the door. The Countess demanded that the curtains be drawn. But there were no curtains, and passengers kept appearing at door and window to stare at the animals in their cage.

When the train had left, Herr Fenyvesi—Imre Fenyvesi from Miskolcz—asked the Countess what language she would like to converse in, German, French, English, Spanish, or Italian. *"Voyez-vous madame,"* he said, *"c'est une chose drôle, le destin.* I always profited by women, and here I am doing it *de nouveau,* in this *situation pénible* because they didn't want to put on a prison car just for me, and I may therefore enjoy the luxury of a trip in the pleasantest company imaginable"—he bowed—"one might say, like a stowaway." He spoke about himself, justifying himself, not without vanity. "My aversion to marriage is a matter of principle. Why should a man have to support the daughter of an absolute stranger? Isn't that the true purpose of marriage, *au fond?* And why should one never want to part from a woman one didn't know until one's wedding day, *désormais et dorénavant,* and adjust to her habits, prefer her cuisine to the infinite variety of a restaurant, adopt her friends, and lie down at her side every night? *Ma foi, c'est paradox!"*

While Fenyvesi philosophized, the Countess looked out the window. She knew the region they were passing through; on her trips to Venice she had usually taken the Pontebba line. Whenever they came out of a tunnel, she could see that the guard had his hand on the door handle. Tioka had loved counting the tunnels—forty to Venice.

The Hofrat had given her a letter from Andrey. He had kept a watchful eye on her, like a pyromaniac listening for a crackling in the beams so as to rush in sanctimoniously and put out what he had ignited. In vain. Tioka was safe. Now she had smuggled secret instructions to Elise Perrier, who had put on a greater show of simplemindedness during the confrontation than the Hofrat had liked. Since Andrey's letter, the Countess had begun to hunger for life anew. Until now, she had always felt hunger for something specific—no hunger, therefore. There was a saying about human beings saving their bare skins. In that case, they saved what was best. It was a dead woman who had left the train in Vienna. After Alexis' death, she hadn't had any time to think things over. All misfortune happened because of lack of time. In prison she had had time. At first she hadn't been able to recall the woman she had been once. Now she could. Prilukov would take all the blame upon himself, but he would never do it if he saw her weaken, even for a moment. She clung to the leather strap at the window. Even in prison you could still wield a whip.

The smell of charred potato plants drifted through the cracks in the window. Maria Tarnovska felt like talking and, with a smile, turned to her companion.

"You don't feel guilty, monsieur?"

"At best, in the sense of a senseless law, madame. In our age of the suffragette, there isn't a less timely law than the one that punishes the marriage swindler. Thousands of women are saying yes to marriage every day, and are doing men out of their little savings, but it would never occur to anyone to accuse them of swindling if the marriage doesn't come off. *Est-ce que c'est juste, je vous demande?* Marriage is the only contract with unilateral benefits, still, it has been renewed over and over again for centuries. The whole world speaks touchingly of the blissful period of engagement because it is a time of wonderful hopes that are never fulfilled. Oh, how women love promises! How they love to embroider on plans! A marriage swindler, madame, is a fairy prince of illusions that would not be fulfilled—in fact, would certainly not be fulfilled if he kept his promises. Marriage, *voyez-vous,* is an institution to help us bear in common those sufferings we would never have suffered if we had not married. . . ."

The track began to rise; the train traveled more slowly. The cars rattled across viaducts whose arches looked like Romanesque church windows. The train moved over the roofs of the domes. Firs stood black among the fleeting colors of autumn, as if reminding one that only that which was dark endured. It had stopped raining; people were turning their faces skyward. They were free, all alike and unlike her. The self-evident was no longer self-evident; it had become extraordinary. She wasn't listening to Fenyvesi by chance; although, like herself, he was a prisoner, he was part of the freedom between two prisons, the illusion of which she was now absorbing. Tomorrow she would be alone again and be no different than she had been in that false freedom that had preceded her arrest.

Passengers got in; new faces looked through the glass door. At the Austrian-border station, Pontafel, the indifferent guard left them. Two *carabinieri* took his place, peasant lads in Napoleonic disguise, with bursting faces of coarse joviality. They brought sex with them; they came into the compartment as if it had been a bordello, their pants taut. In Pontebba, a family—mother, father, and five or six children—took the next compartment, and the dark children, who looked as if they were all the same age, pressed their runny noses against the pane, laughed, pretended to be horrified, nudged each other, scattered, pointed fingers, couldn't seem to get enough of the prisoners.

Maria Tarnovska had put off having to go to the washroom. As she rose, one of the policemen followed her; the children were on her heels; compartment doors flew open; the *carabinieri,* grinning, told her not to lock the door; *libero;* the toilet window was barred. When

26

she came out again, the policeman looked down at her, from the hips. The children were gathered around the door.

It was growing dark. Chiusaforte, Resiutta, Venuone, Gemona, Udine. The evening was mild. The Italian villages lay in a violet twilight; the houses huddled together as if by day they reached for each other's shadows, as if they were afraid of losing each other in the night, forts, castles, ruins towering above them, besieged or preparing for a siege, ruins of the future. Then it was dark, and only the increased thunder of the tracks indicated that one had passed through a tunnel, perhaps the fortieth one.

Shortly after midnight, after seventeen hours and forty-five minutes of travel, they arrived in Venice. The family with the children had got off long before. One of the *carabinieri* was playing cards with Fenyvesi; the other was sleeping, his mouth open, his cheeks puffed, a peevish child. No one in the corridor except a honeymoon couple, fused into one shadow, for hours now. The marriage swindler got Maria Tarnovska's bag down from the rack. One of the *carabinieri* thrust it into her hand.

As she stood on the platform, in the gaslight, she heard someone call out "Madame!" Fenyvesi was leaning out the window, waving. *"Bonne chance et au revoir!"*

3

Women hate women, the teacher in the Rossauer Laende jail had said. Now Maria Tarnovska knows what she meant.

The prison on the island of La Giudecca. *Istituti Penali Femminili, Fondamenta de la Convertite 712.* Domenico, the head warden, is rarely seen. There is the Mother Superior, Sister Angela, his right hand, fat yet bony, with a flushed neck and a beard, a disguised man. The nuns are wearing black habits, the Order of Maria Bambina. Little caps on their heads, gathered at the front, dark nightcaps; sometimes a white apron, like female Dominicans. Sister Rosa, so tall she has to stoop when she enters the cell, a wart on her pointed nose; the wart seems to come in first. Maria Tarnovska's perfume makes her feel sick. Sister Sofia, pale, red-rimmed eyes, with an importunate kindliness, who seems to be bewailing "the poor lost souls" all the time. Keys at the belts of their habits, long, thin keys, with claws like those of lobsters. The cell cold, damp, but light. No skylight, as in the

Viennese prison. A big barred window in a thick fortress wall. On the other side, perhaps, Venice. The stone spiral of Santa Maria della Salute. Behind it, the Doges Palace, St. Mark's Cathedral, the demolished Campanile, the lagoons, wide and dreary. Life rolls past the prison; gondolas, helpers from the market, tourists, processions, fishermen, funeral cortèges, honeymooners. So close, you could touch them. Tantalus. The fish stink, the vegetables stink, the lagoons stink, the prison stinks. And still no hearing. "Just wait." Maria Tarnovska asks for a mirror. Sister Angela refuses. "Intentions of suicide, we know." Sister Sofia brings a mirror. The Countess can't understand why her face hasn't changed. She grimaces into the mirror as if to throw up her soul. "Poor lost soul!" Sister Sofia takes the mirror away again. I shall tame my face with my soul, Maria Tarnovska thinks. Food on a tin plate. Spaghetti, macaroni, spaghetti. She won't touch it. Hunger strike? No, not hungry. Sister Angela has her brought in. A cozy room, red Victorian furniture, Murano glass in a case; in the garden, palms; a cloister courtyard. "Money has come for you." "From whom?" No reply. "Would you like to pay for your food?" That evening Maria Tarnovska orders caviar, *tournedos Rossini,* cream torte, brought from the Savoy. She eats only the caviar. Sister Sofia eats the rest, greedily, with a guilty conscience. The singing of the nuns. The rattling of the keys. Over the dishwashing, other prisoners. A fat motherly woman who has murdered her husband; a jewel thief, dressed elegantly in the style of 1903; a pair of thieving twins, consumptives. And still no hearing. A letter from Tioka, with the stamp of the prison censor. "I am fine, Mama. I am, truly. We shall see each other soon, because Andrey is going to bring me to Venice." Maria Tarnovska cries all night. Every day a new dress; sometimes she changes her dress twice a day, but she is frugal with her perfume. She is more afraid of dreams than of insomnia. Dreams don't know the meaning of purpose; they know only the past. Vassily is sleeping with his mistress, Julia Terletzkaya. A forgotten name. He persuades Maria Tarnovska to come and stand beside the bed. She enjoys it, and dreams on until the prison bell awakens her. Pavel brings her a string of pearls; she doesn't want to accept them. Pearls mean tears. Her pillow is wet. She dreams about Zolotariev, the tutor. She makes him hold the towel for her when she gets out of the bath. She hears her name being called, feels her way to the window, thinks she is dreaming. A full moon. She is not dreaming. The voice of a man is calling out to her from a gondola. Rust and dirty water. The roof of the rust-brown factory where they make spaghetti. She demands to see her lawyer. "Later!" Novels from the prison library . . . young Count marries poor but virtuous governess . . . Mademoiselle Larue and the theater troupe in Kiev. Maria Tarnovska cannot grasp the misfortune of the figures in the novel, for all of them are free. The warnings of the *gondolieri*. The Mother Superior, telling her that a letter has come from Russia and not letting her see it. "Only two a month." A pendulum clock in the Mother Superior's office. The sun rises on the right, sets on the left, all in one frame. Its path is descending, always in the frame. A young Italian priest celebrates Mass on Sunday. Maria Tarnovska can't understand a word, crosses herself at the wrong time, asks to make confession. The priest can't understand her. She whispers obscenities in his ear, in Russian. Her body does not respond. She begs Kamarovsky to forgive her. Kamarovsky is in heaven and knows why she murdered him. She suggests a bargain to the Lord; "I shall enter a convent"; knows that she is lying; perhaps He doesn't know. Her window has six vertical bars and four across—why not the other way around? When after sixteen days she has still not been permitted to see a lawyer, she flies into a rage, smashes her perfume bottle. The whole cell is redolent with rose oil. She lies on her cot and tries to think of a way to destroy Prilukov. That night she dreams of her first night with Prilukov.

At last, on the seventeenth of November—it is a Sunday—Sister Angela tells her that Prosecutor Garzoni wishes to see her on the following day.

CHAPTER 4

I

Lawyer Ricardo Calzini's house was situated in a side street of the Merceria de l'Orlogio, where the noise of business traffic ceded to a hallowed stillness, as if the old part of the city refused to respond to the young one.

Andrey entered the house through a side door in the Calle Morsoni de la Regina e dei Pignoli. It was cold on the stairs, but the tiny waiting room was overheated. In the green gaslight, the walls seemed to move. The furniture, with its *décor* of winged St. Mark's lions, was too large, exiles from legendary *palazzi*. Doubly present here were the unrealness of a city in which people went about their ordinary business between the houses of Dandalos and Desdemona, doing the right thing or pandering to evil, behaving as if they were alive.

Andrey had tried to visit Maria Tarnovska. He had been told to see her lawyer, but for days he was not received. Already he had composed a letter, telling her what was to become of Tioka; suddenly his last effort succeeded.

The man sitting opposite him fitted perfectly into the style of the room. He too defied proportions. His beautiful, slightly gray head was large, his icy beard of stone, his eyes cold fire; yet his body delicate, spoiled, soft.

"You wished to speak to me?" It sounded as if he were saying, "You wanted to speak to me, but I don't know why."

Andrey explained that he had at last been able to locate Maria Tarnovska's sister, Princess Olga Katerinovich. The Princess, who was on the Riviera, had begged him to meet her in Venice, and from there she would take Tioka to Russia. He wanted to add that he was still hesitant about handing the boy over to the Princess, but, faced with the lawyer's mocking eyes, he was silenced. He only mentioned that Maria Tarnovska's father had not replied to his letter or telegram.

"The Count has asked me to defend his daughter," said Dr. Calzini, "but with the stipulation that his name not be mentioned, not even to the Countess."

Andrey wanted to leave, but the lawyer showed no sign of letting him go. His head, standing out against the dark red velvet of a huge Renaissance chair, was like those of the pallid infantas and wicked dwarfs of Velasquez. "Why are you taking an interest in this woman, Father?" he asked.

"I am her friend."

"Is that why you came to Venice?"

"I wanted to tell her about Tioka."

"You could have done that in writing."

"It is different personally."

"You can't see her."

"I can pray for her."

"You can do that any place." He leaned back. "Do you think the Countess is innocent?"

"The court will decide that."

"What would you do if it were up to you to give her back her freedom?"

"Anything that can be reconciled with my vows and justice."

The lawyer's questions didn't surprise him. He was accustomed to the fact that his habit was a challenge to people. They felt that they had to challenge all that pretended to be saintly. He rose.

The lawyer remained seated. "I could convince the Countess that you want to help her," he said.

"How could I . . ."

"Your testimony could be invaluable."

"I know nothing about the details of the complaint."

"But you know Maria Tarnovska's past like no one else. The Countess depends on her beauty and charm, attributes that become incriminating behind prison walls. People fall victim to charm and feel cheated afterward."

"I have seen Maria Tarnovska only rarely since her friendship with Kamarovsky," said Andrey.

"Modern psychiatry looks for the motives in childhood, before anything else. I have asked for a psychiatric examination."

"You are not implying that the Countess is mentally disturbed?"

"Modern psychiatry relieves not only the mentally disturbed of responsibility." He sounded patronizing. "I would like to bring you together with Professor Ceresa."

Modern psychiatry, thought Andrey. He didn't know much about the new science, but Dr. Calzini corroborated what he knew of it. It collected proof according to which a human being was supposed to act under the force of his experiences. Christian liberty knew nothing of such forces.

"If Maria Tarnovska is guilty," he said, "justice must take its course."

"You talk like the prosecutor."

"I am not accusing her."

"But you are a friend of confession and remorse."

Now the lawyer's animosity was obvious to Andrey.

"You, on the other hand, seem convinced of the Countess' guilt," he said.

"It is not a question of the deed, but of the motive. And of the person who commits the crime."

"That may apply to the meting out of punishment. You don't give me much hope, Doctor."

Things were not so bad, Calzini replied complacently. New aspects had come up, much to the disgust of the authorities. One of Count Kamarovsky's doctors, a young but experienced man, a Dr. Menini, had deposed a statement with Dr. Calzini, according to which the Count had not died of his wounds, but had been the victim of an error of the chief surgeon, Professor Cavazzini. For reasons no one could explain, the surgeon had ordered the stitches in the stomach removed and the stomach pumped out just when things were healing nicely, and this was what had caused the peritonitis that had been the actual cause of death. An absolutely crazy thing for the professor to have done—not only according to Dr. Menini. His assistant, Dr. Facta, was of the same opinion. "If this theory can be maintained," Calzini went on, "then—even taking all premeditation for granted—it would not be a case of murder but of attempted murder. We are therefore justified in being mildly optimistic."

Andrey asked himself what chaos was spreading around him. Had the hand of the student Nicholas Naumov trembled . . . had Kamarovsky, although severely wounded, not succumbed . . . if an error on the part of the surgeon could be proved—would Maria's intention then count for nothing, would it then be null and void? They were looking for motives only in order to eliminate them. "For by the fruit the tree is known." Had they so utterly misunderstood the word of the Lord? The tree was the intention, but they saw only what they could reap. It didn't surprise him that people acted contrary to the law, but it startled him to see the law itself oppose the law; to see it submit to coincidence; to observe it weighing, not the motivating force, but the deed; not the deed, but its consequence.

"Attempted murder," Dr. Calzini was saying. "If I could succeed in illuminating the personality of the Countess for the judges . . . You won't testify?"

"If the court needs me, they know where to find me."

As he rose, his glance fell on the desk. He couldn't believe his eyes. A large cut-glass bottle of perfume, L'Origan, Coty; a silk scarf, a picture of Count Tarnovsky with his daughter, a picture of Maria's mother, two or three photographs of Tioka.

The lawyer smiled. "The Countess' wishes. I received permission to liven up her cell a little."

"Tell the Countess that Tioka is well," said Andrey. Hurriedly he bowed; hurriedly he left.

2

That night Andrey lay awake.

"I can pray for her." "You can do that anyplace." The Velasquez dwarf had challenged him. Why had he hurried to Vienna? To Venice? Was he journeying after the Devil? He couldn't help Maria; he couldn't exorcise the Devil in her. Exorcising the Devil—an error of the Inquisition. "Now is the judgment of the world; now will the Prince of the world be cast out." The death of Christ had not freed the world of the Devil, but it had given man the freedom to free himself. Exorcism was liberation by force, therefore coercion. Who was the Devil? What was he? No longer a monster in red, with horns and hoofs? What, then? Philosophy began with divestment, and where philosophy began, the Devil sat in one's faith. Explanation was obfuscation and the end of transfiguration. The Devil was a purse of gold, a naked breast, a teeming city, Babylon, the whore of John's Apocalypse. A beautiful youth, the oppressiveness of a summer evening, a scholar's laboratory. The coveted place taken by another, a mirror, arrogant or sensual or ambitious fantasy, the right thing done at the wrong time. Temptation, therefore. You couldn't depend on the Devil stepping forward to introduce himself. "I recognize him in Maria Tarnovska." Had he recognized him? "I can pray for her." "You can do that anyplace." Why had he come? Was his love free of all carnality? Agape, not Eros? The warning of the dream in Mirgorod. It wasn't the act of love that distinguished Eros from Agape; it was one's presence. Pure love did not require one's presence. Eros was proximity, and that was perhaps all that Eros was. Speak of Maria, stand at the prison gates, send her a message—that was Eros. The Prince of the world . . . didn't he rule any longer? There was daily proof that he did. But since the death of Christ, no longer with God's grace. A constitutional monarch ruling only over those who chose him. Had he chosen the Devil when he had left the monastery in Cracow? One could not be too distrustful of oneself. Prison gates did not shut the Devil out; if they did, then prisons would be heaven. Dr. Calzini. "I received permission to liven up her cell a little." The devil in Maria Tarnovska had taken possession of Dr. Calzini. The man's questions, his vanity, his jealousy. "Prayers do not suffice, Dr. Calzini!" A prayer heard was a mandate to act. No one was damned, not since Golgotha. "What would you do if it were up to you to give her back her freedom?" The psychiatrists' motives substantiated the compulsiveness of an action. They sought the forcefulness of evil; Christ sought the liberation of good. Maria was free. She could choose love. The thing was to bring it to her. His evidence was not what she needed, nor the proof of her innocence—what she needed was the proof of his love.

Andrey rose and knelt beside his cot and thanked God who had led him to Ricardo Calzini. His soul was like a roof, invisible in winter, uncovered by the first winds of spring. It was thawing.

3

Olga O'Rourke, Princess Katerinovich, was to arrive in Venice late that evening. All day long, Andrey and Tioka wandered through the city. Although Tioka had been in Venice often, Andrey was astonished to see how little the boy knew the city. He seemed to know all about the Hotel Danieli, the Grand Hotel des Bains, and the motorboat that shuttled back and forth between Venice and the Lido. He knew the Quadri and Florian, coffeehouses famous for their fancy ices, but he had never been inside the Doges Palace, never visited the Accademia di Belle Arti, nor Santa Maria della Salute, the "savior from the plague."

It was a southern November day, sunny, with a foolish warmth. Only a few pedestrians populated the square, as on the paintings of Antonio Canal, who had seen them through his *camera obscura;* just enough figures to give life to his serious, bright pictures. Shingles, marble and stucco, were spotted, like the silver of a family who had received no guests for a long time. The *"Sci stali! Scia premi! Sci di lunga!"* of the *gondolieri* rang back from the bridges, echoes of solitude.

Tioka listened to Andrey's explanations politely rather than attentively. At last, on the Campo San Giovanni e Paolo, under the statue of the Rider of Colleoni, he said, "I'm tired. Couldn't we sit down?"

They sat on the steps of the Ponte del Cavallo. The boy rubbed his knee. "Where is the prison?" he asked.

"On the Giudecca, a group of eight islands. . . ." Andrey stopped. He was afraid of sounding like a guide.

"Can't we go there?"

"They wouldn't let us in."

"I might see Mother at one of the windows."

"They're high up."

The boy nodded. His comprehension tore at Andrey's heart. In the weeks they had spent together, Tioka had rarely posed questions about his mother, as if he wished to spare Andrey the answers. Yet he had neglected his appearance: his suit was often dusty, and his socks hung down over his shoes. He held his head more to one side than ever, his right shoulder high. Children could be just as sad as adults, but usually they were sad in an angry way, just as they liked to chase away sleep by crying—puppies barking at a stranger. Whenever Andrey looked at the straw-blond boy with the blue eyes and slightly protruding lower lip, it pained him that Tioka had stopped being angry so soon. He wanted to shake the boy—speak, cry, curse, ask questions! But he couldn't be certain where the cancer lay hidden, and if it was bleeding. He saw Tioka as one sees a person who has been unrecognizably ill, and then upon discovery of the sickness, must make up for belated pity. The more he reproached himself for his omission, the more the child's attachment to him touched him, as if Tioka had loved him long before he had loved Tioka.

The autumnal sun fell on Tioka's face. After a while he said, "Why did you become a priest, Andrey?"

God help me, thought the friar. Summer in Otrada, the first kiss, the ardent dreams. The sleigh ride, their hands interlocked under the fur rug. Her flight with Tarnovsky. His conversation with Count O'Rourke. His talk with his father. "I want to enter a monastery." "Disappointment is a poor counselor, my son." Sergey Burintzev's scorn. "And you—would you have found your way to God if she hadn't walked out on you?" Had Christ called the little children only to lie to them?

"It's a long story. Why do you ask?"

"Do you think God would free Mama if I promised to become a priest?"

"You can't strike a bargain with God, Tioka."

"Why not? We promise Him to be good."

"But we're not supposed to expect anything in return."

"We're supposed to be rewarded for our good deeds."

The theologist in the child, thought Andrey. "God is pleased if you give alms to a beggar, but he isn't pleased if at the same time you're thinking that He is going to reward you for it."

"But one does think of it. And it doesn't make any difference to the beggar, after all." He passed his hand across his forehead. "Andrey, is God just?"

"Of course He is just."

"Then why can't I be with Mama?"

"You shall be with her."

"Even if I don't enter a monastery?"

"Even then."

"Well, you must know." A short-lived rebellion. He looked up at the statue of the rider. "What is a *condottiere*?"

Andrey explained, but he knew Tioka had asked only to dispel his own thoughts or to placate Andrey, who evidently knew more about churches, painters, and *condottieri* than about God.

Then they were standing on the square again. A beggar was dozing on the steps; children were playing in front of the coffeehouse; every now and then a gondola glided slowly down the canal, past the gray walls of the hospital where Kamarovsky had died. Andrey was glad Tioka didn't know.

Although he was not supposed to spend money, he took a gondola, because he was afraid the tired child might catch cold. Evening descended upon Venice; all the city's colors were melted down to one— yellow gold: palaces and the tenements and the churches and the hotels and the sidewalks and the roofs. Andrey spread his scapular around Tioka.

"I would like to stay with you," said the boy.

"Your Aunt Olga . . ."

"I can't stand her."

"Why?"

"Because she doesn't like Mama." And he began to cry. He clung to Andrey. "Don't leave me. Andrey, please, please, don't leave me!"

"I shall never leave you," said Andrey.

He felt like an impostor, for he knew that Tioka took literally what he had meant figuratively. In the Book of Mark it said, "Amen I say unto you, there is no one who has left house, or brothers, or sisters, or mother, or father, or children, or lands, for my sake, and for the gospels sake, who shall not receive now in the present time a hundredfold. . . ." But in the same book you could read, "Let the little children come to me and do not hinder them, for of such is the Kingdom of God." Now, which one of the two was valid?

4

A man got up out of an armchair, came toward him; and Andrey knew he had seen the man before. He had been watching the friar for quite some time. They were in the lobby of the Hotel Danieli. Olga's train was late. Andrey was waiting for her.

The stranger wasn't dressed poorly, just carelessly. He adjusted his spectacles on his nose. They were attached to a black silk ribbon. He smiled knowingly. "Friedlieber. Dr. Hugo Friedlieber, from Vienna. *Neue Freie Presse.*"

Andrey was overcome by an unpleasant feeling, not because of the man, but by his own memories.

"Orel," the stranger went on. "The execution of your friend

Burintzev. We journalists are like the Flying Dutchman; meeting up with us never bodes good."

"What are you doing in Venice?"

"Funny that you should ask. The Tarnovska case, of course." He passed a hand through his obstreperous gray hair. "I presume you're expecting her sister?"

"You are well informed."

"That's how I make a living. It would mean a lot to me to get an interview with the Princess."

"For an article?"

"You say that contemptuously."

"I mean it contemptuously." Immediately Andrey regretted his vehemence. "I suppose sensationalism is indispensable."

"What you call sensationalism is nothing but the smoke pouring out of a burning house."

"I don't have to fan the flames."

"Sometimes it's only the smoke that brings the fire brigade to the spot."

"But that is not the purpose of the press. The press doesn't live by quenching the flames, but by kindling them."

"And what does the Church live by?" replied Friedlieber. "The Inquisition—that was really something! Until a hundred and fifty years ago, the Church tried to stamp out what she considered evil, even though she didn't know what evil was. But since then, she's given up cauterizing the wounds. Now she spreads a sheet over them."

Andrey looked at the desk. It had begun to rain. Through the half-open door one could hear the cursing of the *gondolieri*. Friedlieber lit a cigar. The aroma reminded Andrey of Orel.

"I had a long talk with Burintzev in the death chamber," the journalist said. "Would it interest you to know what he said?"

"Anything about Sergey interests me."

"It was a strange year. Dreyfus had been freed in France. That touched me. I'm a Jew. But I don't have to tell you that." He laughed. "Burintzev related everything—even an eruption of Vesuvius—to himself. I wonder sometimes if the end of the world was more sympathetic to him, because it's easier to go down with a ship than end one's days in a lonely boat. By the way, he was full of contradictions. He negated the existence of God, yet believed in the day of judgment.

He spoke about the Flood as if it were written in Karl Marx, not in the Bible."

"Did Sergey speak about the Flood?"

"Our world was being destroyed by a moral pestilence, he said. Anarchist, Bolshevik—I never believed he was either. I think he was something much worse—a moralist. When they hang a moralist, they always have to find another name for him." He followed Andrey's gaze to the door. "The Countess Tarnovska is an incarnation of one of Burintev's visions."

"Do you know the Countess so well?"

Friedlieber laughed again. He had an insulting way of laughing, like someone who tells only half a joke and is amused at the punch line without divulging it. "I have met her quite often," he said. "Don't misunderstand me—I don't hold it against her that she treated me like a Jew of the Middle Ages. I resent what she's done."

"She hasn't been convicted yet."

"For heaven's sake, don't you know how to recognize a bankrupt organization? Its members don't pay their dues: that's how you recognize them. An aristocrat's notes used to be accepted because the creditor could presume that an aristocrat wouldn't use his name in vain. The masses are the creditors of the privileged. When the privileged stop honoring their notes, all credit goes to the dogs."

"Did you know that the Countess Tarnovska was the one person who tried to save Burintzev?"

"She undoubtedly had personal reasons. Besides, the Tarnovskas and Burintzevs aren't enemies. They're rivals. The world of the Tarnovskas behaves so anarchistically nowadays, the anarchists don't know what to destroy. That's the big opportunity for the communists."

"Do you see any great difference between anarchists and communists?"

"You, of course, don't, because both are godless. But Burintzev did make some very fine differentiations. Anarchists create confusion for the purpose of creating order; the communists create order for the purpose of creating confusion. The Countess irritates me because she makes it easy for them. The masses don't see the cause of the plague; they see the disease. And as a Jew, she annoys me particularly. We had become accustomed to those who oppressed us. The monarchy has its pogroms behind it; for the revolution they still lie ahead."

39

"How would it be if you looked at the sensation you are after as a regrettable individual case?"

"Burintzev talked about you," Dr. Friedlieber replied. "You're too intelligent to believe what you're saying. In the fifteenth century you would have come to accompany Countess Tarnovska to the stake; now here you are, come to pour water on the stake."

"Countess Tarnovska must have offended you, Dr. Friedlieber."

"I am accustomed to being offended," said Friedlieber.

A commotion at the desk announced the arrival of the Princess.

5

The children had been put to bed. The Princess and Andrey were alone in the drawing room of the Princess' suite. To Andrey it seemed that she hadn't changed at all. Although she was taller and darker than Maria, she could have posed for a portrait of her sister; thus she was a portrait of life, instead of life itself. In accordance with her father's wishes, Olga had married Prince Gabriel Katerinovich, twenty years her senior, a pale man without features. In three consecutive years, she had presented him with three healthy children. Like all people without troubles, she had plenty of time for the troubles of others, and was considered charitable by the poor. She knew how to conduct a hygienic marriage with a man she didn't love. In her presence Andrey always felt slightly irritated, as if he had just learned about some injustice. The Devil had a sure instinct for amusing himself: there were people whom he passed by because it would be no fun to seduce them. This time, too, Andrey's conversation with Olga opened on a note of irritation.

Not later than tomorrow, she declared, she was going to continue her journey, for she had no intention of getting involved in the "Tarnovska scandal." He could see for himself: that Jew from Vienna had already molested her, and her father had warned her against communicating in any way with Mura. Her brothers, Alexander and Zoa, were of the same opinion. From her half brother Nikolay she had heard nothing—"of course."

"Is no one going to stand by her?" asked Andrey.

"It's her own fault."

"All the more reason for compassion."

"You say that? Why do you help the sick and the poor?"

"Sinners are poor and sick, and guilty."

"Is that why you're here?"

He could hear the challenge in her question. "You hate Mura."

She frowned. She had a peculiar way of frowning. Instead of drawing her eyebrows together, she raised them, making her eyes big and questioning as the folds in her forehead fled to the roots of her hair. "We are not a family like any other," she said. "One of our ancestors was Brian, the first Christian King of Connaught. The Franciscan monk, Cornelius O'Rourke, became a martyr in 1578, together with the Bishop of Mayo. I don't hate Mura; I despise her."

"It's one thing to be proud, another to be haughty."

"Apparently one has to become guilty to please you. You mistake pride for haughtiness. I despise Mura because she has forgotten her obligations to our name."

"You sound like Dr. Friedlieber. He thinks morality is a social obligation; you think it is a family one."

The Princess was standing at the window. Her hands were gripping the silver cross she wore around her neck. It wouldn't have surprised Andrey if she had held out the cross to him. He had to think of Otrada. Maria was gone. Olga had thrown her arms around his neck, weeping. "Why? Why Mura and not me?" Her little breasts had pressed against his chest. The ripe fruit. He would have liked to ask her if she had thought of the Franciscan monk then. Cornelius O'Rourke, 1578. It was easier to forgive the sinners than to believe the innocent.

"I came here because of Tioka," said Olga. "You still love Mura."

He went over to her. "I am asking myself, does one hate the sinner because one envies him?"

"You only became a priest because of her."

The old reproach. As if it mattered. Why did people—women especially—however devout they were, believe that with everyone who chose the Church, they lost something that belonged to them?

"What do you intend to do with Tioka?" he asked.

"I shall bring him up with my children as if he were my own. Unfortunately, he is already twelve. But I hope my children are immune to bad influences."

"Do you know Tioka?"

He tried to ask the question guilelessly, but he was ashamed, because her harsh words were welcome to him. Since his conversation with Tioka that evening, he had a goal, and Olga was making it easy for him to reach it.

"The child was brought up in the gutter," she said. "Mura dragged him from city to city, from hotel to hotel. The only person who ever devoted herself to him was that Swiss prostitute. Whenever a man relinquished the door handle of his mother's bedroom, the next one was there to take it out of his hand. Before she became Kamarovsky's mistress, she was in constant flight from her creditors. Our tailor in Kiev told me that one night she fled from the bailiff out the back entrance of her hotel. Just the same, I intend to make a human being out of her son."

"On the condition that he forget his mother?"

"Her name will not be mentioned in my house."

The rain splashed against the window pane. The Riva degli Schiavoni was deserted. The wind sought in vain for autumn leaves and swept the rain water into the lagoons.

"I shall keep Tioka," said Andrey.

"You are out of your mind."

"The love you are prepared to give him would be worth nothing if he had to forget his mother for it."

"Do you think you are Jesus Christ, that you take it upon yourself to forgive a sinner like her?"

"You don't have to be God to forgive, Olga." Love for the child overwhelmed him, and he didn't ask if it was love for Maria Tarnovska's son.

"I thought you traveled a great deal," Olga remarked.

"There are boarding schools."

"You mean convents."

He had considered Olga religious; now she spoke of convents as if the Church were out fishing for young souls. She said, "Children are burdened with so much guilt in such schools that they can only atone for it by dedicating their whole lives to the Church."

For a moment his enthusiasm ebbed. He could hear Tioka: "Do you think God would free Mama if I promised to become a priest?" He said, "I shall have Tioka brought up in one of the best boarding schools."

"In Russia?"

"No. Not in Russia."

Hadn't he taken vows of poverty, Olga wanted to know. Where

would he get the money? He shouldn't believe that he could count on her or her family. He would find a way, he replied, although he possessed nothing of his own but the few coins he had on him. He wanted to say that the Lord had fed five thousand with five loaves of bread and two fish, but he knew that boarding schools didn't think much of five loaves of bread and two fish. "She will ruin you," said Olga, "even from her cell," and she didn't let go of the cross. But it didn't touch him, although he had thought somewhat similarly about himself in Dr. Calzini's office. He could see Tioka in the Katerinovich *palais:* a leper among three healthy children, an orphan with a mother who was alive; nameless, with a name that rang out in the world; robbed of the only love of which his sinful mother was capable. The certainty that he could save the child from lovelessness, and could save love for Maria, gave him the strength that Olga Katerinovich, growing more and more excited, called "blind fanaticism." She would not give in; she demanded that the boy go with her; now she seemed to be wrestling with her sister over the boy. When she finally threatened Andrey with the intervention of the Russian Embassy, and declared she would denounce him to his superiors, he told her that he would, indeed, welcome such steps, for it had just occurred to him that judgment had not yet been passed on Maria, that she was still her own master, certainly where the disposition of her child was concerned—he had been wrong not to ask her what her wishes were. Now he would do so, and abide by them.

Midnight was near when he headed for the monastery through the deserted streets of Venice, the rain drumming down on the cowl that covered his head. He had a long way to go, but he met no one. Although the streets were dark, he seemed to be seeing Venice for the first time. His steps were sure, as if a radiant star were guiding him. For moments at a time the darkness surged back like the water before the lashing wind. Near the monastery, in the Sestiere di Castello, he saw a beggar sitting in a doorway. But the beggar didn't speak to him. Perhaps he was drunk; perhaps he thought the Dominican was one of his own kind.

CHAPTER 5

I

Maria Tarnovska entered the room of the *procuratore del re* with a feeling of elation. She had stood half the night at her window. Strangers—Russian tourists, most likely—had played a serenade under her window. A few *gondolieri* had joined in. *"Dime mora zogia mia, dime quel che t'ho da far. . . ."* (Tell me, my dark sweetheart, what I may do for you.) The walls had towered mutely above them. Then a woman had begun to sing from behind her bars, a beautiful, clear, nostalgic voice. The men in the gondolas had listened to her; and the prisoners behind their walls. Then the *gondolieri* again: *"Dime mora zogia mia . . . ,"* followed by insults, women with hoarse night voices crying obscenities through their prison windows; the men in the gondolas laughing and replying. Declarations of love interrupted by filth. "Maria! Maria Nikolaevna!" A Russian voice, and from one of the windows: *"Silenzio!"* Voices, spattering against the wall like hail; lights, flashing on in the nuns' windows. The chorus opened up again after having been silenced by the nostalgic voice. The men in the gondolas applauded. The applause ebbed away slowly against the prison walls, like waves. A shrill voice, a woman's, screaming—a cry for help. *"Dime mora zogia mia . . ."* Not until after midnight was it quiet. *"Addio,* Maria Nikolaevna." The sound of oars echoing through the night, a splashing *"Arrivederci."*

The *procuratore del re's* room in the Palace of Justice was not really an office; it was, rather, the study of a scholar, with dark bookcases, two reproductions of paintings—Veronese's "Unfaithfulness" and Savoldo's "Venetian Lady." Wine-red upholstered armchairs, inti-

44

mate lamps. As on the occasion of former hearings, it raised the Countess' spirits even more.

Prosecuting Attorney Giorgio Garzoni, of whom it was said that he belonged to the illustrious family whose *palazzo* on the Canale Grande was a center of attraction for tourists, looked out of place in these fustian surroundings, but he would have looked just as out of place in an office. Like a sketch by Goya, one of those highly accurate yet casual drawings, he was all arrested motion. Perhaps he was at home nowhere. The likeliest surroundings for him would have been in one of the old *palazzi,* but it would have had to be one of those that stood empty now, in which ancestors occasionally stepped out of their picture frames to scurry soundlessly across marble floors.

It had been quite clear to Maria Tarnovska for some time that Garzoni was having her brought before him more often than necessary. Today a reporter and a translator were present. She was to be confronted with Nicholas Naumov. She had hardly given a thought recently to the young man who was brought in now. She had dreamed of Prilukov, Pavel, Vassily, and of Ivan, the stable boy. Now she thought she was dreaming. Naumov seemed spun of the material dreams were made of, transparent, flawless, veiled. His long white hands moved as if he were directing an invisible orchestra. It was impossible to follow his eyes, or to evade them, for they seemed to flutter from out his deep sockets like fledgling birds, and fly back again, startled. When he saw Maria Tarnovska, he began to tremble, not fearfully or excitedly, but like a blue spruce with the wind blowing through it.

"Calm yourself," the Prosecutor said, without being able to hide his disgust. "Please repeat your statement."

Naumov was silent.

Garzoni sighed, then he read aloud, softly, monotonously, as people do when speaking with the voice of another. " 'On the twenty-seventh of August, Madame de Tarnovska asked me to visit the grave of her mother with her, at All Saints Cemetery in Kiev. It was almost dark when we got there. After looking for it for quite some time, we found the grave of the Countess O'Rourke. Madame de Tarnovska sank down beside the gravestone, sobbing; she clasped the marble statue on it and cried, "Mother, Mother, must he die?" Then she got up, looked at me, and said, "Yes. He must die." She began to walk very fast. I had difficulty in keeping up with her. She ran across graves, stepped on wreaths and flowers. By the time I had caught up with her, she had reached the cemetery walls, where those who have taken their own lives lie in unhallowed ground. She stopped beside a wooden cross on which I could make out the name Vladimir Stahl. She leaned over the grave—so low, I thought she was going to kiss the ground. When she finally stood up again, she said, "He orders you to kill him." I tried to bring the Countess to her senses. I had heard the name Stahl before, but I didn't know that he had been one of the Countess' lovers. She told me that Stahl had loved her, and repeated, "He would have rid me of him. He orders you to kill him." Then she demanded that I swear, by the memory of her mother and the salvation of Vladimir Stahl, to kill the man she hated. I raised my hand to swear but had every intention of breaking the outrageous vow. Late that evening we went back to the Countess' hotel. She told me that she had sworn to kill Count Kamarovsky. After she had made this vow, her son, Tioka, for whom the doctors had given up all hope, had been miraculously saved. She also said that Donat Prilukov was willing to kill Kamarovsky, but this would bind her forever to a man for whom she felt nothing but hatred. I had to take for granted that the Countess was speaking the truth, because, in Vienna, Prilukov had told me that Kamarovsky was no more than a "living corpse." I tried to convince the Countess of the monstrosity of her intention. I can remember exactly, saying, "Your life is ruled by the dead; they are the compass that points toward the cemeteries." I must confess, however, that her frenzy had taken possession of me. I was jealous of both men—Kamarovsky and Prilukov. Although in my childhood I had felt no aversion toward Kamarovsky, I could understand the horror Madame de Tarnovska felt for him. And she showed me a telegram in which Kamarovsky insulted me in the most shameful fashion. I wanted to challenge the Count to a duel, but Madame de Tarnovska declared she would not survive my death. Since I felt that Prilukov was quite capable of the deed, I wanted to get there ahead of him, and hurried to Venice the next morning. Now I realize that my action was mainly aimed at getting Prilukov out of the way.' "

Garzoni had finished. "Do you want to add anything to this statement?" he asked the Countess.

Add anything? An evening in August, a leaden sky, a thunderstorm gathering over Lukyanovskaya. The young man helping her to rise from Vladimir's grave. "Only the dead shall be witness to our love, Mura." Baudelaire: *"Nous aurons des lits pleins d'odeurs légères,/ Des divans profonds comme des tombeaux,/ Et d'étranges fleurs sur les étagères/ écloses pour nous sous des cieux plus beaux."* Divans profound as the grave. His translation of *The Flowers of Evil*. The grave a bed and the grave of his sex. The smell of dead earth. His pitiful weakness, strong enough only to silence his conscience. She herself stretched high. "The dead are laughing at you, Nicholas." The willow tree. As she broke off some of its slender branches, he trembled. "Take them, Nicholas." The drive from the cemetery. A naked youth in the hotel room, beautiful as an angel, crawling on all fours like a dog; she still in her black dress, the willow switch in her hand. "Revile me, Maria, I implore you. Punish me." The lashes on his back. "Coward! How long do I have to whip you?" Under the blows, his sex erect. Not a dog any more, a twenty-four-year-old youth, his flagellated body over hers. "Order me not to ravish you, Maria. I am your slave." Signor Garzoni, it is the truth. He may have wanted to break his vow out there on the cemetery, but in bed . . . "Promise me, promise to spit in my face if I fail you again." And she: "If you fail me, I shall never flog you again." And he: *"Toi qui, comme un coupe de couteau,/ Dans mon coeur plaintif es entrée;/ Toi qui, forte comme un troupeau/ De démons, vins, folle et parée,/ De mon esprit humilié/ Faire ton lit et ton domaine;/–Infame à qui je suis lié/ Comme le forçat à la chaîne."* Five minutes alone with Nicholas and he would declare himself a liar, whimpering.

"Signor Garzoni," she said, "you can see that Nicholas Naumov doesn't dare to repeat his lie in my presence. The truth is that he threatened to kill Kamarovsky if I didn't break my engagement. It is true that he accompanied me to my mother's grave and that after that we had a violent quarrel, which upset me so much that I was taken sick with a nervous fever. Next morning my maid told me that Monsieur Naumov had left for Venice, whereupon I decided to beg Prilukov to follow him immediately."

"Why didn't you warn Count Kamarovsky?"

"My fiancé was a jealous man. Any warning would only have added to his distrust."

"You should have taken such a risk upon yourself."

"I didn't take Naumov seriously."

"Then why did you send Prilukov after him?"

"After Naumov left, I began to fear his madness."

"Naumov's testimony coincides with Prilukov's. Only, Prilukov declares that you sent him to Venice to denounce Naumov after the crime. In this way you wanted to rid yourself of two despised men—Kamarovsky and Naumov."

Naumov swayed. An officer offered him a chair. The Prosecutor paid no attention to him. "Signor Naumov has testified that you personally removed all marks of identification from his clothes so that he could not be identified in case of arrest."

The Countess felt that Garzoni was trying to help her. "You yourself say that, on the one hand, I am supposed to have persuaded Prilukov to denounce Naumov; on the other, I am supposed to have helped him to remove all signs of identification from his clothing. I am the victim of a plot between these two men."

"Please face Signor Naumov," said Garzoni. "Naumov, stand up!"

The Countess recalled that Nicholas had told her about Kaefer, the famous hypnotist. If Naumov was a good medium, why shouldn't she perhaps possess hypnotic powers? She wanted to impose her will on Naumov, but she could not do so because she had to think of the man sitting behind his desk, watching her. Garzoni knew all about her; she knew nothing of him. Was he married? Did he have children? Did he drink for pleasure or stupefaction? Did he obey the law or was he a hypocrite? Was he selling, or buying? Did he love his mother? Was he brave, or a coward, courageous by cowardice? Did he envy the riches of others? Did he avoid his own image, or did he enjoy looking at himself in the mirror? What was his weakness? Did he like frigid women, or did he go to whores, for whom he remained nameless? Did he love the light, or feel for the switch to put it out? What excited him—a sentimental word, or a severe gesture? She was sure of only one thing: he had confronted her with Naumov, not to find out the truth, but because he wanted to see them together as they had been together—the woman and the youth. She heard him saying, "Naumov, repeat that Madame de Tarnovska incited you to commit murder." The excitement in his voice satisfied her.

Scarcely audible, Naumov said, "She did."

The Countess said, "Nicholas, confess that you are lying."

Naumov was silent.

"You insist therefore that Naumov acted of his own free will?" Garzoni asked, and she, still addressing Naumov: "Don't force me to say you are a dog, Naumov. Think of your father. Do you want him to hear it said in court that his son is a dog? Wouldn't it be better for him to know you murdered out of jealousy?"

Garzoni interrupted her "I asked if you were going to abide by your testimony."

She pointed at Naumov. He had fallen on his knees and was wringing his hands, imploring the Prosecutor to dismiss him. He couldn't endure the sight of the Countess, he stammered: if he wasn't freed of her presence, he would be forced to lie. His speech was confused—Russian, Italian, French. He accused her, withdrew his accusations, declared himself the murderer, denounced Maria Tarnovska as the instigator, negated what he had just said. He took all blame upon himself, begged for mercy, accused her again. Like a dog begging for a scrap of bread, he crawled to where she was standing, reared up as if to lunge at her, beat his breast, crossed himself, cried out to the Holy Mother, murmured lines from *The Flowers of Evil*. *"Tu n'es pas digne q'on t'enlève/ A ton esclavage maudit."*

Garzoni gave the sign to take Naumov away. After he had dismissed the others as well, he rose and accompanied Maria Tarnovska to the door, touching her arm as if by chance. "We shall continue our conversation at the prison."

2

Two days after the confrontation with Naumov, the prison director presented Maria Tarnovska, in the presence of her lawyer, Calzini, with two letters and some papers. The letters were from Olga and Andrey. Both were short and concerned Tioka. After she had read them, she had a consultation with Calzini. Then she did what he had warned her not to do—signed a document to the effect that she entrusted Father Andrey Antonovich Vyrubov with the guardianship of her son, Count Tioka Vassilyevich Tarnovsky, born in Kiev on April 18, 1895, "for the present and until countermanded."

In the night she could not sleep. She thought of her childhood, as she did often now when fatigue overwhelmed her. It was as if the present fell asleep, a poor watchman incapable of refusing entry to the past. In the center, focal point of her childhood, her father squatted like a gigantic spider. "Terrible O'Rourke," they had called him, admiringly. Everything terrible was always admired. Had he ever loved?

His first wife, the Princess? Twice a month he had had himself driven to the cemetery—black suit, black hat, black cotton gloves. On those days the meals were meager; all piano music was silenced. Terrible O'Rourke sat at the head of the table, taciturn, as if he wanted to punish the living. Twice a month it was funeral time in Otrada. Her father had been drawn to graves, too; his compass had also been pointed by Death.

Her mother. She had faded slowly. They had grown accustomed to her dying; she herself had grown used to it. Death had read aloud to her like a patient governess. How had she been able to endure life at the side of such a man? Was the love life of a mother an enigma to all daughters? Her father had not crushed the flowers; he had denied them water until they withered. To Maria Tarnovska it seemed that since her childhood she had been trying to avenge her mother, although she had not loved her mother more than most children, probably less. Everything a failure.

Fleetingly she smiled. The vision of two aunts came to her—Aunt Anna and Aunt Sonya, twins. One could hear their steps on the stone tiles. They had seemed to be on the go all the time, even at night, and always together, *tripp-trapp;* not four feet, but two, always in time, *tripp-trapp, tripp-trapp.* Maria Tarnovska listened; the prison was still. The two had hardly ever spoken, just stared straight ahead like simpletons. They had always smiled at the same time, and moved their knitting needles in the same rhythm. What had they been knitting? One day their steps had no longer echoed through the halls; the knitting needles lay motionless. They had stepped into a carriage, black sequined bonnets on their heads, had nodded and waved, raising their hands at the same time—au revoir. No, not au revoir. Adieu. Maria Tarnovska could feel rage welling up inside her as she had felt it rise when she had found out her father had sent the twins to an insane asylum in Warsaw. "It is better for them." That was what they had said in Otrada. Everybody always felt that whatever Terrible O'Rourke, answerable only to himself, had decided was for the best. Why had he always known best; why had he always been so infallibly sure about everything? And why had all of them always done what he thought best? Alexander, you will be an engineer. Zoa, you are to stay single; Olga, you shall have children; Katharina, you are to die; Maria, you shall end your days in prison.

Nikolay, her half brother, the only one of them who had rebelled

Her father had loved Nikolay's mother—perhaps; but his capacity to love had been exhausted; nothing remained for his son. Never had he taken Nikolay with him to the cemetery. Where was Nikolay? A name in political arrest warrants. Or Uncle Edward? He could have helped her, but, like her mother, he was dead. The darkened library, in which he had led her out of darkness. What had been the doctor's name? Maria Tarnovska believed that all might not be lost if she could only remember the doctor's name. Superstition grew rank behind prison walls, entwined itself around a name. Why were all of them dead or gone—her mother, the doctor, Uncle Edward and the aunts, and Nikolay?

The darkness of her cell was different from all other obscurities, because no will could penetrate it; it was a blindness that came from outside. In it her childhood lay on the floor like a toy abandoned that somebody had forgotten to put away. Maria Tarnovska did not fall asleep because she feared the awakening. The woman in the Vienna jail had told her it would be like this. The mornings should have counted double—one morning, two days. When the bars began to stand out against the sky, a convict's gray covered the furnishings, common sounds stole through the walls, and one realized that the night had brought no miracle. One was awake, but one's instincts were still asleep, and one's self-deception. Every morning held its own verdict.

Olga's letter. That was why her childhood had returned. She could read the same hateful certainty in Olga's letter, the assurance of Terrible O'Rourke. Why should this be right and that be wrong for Tioka? Why had everything been all wrong? How did Olga know? How did she know that a murderess could not love her child more than the cocksure O'Rourkes? Those were the enemies—the benevolent who knew to whom they were giving; the punctual who did not have time for their children; the indolent who never faltered; the devout who kept confession in mind as they sinned; the fearful who knew the law; those so sure of themselves, they smiled at the doubter; the faithful who didn't deceive their women but murdered them.

Maria Tarnovska sat up. That she could think surprised her. Was it possible that she took after her father? Had he done what was wrong for the sake of evil, or for the delight it gave him? Had he wanted to torture others or to test his own power? Didn't the weak, who carried the strong, also carry their guilt? You could trample on the weak; but because they were weak, the ground gave way beneath them, and you sank into the mire yourself. She had sunk deep. Now she thought she could feel firm ground under her feet again. How had it happened? What had freed her? Pavel's death or her imprisonment? Her eyes filled with tears. She rarely cried, and then only with rage or for joy. She wasn't angry now. A feeling of bliss flooded her. It was not Pavel's death, nor her imprisonment. It was the certainty—for once and incredibly granted her—that she had done the right thing. She had thought only of Tioka, acted only for him. She was not her father. Tioka was with Andrey. He was safe.

3

She arranged her cell like a boudoir. Pictures in silver frames stood on a small table beside her cot. Since all she had were rough blankets, she spread a velvet dress across the cot; on one of the two chairs, a silk scarf. There was the scent of L'Origan.

It grew dark early. The December wind hurried past the prison walls as if it feared the sight of La Giudecca. The lights swayed back and forth. Every now and then their rays mingled with the tired light in the cell.

One of the women let the Prosecutor in. He waited until she had closed the door, then he went up to Maria Tarnovska and took her hand. "This visit is quite unconventional," he said. "An inquiry in a cell is permissible only in exceptional cases. I have been given permission to hold an on-the-spot investigation."

"An on-the-spot investigation?"

He hesitated, undecided which of the two chairs to sit on, sat down finally on the one that was not covered. He was breathing heavily, as if he had come a long way fast. "The evidence against you is overwhelming," he said. "Your relationship to Naumov is clarified. There are various interpretations for your relationship to Prilukov, but one is just as incriminating as the other. The only one who exonerates you is your maid. But your motives are unclear, unless it was an insurance murder." He spoke quickly, in fluent French. "I want to confront you with Kamarovsky."

She paled. She had thought Garzoni was her friend. Perhaps he was even more malicious than the oily *chef de réception* in Vienna. "Pavel is dead," she said.

"You went to your mother's grave with Naumov."

"Yes."

"And to the grave of Vladimir Stahl."

"Yes."

"Didn't you say that the dead speak to you?"

"Naumov said that."

"I don't think he lied. The dead speak to those who want to hear them. My wife died three years ago. Our son was barely two at the time. One August evening I drove out to the cemetery where Pavel Kamarovsky also lies buried. My wife and I were very much in love. Since her death I haven't touched another woman." His voice was trembling with excitement. "As I leaned over her grave, I heard her voice. 'Hurry home,' it said. 'Francesco is in danger.' I found my son with terrible burns. He had spilled boiling water over himself. In the excitement no one had called a doctor. An hour later and it would have been too late."

"You want to take me to Pavel's grave?"

She no longer distrusted him. They were kindred spirits. Peter and Donat and Nicholas and Pavel and Vladimir—kindred spirits. They met in mysterious ways and on mysterious paths, recognized each other, walked arm in arm, until death parted them. But death did not part them. They met again in space, recognized each other, wafted through space arm in arm. The murderess, the murdered ones, the prosecutors . . .

"We are kindred spirits," she said.

She took her traveling coat, her small hat, fastened her scarf under her chin. She dressed as slowly as if she were undressing. "I don't have a mirror," she said.

"You are beautiful," he told her.

Sister Sofia opened the door of the cell. There she stood, eyes lowered, pressed against the wall, a black relief, as if she wanted to let sin pass by, like the pious letting the monstrance pass them. "Your permit . . . ?" she asked.

"I have already given it to you." Garzoni's tone was harsh.

Sister Sofia fiddled with her keys. "I need your signature, Signor Garzoni."

It took a while for her to find pen and ink. Maria Tarnovska and the Prosecutor stood in the open doorway of the cell. It's as though Elise had to run back into the boudoir to fetch a forgotten handkerchief, thought Maria Tarnovska. The corridor was empty. The doors of the cells looked like gravestones. Sister Sofia came back; the Prosecutor signed.

The front of the prison faced a narrow canal. On the opposite side, dark suburban houses, warehouses of misery. A gondola was waiting at the steps, its long side slapping against the heavy stones. The *gondoliere's* white collar stood out in the dark. He had on a sailor suit, like the *gondolieri* of the *grandes familles*. Maria Tarnovska put her hand on his arm, and he helped her across the carpeted step of the gondola.

The night was cold. She breathed deeply. Only her fingers were cold. She had forgotten her gloves. It was as if she were breathing for the first time in weeks. In the prison courtyard, even the air was prisoner. Garzoni, in a black coat, bareheaded, turned to face her. It occurred to her that she had never seen him in profile. The back of his head slanted sharply down to his neck, rather like the roof of a Swiss chalet. It touched her that he tried to hide this little defect.

"Are you related to the Garzonis whose *palais* is next to the Mocenigos?" she asked softly.

"We are an old family," he said, "and dying out fast, like the O'Rourkes. Our children live, but they are doomed to die."

The lights of the miserable houses of La Giudecca sank into the water like old gold coins in the Fontana di Trevi. The gondola crossed the Canal della Giudecca and glided toward the living lights. To the right, the island San Giorgio Maggiore. The city, St. Mark's Square, the Doges Palace . . . did the *gondoliere* have to go under the Bridge of Sighs, that stone sarcophagus, resting on the banks of the canal at either side, as if being borne by the stony dead? Maria Tarnovska counted the strokes of the oar. Sleeping palaces, small balconies above the water, steps echoing over their heads. Every now and then they met another gondola. The *gondolieri* cried out greetings and warnings to each other.

"They think we are a bridal couple," whispered Garzoni.

"At this time of year?"

"At any time of year."

She followed his gaze. The Condottiere came riding out of the dark. A closed church. God locked himself in at night in Venice. Next to it, a lighted portal in gray marble, two lions turned from each other, a cold mosaic—the *ospedale civile*. A few lights behind grimy panes

That was where Pavel had died. Her distrust was aroused, died down again. There were the lagoons. A breeze from the open sea. She breathed more freely. In front of them lay the cemetery island of San Michele.

The gondola had to circle the island, past brick walls interrupted by heavy iron portals; steps in front of them, a ramp, as if to let coffins glide into the water. A smell of death? Perhaps it was only the stench of the lagoons.

"Like a prison," said Maria Tarnovska, shivering.

"How little room the dead of a whole city need," said Garzoni. "They are unassuming, the dead."

Maria Tarnovska noticed barbed wire on top of the brick wall. "Are they afraid the dead might get away?" she asked.

The gondola came alongside. The *gondoliere* took one of the torches out of its brass holder. Garzoni lighted the way. Maria Tarnovska lifted her skirt so as not to slip on the damp, moss-covered steps.

The entrance was of white marble, a gigantic tomb; above it, an angel with a scale in his hand. She had seen a figure like it over the portal of the prison, only not an angel but the goddess of justice. Did even angels weigh good against evil? Were the angels so strict with the dead?

Slowly she followed Garzoni. The slower she walked, the longer her freedom would last, even if it was only the freedom of a graveyard. She had thought they would find the cemetery in complete darkness, but it was sparsely lighted. Like the angel over the portal, it was stern. A field of white crosses, one exactly like the other—only nuns rested here, only priests there, cloisteredly separated even in death. Steps leading up a marble semicircle, magnificent plaques on the walls, ivy hanging in wrought-iron urns, in front of them vases filled with chrysanthemums, asters, winter flowers; the graves of the rich. Garzoni led her through small courtyards. Not a tree anywhere. The courtyards were surrounded by white stone walls, lined with marble and alabaster. Reliefs with stone faces—a beard in stone, a virginal smile in stone, a child's face, an old man's, in stone. 1810 to 1882, 1840 to 1851. The aged and the young who hadn't found a place in the stingy ground; their names side by side as on the back of a file case.

Maria Tarnovska screamed. A cat had run across her feet. Garzoni held out his hand to her.

An open field, an avenue of cypresses. The Prosecutor went on ahead between the trees. A huge stone cross stood in the middle of a field, with freshly dug graves all around it, wooden crosses.

"Count Pavel Ergrafovich Kamarovsky, 1868–1907," was inscribed on one of the wooden crosses. The wind tore into the silk scarf around her throat.

It was difficult to imagine people one had known in the narrow confines of a coffin. What had surrounded them in life belonged to them; perhaps they had only existed through what had surrounded them. How could they be if nothing surrounded them? Here they were turned to sand without surroundings. Something devised by carpenters separated them from the earth. Strange that she could imagine Pavel dead. The bed had been his coffin; now the coffin was his bed. *"Dushka, dushka!"* Every night he had wakened her out of sleep. "Tell me about Prilukov! . . . Look, I had this sent from Paris, *dushka*. You'll enjoy it. . . . How did Tarnovsky love you? . . . Get into the bath, *dushka!* . . . Tell me about Bozevsky!" And afterward, his exhausted sleep, as if dead. Sleep well, Pavel, she thought. I did not murder you.

The wind tugged at the cypresses and inflamed the clouds; their edges burned like pieces of cloth caught fire. The lantern in Garzoni's hand swung back and forth. Maria Tarnovska wondered why she was afraid only of the cats. She had been taught that superstition was a sin; but that couldn't be, because now, with her belief, she had lost all false beliefs as well. Ghosts were not at home in cemeteries; only cats were at home here.

The lamp cast its light on the grave beside Kamarovsky's cross. Flowers in an earthenware vase stood nearby, as if by chance. Maria Tarnovska stepped up to the vase, took the chrysanthemums out of it, laid them on Kamarovsky's grave. She was grateful that he could not speak. If he had never spoken, he would still be alive. As she leaned over the grave with the stolen flowers, she was overcome by disgust, as if the coffin were a bed. She could feel Garzoni's breath on her neck.

"Won't you confess that you murdered him, Maria Nikolaevna?" he whispered. She shook her head. "Why did you do it?" She shook her head. "Don't you fear God?" She shook her head. "God is omniscient."

She nodded. Since God was omniscient, he knew why Pavel Kamarovsky had to die. She didn't. Because of the vow by Tioka's life?

56

Because he had been one of three men? A test of power, accident, madness? It was good that God was omniscient.

Then they were walking through the cemetery again. The grave-stones were like prison doors. The wind was heavy with the scent of dead flowers. Little red oil lamps lighted the way as if borne by invisible dwarfs. In one of the courtyards, the Prosecutor suddenly stood still. It must have been the graveyard of Venetian patricians. He said, "I don't want you to confess. I shall conduct the prosecution so that you are acquitted."

She turned to him. For the first time she was startled. She was afraid of seeing Donat appear from behind Garzoni. He put the lantern down on one of the gravestones. His hands grasped her hips, moved up her back. "You shall belong to me," he said.

She responded to his kiss with shut lips.

"I must possess you."

"When I am free."

"Now!" His hands touched her breasts. "You loved Naumov in a cemetery."

"How do you know?"

"He confessed it. He will confess anything I tell him to."

He dragged her down onto the gravestone. The lamp tipped over, the glass broke, the light went out. He sought her body. Gently she freed herself. "Later," she said. "When I am free."

"Now!"

"Later."

"You swear it?"

"I swear."

"By the dead?"

"By the dead."

"And by your salvation?"

"And by my salvation."

She looked up and saw a stone woman leaning over her.

Between graves and wreaths and stones and trees, they groped their way through the cemetery, back to the gondola.

4

This was the evening Maria Tarnovska had dreaded—Christmas Eve, 1907.

57

Her plea to be allowed to remain in her cell was denied. On Christmas Eve the prisoners were given privileges. Privileges were like punishments.

It began with a communal dinner, a feast. The sheep were herded into the big hall. Since those still to be tried were in a section of their own, Maria Tarnovska had not met many of the convicted. Even now, those under investigation sat at a long table separate from the rest. But the condemned were not far away. In between sat the nuns. Those under investigation wore their own clothes, and although they were for the most part shabby and dirty, still they had the effect of a provocation beside the brown uniforms of those who had been sentenced. Long brown sacks—from shoulder to floor—and over them a gray-white apron, like the scapular of a monk. A few years ago, according to Sister Sofia, on Christmas Eve, the regular prisoners had fallen upon the colorful birds for no good reason, and had torn their poor finery off their bodies. That was why the nuns now formed a black cordon between finality and hope.

Maria Tarnovska had put on her simplest dress. She sat between the motherly Venetian woman who had killed her husband with a flat-iron, and a young creature, a coarse beauty, who had stood watch for a bank robbery. The food tasted good to the fat mama; she appreciated everything about the jail; she even found the nuns charming. She also liked to speak of her blessed husband, as if she had not been the one to dispatch him into his blessed state. Stubbornly she had talked herself into the belief that the Countess had also killed her husband, so she looked upon her as a colleague. Maria Tarnovska was revolted by the woman's resignation; she preferred the animosity of the burglar's moll. In the hatred of the slimy creature with the sensual mouth, she recognized the distance she was accustomed to being granted by members of the lower classes.

The Countess was the focal point of attention. The condemned prisoners called out to her from various tables. She couldn't understand what was being said; only the word "Contessa" could she distinguish clearly. She was the prima donna of the evening, welcome because she was proof that even the mighty could fall. One of the prisoners, a tiny old woman with skin like papyrus covered with hieroglyphics, was showing off as a great wit. She got up, stretched out her tin cup filled with red wine in her yellow hand toward Maria

Tarnovska, and toasted her amid lively, scornful acclaim, for humans despise those they consider their equal. Even the nuns smiled. And now Maria Tarnovska smiled graciously, as if thanking the table from which the toast had come, and raised her cup to her lips—with astonishing success, for at once all the defiant jeering was silenced. Some of the women applauded; others dragged the old woman down on her seat again. Maria Tarnovska came within an ace of having to take a bow.

Then the prisoners were herded to the distribution of gifts, nuns in front of them, nuns behind them, and a few policemen who formed the guard. It took place in a hall, the original purpose of which was hardly discernible any more. With its stone arched ceiling, thick walls, and embrasure-like windows, it reminded one of a hall in an abandoned castle. A Christmas tree stood in the corner, decorated with a few candles and red apples that looked as if they had been forgotten on a stripped tree; one of those Christmas trees meant for everyone and delighting no one. The young prison chaplain spoke a few uplifting words. Then the director of the prison rose. Taking advantage of the introspective mood, he tried to convince the women that the Savior had been born only for those who were good, and reminded them of their families, whose Christmas they had spoiled. After the director had thus celebrated the birth of Christ, the chaplain started a Christmas hymn. The prisoners joined in the chorus.

Maria Tarnovska stood against the wall, far back. The shadows of the women rose to the ceiling, where they were bent—gigantic broken women. The heads flowed together and bobbed up and down; the hoods of the sisters of Maria Bambina were little waves among big ones. The surging waves above her head made Maria Tarnovska feel sick. Sister Angela, bearded, her puckered cap on a too-large head; a young girl in a transparent summer dress, her voluptuous breasts as if naked; the consumptive pair of twins; two young Italian girls, beautiful as angels, in close embrace; a guard in gray uniform; a young nun, half child, looking about her in consternation; the old woman with the papyrus face. All of them were singing with a guilty fervor, nearer to God because he had punished them; some had mouths that were twitching; others were filled with hate; every now and then the prisoners looked up at the Savior on the cross, whose plaster image hung beside the Christmas tree. Maria Tarnovska looked up too and thought that Christ had chosen death on the cross, because even in death he had opened his arms wide to receive those who had crucified him.

She could feel a thigh pressing against hers. She had felt it before but thought it was an accident. Now the soldier in the gray uniform of a guard, big, coarse, with the apelike features of Neanderthal man, began to move his leg up and down; he was trying to wedge his knee between hers; he rubbed against her like an itching animal against a tree, without looking at her, singing, his eyes on the Christmas tree. Maria Tarnovska suppressed a cry and thrust the man from her.

And then her misery overwhelmed her. Tioka, their last Christmas in Vienna. The two children, Tioka and Granya Kamarovsky. The snow covered Ringstrasse under the windows of the Hotel Bristol. Thick carpets, mountains of candy, fruit, toys. "We shall celebrate next Christmas at the château, *dushka*." And the year before that. Kiev. The pealing of the church bells of Lavra, the sleigh bells. That afternoon, a letter from Andrey to Tioka. "I am on my way home. The war is over." Would Andrey bring something home from the war? Tioka had asked. Elise had come in from the street. "It's quiet outside. Even the revolutionaries respect the day of our Lord." Christmas, 1904. The pearl necklace. "I must spend the evening with my family. Can you forgive me, Mura?" Signed: D. Donat Prilukov. And a letter for Tioka. "You are going to get a pony from me." Just one more lie.

Maria Tarnovska didn't want to remember any more. Least of all did she want to think of Andrey, just as there were moments when one simply could not bear to see the picture of a beloved friend. Again the man's leg moved against hers, at first up and down quickly, regularly, like a butt, then convulsively. She kicked him so hard in the shins that he yelled aloud. Prisoners turned around. The guard behaved as if it were no concern of his; his eyes were still fixed on the Christmas tree. The singing stopped. You could hear the sound of church bells.

Maria Tarnovska tried to move toward the exit, but Sister Angela took her by the arm and forced her into one of the rows of women. The presents were spread out under the tree. On the Savior's birthday, no one was allowed to leave with empty hands. Slowly the rows moved forward. A gift for everyone. *"Lieto natale!" "Dio sio laudato!"* The old woman in front of Maria Tarnovska; the two beauties, still with their arms around each other, behind her. Where was Tioka?

Who was giving him presents, kissing him? What was he thinking of? Was he thinking of her? *"Dio sio laudato!"* Was Andrey with him? Didn't he hope secretly that she would come? Did he go to bed crying? Or had he forgotten her? The old woman took her present. *"Lieto natale!"* It was Maria's turn.

And then she was back in her cell. The light was still burning, courtesy of Christmas Eve. Here you could hear them clearly, the bells of Chiesa del Redentore. Maria Tarnovska opened the little package. It contained a cake of soap.

5

The beginning of January. Maria Tarnovska had not been interrogated again. Had the on-the-spot investigation been a pretext; had Garzoni only wanted to put himself in Nicholas' place? Cemetery in Kiev, cemetery in Venice. But then why had he wanted to wring a confession from her? How had he succeeded in getting permission from the court? The quiet was eerie.

The cell was cold. It rained almost every day. The fog rose to the bars of the windows like a flood. Sometimes Maria Tarnovska thought the fog was going to flow through the window and take her along. But for the most part she was only bored.

She had always known one could suffer from boredom, but never believed that one could be bored with suffering. She began to believe that the present and boredom were one, not only the present she was experiencing now. The present was a step within emptiness, like stairs in an unbuilt house; one could not sit down on them with impunity. A present that led nowhere was boredom. The present was bearable only when it passed, facing the future. Since her present was without a future, she turned toward the past. The boredom remained. Her past had been a present with no future.

Maria Tarnovska was glad when her lawyer's visit was announced, although her aversion to Calzini had grown with every encounter. His haste to sit down, because seated he gave an impression of greater power; his pompous behavior, which wouldn't permit him to admit a mistake; the mixture of wanting to play guardian yet at the same time begging for recognition. If she had been free, she would have found him ridiculous; now his behavior was an insult.

In the reception chamber, he came to meet her, then sat down quickly at the bare table that ran almost the entire length of the narrow room. She sat down opposite him. A single lithograph hung behind him, a glassy blue—a warrior with a gold helmet, half Roman god, half wrestler, staring up at a supernatural vision, the Madonna in effulgence. The patron saint of prison wardens praying to the Holy Mother of God

Calzini spread out his papers. "The sense of orderliness of my 'colleague' Prilukov," he began, "has put a crimp in our sails again. The Vienna police suspected that the papers found on him weren't all he had. Hofrat Stuckart wouldn't give up until further pieces of luggage were located at a railway depot. They contained your entire correspondence with Prilukov, or if it isn't the entire one, it certainly suffices. What methodicalness! He who earns his living honestly doesn't always keep his books in order, but the embezzler always does."

His accusations against Prilukov were nothing new. He seemed to be basing his entire defense on the annihilation of Prilukov. Maria Tarnovska had the feeling, however, that he hadn't come to speak about Prilukov. Hesitantly he put on his glasses. They made him look older. He took up one paper after the other, then, not waiting for her permission, began to read from copies of the letters.

" 'My beloved, today I dreamed of you again. I was sitting naked in front of the mirror, and you were naked, too. You kneeled before me, your head was in my lap. A shameless light was reflected in the mirror. I awoke as if shaken by fever, in a state of incredible bliss.' " A look from behind his glasses, then Calzini read on. " 'I couldn't go back to sleep. Always when we are separated, I have the wildest dreams, and I promise myself to transform them into the happiest reality the next time we are together. Why shouldn't reality once follow the dream? But when you lean over me, I don't dare to use all my seductive powers. But that is going to change.' "

Rage overwhelmed Maria Tarnovska. She was naked, and bound, and a man was having his fun with her. What did Calzini expect from this humiliation?

His face red, and in a shrill voice now, he went on. " 'I am driving Kamarovsky to desperation. Yesterday I told him about our night in Nice. I embellished the story a little, although the truth should have been enough to kill him. I told him that you stayed inside me for one whole hour! You know him—he goes limp when I wear a deep décolleté.' " Calzini was reading like a comedian. " 'I think I could torture him into suicide . . . but is that what we want?' "

Maria Tarnovska wanted to jump to her feet, but weariness dragged her down. He was ridiculous. Men were jealous of each other, yet they took delight in imagining a woman in the arms of another; so closely allied were ecstasy and suffering, so much were all of them like Nicholas Naumov, whom they considered damned.

" 'Yesterday' "—the lawyer was reading another letter—" 'the Baroness Staniskaya was telling about a young man of good family who forced his masseur to flog him, until one day the man became so enraged that he almost beat his master to death, and he had to be taken to the hospital with broken bones. It could have been Naumov.' " Calzini took off his glasses and leaned back as if exhausted.

She couldn't remember the letters; old letters always seemed to have been written by a stranger. She detested lascivious servants who watched their masters' orgies through keyholes.

"Why do you read these letters to me?" she asked. "They have nothing to do with the case."

"You are mistaken. Jurisprudence judges the accused not by his deeds but by what he is capable of. The victim of a miscarriage of justice was capable of committing the crime—he just didn't commit it. The Prosecutor will put these letters to good use."

"Are you trying to frighten me?"

He laid his little hand over the papers, as if protecting his property. "Don't count on the prosecution waiving such incriminating material. Garzoni won't get the case; they know about your nocturnal excursion."

"It was an on-the-spot investigation."

"And what was being investigated? The scene of the crime? Nobody maintains that you were ever there. The room of the culprit? That offers no explanation. No one believed Signor Garzoni's fairy tale that he wanted to wring a confession from you at the victim's grave."

"He had the permission of the court."

"Strangely enough, he had. I don't know how he managed to convince our senile president of the necessity for this hoax."

"But he did."

"He blundered over a formality—as usual. Certain court officials have to be present at an on-the-spot investigation. And unless there is a compelling reason, it may not take place at night. I have requested that Signor Garzoni be relieved of his duty."

"You? You rejected him?"

"And why not?"

"But you are my lawyer."

"I represent your interests. I have to destroy the picture the court has formed of you. If you insist on practicing your 'seductive powers'—as you call them—even in prison, you are only giving the court the proof they want."

"I refuse to let you defend me."

"You have no money."

"The court will assign me a lawyer."

"A nobody. Only I can save you."

"You are mad."

"If I lay down your defense," said Calzini, "your relationship with Garzoni will be made public."

"I have no relationship with Garzoni. You are jealous."

Calzini leaned across the table, close to her. "You are right, Maria Nikolaevna. Your life lies spread out before me. That is why I know you are innocent. Guilty are the men you loved. How could you waste your beauty, your youth, on such miserable creatures? I am jealous of the lost years. But it is not too late. I shall prove that you were Prilukov's victim. You will leave the court on my arm. I shall buy you a house in Toscana. For you and your child. I shall ask for nothing in return. You will soon forget."

Maria Tarnovska felt a leaden weariness. Her life lay spread out before Calzini, yet he had no idea how often she had heard the same words from the men he despised. Their weakness began with the declaration of their strength, miserable saviors. And she had thought Calzini wanted to humiliate her. It had only been a curtain raiser for his own humiliation. He envied the living and the dead the suffering she had brought upon them. What good would it do to upbraid him? Of what use was it to tell him that she had learned to hate her own weapons? Between her and prison for life stood only Dottore Calzini.

She held out her hand to him with a gesture that was as distasteful to her as all gestures one knows too well. When he covered her hand with kisses, she closed her eyes. She blessed the walls of her prison, the bars, and the spying nuns.

CHAPTER 6

I

The houses of the oldest part of the city appeared careworn as Andrey looked out the window of the Geneva library. It was a dismal February afternoon. Melting snow dripped from the steep roofs onto the street. The gaslight from a little antique shop collected in the puddles.

This was the city where Jean Jacques Rousseau had lived—Calvinist, Catholic, Calvinist again, the gigantic hypocrite, chasing faith as if she were a whore. In his lasciviousness to see himself naked, he had unmasked himself; had pronounced the postulate of a return to nature because he had looked upon his uncontrolled instincts as natural; incapable of rearing his children, he had declared that everything in man's hands must rot. A miserable wretch who had loved God only because he had seen himself as God. Rousseau in the city of Calvin. And Andrey had had to follow the trail of the pastor of Pont l'Evêque, the heretic who had actually believed that God had created the world only that it might be a showplace for his "integrity," an ambitious idol. And wasn't this the city in which Dr. Michael Servetus had been burned at the stake, not by the Inquisition, but by the anti-Inquisition of John Calvin?

During the last hours, Andrey had been leafing through the Rousseau *Confessions*. That evening he was to lecture in the Cercle Catholique on this famous son of the city. A bold effort, even in Catholic circles, since this vagrant, hero of whores, miserable father, philosopher, calumniator, the genius Rousseau, had been dead for one hundred and thirty years, and was therefore bathed in the sanctified aura that is eventually bestowed on enduring sin.

Today Andrey was finding it difficult to elevate himself over the hypocrite. In an hour he intended to visit Tioka for the first time since he had taken the boy to the boarding school on the Lake of Geneva. Whenever he thought of Tioka, he had to think of his own hypocrisy.

Thirteen years ago, when he had taken his vows, he had renounced his father's inheritance—the palace in Kiev, properties, jewelry, a fortune in cash and securities, plus the payments from the estate of his mother, a French Princess L'Ardennois. These gifts to his Order could not be made with one stroke of the pen, because of their changeable worth, and because he had to share them with his mother's kin. That had been the temptation, and he had succumbed to it. Instead of making over the sums to his Order semiannually, he had taken advantage of the ignorance of his superiors as to the amounts involved, and had used a part of the income to open an account in the name of Tioka Vassilyevich Tarnovsky at the Bank Commerciale de Bâle. In other words, if he wanted to be just, he had robbed his Order. Fruitless were all explanations that he hadn't enriched himself, that he wasn't the owner, not even the administrator of the money, that every centime went into Tioka's schooling. Only he could donate who owned.

Confession, prayer, mortification—they were no refuge. Nor were all justifications—that the child's soul would have been exposed to fearful shock, that the inimical atmosphere in Olga Nikolaevna's house would have proved unendurable. Everything wrong could be explained away. The search for the motive contradicted the law. Institutions, however dubious, had been created to prevent arbitrary interpretation of the law, since one's will—the product of secret desires and failings—was a twin of caprice. Mitigating circumstances opened the way to barter.

Why hadn't he left the care of the sinner's son in the hands of his Order? Because Saint Dominic had founded the priestly Order to convert the Albinghese, not to abuse his victory over them. Because a mother's misfortune could not have been foreordained to lead her son to the Church. Because John Calvin's heretical teachings of predetermination made partners of God and Devil, who divided souls between each other like brothers. Good answers—if Tioka had not been the son of Maria Tarnovska. One should never stop mistrusting oneself.

His soul could not find peace. It was possible that the Devil, unable to slip through the portal woman, had made entry into his heart through the portal child. There was no denying the fact that during the last months, in which his missions had led him through four different countries, he had never ceased to think of Maria Tarnovska—of Tioka, to be correct, but via Tioka, of course, of his mother, so that the Devil was perhaps leading him on a long leash in a vicious circle as a groom leads a horse; he, who thought he was driving out the Devil, was perhaps being driven by him.

Andrey put the books back on the shelf, thanked the librarian, and left. Twilight was descending on Geneva's old city. Gas lanterns were tired eyes in the dark. The friar hastened across the cobblestones, along the narrow streets, a refractory figure in the town of Rousseau and Calvin.

2

La Glycine was a famous boarding school for the children of aristocratic families from Austria-Hungary, France, Italy, and for the wealthy Swiss; it was religious but not bigoted. The prefect, Monsieur de Vauthier, had prepared Andrey for the fact that Tioka was depressed. Children, he explained, were rather like those who had declared bankruptcy; they lived from day to day, devoted to the pleasures of the moment. They were thick-skinned; in them the sources of self-preservation still bubbled and were fresh. But Tioka didn't show any signs of being thick-skinned or blithe. And how could it be explained that it was Tioka who, only yesterday, had again provoked trouble? He had been the one who had begun to speak of his mother and had threatened his schoolmates, who doubted her innocence. "You should try to influence him," the prefect had told Andrey, "so that he doesn't put himself in the wrong."

When Andrey entered the visitors' room—cold furniture, cold rubber plants, a cold tiled stove—Tioka ran to meet him, overflowing with joy. Andrey pretended not to notice the little bandage over the boy's eye. They talked about the progress he had made, an outing on Mount Salève, a sleigh ride to Nyon. Then Tioka noticed Andrey's questioning look. "I was in a fight," he said.

"What about?"

"One of the boys said something about Mama."

"Who began it?"

"I did. But only because he put a newspaper on my bed, full of lies." He moved closer to Andrey. "Are you sure they were lies?"

"What do you mean?"

"She didn't want to marry Uncle Pavel, not really. I couldn't stand him. And I didn't want Granya for a brother."

The boy's honesty pained Andrey. How much suffering other children must have caused him that nothing was left him now but honesty.

"Why did Mama divorce my father?" Tioka asked.

"Your mother was very, very young when she married your father. She didn't understand him, and he didn't understand her." And he thought: Now I am not even defending the sacrament of marriage any more.

"Of course the boys think he's paying for me here," Tioka went on. "Why are you doing it?"

"Who told you . . ."

"The prefect." He dug into his pockets and brought forth the sort of objects to be found in a boy's pockets—a pocket knife, a slingshot, marbles, an old calendar, and finally, two carefully folded letters. "You may read them, Andrey. You are the only one who may read them."

He didn't read the letters. "Your mother can't spend any money right now."

"She doesn't have any money. That's why she was going to marry Uncle Pavel. Do you know that I once loaned Uncle Donat money?"

Tarnovsky, Prilukov, Kamarovsky—Andrey wondered how many more the boy would name.

Tioka laughed. "It was really his money. He used to give me money. Then one day he wanted to go out with Mama, and he didn't have any money on him. He asked me if I'd saved anything. We broke open my savings bank together. I liked him." He fingered the bandage over his eye. "Do you think I'll ever be with Mama again? I mean honestly now."

"I am sure you will. Some day . . ."

"But if she's convicted?"

"You must believe in her innocence. We have to believe in the people we love." Hollow phrases, clichés for adults. "You see, guilt can be proved, but innocence . . . that's a different matter. When I was about your age, we had a servant. One of our gold plates disappeared, and the entire staff accused old Ivan. The police came, and they did, too. Only my father said it could not have been Ivan. 'Why?' everyone wanted to know. 'Because I know Ivan,' said my father

68

But the officers shrugged their shoulders, for that was no proof, of course. Many years later the plate was found. My father was right because he loved Ivan."

The boy's thoughts seemed far away. "But you promise to tell me the truth?" he asked.

"I promise." Andrey pressed the boy's hand. "And you must avoid quarrels. Remember that the boys don't know your mother. They read a lot of nonsense in the papers or snap things up that their parents say. Monsieur de Vauthier tells me you are the third-best in your class. That's fine. Very fine. Be first. That's the best answer you can give them."

"Right. Could you get me a Russian math book? I don't understand the French one I've got."

"I'll see to it." And they didn't mention Maria Tarnovska again. Andrey thought the boy had forgotten her, but that evening, when he was accompanying the friar to the gate, Tioka said, "Wait a minute while I run up to my room. I've written Mama a letter. I'd rather you mailed it, Andrey."

3

A few days after his departure from Geneva, Andrey received a letter from Dr. Calzini in which he informed the friar that his petition to visit the Countess Maria Tarnovska had been granted. Andrey was in Paris, attending the discussions for the founding of a Dominican monastery in Russia. Although again nothing had come of the plan, he had to postpone his trip to Venice. On the tenth of March, the Prior granted him permission. Three days later, Andrey was in Venice.

He arrived in a pessimistic mood. Since the end of the year, the papers had mentioned the Tarnovska case only occasionally, but for two weeks now, columns had again been given over to it. One especially, in the *Neue Freie Presse,* had attracted Andrey's attention. It was dated Venice and written by Dr. Hugo Friedlieber.

Various events have brought the Kamarovsky murder case into the spotlight again, and they form a rather unpleasant mosaic. As already reported, the Prosecutor for the Crown, Dr. Giorgio Garzoni, was replaced some time ago by the Venetian public prosecutor, Commendatore Randi, which gave rise to the liveliest comment, since the latter intended to retire this year because of ill health. And now we hear that—to make things worse—the famous and highly respected lawyer, Dr. Ricardo Calzini, has also given up Maria Tarnovska's defense. In Venice they say that he came to this decision as the result of personal misfortune. The explosion of a petroleum stove in his home in the Calle dei Fabri resulted in a fire in which his wife, who had been in a wheelchair for years, was burned to death, and a maid suffered third-degree burns. Several prominent lawyers have refused to take over Maria Tarnovska's case, and the Venetian authorities had to admit today—after some hesitation—that the former Moscow lawyer, Donat Dmitrievich Prilukov, who is also accused, tried to commit suicide by slashing his wrists after a confrontation with Maria Tarnovska. They were able to save his life, and he has been admitted to the Inquisition Hospital. These events have thrown the Venetian population—who, surprisingly enough, were at first sympathetic to this seductive woman—into a turmoil. We must not forget that all this is taking place in Italy, a country where superstition is still deeply rooted. The populace is convinced that Maria Tarnovska has the evil eye—*malocchio*—and brings disaster on everyone who comes in contact with her. The Catholic Church is not countering this superstition with appropriate energy; on the contrary, the Church, indirectly, seems to be feeding it. The Superior of the Penitentiary for Women, on the island La Giudecca, a man named Domenico, has, for instance, declared that two nuns, after their keys had disappeared in a "highly mysterious fashion," refused to set foot in the quarters where the Russian aristocrat is housed. Of course, no one wants to admit that the growing animosity is an expression of social unrest or in any way connected with the rebellion of the lower classes against a frivolous aristocracy, which is constantly embroiled in love affairs, duels, brawls, and scandals. Everybody pretends that a strengthening of the guard in front of the Istituti Penali Femminili by four extra men should suffice to cope with all eventualities.

Dr. Friedlieber was not exaggerating. When Andrey arrived in Venice, the newspapers were offering a new sensation. Four Russian students had plotted to abduct the Countess. Two had been arrested; the others had succeeded in fleeing across the Austrian border. Caricatures of Maria Tarnovska as a man-eating octopus looked out at Andrey from shop windows, a seductively beautiful head, men wriggling from her tentacles. And in the streets a song pursued him across the Rialto Bridge and through the Merceria:

> With Maria Tarnovska, Calzini spent the night,
> Found a witch in his arms when next he saw the light.

Prosecutor Garzoni has slept with her too,
Now he's in the dock, and his rashness may rue!

A flag with a death's-head and the words "To the gallows with the Countess!" hung from the house in the Campo Santa Maria del Giglio where Kamarovsky had been murdered. In the monastery on the Sestiere di Castello, a monk told Andrey that a sermon was going to be preached in the church of San Moise against "The Witch of Kiev." The more Andrey heard and saw, the more he felt drawn to the prisoner, as someone may feel close to a drowning man, even if he doesn't know whom he is saving.

It was a cold March. The wind swept across the city from the lagoons, scurrying through the narrow streets like a murderer stalking his prey, hiding in dark corners and under archways, a crazy, searching wind. The pigeons on St. Mark's Square fled to the colonnades, huddled together, warming themselves, flew spasmodically across the square like dead feathers scattered by the wind. The walls of the law courts were gray, the streets were black pen drawings, the *palazzi* without perspective—a single, flat wall with glassy paper windows, like an Advent calendar. Andrey drew his coat closer, hurried past shop windows and newspaper stands, head lowered.

He had to wait a long time for someone to answer at Dr. Calzini's office. In the end an elderly woman came to the door. Her hair was unkempt, her expression horrified, like something creeping out of its lair. She thought he had come to beg, gestured him away, then recognized him, and was startled because she recognized him. Dr. Calzini wasn't in, she said; she didn't know where he was or when he would be back. She was a poor liar. Andrey showed her the letter. That was written before it happened, the woman said, without explaining what she meant by that. Andrey asked if the *dottore* had left a message for him. He should wait, please, the woman said, closing the door in his face. Then she came back with a piece of paper. He was to go and see Professor Ceresa, Campo delle Veste. A lawyer? No, a doctor. And she shut the door.

4

Professor Ceresa's *palazzo* was on the corner of the Campo delle Veste, near the Teatro Fenice. Although it was a large, elegant house, the professor answered the door himself. He seemed to be alone.

71

"I am a friend of Dr. Calzini," he explained, with a labored smile. "The court has called me in on the case, as psychiatrist, quite by chance. But that my friend was agreeable to your coming to see me is no coincidence—I asked his permission. I wanted to meet you, Father."

The library was veiled with the venomous gray of the afternoon. A few small logs burned in the fireplace, but you could feel their warmth only if you sat close to it.

"I need your help," said Professor Ceresa. "You are the only person the Countess trusts. Tomorrow you will see her."

"Have you talked to her?"

"Several times. With very little success. She doesn't trust me, in spite of the fact that I am probably the only one who does not agree with the prosecution." He was fiddling with a brown chrysanthemum in his buttonhole, tearing out one petal after the other with nervous fingers and letting them flutter absent-mindedly to the floor. "Medicine and jurisprudence have declared war on each other in this new century," he went on. "Judge and doctor both come in contact with the human being just at the moment when he has deviated from what is commonly accepted as normal, but the judge hates the accused; the doctor loves him. The judge investigates whether the accused has transgressed against society, the doctor whether society has transgressed against the accused."

Andrey felt that, although he didn't know the doctor, he had seen his eyes before. They lay in deep dark sockets, but because they were bright, they shone like the faraway light at the end of a tunnel. It was not a comforting light; it was as if one could see the end of the tunnel but not reach it.

"You think the Countess is ill?" he asked.

"In the Middle Ages, those suffering from the plague were treated like criminals. Modern psychiatry treats criminals like the sick."

"Are you convinced that the Countess is guilty?"

"I am convinced that she incited Naumov to the murder."

"So is the prosecution."

"The prosecution seeks the motive for the action; I seek the motive of the person involved. It is quite possible that Signora di Tarnovska, as overcompensation for a feeling of inferiority, was seized and in the end overcome by a power complex that forced her into a constant testing of her powers. It is possible that she persuaded Naumov to commit the murder only to find out if he was capable of murdering for her sake, without seriously intending Kamarovsky's death. I am not making a diagnosis; this is only a possibility among many others. If you could persuade the Countess to confide in me . . . Without the facts, the investigation is useless. The facts—by that I mean her past, her youth, her childhood."

"The prosecution speaks of quite different facts."

"You are right. I must explain what I mean. Have you ever heard of Professor Freud?"

"I know the name."

"Professor Freud has revolutionized the science of the soul. Just as the human body has had to surrender its mysteries to the advancement of medicine, the human soul is now divested of its secrets." He said that it was impossible to explain the new teachings to the friar in a few sentences, but he contradicted himself by embarking on a lecture on sexual inhibitions; spoke of "libido" and "Oedipus complex," about dream analysis and the subconscious, of discord and failure.

As Andrey tried to follow, he realized suddenly of whom the doctor's eyes reminded him—Sergey Burintzev, his friend, the executed revolutionary. The same glow; the same compulsion to convince; the same sense of infallibility. It provoked him to reply.

"Let us say that I could persuade the Countess to reveal her past to you, and her dreams—would they excuse the deed?"

"I thought you were a friend of the Countess?"

"Dr. Calzini had his reservations about that, too. I am her friend, but that doesn't mean I intend to stand by her the same way a psychiatrist does. You seek the motives; I am concerned with remorse. A century of motivation would be a remorseless century. A criminal could place a dossier explaining his action and justifying it alongside the body of his victim. The new confession you are speaking of would be a farce of a confession, since it does not aspire to a forgiveness of sins but to their resolution into collectivity."

"I can't believe that the Church will oppose progress," said the professor.

"Throughout the ages there has been talk of progress. More often than not, it was a good word for arrogance."

"The Church made the mistake of giving us permission to heal scarlet fever, measles, rabies; it can't very well forbid us to heal the sick soul. There is no denying it any longer—God has banished the human race from the paradise of ignorance. We may say therefore that it was God's will that man should become knowing. We know what we know about the soul; and there's no praying it away."

"I am no enemy of science," said Andrey, "but our vision of the twentieth century differs. More and more science is losing its way in a labyrinth. When it finds out the truth, it will have arrived at a point reached by the Church long ago—God. I believe that the new teachings are making the way that leads to the truth of the ten commandments and the postulate of the love of our Lord Jesus Christ very much more difficult. The curse of mankind began with the expulsion from Paradise, but it was fulfilled at the Tower of Babel. I feel that your professor has simply added another language to the many languages that serve to confuse the truth; one of the architects of Babel."

Professor Ceresa, whose mind before had only been busy with formulating his next thoughts, was now listening to Andrey attentively. He was still toying uneasily with the flower in his buttonhole. "The Countess Tarnovska is thirty," he said.

"And what does that imply?"

"That salvation still lies in the distant future. Psychoanalysis is a healing science. We want to save Signora di Tarnovska—not only from the highhandedness of the court. We want to make it possible for her to live with herself, behind prison walls if necessary, in freedom if we succeed. Please forgive me if I put it bluntly—we are dealing here with a sexual-pathological case. I have spoken to Naumov and Prilukov, and I know Dr. Calzini."

"Dr. Calzini? I don't see the connection."

The professor lowered his voice. "Try to picture a woman who, while in jail, still succeeds in ruining a man. And the case of Prosecutor Garzoni . . ."

"Now it is my turn to ask—are you accusing the Countess or trying to justify her?"

"Haven't you noticed that I have been speaking about the men who loved her? I don't know who Kamarovsky was, but I can visualize him. The century that has just ended was a guilt-ridden century. It was also, perhaps, the last one in which the male bore the major burden of guilt. Hence the emancipation, which is the effort—emanating, by the way, from the male—to place a share of the responsibility on the female. But we haven't come to that point yet. The guilty male still wants his punishment, but wants it of course to be as pleasant as possible. He wants to atone by becoming woman's slave. But not every woman is suited to be a merciless slave driver. We may speak of 'a perfect pair' only when a man's longing for subjugation is coupled with a woman's will for power. I hope you understand how I mean that. Naumov wanted to be flogged; only when he was being flogged was he capable of sexual satisfaction. Signora di Tarnovska kept a whole arsenal of instruments of torture for him."

"That is impossible!"

"That has been proved. But it doesn't answer my questions. It doesn't satisfy me, either, that there seem to be more and more women ready to inflict on men the suffering for which they hunger. I am one of the psychiatrists on the Tarnovska case; it is therefore up to me to find out how this woman's perverse impulses—which at the same time satisfy perverse impulses in others—originated."

An inexplicable excitement captured Andrey. "You just said 'no diagnosis.' What are you doing but stating a diagnosis? You don't seem to have any doubts about anything; I doubt all things, except God. I had a friend, you see, a revolutionary. He too thought he had a key that could open all doors; only his key fitted a little higher up, in the stomach. You use yours lower down, where human life has its origin. My friend wanted to penetrate the soul through a man's stomach; you think you can do it through his sex."

"I doubt very much if your friend was at all interested in healing souls," the professor said. "To fill the stomach and to appease the soul are two very different things. Since Freud, the number of incurable diseases of the soul has grown less. As soon as the patient recognizes the nature of his illness, he is already on the way to its cure. Believe me, it is not at all impossible that Signora di Tarnovska may end up a healthy, even a happy, woman."

"And you think all this is new, Professor? We were expelled from Paradise through knowledge—now Paradise is to be regained by it? Your Professor Freud has discovered sex? Hasn't he read the Bible? Right at the beginning it tells us of sex: 'Then the eyes of both were opened, and they realized that they were naked; so they sewed fig leaves together, and made themselves coverings.' But now comes a new teaching, and tears the fig leaves from our bodies as if our shame were the cause of our illness, when actually our desires are—desires

75

that began with the revelation that there was love, but also with another, that adjectives might be attached to it, such as, for instance, 'sexual.' That man and woman, like God Himself, may beget love in others. What happiness do you mean? God, whom you would like to emulate, isn't happy. The Holy Scriptures speak of an angry or a merciful God, of a wise God, or of the Omnipotent One who sits in judgment, but only heathen mythology speaks of a happy God. Since the creation of the world, our Lord has been a disappointed God. Happiness on this earth has at all times been promised us only by the Devil. If your Professor Freud promises us happiness, then the Devil has entered into him."

It had grown dark. You could hear the bells of the nearby church of San Fantino. The books were receding slowly, as if a dark hand were pushing them into the background. The professor opened a drawer, took out a slip of paper, laid it on the table. Then he struck a match and lighted one of the gas lamps. The objects in the room took on shape; unclear, vibrant shape, as if mirrored in water.

No answer of Ceresa's could have upset Andrey as much as the man's silence did. The fanatic saw him as a fanatic, and in all probability he was right. Was he so certain that the professor was acting in a less Christian way than he? Had the mention of sex startled him, and why, if he was so sure of himself? He had had every intention of supporting the lawyer, why not the doctor? Because he had nothing to fear for the Church from jurisprudence, but could not feel the same security when faced with this new philosophy of healing? Did his love for Maria mean that she would have to spend the rest of her life behind bars? Who said there could be remorse only behind prison walls? And Tioka. Shouldn't a life, however worthless, be spared for the sake of another?

"Tomorrow I shall visit the Countess," he said, rising, and stood still because his heart had begun to beat fast. "I am afraid we let ourselves be carried away, Professor. I know only what I have found out from others, that is to say—nothing. I don't know whether she is guilty or sick. I came to Venice to offer her consolation. Don't ask me to promise you anything, but I am not going to say no, either."

"May I expect you after you have seen her?"

Andrey nodded.

The professor handed him the paper. "Tomorrow, between ten and eleven, at the Women's Penitentiary of La Giudecca."

76

He accompanied Andrey through a dark hall to the anteroom, and walked out the front door with the friar. It was evening. Men and women, festively clad, were hurrying in the direction of the illuminated columns of the Teatro Fenice. Women with black shawls over their heads, men in work clothes, a few beggars moved slowly toward San Fantino. The former were going to a performance, the latter to vespers. The theater bell could be heard ringing amid the tolling of the church bells. Andrey and the professor shook hands. Dr. Ceresa was smiling. Only stem and chalice were left of the chrysanthemum in his buttonhole. He threw the flower away. Andrey walked in the direction of San Fantino.

5

Domenico, the senior warden, was a plump man whose head didn't seem to go with his body—a tough little birdlike head, as if stamped on him, to go with his office. He examined Andrey's permit to visit the Countess with the pompous air of the bureaucrat to whom a seal means so much that he is forever doubting its validity. Finally he accompanied Andrey to the barred gate, where a policeman was standing, told the man to open the door, and handed the visitor over to Sister Angela, who had been waiting behind it.

In the corridor—cells on either side—female convicts were scrubbing the floor. They wore brown uniforms, with dirty aprons that came to the shoulders, like nuns of a convict Order. They looked up, surprised to see a man, disappointed when they saw he was a priest. At sight of the female warden in her boots, they bent hastily over their buckets.

Maria Tarnovska was living in one of these cells. Perhaps there was such a thing as worldly justice, but if this was it, what was left for purgatory? Simon Magus, Basileidos, Karpocrates, the Gnostics had harbored such thoughts, and the Church had denounced them as heretics. Since the dead did not know that they had lived, since they were freed from past sorrow and all kinship, wasn't it possible that the living were dead and the poor truly the poor souls of whom the Holy Scriptures spoke? And the apparent injustices of God—the suffering of the good; the death of a child; seduction by the senses; illness, poverty, disappointments, even the false happiness of those who were happy—as the punishments of such a cool purgatory, all

77

these things were suddenly comprehensible. War and fratricide, hail and drought, the wrong way and the wrong teachings—suddenly comprehensible. Not everyone had sinned to the same extent in first life, not all were similarly punished, yet all in purgatory—suddenly comprehensible. The earth a hell of angels, explicable by the role of Satan, who, in that case, no longer dwelled among men, mysteriously tolerated by Almighty God, but ruled in this intermediate space according to his will and mandate, in a purifying purgatory, in which only Azazael remained unclean forever. Prince of the world? Master of purgatory. Even death became comprehensible as a deliverance of all earthly burden, as promise and mercy, when it freed man of this second life in purgatory. Death in the first life—the surrender to Satan; death in the second—the surrender to God. Heretical thoughts, for they cast doubt on the manifestation of the Savior, who had descended into the underworld only after his death; heresy, too, because they explained the inexplicability of being. Maria Tarnovska was atoning on earth for her sins. The earth was not purgatory, but its flames flickered on this earth.

The nun opened a door. The room they entered was not like the reception room in which the prisoners were allowed to see their lawyers. It was a room with no windows; cold, damp, gaslit by a lamp that was caught in a wire net, as if its light too were captive. A third of the room was partitioned by a wall in which there was a barred window, behind it a chair, the only piece of furniture.

"I shall leave you alone," said Sister Angela. "It is against the rules, but in your case . . ."

Andrey stood still. Why had these forbidden thoughts occurred to him? Was he close to the Devil because he was close to Maria? Why journey after the Devil if one feared to encounter him? "Now is the judgment of the world; now will the Prince of the world be cast out." And "now" was the moment in which love could prove itself.

CHAPTER 7

Maria Tarnovska had been notified of Andrey's visit only half an hour ahead of time. She had been reading a travelogue written by Marco Polo, which had carried her off to Baghdad and Ormus, to Kanibaluk and into the province of Kiangnan. It was the only kind of reading she could tolerate, because it had as little to do with reality as a fairy tale. Now she undressed under Sister Rosa's watchful eyes. The tall nun looked at her as one looked at sin, full of hatred and envy. What was she thinking? The witch is making herself beautiful for the priest. Since the Countess had found out that she was considered a witch, she enjoyed startling the good sisters; and since she couldn't ride through the night on a broomstick, she stood there as long as she could in her transparent underwear, choosing something to wear. She finally put on a high-necked black dress, powdered her nose, dabbed perfume behind her ears. As the hypocrite tries to hide his unclean thoughts, she tried to conceal her innocent ones. She smiled coquettishly—and was thinking of Tioka. Not until she was being led past the other cells did fear of seeing Andrey overwhelm her. Who had said that sorrow shared was sorrow lightened? Shared, it grew heads, like the Lernaean hydra. Had Andrey come to share her suffering? Perhaps he had come only to collect the bitter tithe of his warnings, a usurer of integrity. If only he didn't exhort her to pray! She had prayed to a deaf God. What did He want her to do? He was punishing her because she had sinned, but why had He let her become a sinner? If Andrey spoke of Tioka, heaven may have sent him; but if he told her to search her soul and repent, then he would find out that she had no hope left but in an alliance with demons.

Sister Rosa opened the steel door, and the Countess found herself in the barred part of the room. All she could see through the hole in the wall was a white spot. Not until she was alone, and had sat down, did she see Andrey; not until he had said "Maria" did she recognize him.

"We don't have much time," he said. "I want to talk about Tioka."

He drew his chair up to the barred window. An animal behind bars, he thought. A tiger, a panther, or a hyena? But she reminded him only of a deer or a gazelle, kept behind bars in a zoological garden not because it was dangerous but because it needed protection. She looked younger; she no longer resembled Vassily Tarnovsky's wife, or Pavel Kamarovsky's fiancée; she was the girl he had known in Kiev, only then she had been branded with the curse of the future, today with the curse of the past. It seemed to him that he should be able to take her by the hand and lead her out of the prison, and show her what lay ahead, so that it might not happen; then he remembered that it lay behind her, and had happened.

He began with the day on which he had decided not to let Tioka go back to Russia with Olga. "She wanted to take him from you; that's why I kept him." He spoke about Tioka's development, his progress, his studies—a preceptor reporting to a mother about one of his pupils. He told her about the boarding school, but he didn't mention the means that were making it possible to educate Tioka in the Geneva school. "Believe me, he is not unhappy. He knows everything, but he is not unhappy. He believes in you."

"He believes in me? What does he believe?"

"That you are the victim of an error of justice."

"And if I am convicted?"

"He will always think of you as a victim."

"Do the other children torture him with it?"

"He has learned to defend himself."

She gritted her teeth. There were a thousand things to ask, but her mind was a blank. Autumn to winter, winter to spring, the seasons had passed by her window, but the seasons were treacherous; they simulated the passing of time, yet time stood still. Now she wanted to hold the minutes fast, but time, gone wild, drove her along, headlong.

"Does he know you are visiting me?" she asked.

"Yes."

"Don't tell him about the bars."

"Of course not."

"Have you heard from Olga?"

"She is angry with me, because of Tioka."

"And Alexander?"

"He is traveling."

"And Zoa?"

Andrey looked away.

"I should have let him drown," she said.

"I can understand your bitterness."

"Oh, you can? And can you also understand the O'Rourkes? Not a human being among them, not a single human being. I am the only one here who has no visitors. For half a year now, I haven't heard a word of Russian, not a familiar voice. Where are my friends?"

"I never knew them."

"No one has written to me, not even a few lines to say 'I am sorry . . .'"

"What good would it do for me to tell you you had the wrong friends?"

"There are no right ones. Has my father answered your letter?"

Andrey shook his head.

"He always hated me," she said. "And he was right. I hated him."

"He is paying for your defense."

She began to laugh, laughed loudly, half sob, half laughter, like those who, as a last resort, find mankind ridiculous. Her laughter seemed to shake the life out of her, leaving her depleted, inanimate. Andrey wanted to take her hand, but she was clutching the bars with both hands as if they were the only support she had.

"He knows he hasn't much longer to live," she said. "He wants to buy his salvation with rubles. If I could still pray, I would beg God to punish and destroy him."

Andrey was silent. The bars had daubed lines on her face, wrinkles in the shape of prison bars. She didn't look young any more, only small. "Why did you come?" she asked, running her fingers through her hair.

"I thought it might comfort you."

"Of course. You are charitable."

"I wanted you to hear about Tioka."

"And you? Do you believe in me?"

"I don't know if you are guilty or not."

"But you think it is possible."

"That is for the court to decide. By the way, I saw Dr. Ceresa. I think he wants to help you." He was astonished to find himself complying with the doctor's wishes.

"Nobody wants to help me," she said. "I don't even have a lawyer."

"I will find one."

"The prison is full of murderers. Why do they hate only me?" She leaned closer to the bars. "They don't have to be afraid of me any more. Tell them that. I will be old and ugly by the time I leave this prison. I shall make no one happy any more, and no one miserable. They should leave me in peace. Tell them that. And tell them that I shall never confess, never. Do you understand?"

"Because of Tioka?"

"That, too."

"Tioka's belief in you does not depend on your confession or conviction. He loves you. That is why he believes in you."

"And you? Do you still love me?"

"I shall never stop loving you."

"You should have thought of that in Vienna."

"You were talking of another kind of love then."

She shook her head, but he didn't know what she meant. Did she want to express that she didn't believe in his love or that she didn't understand it? "You are wise, Andrey," she said. "You have always done the right thing. Can you tell me how all this happened?"

"I wasn't able to find an answer."

"I know thousands, but all of them are senseless. Perhaps because I didn't hold the horses back when they bolted with Nikolay, or because Vassily took singing lessons, or because there were snakes in Kossino Park, or because they cut off my hair, or because I lost the amulet, or because the furniture was so hideous in Baden-Baden. Because . . . because . . . because . . . At some time or other something must have turned out right for me?"

"You love Tioka."

"All mothers love their children."

"Not all of them."

Her hands, small, yellowed, the only part of her that was old, were resting in her lap. Now she clung to the bars again. "What will become of Tioka? Andrey, it is late, you must tell me. You can't leave until you have told me. He can't stay in Geneva forever. Is my father paying for him?"

Andrey reflected. Should he lie? "No. He isn't paying for him."

"Is Vassily?" She was horrified.

"No."

"Then who is?"

"I am."

"The Church? Have you sold him to the Church?"

"I inherited some money from my mother."

"But you have to give that to your Order. Did they give you permission . . . ?"

"They can't do that."

Silence. "You broke your vow," she said. "For me."

"For Tioka," he said.

She was staring at him as if she had been staggering through the night and suddenly seen light; as if she had been walking through the fog and suddenly seen the heavens open up; as if she had been reeling through chaos and suddenly her feet had felt firm ground; as if she had fallen and suddenly a hand had stopped her. She began to cry, sobbed without covering her face with her hands, abashed at first, incredulously, then more and more violently and unrestrainedly and credulously. She stretched out her hand through the bars. When he gave her his hand, she kissed it.

"If you want me to, I will confess."

"I knew it," he said. "When you began to ask questions . . ."

They could hear the grating of a key in the lock. He didn't take away his hand because he was afraid she might misunderstand, but she let go of it with the smile of an innocent girl whose innocent gesture might be misinterpreted. Sister Rosa came in; her long shadow falling between Andrey and the prisoner. She stood there, disappointed, because there was no need to remind Maria Tarnovska that the time was up; the prisoner was already standing.

"I shall come to see you again," he said.

"Go to see Tioka."

"You may be sure of that."

83

Sister Angela came to fetch him. He followed her through the empty corridor. Only one nun was standing beside a peephole, talking to one of the shut-in animals. Andrey's heart was light and happy. He thanked God for having made him guilty, for guilt was a burden no one could shake off without burdening someone else with it.

BOOK II

❦

THE FACTS

CHAPTER 1

I

Maria O'Rourke was twelve years old when she saw the light of day for the second time.

For years she had lived in the dark. Measles, the doctors had said at the time. The illness passed, but the light did not return. When it did come back, four years later, it was a light without shape. Trees, animals, people were mirrored in deep water, constantly in motion, waves breaking over them. Moss grew in the water, an opaque light, like spilled milk. She never saw the morning. Servants tied a bandage over her eyes and told her if the weather was good or bad. During the day she wore dark glasses, shut at the sides. She never took them off because she had been told that in the light she might become totally blind.

Rarely did she play with children. She knew the patient hand of Anna Dobroyubova, her governess, every curve of her palm, the hardness of her nails. Her hearing became more acute. With the first notes from the music room, she knew whether her half brother, Nikolay, was having a lesson, or her sister, Olga. If a child was crying, she knew if it was Alexander who had fallen down, or Zoa who had been naughty. She heard what was being whispered behind her back. If the words were compassionate, she covered her ears, but the voices trickled through her protective fingers. The present had begun with her illness; behind it lay the past. The past was tangible, and she longed for it; the present burst like a bubble. Later, some day, she would see again. That was the future.

She loved autumn and winter because the days became shorter. The night put dark glasses on everyone; she became like the others.

She lay in her bed and waited until the noises of the house had subsided, then she leafed in the past as if it had been a fairy tale. The turreted house, colonnades, balconies, arched windows; in the dining room, a picture of her ancestor, the Irish King Feargal; gold-glittering icons, kneeling servants, cupboards filled with silver and porcelain; the brook with acacia branches trailing in it; firs, birches, oaks; the frozen pond; the meadow with the swing—nothing stirred, even the swing hung still.

One night she groped for matches and candle, stood up and felt her way to the mirror, held the candle high and so close to her face that she could feel its warmth. She saw her thin little body in a long nightgown; saw her blond hair and blue eyes; marveled that one could see one's own eyes when, after all, one was looking with them; and marveled that she could see. More and more often she would get up in the night. At first she saw only herself, made faces at herself, stuck out her tongue; then she dragged books, shoes, toys, to the light, and found she could see them too. At first she thought the blind could see only by candlelight, but gradually she could see also in the daytime, all things that were still and near. She mentioned her observations, but she told no one about her secret rendezvous with her image in the mirror. Her mother told her father. Nikolay O'Rourke flew in a rage. "Now Mura has gone crazy!" Maria—only they had always called her Mura—heard every word. They always spoke as if she were deaf. "Dr. Orlov knows better," said her father, and everyone nodded. She said nothing, and flew back to her candlelight image.

Every now and then her governess took her to Kiev to see the doctor. Her father didn't go along. He owned vast estates, was Knight Marshal of the province, a governor of the Czar, a busy man. Her mother feared heat and cold, the excesses of nature. The doctor examined Maria in a darkened room. His hands smelled of leather. A tiny light burned, an angry eye. Dr. Orlov also had angry eyes. He was small, bald, wore a goatee—a gnome in an Irish fairy tale. He asked her to read the letters on a long board. "You guessed that one," he said when she got it right, and the letters ran together. The smell of leather made her feel sick. Oh, to get out of the place, was all she could think of, and saw nothing more. He put her dark glasses on her again. In the night she got up and tiptoed to the mirror.

She began to believe that supernatural powers were playing a game with her, and that they were allied with her family. They wanted to keep her in this tremulous darkness. The suspicion tortured her; but then it filled her with an elfin spite. She could see, but she didn't want anyone to know it. She nodded at herself in the mirror, and laughed at all mean adults and foolish spirits. The girl in the mirror joined in her laughter; the two of them knew best.

2

On a bitter cold February day in the year 1889, all this was abruptly changed. The night before, Uncle Edward had arrived. Count Edward O'Rourke was the only member of the family who lived in Ireland, where the O'Rourkes had originated, descendants of the first Christian Kings of Connaught, champions of liberty, heroes of the battles of Blackwater, Fontenoy, and the Boyne, exiles finally, and officers in foreign regiments, split up into French, Livonian, and Polish lines. The father of Nikolay and Edward O'Rourke had been a Major General in the Russian Army. Edward, the younger of the two, had been named after his uncle on his father's side—the Bishop of Danzig. Driven by nostalgia or pugnaciousness, he had returned to Ireland as a youth. No people, he liked to say, had ever gained their freedom by remaining outside their country. He was five years younger than Maria's father, fifty now, a bear of a man, a hirsute giant. Everything about him was red—hair, mustache, hands—even his eyes seemed red, although they were really violet-blue. Once, during a quarrel with his brother, he had pounded on the table with his fist so hard, the top had been split in two as if by an ax. He had never married, and because he liked to boast, he vaunted his loneliness too, yet sometimes he fled from what he claimed to love. He turned up in Otrada unannounced, laden like Santa Claus.

This time he didn't come alone. He jumped out of his sled—no one could fathom how he could have stood the ride from Kiev in an open sled—and helped an elderly man out, that is to say, lifted him out, which was like Edward O'Rourke; he had a way of standing people around as if they were things. He paid no attention to his brother, nor to the servants, nor to any of the other children, but walked straight up to Maria, who had remained in the background, clinging to Anna Dobroyubova's hand. After he had kissed her so that her little face was reddened by the stubble of his beard, he introduced Dr. Frithof as "the greatest eye doctor in the world."

That night, Maria couldn't sleep. During supper she had listened to the loud voices of Uncle Edward and her father in the next room. Her father had referred to Dr. Orlov, and had told Uncle Edward he was being presumptuous; they didn't know more in Moscow than in Kiev; Edward was interfering in matters that were none of his business; besides, Frithof was a Jew and could sleep in the servants' quarters. Maria had looked down at her plate and waited for Uncle Edward to pound on the table and split it wide open.

Now she groped for the matches again. Would the mirror fail her? If her image in the mirror didn't fail her, Uncle Edward wouldn't either. On the way to the mirror, she had a bold idea. She felt her way along the furniture to the window, put down her candle carefully. She wanted to raise the roll-shades, but she wasn't strong enough, so she let herself hang by the cords with her full weight. At last she was able to raise the narrow slats a little. She blew out the candle and pressed her forehead against the window. In front of her, in the opalescent light of the moon, lay the park. The glittering light hurt, but she grew accustomed to the pain and was happy, because eyes that hurt couldn't be dead. Her heart responded to everything she could grasp with her eyes, and grew wide with the landscape. Snowflakes settled down like white birds on the lonely oak tree; the wrought-iron railing sparkled like spears; the basket held by the statue of a young boy was full of white apples. She couldn't see the sky, but that was just what she wanted to see, so she lay down on the floor and face upturned, found the source of all light. Crossing her hands behind her head, she sunned herself in the moon. When she tried to lower the roll-shade, she found that she couldn't. In panic, she pulled the cord into the middle of the room, tugged at it, but in the end, exhausted, she had to let it slide back.

She slept fitfully, in fear of being discovered, but in the morning Uncle Edward woke her. He sat down on her bed. "I have brought a friend with me from Moscow," he said. "Dr. Frithof. He is a famous eye doctor. He may prescribe new glasses for you."

"Don't you think I'll have to wear dark glasses any more?"

Uncle Edward raised his big red-haired hand high. "How many fingers do you see?"

"Four."

"And now?"

"Two."

He laughed. "I noticed it this summer. I have an idea that you may not need any glasses at all."

"But Dr. Orlov . . ."

"Don't tell a soul, Mura, but I think Dr. Orlov is an idiot."

She threw her arms around Uncle Edward's neck.

After breakfast, he led her into the dimly lit library. The doctor had hung up his reading charts there and set up his ophthalmoscope, lenses, and instruments. Maria was startled. She thought she could smell leather. But when she didn't have to look in any glassy eyes or decipher letters, she began to trust the little man, who seemed to be almost as sad as she was. Even his soiled tie and shy way of speaking Russian were sad and made her feel confidence in him. He spoke with her about animals and plants, butterflies and polar bears, but he didn't speak about people.

"I'd like to see your glasses," he said at last. "Do you have them with you?" No, they were in her room. "Well, then go and get them."

She looked at her uncle, who stood near the tiled stove.

"Go on. You can go by yourself," said Dr. Frithof. "You don't have to hurry. We have time." She felt her way along the furniture. "It's a little dark in here," he added.

Outside, she looked about her because she was afraid of being caught without her bandage and her glasses. When she met no one, she felt sure that Uncle Edward had spirited everyone in the house away. Stairs, walls, pictures, doors were veiled, but they were motionless. It had stopped snowing, and a ray of sun fell through the window. She looked out and wasn't afraid of the sun.

When she had found her glasses, she felt her way back along the wall. She had to be cautious; only Uncle Edward wanted her to see.

"You see, you found them," said Dr. Frithof. He examined the glasses, put them under a lens, shook his head, put them in his pocket. Then he examined Maria with the help of an instrument she had never seen before, asked a few questions, mumbled something in a foreign language. "And now you are going to try to read these letters," he said. "You don't have to recognize all of them. I don't recognize all of them myself."

She recognized the big letters at once. The doctor put a pair of glasses on her nose with no lenses in them. Out of a velvet case he took various lenses, which he slid into the semicircular frames. Every time she got a letter right, Uncle Edward clapped his hands and bellowed "Bravo!" Maria would have liked to go on playing this game, because it was the first game in which she always won.

The doctor parted the drapes. "I am going to prescribe new glasses for you," he said. "Wear them only for reading, or if you are tired. You are a big girl and can decide for yourself when you need them. And you don't have to be afraid of the sun." He opened the window, and the February air streamed bitingly cold into the room. He threw her glasses out of the window.

Maria ran to the window. Her glasses were lying on the firmly frozen snow. She was afraid someone would find them; she would bury them, or smash them. Dr. Frithof took her hand. "Soon you won't have to wear any glasses at all," he said, and closed the window.

She looked at Uncle Edward. "Will you tell Papa?"

"I certainly will!" he roared. "And you don't have to go to Dr. Orlov any more. He is an idiot."

3

1889 to 1890. Seeing what one had never seen before, experiencing things new! Nature and animals and games and books and children and contests.

Maria O'Rourke takes riding lessons, soon doesn't need any, rides like a devil and as if devils were driving her. A groom rides with her, although it is forbidden. Ivan is blond, blue-eyed, and twenty years old. He obeys her like a slave. His obedience trickles through her, a pleasant sensation, as if she were pressing the flank of a horse between her thighs. They ride across the steppe. The sand is like a sea of hot water, the dust like hot waves. They ride through villages. Old people, former serfs, bare their heads; the young ones spring aside. It makes Maria ride faster; she hates the fearful. Why does he ride with her? she asks Ivan. "So that nothing should happen to you, my lady." She doesn't know what could possibly happen to her, but she asks, "Would you die for me?" Happily, he nods.

She reads a great deal. She wheedles trashy novels from the servant girls and hides them between the pages of a book about Napoleon. "You should be reading the Bible," her father barks at her. So she hides the trashy novels between the pages of the Scriptures. They are love stories—love, threatening parents, rivals, brothers and sisters envious enemies, a victorious ending. The lovers get married. End of the story, end of love.

She cannot imagine that her parents ever loved each other. Twice a month her father has himself driven to the grave of his first wife. Maria persuades Anna Dobroyubova to go to the cemetery with her. The first Countess O'Rourke is interred in a mausoleum; that is the way princesses live. "Born Sofia, Princess Ghika"—the inscription on the gravestone. "My stepmother," Maria explains to the governess. Anna Dobroyubova crosses herself. "If your mother was dead and she was alive, she would be your stepmother." Maria is convinced that twice a month the Princess rises from her grave. Her portrait hangs in the big salon above the sofa. Maria wonders if she should take a knife and cut up the picture. Once she gets up on the sofa, but doesn't dare.

The time of her blindness is now a thing of the past, and she recalls it with pride, as the victor recalls a bloody battle. But why had they kept her in darkness? Her father had done it. Why? She doesn't want to forget it. Who had played this cruel game with her, who had not? She wants to punish Olga, do evil things to her, but her older sister avoids her. Olga is flawless—that's what everyone says. Maria despises Alexander, who is three years younger than she and worships Olga. Because he, too, is flawless, she hides needles in his sheets. Of Zoa, born four years after her, she is afraid, because he creeps through the house, listening. She loves her half brother, Nikolay, because he played with her. He is seven years older than she, studying at the University of Kiev. When he comes home, he brings presents only for her. He spends most of his time in the servants' quarters. She loves the servants because they used to play with her.

She rarely sees her mother. She knows that her mother is younger than her father, yet to Maria she seems aged. Whenever Maria embraces her fervently, she complains of a headache. The aunts, Anna and Sonya, who patter through the house all day, put their fingers to their lips when they pass Katharina O'Rourke's bedroom. At times Maria's tenderness burst forth, and her mother cannot restrain her. Once she dreams that the house is on fire. Only she and her mother escape.

She still loves the night. In the summer, she stands at the window and looks up at the stars. God sees all things, for the stars are His eyes, and they are countless. She chooses a star. That is the eye watching over her. She tries to find it again, but it has disappeared among the many other shining eyes. In winter, the Milky Way is God's long white beard, and the stars are blue, gold, yellow, even pink. The snow covers everything. She wishes it would never melt.

Every Sunday, the priest comes from Kiev to celebrate Mass. He is an old man and reminds her of the Buddha Uncle Edward brought back from his trip to India. With his short arms, he reaches greedily for his food. Maria is afraid he might drink too much and betray her confession. In the courtyard she sometimes meets *hiereyis,* the Greek Orthodox priests, who wear long beards and are even dirtier than the roving soldiers. On Palm Sunday, Anna Dobroyubova takes her to a Greek Orthodox service, and the priest is magnificently clad. Willow branches, gleaming silver, are being blessed; hundreds of candles flicker above golden icons. One day her father gives orders to drive "the bearded dogs" away, for they steal everything that isn't fastened down. Maria believes that the servants have a God of their own, with priests of their own, and she imagines the God of the servants as a gigantic Greek Orthodox priest, dirty, with a black beard.

She still doesn't have many playmates. The older children visit Olga, the little ones come to see Zoa and Alexander. People say she is domineering. Once a boy is lying in front of the fireplace, reading, and she plays that he is a bridge, and walks up and down on his back. He kisses her shoes. She confesses it to the priest; she doesn't know why. She prefers the company of boys, because they obey her.

Sometimes Count Vyrubov comes over, with his son, Andrey. He is in high school, and wears a colorful student's cap. Olga gets all dressed up for him. Maria's heart flies to meet him because he pays no attention to Olga. On a Sunday in August they go fishing, and she remains alone with Andrey. She sits on the river bank, her skirt pulled down to her ankles. "You're not supposed to speak," she tells him. "I like to sit next to you," he replies. The frogs in the stream bed croak, the birds in the trees answer. Maria laughs. As she rises, she stumbles and lets her fishing rod fall, and the stream carries it away. On the way home, they meet her father. "Where's your rod?" he asks. "I lost it," Andrey says quickly. When she reads novels, she skips all descriptions of the hero. She sees all of them as Andrey.

In June, shortly after her fourteenth birthday, she is in the stable, about to ride out with Ivan. A storm is gathering over Otrada; the clouds are converging from all sides, like peasants to the *mir.* Ivan doesn't want to saddle her horse, and she is upbraiding him. Her father finds her alone with Ivan. He discovers that they often ride together. He strikes the boy in the face with his whip. The blood spurts from his nose. When the boy doesn't move, the count strikes him on his back, on his buttocks. He doesn't stop until the boy cries out. Maria is ashamed because she doesn't throw herself between her father and Ivan, but a feeling of bliss overwhelms her such as she felt only once before, when she saw Olga crying. She decides to slip out of the house that night and comfort Ivan, but she doesn't know where he lives. She wants to ride out with him again, and hopes her father will catch them and punish Ivan again. That night it takes her a long time to fall asleep. More than ever she senses that what she is doing is forbidden, but when she finally falls asleep, exhausted, her hands are still resting on her soft pubic hairs.

Next morning, she looks for Ivan, but he has disappeared.

That September, she is sent to a finishing school for the daughters of the aristocracy in Moscow.

4

The school lay in a part of the city called Bjely Gorod, "white city," on the corner of the Tverskaya and Chernishevsky boulevards. Like most of the houses, palaces, and villas in that area, it was white, a big snowman towering over a lot of smaller snowmen. If you were lucky, you slept in one of the dormitories on the upper floors, where you could look out over the park walls onto the boulevard, with its cabs and sleighs, clanging fire trucks, and cries of the boys selling the *Moskovsky Listok*, with its perils and mysteries; where you could see priests and men of the world and murderers and pedestrians and honorable citizens and children and courtesans.

Maria, with Anna Dobroyubova, entered the room of the head of the school as if she were walking behind her own hearse. The governess was not returning to Otrada; she had accepted another position and was on her way to St. Petersburg. Even from a funeral, those left behind went home, but since Anna Dobroyubova wasn't going home, life could not go on. Perhaps Otrada had never existed.

Soon her tears dried. The girls came from Orel and Tula, from Tver and Charkov and Poltava, from Lake Ladoga and the Black Sea. They were blonde, brunette, and dark; they were fourteen and fifteen, there was one who was seventeen; princesses and countesses and baronesses; and there was the daughter of a famous singer who was married to a countess. Some were frivolous, others were melancholy, but they all had their nostalgia in common: they were homesick for mountains, steppes, woods, fields, or lakes; different homes, but the same nostalgia. At first they boasted of their horses and servants, their clothes and parties, of rich fathers and beautiful mothers, but soon they boasted only of parties, clothes, servants, and horses; they no longer boasted of their mothers and fathers. At night they sat at the windows of their dormitories and talked softly, or they crept into each other's beds, whispering, giggling, laughing. One admitted that she hadn't seen her father for years, another that she had caught her mother with the tutor, another that her mother was sick and her father only came home to brag about his conquests. They warmed each other like birds in the rain and were convinced that they were here only because they were unwanted at home. They were being "prepared for marriage"—that was how Miss Stotsbury, the English teacher, put it—but they didn't think much of marriage, and sometimes they wept like the servant girls who cried from engagement to wedding day and had to sing *svadebniye platshi,* the old laments. Family photographs stood on bedside tables, but very few of the girls ever looked at them. They longed for mountains, steppes, woods, fields, or lakes, but the landscape held no people.

They were at an age when young girls began to be knowing, but the things they discovered were not alike. When the little Countess Golitzin, the anemic child of a bigoted family, began to bleed, she didn't dare own up to her shame; she would rather have died than be female like the others. Before her history class, Princess Anna Nikolaevna Romodanovskaya rubbed her little breasts with ice-cold water so that the nipples might become visible under her loose school uniform and attract the teacher's attention. When they sat on their beds at night, the Countess Czartorskaya—a beautiful redhead—told of her dreams, in which she had made love with her cousin, and although the others knew that she couldn't dream every night, they demanded more and more dreams, which Anita Ivanovna then began to invent because she saw that they envied her hoard of dreams. There were girls like the general's daughter, Petrovna Apraskin, who incited her schoolmates to play sinful games, and girls like the Baroness Blumberg, who took part in them but went daily to confession, grown one with her guilty conscience like a Siamese twin. They were virgins, and only a few had experienced their first kiss, but in all of them their blood was boiling at fever pitch. They were pawing the ground like impatient race horses at the starting line, ready to race off with all their passions and desires, delights and disappointments, as soon as the thin rope was cut.

5

The fires burned around the Countess O'Rourke, but her body remained cold. Sometimes her breasts hurt as if they would burst their delicate skin, for she was almost sixteen, yet she had not yet experienced what had shocked the pallid Countess Golitzin. Furtive talks, caresses, jokes, ambiguous scenes in books excited her, but it was like someone discovering a scar and not knowing how or where he had hurt himself. In the eyes of her schoolmates, however, the effect was quite different. The superiority of an ignorant girl could hardly be told apart from the blasé attitude of the knowing, and Maria knew how to take advantage of this. If you didn't tell anything, you were told everything. If you hid, they looked for you. If you didn't court anyone, you were courted. She distributed her favors like the Czar his medals, smiling and aloof.

The desire to dominate grew stronger and stronger. In this respect, school and circumstances favored her. The academy was famous all over Russia for its strictness. The Countess Narishkin, widowed in the first year of her marriage forty years ago and still in mourning, ruled with an iron hand. She came from a small middle-class family, and she hated her pupils, not only for their youth, but for their social positions as well. She made no secret of her hatred, converted it into discipline. It was forbidden to punish the older pupils, but she personally chastised the younger ones, resorting to the rod in a disciplinary ceremony. The fourteen- or fifteen-year-old girls who were to be punished had to present her with it on a velvet cushion; you could see them parading through the halls, red-faced, holding the cushion with the rod on high, as if it were a royal insigne. The widow liked and trusted Maria O'Rourke; she was never punished. Over tea and *kalatshi,* she told Maria about the sins her schoolmates had committed, for the most part sins of the flesh. Once she let Maria take part at a disciplining. Maria wanted to look away, but couldn't.

In her imagination, she found herself changing places with the principal more and more often, without hating the woman any less for it.

She felt the same excitement when she confessed her sins. The greater the sin, the greater her delight. She left the confessional pale and depleted, feeling more guilty than when she had entered it. Still, she went often to confession, and Countess Narishkin spoke highly of her piety.

The girls knew that Maria O'Rourke held a special position. They sensed that the teachers urged her to denounce her schoolmates, and respected and loved her because she denounced no one. She enjoyed power in its most attractive form—unused. When the Countess Czartorskaya secretly received flowers from the young gardener; when, in the bed next to hers, the Countess Kritzkaya pleaded and finally sobbed until Katharina Petrovna would let her kiss her, Maria reveled in the knowledge that she could have told if she had wanted to. And sometimes she wondered what had become of Ivan, the groom.

6

That spring, the authority of Maria Nikolaevna O'Rourke was enhanced by an unexpected incident.

The entire school had gone on an outing in the outskirts of Moscow. They had driven in landaus to Ismailovo, a country estate of the Czar, ancestral home of the Romanovs, where they were to be shown a model farm. Two women and one male teacher were in charge of the excursion. It was May, a day of early summer warmth. The meadows all around were in scented bloom, as if spring had conquered all winters and would possess the earth from now on and forever. The stillness contained no sound but the clip-clop of the horses' hoofs and the singing of the birds. The girls were thinking of the landscape at home, of which all this reminded them, as all beautiful things did.

Maria was sitting opposite the male teacher. Ilya Mihailovich Gorelin taught French literature. He recited poems in a falsetto voice; at the word *"l'amour,"* he would redden. It couldn't have been by chance that the knees of the young peasant's son pressed against Maria's, because whenever he spoke to her, his eyes behind his bureaucratic pince-nez became glassy; he blushed to the roots of his hair, and his gestures became expansive, as if his arms wanted to fly off and leave him. She paid scarcely any attention to him; she was too busy being homesick.

She didn't really become aware of him until they were looking for a boat on the Vinogradny Pond, at the edge of the park, and she found herself suddenly alone with him. He was standing as if rooted to the spot, staring at her. She was startled, and asked him what was the matter. Without blushing now, but with great pathos, he declared his love for her as if he were reciting a poem; his large Adam's apple bobbed up and down; he coughed, went on reciting. She had to laugh, but he stretched out his arms to her and pressed his mouth to her lips. She was overwhelmed with revulsion, especially since the wet, greedy mouth on her lips didn't seem to belong to him. It was as if he had pressed a dog's snout against her lips. She pushed him away, slapped his face. His glasses fell to the ground. She could hear girls' voices, coming closer, but she didn't run away. She watched the shortsighted man, on his knees, groping for his eyes. The glasses glittered in the grass, but she let him crawl around on the ground; and that was how the others found him when they came to the edge of the wood.

That same evening, Maria told the principal what had happened. She didn't know why she did it, because she wasn't afraid of Ilya Mihailovich. Was she insulted because he had believed she might give in to him? Did she feel cheated of her first kiss? Did she believe what she was saying? Her excitement grew more and more intense, so that in the end she felt nothing but the wish to destroy Ilya Mihailovich. Originally, she had intended to tell the truth, but now she elaborated the incident; declared that the teacher had gone down on his knees in front of her and embraced her legs, and that he had whispered something about elopement; lied finally that he had felt for her breasts and reached for the hem of her dress. She was trembling from head to foot and sank down in a chair. The principal brought her a glass of water. Maria would calm down only when the Countess said she would call the doctor.

The dismissal of the teacher made Maria O'Rourke the queen among her comrades. She had to repeat what had happened over and over again, and nobody seemed to notice the fresh details of her invention.

A few weeks later, the principal told Maria that her new governess, Mademoiselle Larue, was coming to fetch her home, not for the holidays, but to remain in Otrada. Maria didn't know if this was because of the incident in the park of Ismailovo.

CHAPTER 2

I

The ball rolled into the pocket. Andrey Antonovich Vyrubov put his billiard cue to the side. "Now let's go to the Uvarovs," he said.

"The way I'm dressed?" Sergey Burintzev was smiling.

"I'm not very presentable myself. Nobody'll notice. They'll all be drunk."

"Then why go?"

"I promised Sonya Petrovna that I'd come."

They left the coffeehouse. On the Kreshchatik Boulevard, they looked for a cab. The driver steered them across the Nabereshnoye Chaussee, along the Dnieper. It was the middle of April. The ice had begun to melt, but Sergey was cold in his threadbare coat. The river was dirtier than usual. It had overflowed its banks and eaten away some of Kiev's clayey soil. The water was yellow, like a gigantic lump of clay.

"The Dnieper looks sick," said Sergey. "Like a sick man who dies hard."

"You're a poet, Sergey. Why don't you write poetry?"

"It isn't a good time for writing poetry."

A waning moon shone peevishly above the rooftops. Andrey wanted to talk about Sonya Petrovna, but he was ashamed because he knew Sergey had other worries. Out of a feeling of shame, he had secrets from his friend. But Sergey had secrets from him too. Andrey couldn't understand this, since Sergey had nothing to be ashamed of.

For weeks now Andrey had been intending to break off with Sonya Petrovna, but it was difficult to break something that had never been whole. Sonya, dainty, blonde, with the face of a Trecento angel!

When Andrey thought of her, he thought of her breasts, which were white and taut and a little too large. In all probability she didn't have a soul, only breasts. Like him, she was twenty-two years old, and had been married to Prince Uvarov for six years. It was all the Prince's fault. Why did he have to dig for gold in the Urals?

"Would it bother you to have an affair with a married woman?" Andrey asked.

"I've never thought about it."

"Do you know Maria O'Rourke?"

"But she isn't married."

Andrey laughed. "She's barely sixteen."

"Then why do you ask?"

"I was in Otrada on Sunday." He couldn't explain how he had gotten from Sonya Petrovna to little Maria O'Rourke. "Did you read Tolstoy's protest?" he asked. He wanted to show Sergey that he wasn't indifferent to those things. He was always wanting to prove something to Sergey, and being irritated by his own zeal.

"He begs for alms," said Sergey. "And if all who were starving to death were to be given alms, what good would it do? I was in Tripolye. Our Little Father is a criminal and an idiot."

Andrey had lost all desire to go to the Uvarovs. Caviar, salmon, suckling pigs, *kulebyaki, pelmeni, kotletts pojarsky,* hot cakes—as if the kitchen wanted to throw up. Rejected food and spilled wine. *Zakusta* and *subrovka* and *perzovka.* Servile servants and servile musicians. He bent forward to the carriage door, then hesitated.

"Don't mind me," said Sergey. "I'm not squeamish."

The Uvarov palace was on Castle Park, at the corner of Yaketerinsky Street. As Andrey was paying the driver, a second cab drove up. Andrey recognized Dr. Sipyagni, the heart specialist. He had been called to the old Princess, the doctor explained. "A priest is what she really needs, my dear Andrey Antonovich. Natasha Pavlovna has been *in extremes* for days now. God only knows why her heart is still beating."

In the drawing rooms, about fifty or sixty people were chatting or dozing, nearly all of them drunk. Sonya Petrovna kissed Andrey on the mouth, saw that he and Sergey were served champagne with vodka, and disappeared again among her guests. Everyone was crowded into a green silk tapestried salon, for this was where they could find Professor Delphinius, a clairvoyant who had toured all of Russia and was in Kiev now for the second time. With his long neck and head held forward, he looked like a black umbrella. His spotty dinner jacket was covered with medals of suns, lions, palms, the honors of unknown kingdoms; yet if you were gullible enough to believe the professor, every medal told a story of the gratitude of a prince saved, a potentate warned.

As the two friends entered, the professor was reading the palm of young Count Peter Tarnovsky, whose small feminine hand was lost in the hairy paw of the chiromancer, as if a larger destiny were grasping his small fate. Now the Countess Rautenfels forced her way to the future, holding out her bejeweled hand to the fortuneteller. An old man grabbed her by the arm and cried, "I don't want to have anything to do with that damned quack!" to which the professor responded with a scornful smile. Hands were stretched out to him, but he took none of them. He stared down at the table, blinked at the light coming from a tasseled hanging lamp, then looked up suddenly and pointed at Sergey, who had remained in the background. This time it was the clairvoyant who held out his hand, mumbled something, finally whispered, "Come to see me. I'm staying at the Hotel National. My young man, you are in danger."

Sonya Petrovna appeared and urged her guests into the ballroom. Through the open doors, you could hear the gypsies starting a czardas. She took Andrey by the hand. "Will you dance with me?" He laid his hands on her hips.

She showed her little pearly white teeth. "It's boring tonight. Most of my guests were at the Godounovs until six this morning. Of course, Anna Alexandra arranged it like that on purpose, to spoil my evening." She looked toward the doorway, where a lackey had appeared. "I must go to the Princess."

"You should have canceled the party."

"The year of mourning is going to be long enough. Come with me. I'm afraid to go alone." On the way, she pressed a bottle of Veuve Cliquot into his hand.

They had to traverse the palace to reach the suite of the Princess Uvarov. It was cold. Candles fluttered, and the heads of the ancestors seemed to move in their thick gold frames. The Uvarovs were shaking their heads because a Princess Uvarov was deceiving her husband. Sonya Petrovna pressed close to Andrey, as if she were afraid of the dead Uvarovs, and of the Princess who was now very nearly one of them.

An aged lackey stood at the door of the bedroom, pale as death, yet as if warding off death. He looked the young man with the champagne bottle up and down, but deferentially he led Andrey into the neighboring salon. Andrey uncorked the bottle of champagne. Sonya Petrovna had forgotten to bring glasses. Dark red Bohemian goblets stood in a glass case. Andrey washed two with champagne, and emptied them out the window. The cold night air struck his face. Far away he could hear dance music. He closed the window, poured himself a drink, lighted a papirossa, and stretched out on a red velvet couch. Was he really tired of Sonya Petrovna? The glowing, sensual creature was not the first woman in his life, not the first married woman, either. One collected love adventures like butterflies. Under glass they were colorful; in the air they fell to dust. The pity of it was that this time he couldn't talk himself into believing he loved the woman he desired. It was convenient to behave as if one were in love; the next thing one knew, one was. So why hadn't it happened with Sonya Petrovna? Just as he had done a while ago in the cab, he suddenly saw the face of Maria O'Rourke, only this time it was as if he were nearing the explanation of an inexplicable feeling. He could hear the gasping cough of the old woman in the next room. He felt uncomfortable, but then there could be so many reasons for his discomfort. Death agony and champagne? Sonya Petrovna and Maria O'Rourke? The clairvoyant's prophecy? Not long ago, when one of his stableboys had lain dying, Andrey's father had watched at the boy's bedside all night. He, Andrey, had gone to confession only yesterday, and today he was drinking himself sodden while in the next room a woman lay dying. Did God look into the human heart, and what did He find there? Was it a good thing to think, or was only that which was not premeditated pardonable? Only somnambulists trod surely.

The door opened. He sat up.

"Don't get up," said Sonya Petrovna, and sat down beside him.

"How is she?"

"We have sent for the Bishop."

He picked up the bottle he had placed beside the couch and filled her glass. She looked at it and laughed.

"Won't you wait for him?" he asked.

"She doesn't know me any more."

"You must go to your guests."

"You must give me a kiss first."

Her tongue tasted of champagne. Her shoulders were as naked as if she were wearing no dress. He thought of Sergey, waiting for him; of the dying Princess, but he didn't dare restrain Sonya Petrovna, because women had peculiar ideas about love and considered men, who felt more strongly for death or duty, traitors or weaklings. He kissed her breasts and forgot that it had been his intention to break with her. He hadn't been fair to her, for there were few women with the courage to unveil their bodies without veiling their souls. She lay down beside him. In the next room it had grown still. Perhaps Natasha Pavlovna needed neither heart specialist nor bishop.

Later they went downstairs again. Sonya Petrovna hurried to her guests; Andrey remained standing in the doorway, looking for Sergey. The game with which the guests were trying to dispel their boredom wasn't new to him, yet it shocked him a little, for he felt like a child who wakes up one morning to discover that his toys have become childish. The Countess Rautenfels had promised a kiss to the winner of the "frog race," and fifteen or sixteen men in dinner dress and uniforms were squatting at the end of the room in a deep knee bend. The gypsies had played a flourish. Now the gentlemen began to hop toward the Countess like frogs, their hands on the parquet floor, while the women stood in a circle around them, clapping their hands to urge the frogs on, making bets, laughing when one of the frogs fell down or stood up straight because he was muscle-bound. Andrey saw the men's bent backs—a few were croaking and quacking—saw the flushed faces of the women; saw their goal, the Countess Rautenfels, standing motionless, her face coldly serious under her red hair. His sense of shame deepened. He could still feel Sonya Petrovna's warmth under his skin. Was this the sobriety after delight that was supposed to follow when one had made love without loving, like animals—*omne animal post coitum triste?* Or was he looking at his surroundings with Sergey's eyes, as though the personality of his friend had drawn a cloak over his own? The frogs were hopping toward the Countess. Bored, tortured eyes. Porcelain figurines from glass cases come to life, but only very slightly, on a holiday from the showcases. The men really looked like frogs, scarcely any difference. At every party, the same faces. Although they had seen each other yesterday at the Godounovs or the Yustikovs, they hurried up to each other, as if afraid of not being able to recognize themselves if the other did not recognize them. They kissed one another as a sign of how intimate the relationship was, although they weren't really intimate with anyone. They would go on to tell what a good time they had had the day before, and would have again tomorrow; it just happened to be boring today. They gossiped about somebody who had only gossip to thank for his popularity; cuckolded husbands were the most popular theme. They fell in love with women they had known for years without paying any attention to them; they talked about politics, the theater, and literature, dead phrases aroused to renewed agony. They played the parts assigned to them—were jokesters, charmers, paradoxes, conformists or revolutionaries. They drank until their tongues became thick and their eyes dim. There was always someone who helped you get home and handed you over to your waiting valet. Or you woke up beside a woman who had turned into a stranger while you were sleeping. Next morning you sent her flowers, and if you were in danger of stifling in your own boredom, you got yourself mixed up in a quarrel and fought a duel to recover an honor of which you were reminded only when blood flowed.

One of the frogs, a bearded giant, had reached his goal. He straightened up with difficulty, but he took his prize seriously. The slender Countess was swallowed up by his powerful arms. He kissed her on the mouth to the accompaniment of wild applause.

Sergey was standing beside Andrey.

"I think we can disappear without being noticed," said Andrey.

"I've had a wonderful time," said Sergey. "The professor prophesied that I would end on the scaffold."

In the hall they met the Bishop. A lackey told him, "Your Excellency is too late. Her Grace passed away a few minutes ago." The Bishop and the lackey crossed themselves.

2

The news that Sergey Burintzev had been arrested in Shitomir, the capital of the province of Volhynia, west of Kiev, reached Andrey not quite a week after the party at the Uvarovs. He left at once.

After a tedious journey by carriage, he took the local train, which was supposed to do the stretch from Berdichev to Shitomir in two and a half hours. There was only half a compartment for first-class passengers. He was alone. It had been raining for days, a heavy rain that beat against the long narrow windows as if strings were being slung across them from the sky.

Sergey's arrest had horrified but not surprised Andrey. He had had the feeling that one day it would have to happen, but had avoided the question of how he would behave when it did. He could see Sergey, with his short dark hair; the face of a peasant in which every feature was too broad, nose, mouth, forehead, cheekbones; in which the eyes shone, a deceptive light on the steppe. A great tenderness crept into Andrey's heart, as happened when fate overwhelmed someone strong. He had been fourteen when they met. A long illness was keeping him in bed, and Burintzev, four years older, had tutored him. They had remained inseparable—the son of the wealthy Count Vyrubov, and the son of the seamstress. They were friends, the best, a unique friendship—or were they really friends? There were moments when one of them covered the other's eyes with his hands. Sergey, who was constantly recruiting followers for his revolutionary ideas, had never tried to convert Andrey, or tempt him, as the case may be, and Andrey had never confided his pleasures, adventures, and love affairs to Sergey. Sergey sheltered Andrey from what was perilous; Andrey sheltered Sergey from what was dissolute. Was such a cautious friendship possible? It was useless to keep small chambers, or cellar, or attic, locked in the house of friendship. One day they opened of their own accord. What would he see then? Andrey asked himself.

3

It was three o'clock in the afternoon when Andrey arrived in Shitomir. The leaden sky was simulating an early twilight. Three cabs were waiting in front of the station, but not a cabby was to be seen. They had taken shelter under their wet tarpaulins. The horses stood there dripping, as if forgotten.

The city was quite a distance from the station. The nearer the cab drew to it, the more deserted it looked. An unhealthy Sunday hung over Shitomir. "What has happened?" Andrey asked.

The driver's back moved imperceptibly. "It's still happening."

"How did it start?"

"The gendarmes wanted to get the rabble off the streets."

"And why was the rabble on the streets?"

"That goes on here all the time, *vashe prevos'choditelstsvo.*" He addressed his noble fare as "your Excellency," in spite of his youth. "The people loaf in the streets or lie around in doorways."

The suburbs were deserted, roll-shades down, doors barred. Gendarmes and *gorodoyovs* patrolled the streets in pairs. Nothing to be heard but the drumming of the rain and the steps of the policemen on the cobblestones. An empty streetcar rattled past as if driven by a ghostly hand. There was a smell of smoke.

"It's the Jews' fault," the driver mumbled.

"The Jews?"

"There are forty thousand Jews in Shitomir, your Excellency, and that's the trouble. They have enough to eat; still they hold to the rabble. The gendarmes couldn't manage them, so they had to call in the Cossacks. Almost twenty Jewish houses have been burned to the ground. A blessing that there was no wind." He looked up at the sky. "The wind doesn't know what it's doing, that's the trouble. It carries the fire into Gentile houses." He cracked his whip. "Where are we going, *vashe prevos' choditelstsvo?*"

"To the Chief of Police."

The bearded man on the box said nothing more. His broad back was bent so far forward, he almost looked slight. He pretended not to hear Andrey's questions.

A group of riders appeared, Cossacks in green uniforms with fluttering sleeves and narrow leather belts, baggy trousers, boots, green *papachas*. They rode through the city as if it were the steppe; they rode through the rain like the wind. Near the main square, a group of Cossacks was herding some bound Jews in front of them. On the steps in front of the church lay a few people, reduced to skeletons. Others sat with their legs crossed, staring idiotically straight ahead. They stretched out their hands, begging for alms, but no one was walking past them. Perhaps they were stretching out their hands to God. But God didn't pass them, either. Not a human voice to be heard, as if dead Cossacks had been roped into saddles and dead Jews were being led on a leash, as if the dead were starving.

Two local policemen planted themselves in front of the cab. The horse shied, startled by them. They asked Andrey where he was going, then launched into a long-winded discussion. "I'll walk," said Andrey, and paid the driver.

He took the way the policemen had pointed out. They looked after him; they were still deliberating what to do. As he rounded the corner, he was met by a clamor. Many people were shouting, but one was screaming louder than the rest. There was the red brick wall of a tobacco factory; people lay along it, some face down in puddles. The rain was falling; they didn't notice it. A hearse stood in the middle of the street, four or five corpses piled on it, the legs dangling down, discarded dolls. Gendarmes, shouldering their rifles, were policing the wall. They bent down to pick up the corpses by the collar, but every time they touched a body, the man began to scream. Men were afraid of being taken for dead and buried alive, so they screamed, nothing still living in them but the voice. The gendarmes lifted the screaming men by the collar, then let them drop back into the puddles, where they didn't scream any more. They didn't fear to be taken for dead any longer—they died. The gendarmes kicked them to find out if they could still scream. Then they continued pacing the wall. The driver of the hearse cracked his whip. The horse didn't move, just as the people along the wall didn't move.

Andrey asked a gendarme the way to the police station. By now he knew the way, but he had to speak to someone. "The Cossacks won't let you through," said the gendarme.

"Why not?"

The man shrugged.

"What have these people done?" asked Andrey.

The gendarme frowned. He had thick eyebrows, like a mustache over his eyes. After he had asked for Andrey's pass and examined it, he said, "Turn to the right, your Excellency. Then you don't have to see the Jews."

Andrey walked in the opposite direction. He wanted to see. A man was being dragged out of a narrow house; two Cossacks had him by the wrists; his face hit the ground, blood was pouring from his nose. A woman had thrown herself in front of the Cossacks; she was clinging to their filthy boots, and their boots dragged her along.

At a wall, the Cossacks stopped Andrey. The air was thick with smoke. You could hardly see the soldiers. They were green spots in a fog. Behind the wall, the houses were burning. The rain fell into the fire, pattered on burning beams, a powerless rain. Silver sparks fell from the sky, a mighty rain. A red pair of scissors cut a hole in the wall of a house, slowly, with scorching points. A bearded man on one

108

of the top floors tried to grasp a burning child; his beard caught fire. Now he was burning with the child. A fiery beam struck them both. A woman screamed. Andrey could hear her screams long after they had ceased. She fell out of the window of one of the houses, her clothes on fire, as if someone had thrown a torch out of the window; her body fell on the wall and went out.

Andrey's pity was drowned in the lust to kill. He didn't want to save but to murder. He was seized by the passion of his impotence, and it threatened to choke him. He hated himself because he could not kill. At the same time he was pursued by visions that were inexplicable: Sonya Petrovna's naked breasts, the dying woman in the next room, Professor Delphinius under the tasseled hanging lamp, an epileptic maid who had once had a fit at his feet in the garden, a pamphlet he had found in some autumn leaves, Sergey on the steps of the university, the father confessor of his childhood. He wanted to stretch out his hand to a Cossack, but the green spot had vanished in smoke.

He walked back the way he had come. Suddenly it was as quiet all around him as it had been noisy before.

4

A police inspector, substituting for the Chief of Police, received Andrey. Like most bureaucrats, the man had plenty of time to complain about how little time he had. He hadn't heard a thing about Sergey Ivanovich Burintzev. . . . "We had to arrest sixty-two students." He sent one of his underlings, however, to find out if Burintzev was in the city jail.

It was still. Through the dirty window you could see a piece of gray sky, as much as one can see from a police inspector's room. The rain trickled desolately across the pane. It was impossible to imagine that houses were on fire in the city, that the starving were screaming, that human beings were being thrown out of windows, and that blood was flowing in the gutters. The police station stood like a colossus in the midst of suffering—blind, deaf, dumb.

Andrey moved restlessly in his chair. Since he had sat down opposite this shortsighted little man who coughed incessantly, he had been thinking only of Sergey. The student who had brought him the news of his friend's arrest had advised him to put fifty rubles in an envelope and pass it on to the police inspector. It took Andrey a long time to make up his mind to lay the envelope on the man's desk, casually. The man looked at the envelope out of the corner of his eye. Temptation almost made him humane.

"Our young people are not at fault," he said. "At fault are the professors."

He spoke abusively of teachers who put all sorts of bees in the bonnets of their students. Like all semieducated people, he hated the intellectual more than the uneducated man. Andrey looked at the door. Would they find Sergey? Was he still alive? Now it seemed to him that, actually, Sergey had not kept many secrets from him; it had been he, Andrey, who had not wanted to hear. The execution of the student Alexander Ilyich Ulyanov; the assassination of Alexander III; the arrest of Vera Figner; the terror organization Narodnaya Volya; the "Sacred Host"; the memory of the murderer of the Czar, Nicholas Rysakov. It had been convenient not to understand.

Then he sat up. A scream echoed through the building. The police officer looked up from his book and blinked in the direction of the window, as if he wanted to censure the fact that such things could happen in Russia—nonsoundproof windows in a police station.

"The Cossacks are with us," he said. "They are bunglers."

Again it was still. A big white alarm clock, the kind you usually found in kitchens, was ticking on the desk. "Your friend probably got mixed up in the revolt by chance," said the officer.

"Probably," said Andrey.

"Very unfortunate. Of course we proceed in an orderly fashion, but the Cossacks . . ."

He was looking at the envelope. Andrey pushed it a little nearer.

"I'm sure you'll be willing to guarantee that your friend won't enter the city of Shitomir again," said the officer.

"Of course," said Andrey, and was ashamed of his cowardice.

The policeman picked up a pen to prepare the release. You could hear nothing in the room but the ticking of the clock and the scratching of his pen. Whenever he put down Andrey's name, he mumbled, "Count Andrey Antonovich Vyrubov," letting the name roll off his tongue. Then he frowned. His trained ear had heard something that reached Andrey's a little later. The shuffle of heavy boots. A man screamed again; this time the sound was close by. A man was being dragged across the floor. Andrey jumped up.

The police officer rose and walked toward the door. Through it

Andrey saw the collapsed body of a man, streaming with blood. A policeman was standing over him, a leather strap in his hand. Then the door was closed from the other side.

Don't do anything rash, Andrey thought. He could feel his nails cutting into his palms. Was he powerless, or was he only telling himself he was powerless because he didn't want to admit to his own cowardice? When the police officer came back, Andrey was standing with clenched fists. The little man looked to make sure that the envelope was still lying on the desk.

"They have found your friend," he said. "But it's complicated. They tell me he made a provocative speech."

Andrey took out his pocketbook. When things were going downhill, they tended to move rapidly. He was no longer ashamed to take another fifty rubles out of his wallet. "I don't want to have to go to the Governor about it," he said, and laid the ruble notes on the envelope.

"Your friend is outside," said the officer. "They're just washing him."

They're just washing him. A human being washed himself; a thing was washed. Andrey left the room without another word.

It wasn't true that they were washing Sergey. He was standing all alone in the dimly lit corridor, at a faucet, his head bent forward. Andrey stopped behind him. When Sergey straightened up and turned around, Andrey saw his disfigured face. One eye was stuck together with blood; the lid was split. Water was running from his hair down his forehead; his blood had dyed the water red. His lips were swollen, dark blue. Around his nostrils—Sergey's prominently large nostrils—a crust of dried blood had formed.

Andrey flung his arms around Sergey. He wanted to support his friend, but Sergey needed no help. He stood erect, smiling. He smiled with only one corner of his mouth, like someone who had had a stroke. When Andrey couldn't control a sob, Sergey pressed his friend's head to his breast.

"It's all right, my boy," he said. "Let's get out of here or we'll miss the last train to Kiev."

111

CHAPTER 3

I

Without any transition summer had come to Otrada. The sky was clear, as if the Lord had pushed all clouds aside so as to see better. It was already hot in the morning. The wistaria was a violet frame around Maria's window.

On the morning of her sixteenth birthday she breakfasted alone, as usual. Then she put on her prettiest dress, all pink. It was a very young girl's dress, the last one, a farewell dress. The ceremony was to take place in her mother's boudoir punctually at nine.

She stood still for a moment in front of her mother's bedroom and looked back, telling her childhood, as though it were a puppy, that it must remain behind. This part of the house had always been still.

The family was assembled. Father, Mother, Olga, her three brothers, the two aunts, and, in the background, her governess, Mademoiselle Larue, and Monsieur Patenôtre, the hairdresser from Kiev.

The members of her family rose to their feet. One after the other, they kissed Maria on the cheek. The two aunts took her between them; Aunt Anna kissed her from the left, Aunt Sonya from the right, all the time smiling apologetically. Only her mother remained seated in her armchair. She was wearing a light blue dressing gown, and her pinched little face was red. She looked like a wax figure in a village church. Maria leaned over her. She wasn't allowed to open her presents yet. The roll-shades were down. It was almost dark.

Maria sat down on a velvet hassock at her mother's feet. The same ritual as on Olga's sixteenth birthday—she knew all about it. Maria could feel Katharina O'Rourke's ice-cold hands on her forehead. The

Countess took her daughter's dark blond hair in her hands, lifted it, and wound it into a knot. The hairdresser handed her some hairpins. A few stubborn little hairs eluded her; she stroked them into place, and Maria's white ears became visible. The Countess leaned back, exhausted.

Monsieur Patenôtre finished the job. He juggled with comb, brush, and curling tongs, stepped back, head to one side, a painter admiring his picture. The family had meanwhile taken their seats in a semicircle. No one spoke. Her father's cold blue eyes, Olga's mocking, Alexander's and Zoa's, overawed. Only Nikolay's eyes were smiling, and the two aunts were moving their heads in unison as if they wanted to say that something extraordinary was taking place, something incomprehensible. There was a slight smell of petroleum in the room. Maria became suddenly aware of the fact that all of them had the same blue eyes except Olga. She, Maria, did too. She was reminded of one of the cheap novels she had read. The story was about a woman who had murdered her child and had stood before her judges. Maria felt accused, and her father was the presiding judge. All the others were judges, too, even the two boys with their bare knees. But only her father passed judgment. The rest just nodded their heads.

She made a sudden, vehement gesture. The hairdresser almost burned her; Mademoiselle Larue screamed. They were going to have her burned, Maria thought. They were putting up her hair, baring her neck, leading her to the stake. What was the meaning of this heathenish ritual? As long as she had been a child, nobody had held her responsible; now they put up her hair, bared her neck, and held her responsible. The judge was looking at her; the rest were nodding; the executioner in white was brandishing his torch.

The hairdresser, in his white coat, was pleased. He bowed, waited for a word of recognition, withdrew disappointed. Mademoiselle Larue followed him like a defense lawyer leaving his client to his fate. One of the aunts giggled; at once the other one did, too. The Count moved his head and glared at the twins.

"You know what your new coiffeur means," Katharina O'Rourke said softly. "You are a young lady now, Mura, and ready for marriage. Your father—all of us—" she corrected herself, "expect you to be worthy of being considered a lady." She was exhausted. "God bless you, my child." She took Maria's head between her hands and kissed her daughter on the forehead.

In the afternoon they played games in the park. More than twenty young people had come from Kiev and the neighboring estates to celebrate Maria's birthday, most of them friends of Olga's. Maria's impatience grew. She was expecting Andrey Vyrubov. Although in the last days she had heard nothing from him, she couldn't imagine that he would forget her birthday. Since she had returned from school, he had come to Otrada, at first every week, soon nearly every day. Nobody pretended to notice anything, but the fact that Andrey was courting couldn't possibly have escaped even the residents of this cold household. To Maria it seemed that she had always loved Andrey. In Moscow she had yearned for Otrada; it had only been a yearning for Andrey.

She looked the young people over: Yuri Tolstoy had the coarse manners that usually went with the country gentry; Peter Tarnovsky was interested in nothing but his sentimental poetry; Prince Meshchersky was too short; Vladimir Mstislavsky too proud, because he was descended from Saint Vladimir; Ivan Trubetzkoy, although he was only a few years older than she, treated her like a child. Andrey was handsome and clever, and infinitely lovable. Olga adored him. It was going to be Maria's happiest hour when she could surprise her sister with her engagement to Andrey.

The thought that Andrey knew nothing of her marriage plans didn't bother her in the least; on the contrary, she found it amusing. Olga had told her about his wild life, perhaps to discourage Maria. The idea that he had possessed Sonya Petrovna, the most beautiful woman in Kiev, only excited Maria all the more. He hadn't sat hand in hand for hours with Sonya Petrovna, hadn't recited Pushkin's *Onegin* to her, hadn't hesitated to kiss her. But he couldn't deceive Maria. That he lost courage just with her was a tribute to his love for her. His hand trembled when he touched hers. After their first kiss, things would be different. He would find out that with imagination she could make up for the experience of the ladies of Kiev. They wouldn't live like the other young married couples in Kiev, whose love ended at the altar. She would become his wife and remain his inamorata.

"Where is Andrey?" asked Mademoiselle Larue.

The governess had noticed Maria's uneasiness. She noticed everything Maria did. Denise Larue, in her middle twenties, old enough
therefore, yet sufficiently young, was Maria's first friend, was her accomplice, her adviser, her ideal. A friend of the Count's in Paris had
recommended her, which was probably why she hadn't been dismissed
right away, although from the beginning she had given rise to vexa-
tion. Her clothes, lingerie, and hats were not only the chic French
attire of a Parisian, they were always, like everything chic, one step
ahead of what was *en vogue,* and gave the ladies of Kiev plenty of
material for malicious gossip. Mademoiselle Larue's pretty, intelligent
face was slightly marred by a scar on her forehead, which she declared
had been caused by a riding accident, but, as she couldn't ride, no
one believed her. Maria, however, believed every word she said. The
French woman was her prize possession, and instead of controlling her,
Maria was like a fetishist who became a slave of his possession.

Mademoiselle Larue was the first to see Andrey. Maria left her guests
and ran up to him. He was carrying what was apparently a fragile
object, clumsily and rather touchingly. It was covered with a silk
cloth. He put it down on the grass in front of Maria, smiled, and
whipped off the cloth like a magician—hocus-pocus, there was a
bird cage with a little finch in it, with blue head, pink breast, and
brightly colored feathers. Maria's canaries, titmice, and bullfinches
were housed in primitive cages, but Andrey had found an old Spanish
bird cage made of painted wood, with doors and turrets and arched
windows that made a princess of the little singer inside.

While the lackeys brought the samovar, Maria had nothing on her
mind but how to get a moment alone with Andrey. Her guests no
longer irked her; now they were a framework in which she could show
herself off to Andrey. The air was gentle, the hands on the sundial
were bedecked with bright flowers, a thin line of smoke rose from the
chimneys, and one could hear the whinnying of the horses outside the
gate. Maria was glad she was wearing her hair up, because that, of
course, was the only danger—that Andrey, who had always known
her as a child, might still take her for one.

When the guests were leaving, she found a way to hold Andrey
back. Mademoiselle Larue followed them into the conservatory, where
the bird cages hung, but she remained in the room next door, ready
to join them if any member of the family should appear. They stood

at the window, looking out at the park with the violet clouds of a June evening descending on it, a last glow above the shadows of evening.

"Why haven't you been here for such a long time?" she wanted to know.

"That wouldn't interest you."

"Was it a woman?"

"No. It wasn't a woman."

"Did you know I was jealous?"

She hoped he was going to say that she had no reason to be jealous; she longed for a declaration of love, a kiss, perhaps even a proposal— all on her sixteenth birthday. When the peasant girls became engaged, they sang a lament and implored their parents not to deliver them to "the wicked enemy." Peasant girls were stupid. The wicked enemy was Otrada. Andrey would liberate her from Otrada.

Women were the last thing he was thinking of at this point, he told her. All pleasures were distasteful to him. "I wish I could forget my whole life until now."

"I know all about you," she said, interrupting him, "or almost everything." She smiled at him. "It doesn't bother me."

That wasn't what he was talking about, he explained, and began to speak hesitantly of Sergey, about the events in Shitomir, of people who were starving for bread and thirsting for freedom. She listened to him, strangely moved, although she wasn't at all sure she knew what was moving her—the injustice of it all, his description of the tormented, or just the fact that he looked like a beautiful angry angel. It became quite clear to her that fantasy could not take the place of experience, and that one did not reach one's goal on prescribed paths. She could not give him what the women in Kiev had given him—not yet; she had to win him with her understanding. He had thought she was a child, but she too had had a wrong conception of him. He was not young; he didn't long for a bride—he longed for a wife.

"You must tell me more, you must tell me everything," she said.

He called what had happened to him in Shitomir a revelation, an enlightenment, but didn't hide the fact that this very enlightenment had served to plunge him into darkness. When one began to believe in the cause of the rebels, one stood alone, because one still remained a Count Vyrubov. Then he stopped short, as if afraid he was risking his all with such serious talk.

"I would like to listen to you for the rest of my life," she said.

Both of them were as excited as if they had been kissing all afternoon. Their excitement didn't demand an explanation. He was fired by his own words, drunk with her understanding of them. She felt his wounds and his suffering, and he was like her because of them, in spite of alien and incomprehensible sufferings. And she could sense that he was happier now, much happier than he had been under the trees when he had held her hand and recited love poems to her. She was happier, too. It was as if she had been looking for the door to his heart for a long time and found it at last.

"I could spend a lifetime telling you all about it, Maria," he said.

He was the only one who called her Maria. He made no declarations of love; he did not propose. He took her in his arms, and she kissed him as if everything had been said long ago.

3

On his next visit, Andrey proposed. She begged him to leave it to her to speak to her father about it. This satisfaction she wanted to experience herself.

The first one she told that she was engaged was her sister. Olga had become entangled in the mesh of her own hypocrisy. Obviously, she would have liked to weep and storm, but anyone who presented such a flawless front to the world couldn't afford to fall out of character. Maria pretended to believe her; regretted that she, the younger, was going to marry first, and brought things to a head of spite when she begged her sister to intercede with her father on her behalf.

When Maria entered the library, her father was sitting at his desk, bent over his papers. The sight of him—his balding head, with a tonsure of hair that had grayed early in life; his eyes, transparent yet somehow opaque; his full beard, parted in the middle, an upside-down V—the sight of him sufficed to irritate Maria. She was irritated most of all by his hands. You never saw the palms, only the backs. He would stretch out his hands as if in a blessing, but his blessing lay heavily on the recipient, and oppressed what it seemed to be uplifting.

He began to speak highly of Andrey's father—a remarkable man, wealthy, and deeply religious. It was a bad thing that the Catholic families in Russia were fast becoming a disappearing minority. Andrey's mother was a born L'Ardennois, of the highest French nobility. Of course he would rather have seen Mura become a Princess Trubetzkoy, and when he had said that, he paused for a moment with a piercing glance at her. The engagement? He thought the beginning of the following year would be a good time to announce it. The wedding would take place in July. He asked no questions. Andrey was not mentioned.

The summer afternoon was glowing hot outside, but in the library it was cold, as if the head of the house stood above any influences of the seasons. The books on their shelves looked frozen together, the flowers in their vases artificial; even the birds, whose warble you could hear outside the drawn blinds, sounded like the mechanical birds in a music box.

Maria wanted to ask why the engagement couldn't be announced right away, but she didn't dare, and hated her father all the more because of it. Everything she wanted to say would come to her only after she had left the room. He would have been opposed to her happiness if he had recognized it. He didn't think that she loved Andrey or that Andrey loved her. He didn't congratulate her, because he didn't see happiness as something desirable. His only desire was for order, and because love was disorderly, one did not mention it. "One." One did what "one" did; what "one" did not do wasn't done. One was arrogant, yet never so arrogant as to despise "one."

Disappointed, all satisfaction denied her, she ran to her mother. For years now, Katharina O'Rourke had spent most of the day in bed, the deceptive asylum of those who are unhappy. She had her hair done in bed, often took her meals in bed, wrote letters and played solitaire in bed. And, in bed, she looked healthy. Here she had never had one of her epileptic fits, of which the whole house was afraid and which drove the Count away for days. She felt safe only in the coquette lace cushions of her virginal bed.

Although she was accustomed to finding her mother in bed, Maria stopped, flabbergasted, when she saw her now. Half a dozen hats lay scattered over the blue silk coverlet, big hats, little hats, felt hats, straw hats trimmed with flowers and ribbons. The bed looked like a meadow in bloom. Katharina O'Rourke laid the silver mirror aside, but she forgot to take the straw hat with its black cherries, opalescent grapes and red leaves off her dainty little head. She didn't take it off until she saw her daughter's perplexed expression. Yes, she said, Olga had told her. Was it really true that her little Mura was going to marry

118

handsome Andrey Antonovich? She spoke hesitantly, with a smile that was ready to withdraw, and as if she were afraid Maria might read consent into her question. But as soon as Maria had told her that her father had agreed to the marriage, had even set the date, Katharina O'Rourke burst into tears and laughed and drew Maria to her, overwhelming her with girlishly curious questions. She pushed the hats aside; her hand mirror fell to the floor. Her cheeks red, she begged her daughter to open the window. "What a wonderful day! Oh, Mura, from now on every day will be wonderful!"

4

The summer passed, a hot summer, "the hottest summer in memory," the old people said. Maria slept with her windows open. Glowworms danced like terrestrial stars, and the stars in the sky danced with them. When Maria drove to the neighboring estates, the horses' hoofs sank deep into the dust. The smell of dust mingled with the scent of the linden trees, which were peeled at this time of the year, their bark being used for thatching or to weave *lapti* for the peasants' feet. There were thunderstorms, hot thunderstorms. The gravel made gritty music under the servant girls' bare feet. Feast days were celebrated in the village, and the *korobeyniki* came, peddlers laden with scarves, lace, beads, linen, and rings.

The Count often invited Andrey to dine. Since the engagement had not yet been announced, it was not mentioned. Maria watched Olga, who cast down her eyes as if she had seen sin; watched her mother, who wanted to say something, but didn't say it; watched Alexander and Zoa, mustering Andrey as if he had been a strange animal; watched her aunts waggling their heads; her father, who seemed to be waiting for an unseemly word to fall.

In the autumn two things happened to make Maria conscious of the fact that she was still in Otrada, chained to her childhood.

At the beginning of September the aunts left the house suddenly, without saying good-by, like lepers who had to be disposed of in secret. Maria found out only later that her father had had them taken to an insane asylum in Warsaw. Her mother had one of her epileptic seizures; Dr. Lissovski came from Kiev and stayed two days. Nobody would answer Maria's questions. She had to depend on what one of the maids said—Aunt Anna had refused to wash for days, and Aunt

Sonya had been sent away with her because, of course, she would sooner or later do what her sister did. Maria couldn't sleep. The old women had been shadows, but where there were no shadows, there could be no sun. She visualized how she would appear before her father next morning and what she would say to him. Morning came, and she said nothing. Her impotence shook her like a fever. She tried to stir up her mother, Olga, even her brothers and the servants, against her father; but they just looked at her as if she had lost her sanity, too. Her words echoed emptily. And she discovered that she hated her father less than before; her rage was not directed against his power any longer, but against her cowardice.

A fortnight later, the Chief of Police of Kiev turned up in Otrada. He came with a lot of men; gendarmes searched the park, eyes downcast, as if they expected to find what they were looking for in the colorful autumn leaves. The servants leaned out the kitchen windows, whispering to each other. The Chief of Police stayed for two hours. After he had gone, the Count had the whole family assembled in the big drawing room, under the portraits of his Irish ancestors, ceremoniously, a ceremony of bereavement. He announced that he had cast off and disinherited his son, Count Nikolay Nikolaevich O'Rourke; directed that anyone who saw Nikolay anywhere near the estate should report it; ordered that no one was to shelter Nikolay, even if he begged for it. He looked terrible, a fierce judge pronouncing a terrible sentence, but he didn't explain what Nikolay had done, as if his sentence didn't require an explanation. Maria's heart went out to her half brother, although she could not pity him. Whoever was forbidden to set foot on Otrada again was not to be pitied. Her father suffered only because Nikolay was the child of his first marriage, his true son. It was good to see him suffer.

5

Andrey came in the afternoon. Mademoiselle Larue withdrew with a smile that was half motherly, half lascivious—the latter seemed to be amused over the former.

"Did you see the police?" Maria asked. "They are looking for Nikolay. Have you any idea what he has done?"

"They are arresting students everywhere. They're supposed to have planned the assassination of the Czar."

"But do you think Nikolay could possibly . . ."

"They're saying something to that effect at the university."

"And you can say that . . . just like that?"

"I know Nikolay. Whatever he does, he does out of conviction."

"What would you say if your brother wanted to murder the Czar?"

"I told you what I saw in Shitomir."

"The Czar doesn't know what goes on in Shitomir."

"It is the duty of the Czar to know what is going on in his empire. There wasn't a word about it in the papers. A hundred dead—and not a line. The censor wouldn't let it through. Censored, censored, censored—as if there wasn't another word in the Russian vocabulary. We have abolished slavery, but the peasants can't pay their ransom. Thirty rubles for a man, ten for a woman. The Volga boatmen drag barges from Astrakhan to Nishni Novgorod for seventy-five long days, and what do we do? Did you know that the Princess Urossov prides herself on the fact that she bathes in champagne? Prince Trubetzkoy has his racing horses shot when they don't win. The Princess Repin has two chiropodists—one for each foot."

"Don't tell me you are one of the conspirators?"

"I am too much of a coward."

"It is the assassins who are the cowards. Of what concern are the peasants to you? They get more impertinent every day."

"They get more wretched every day."

"You don't know me, Andrey. I would find it terribly amusing to bathe in champagne."

"It is not fun to bathe in champagne—it is a sin."

"You should have become a priest."

"For that, too, I need more courage than I have."

"You only want to marry me because you are too much of a coward to throw bombs or become a monk?"

"I want to marry you because I love you."

"You don't know what love means. You love me as if I wasn't there."

That was it. Every time she thought she had him, he eluded her. Her kisses excited him, but he never lost himself in them. He listened attentively to everything she had to say, but did what he thought was right. She thought of ways to hurt him. When he was away, she longed for him, but the need to hurt him grew stronger and stronger. With most people it was the other way around: when they were near, they became bearable. But Andrey's proximity was a challenge. He didn't speak of love because the fate of some dirty Jews was more important to him. She had fallen in love with his picture; he was destroying it. She had to give him pain to rouse him out of his equanimity.

"I don't want to become like my mother," she said. "You're very mistaken if you think that I'm willing to bury myself in some provincial nest. You kiss me as one kisses a child. You didn't even protest when my father set our marriage for July. Can you wait that long?"

She wouldn't let him interrupt her. She knew his sore spot. She told him that she did not feel guilty just because she wanted to be richer and more distinguished than other people; that she hated her father but admired his arrogance; that she was one of the women Andrey despised; that hunger might be painful, but it was also boring. She reproached him for the hours they were wasting, for the milk that flowed in his veins, for the fact that he treated her like a sister.

That evening he left early. He seemed sad rather than angry. Her needling and her tongue-lashing had missed their objective; he had not contradicted her, but he had not given in, either. He didn't want to fight, so she could not be victorious. She wanted to dream of his kisses, and accused him because her body remained cold. That night, for the first time, she dreamed of her wedding. At the altar she began to bleed. She had married and was not yet a woman. Now her blood dyed her white dress red. The crowd jeered. In the first row sat Ivan, the groom, beside the anemic Princess Golitzin.

CHAPTER 4

I

"A gentleman is waiting for you," the lackey said as he opened the door to Andrey.

Andrey looked at the clock. He had left Otrada feeling distraught. It was almost eleven. In his study, Nikolay O'Rourke came forward to greet him.

"You are surprised, Andrey Antonovich. I can quite understand it," he said. "You must excuse me. I won't keep you long."

"Do you know that they are looking for you?"

Nikolay smiled. "And you would be implicated if they knew I was here. Please don't worry, the police are much too stupid to find me. I hope to be across the border in a few days." He lighted a papirossa. "I wouldn't have come to see you, but I promised Burintzev that I would."

"After Shitomir, Sergey disappeared. Where is he?"

"I'm not allowed to tell you that, but he is safe, if you want to call it that. He asked me to bring you greetings. That was of course before the warrant went out for my arrest."

"Can I do anything for him?"

"His mother has been unable to find work for a long time. He begs you to do what you can for her. I'd like to have attended to it, but I have nothing myself."

"If there is anything I can do for you . . ."

"Thanks, but you've done quite enough to endanger yourself. By the way, I don't want you to misunderstand—my trip abroad is not flight. I am leaving on a specific mission for the comrades."

The calm, the brightness, with which Nikolay spoke, impressed

Andrey. How the rebellion must be prospering to embrace two such different people as Sergey Burintzev and Nikolay O'Rourke. This handsome young man, very like Maria—the same dark blond hair, the same blue eyes, even the same lower lip thrust forward a little— was no fanatic. Hatred of the oppressed wasn't driving him, nor the hunger of the poor, nor the ambition of the hopeless.

Nikolay sat down and crossed his legs. "I can see you are astonished. The motives are different, but the goal is the same. Sergey is a revolutionary; I am a patriot. Only a revolution can save Russia."

"Do you really believe that the throwing of bombs can save Russia? What has changed since Alexander II was murdered? Thousands are languishing in prison, and hundreds of innocent men have been sacrificed."

"Your question isn't new. Let's say you find yourself in prison, and innocent, and the men who know you are innocent and plan to free you light a fire near the prison. It might be only a small fire, easy to put out, but the men would know that its glow lit up your cell. Russia is a prison. We light fires so that those who are captive may see they are not forgotten. The fire of a bomb in Odessa shines through the bars of a prison in Taganrog. Take yourself! If we hadn't incited the starving in Shitomir to rebellion, you would never have even encountered misery."

"I can be of very little use to you. The most I can do is give some money to the mother of a friend."

"Don't underestimate what it would mean to the Czar to lose a Count Vyrubov. Nothing brings two people closer than the rejection of a third."

"Of what use is it to incite people to revolt when they are going to be trampled to death by Cossack horses? Sometimes I ask myself if idealism that can have no hope of achieving its goals doesn't degenerate into cynicism."

"If they hadn't murdered the hungry in Shitomir, they would have starved to death. A man who dies without protest today, dies twice.' For the first time an expression of pain became visible in his narrow face. "How did they take the news in Otrada?"

"Your father has disinherited you."

"And Mura?"

"Maria loves you, but you can't expect her to understand you."

"It would surprise me if she loved me. She has known so little love —there's really nothing much left for her to love but herself. The people we hurt become egoists. My father hates Mura only because, of all his children, she is the one most like him. She has fine qualities, but both the good and the bad in her are excessive. Women can be dangerous," he went on, "because they want to do in their small world what we do in our large one. Their wars and revolutions take place between four walls; they seek their adversary in the bedroom. Mura isn't like any other young girl I know." He laughed. "My father is lucky. If Mura had been a boy, he would have lost two sons. And Mura would do more for my comrades than I can. I am going to miss her. In our society, people attend to life as they attend to their mail—they answer because they have to. Mura is one of those few people who really live. She will either make you very happy or utterly miserable." He rose.

"Did Sergey really send no other message?"

Nikolay shook his head.

"I'd like to ask you something," said Andrey. "It has been on my mind ever since Sergey's disappearance. Do you despise me because I can't be one of you?"

"You have been educated in the Christian tradition. Your faith stands between you and Sergey, but it doesn't stand between you and me. Although I despise the corruption of the Church . . ."

"The Archbishop of Warsaw hurled himself against the Cossacks."

"And the Archbishop of Lublin blessed their weapons. The Church is like a roulette player who places on *rouge et noir* at the same time. But I am not speaking of the Church. You were fortunate enough to grow up in a house where they practiced what they preached. I grew up in a house where the word 'love' could only be found in the Bible. Your father took Sergey in after Shitomir. We are not so far apart as you think. You are a patient Christian; I am an impetuous one. Patience and impatience—it may well be that therein lies the whole difference." He stretched out his hand to Andrey. "Farewell, and good luck to you and Mura."

Andrey accompanied him to the garden gate, and went on ahead to see that there were no gendarmes about. The street was deserted.

Andrey goes back to a sleeping house.

His conversation with Nikolay leaves him no peace. He has not known the meaning of peace since Shitomir. He had brought Sergey to his house in the Lindenallee. Long nocturnal conversation; Sergey held nothing back. Then Sergey's return to his mother, his disappearance, the great emptiness. His old friends? Their chatter is an insult. They are like mirrors that maliciously preserve an earlier face. Nothing is harder to bear than people who can't tolerate that one has changed. The Cossacks defend their arrogance and sloth. Arrogance is the vice of cowards. Why doesn't he follow Sergey? Sergey and his father, the agnostic and the believer—they understand each other. Both believe in a power: the one in a supernatural power that knows why it tolerates injustice; the other in his own, which would do away with injustice. Sergey wants to free the slaves, but of what use is it when new slaves are to be made out of slaveowners? The Cossacks today, the rebels tomorrow. His father relies on love, but how difficult it is to tell long-suffering love from cowardice. The hope that force will capitulate before charity is slight. Nikolay acquitted him, but the impressions of Shitomir will not stop pursuing him. Helplessly he had watched force in action. If one decides for love, one leaves the way wide open to force; if one decides for force, one no longer acts in the name of love. The conversation with Nikolay might perhaps not have struck so deeply if the talk with Maria that preceded it hadn't disturbed him so much. He had burdened her with all his hopes. How could a single creature bear such an onerous love? It is his fault. Her beauty has captivated him, but what he is demanding is her understanding. He has saved himself from the mire, and is surprised to find innocence unsuspecting. Is it possible that he has become sexless in the very moment when he thinks he loves? He desires her, yet he cannot accept happiness in such a sea of woe. Shouldn't he have become priest or rebel? The old books speak of Eros and Agape, of carnal and pure love. He believes in one love only—Eros carries Agape under her heart, and Agape, Eros. But the old books know better. The young girl knows better. Eros knows nothing of compassion, and Agape is sexless.

The clock is striking four. Clocks are striking all over the house;

only lifeless life goes on. The cold that heralds sunrise creeps through the cracks in the windows.

3

In the week following Nikolay O'Rourke's visit, Andrey vacillated between joy and misery. One day Maria persuaded him to visit the grave of her father's first wife with her. It was a late autumn day. A glassy mist veiled the crowns of the trees and rose out of the ground. Earthly and heavenly glasses wanted to toast each other. Andrey's and Maria's feet sank deep in fallen leaves. They were no longer colorful, nor did they crackle; they were spongy and drab. Halfway to their destination, Maria stopped and begged him to turn back. Because of the weather? he asked her. But she whispered that the Princess was wont to rise up out of her grave to break off willow branches and make a switch of them. Today was a day like that, she insisted. She knew it was because she knew it. When he asked her why she hadn't known it before, she didn't answer, but fled trembling into his arms.

Another time he found her in a great state of excitement. One of her father's favorite horses had fallen and broken its legs, and was going to be shot. He thought she was excited by pity, but she was on her way to the stable, where they were going to shoot the horse. Rigid with astonishment, he stood at her side and saw ecstasy fill her eyes, and could not explain it to himself. He wanted to cover her eyes with his hands, drag her away, but she insisted on staying until the animal had drawn its last shuddering breath. She said nothing about the gruesome episode, but all that evening she was overwrought, joked more vivaciously, and was more affectionate than usual.

No sooner had this streak of cruelty in her dismayed him than Katharina O'Rourke told him—but Maria's father was not to hear of it —that Mura had gone every day to the window of one of the maids who had scarlet fever, because no one else had dared go near. The servants had refused to bring her her meals, and it was Mura who had gone to the kitchen three times a day, prepared a tray for the girl, and carried it over to the servants' quarters. It was a miracle that she hadn't caught the disease, but when Andrey reproached her, she only laughed. "When you do a good deed, a good angel watches over you," she said, and went right on looking after the girl.

Melancholy was paired with frivolity, superficiality with seriousness,

127

honesty with lies, sentimentality with frigidity. She apologized for what she had said to Andrey on the day the police had searched Otrada. She sat beside him for hours while he talked of a house he had found not far from Kiev and intended to rebuild for them, a home in which there was to be no injustice or ugliness. Once she spoke with admiration of a friend from boarding school who was planning to divide an estate she had inherited from her grandfather among the peasants; but right after that, she wanted to know if Prince Golovin really owned thirteen houses in which he kept thirteen mistresses, and whether Count Lopuchin actually had ordered the gypsies to follow him to the cemetery where, after an orgy that had lasted three days and three nights, he had dropped dead? Once she surprised Andrey with a list she had made, of the guests she wanted to invite to their engagement party; when he mentioned it again later, she had forgotten all about it and said the New Year was still far away. She asked him why he loved her, and when he told her love needed no reasons, she couldn't understand that he loved her. When he admired her purity, she intimated that he didn't realize some of the things she knew; if he told her that he desired her, she asked him why he hadn't stayed with the demimondes of Kiev. She often managed to shake off Mademoiselle Larue. Once she led Andrey to a stall where a cow had just calved, threw her arms around his neck, and dragged him down, laughing, into the hay; let him kiss her and kissed him till his lips were sore, and he had to beseech all the good spirits in heaven to keep him from touching her body. But then weeks would go by without the governess leaving her side; and when he got up enough courage to mention it, Maria accused him of being impatient.

As the first snows began to fall and the days became shorter, and only four weeks remained to the announcement of their engagement, Andrey admitted to himself that the riddle she was attracted him more than Maria herself. He was not sure that he would ever solve it.

CHAPTER 5

I

At the beginning of December Maria departed for Kiev with Mademoiselle Larue. The excuse was to buy Christmas presents. The two had been plotting and preparing the trip for a long time. A month before, the governess had confided in her ward that an old friend, a certain Baron de la Motte, former diplomat and an immensely wealthy man, had written that he was coming to Kiev in December. She had to see him. He would not only take both of them to the theater but, after that, to the famous Château des Fleurs.

It had not been easy for Maria to get permission to go to Kiev, for she had no relatives in town and they were going to have to stay at the Grand Hotel. At first she was disappointed because Andrey was not there—he had had to go to a funeral in Moscow—but her disappointment soon went under in a whirl of new impressions.

A French opera company was giving Massenet's *Le Roi de Lahore*. Maria was not very musical and didn't hear much of what was going on. She was far too fascinated by their host, a man over fifty, with tear sacs that drooped over his cheeks like the ears of a dachshund, who busied himself with Mademoiselle Larue's knee through the entire performance. Also, the clothes the women were wearing enchanted her. Compared with them, the effect of her own dress, although Mademoiselle Larue had altered it and reduced its decorum considerably, was still quite provincial. She was far more interested in the conversations carried on in the marble foyer, which were peppered with the powder of intrigue, flirtation, and jealousy.

She entered the Château des Fleurs on the arm of the Frenchman, with nothing on her mind but to conceal her astonishment. It turned out to be easier than she had thought. The Château des Fleurs, restaurant and night club, had a dubious reputation, although there was really little reason for it, since all intimacy went under in a show of pomp, all secrecy in noise, and anything illicit got lost in the dimensions of the place. Dark red plush furniture, fountains playing, vodka and champagne on ice, gypsies and balalaika players, exotic flowers that looked like cranes and flamingoes, artificial grottoes, and gypsy girls everywhere, in their full skirts and tight bodices, colored kerchiefs around their heads, gold coins dangling from their ears, shamelessly trying to please their hosts. The Baron's guests, ten or twelve, were already assembled, but a few seats were still empty. He was expecting some of the singers from the French opera company.

Maria knew the man on her right, at least by name. Peter, the brother of Count Vassily Vassilyevich Tarnovsky, had come often to Otrada. She therefore found Count Vassily all the more surprising. Peter had impressed her with his delicate, dreamy nature, whereas his brother was aggressively male. Peter was blond and smooth-shaven; Vassily was dark and wore a French-clipped mustache under a nose that was a little too short. Peter was a gentle shepherd; when you looked at Vassily, you thought of a bold and ruthless hunter.

"Have a drink, Countess," he said, laughing. "That'll help you over the first shock."

"I am not shocked."

"You are not trying to tell me that you frequent places like this."

"No, but . . ."

"How did Mademoiselle Larue get to you?"

"A friend of my father's recommended her."

"Denise Larue as a governess. What an idea!" And he was off on an account of her circumstances. She had been one of the most popular—"well, let's face it"—demimondes in Paris. Once or twice she had struck it rich, but easy come, easy go. In the end she had made up her mind to pry an old Assistant Secretary of State loose from his wife; the woman had called in the police. Hence the desire for a change of climate. "Your father's friend was probably one of her patrons. Still not shocked?"

Not at all. On the contrary, she was thinking of what her father would say if he ever found out the truth. He had forbidden her to read French novels, and had put her in the safekeeping of a cocotte! Of course she would talk to Mademoiselle—to Denise, that is—about it. Before Denise had kept up appearances and only loosened the reins under protest; now she was in Maria's hands.

He had really come only because of the singers, Vassily Tarnovsky explained, for he was studying singing. "I'm a bloody dilettante, of course. Do everything by halves." She liked the way he didn't take himself seriously. He had an amusing way of mocking himself yet at the same time taking the spotlight—peculiar to people who stood above themselves, and therefore seemed to stand above others. "You just listen to me," he said as she urged him to talk to the artists. "Let a man talk about himself long enough, and he'll promptly fall in love with you." And he went on talking about himself. "I read a Chinese novel the other day, not very thoroughly of course. *The Dream of the Red Chamber*. It said about one of the men, 'He carried the wind on his shoulders and moonbeams up his sleeves.' That's me." He poured vodka from a small flacon into her champagne.

As she listened to him, she could feel herself growing bigger and bigger. She was reminded of a circus artist she had seen once who had blown himself up, flexed his muscles, and stretched until the chains that held him had broken. But she seemed to be growing of her own accord, and she grew until her bonds burst. At the same time she could feel her body, her breasts, her knees, her thighs. Because usually one felt one's body only when it hurt, she was astounded to find that it was a pleasant feeling. The strangest thing about it was that she felt just as she had when she began to see again. The balalaika players and lovers, the gypsy girls and guests, the champagne bottles and the chandeliers were as if mirrored in deep water, shivering and weaving; yet she knew that they would suddenly stand still and be revealed in beautiful outlines. It was as if all her misery were suddenly ended and she dared to look it in the eye, like the eye of a defeated dragon.

"Let's dance, Maria Nikolaevna," said Tarnovsky.

They squeezed their way through a narrow grotto lined with colored shells, cave and fairground at the same time. A women's orchestra was playing in the next room, scantily dressed girls. Every now and then the conductor raised her baton; one of the girls left the stage, another took her place. One of the girls was sitting on an officer's lap. She had forgotten to give up her instrument and still held her flute in one hand.

Tarnovsky had his hands on Maria's hips. They were playing a waltz. "Is it true that you are engaged?"

"Not yet."

"Marvelous! I am going to visit you in Otrada."

"You will find the doors barred."

"Did I forget to tell you that I am a magician? I can open barred doors."

When she got back to their table, she asked for more champagne. She knew she was drunk. How could she be drunk if she knew it? The Baron had laid his head on the bosom of one of the singers; his head seemed to be growing out of it. Mademoiselle Larue waved to her—oh yes, there she was, Denise, the fancy lady. One of the guests was dribbling champagne into the blouse of one of the gypsies. Maria was suddenly captured by courage, in the way one was usually only captured by fury or longing. Since you couldn't very well be courageous for the sake of courage alone, she looked about her for something on which to prove it. If only her father would walk into the Château des Fleurs now, or Andrey! " 'Wind on his shoulders and moonbeams up his sleeves.' That's like me, too," she told Tarnovsky.

It was three when the party broke up. "Button up your coat," said Mademoiselle Larue. Tarnovsky buttoned up Maria's coat and held her close. "We are all going to the hotel for coffee," he said.

The sleighs drew up to the door. A score of doormen helped the guests get into them. "I am taking the Countess in my sleigh," said Tarnovsky.

It hadn't snowed for days. The sleigh tracks on the icy streets looked as if they had been drawn by children. The sky was spacious, and the stars looked gay, as if unreal. The moon hung in the trees of the Nabereshnoye Chaussee.

Maria saw herself as in a mirror: a young woman letting a handsome man lift her into a sleigh. She was part of a laughing, tipsy company; all of them were rich, distinguished, and merry. The whole evening the young woman had been admired; now she was driving to the palace of her lover. The handsome man spread his coat across her shoulders; he took her in his arms and kissed her. Her body was awake as in the dreams she had not dreamed for a long time.

2

For months she had been asking herself why her body, which in the nights at boarding school had seemed to be so roused, now seemed to sleep. She asked herself if she was like those children who had to take a long nap after lunch when they were to stay up late in the evening, whether her body was slumbering toward an awakening. Her quietude had been disquieting.

Now she dreamed again. Vassily appeared in her dreams. She was bathing, naked; he pursued her at the edge of a wood. They made love. Wind on his shoulders, moonbeams up his sleeves. She entered the Château des Fleurs. Everyone was dressed festively; only she was naked. Vassily walked up to her, kneeled down, kissed her knees. On the stage, where the female orchestra was playing, a bed was waiting.

One day, when the dream of the night before was still so alive in her that it kept accompanying reality, Vassily Tarnovsky appeared in Otrada. He came with Yuri Tolstoy, whose parents owned a neighboring estate. He winked at her, and she pretended to be seeing him for the first time. She became his accomplice.

The following days, with all sorts of excuses, he came again. He knew how to manage it so that he never met Andrey, and he knew how to corrupt his surroundings. He admired Olga's drawings, ran errands in Kiev for the Countess, talked about steam engines with Alexander, and gave Zoa sweets when no one was looking. But with Maria he was perfectly honest, and made fun of those who succumbed to his charms. He didn't have to bribe Mademoiselle Larue. One look out of his dark eyes, and she was off like a trained puppy.

In the middle of December, Vassily came to fetch Maria in a sled he was driving himself. He had told her on an earlier visit that he wanted to show her his *dacha,* which was only about three miles from Otrada. On the way there, in Borispol, he stopped at a tavern. Mademoiselle Larue got out. Propriety demanded that Maria protest, but Vassily and the governess acted matter-of-factly about it, as if Maria's consent had been a foregone conclusion.

It was unusually warm for the time of the year. Snow fell in thick flakes that were so soft, one felt they should be warm. Under its white cover the landscape had lost all identity; still, Maria felt that this piece of earth was home. She thought she knew every tree, every fence; and the ravens, God's truest creatures since they starved, yet never starved to death—she thought she knew them too. She was no longer afraid—that was why she felt at home.

The sleigh drove along a narrow side road. The summer pavilion rose up out of the snow as if drawn with a pastel crayon, its colors foolishly innocent against the white. As Vassily helped her out of the sleigh, Maria thought she recognized the *dacha,* and she definitely knew the lackey who opened the door and led them into the single large room, threw a few logs on the fire, and disappeared without a word.

"Isn't that one of Yuri's servants?" she asked.

"Of course."

"And isn't this Yuri's house?"

"Of course." He was helping her out of her coat.

"I thought you were going to show me your *dacha.*"

"I don't even own a *dacha.* I'm probably the poorest rich fellow you know."

He made no bones about having lured her to Yuri's place under false pretenses; didn't even deny that Yuri knew about their secret tryst; compromised her, and didn't apologize for it. She sat down in one of the colorfully carved armchairs by the fireplace. His honesty was disarming. Just as he had initiated her into his deception of others, he now made her an accomplice in deceiving her.

He brought her a glass of vodka, poured a large glass for himself, and began to talk about Andrey. She had been thinking of Andrey. He didn't ask her if she loved Andrey; he said, "You have fallen in love with me, so you don't love him." According to him, young girls married the first man who proposed; but in civilized countries, like France, for instance, hasty marriages were considered ridiculous. "In France they think of marriage; here they think only of the wedding." And Andrey? "He loves you, but he's not mad about you. I can tell you just what's going to happen. I know it from my father. He was the perfect fiancé; now he has a new mistress every month, because it never occurred to him to make a mistress of his wife. He is thoroughly moral, naturally only for home-use."

She didn't defend Andrey. One's conscience was a hungry Moloch, and one stuffed its mouth with reproaches against the person one was about to betray. It was Andrey's fault that she was here in Yuri Tolstoy's *dacha* with Vassily.

Vassily sat at her feet. He embraced her knees. "You look like a Botticelli angel. I wish I hadn't fallen in love with you; but it did happen, the moment you walked into the Château des Fleurs. I've got to get back my sleep, of which you've robbed me. What a pity you are afraid of me, Mura."

"Why should I be afraid of you?"

"Because I know all about you. You are like me, and I don't think very highly of myself."

She compared his face with Andrey's. He was closer to thirty than twenty, and looked older than that. His features were dominated by his mouth: when he laughed, his face brightened; when he was serious, it darkened. When he was speaking, it was difficult to watch his eyes. His mouth was like a prima ballerina who overshadowed all the other dancers on stage.

He drew her down to him onto the bearskin. She closed her eyes, but he didn't kiss her until she had opened them again, as if he wanted to prove that he could hold his passion in check, as a good driver held his fiery steeds; as if he wanted to force her to admit to her own passion, instead of fleeing from it in a hypocritical fainting fit. She looked him in the eye, laughed, pushed her lower lip forward. He took her face between his hands; slowly his lips approached hers.

But then, when he had kissed her, a change came over him that aroused everything that had been stifled in her since they first met— her upbringing, her faith, her loyalty, her innocence. He kissed her throat, and shoulders, breathed his warm breath into her ears; his fingers moved down her spine, and before she could stop him, he had opened her high-buttoned blouse. Then he tried to undo her batiste chemise. She withdrew from him, hesitantly, not completely. He didn't go on undressing her, not yet. His hand touched her breast, sought her swelling nipple as he covered her other breast with kisses that sought the other nipple. For just a moment she delighted in his love with a painful vehemence; her lips hurt and her breasts, and the skin over her knees, but the weakness that overcame her with this quick and sudden fulfillment gave her, even while it was taking place, a cool strength. She pushed Vassily away, struck him, tried to get up; but he took this to be just another part of their game of tacit agreement and wouldn't let her go. She kicked him. He rolled away from her, screaming, but when he again sought her mouth, beside himself now, she dug her nails into his flesh. His forehead and cheeks began to bleed, and even though he withdrew now, cursing, her nails remained imbedded in his face as if she wanted to leave her mark on his features forever.

On the way back to Borispol, Maria was excited, but no longer roused. It amused her to think of what Mademoiselle Larue would say when she saw Vassily. The pleasure she had felt in his humiliation let her forget the outrageousness of his behavior. She had hurt him, and she had conquered. As she looked at the man sitting silent at her side, gritting his teeth and flogging the horses mercilessly, she was filled with an inexplicable tenderness. He loved her. What did it matter that he had thought she was so stupid as to become his mistress?

3

The traces of her violence are barely healed when Vassily turns up in Otrada again, smiling a little mockingly. The hunter, wounded, goes on hunting. "Mura, you are a child." She cannot stop thinking of him. Whenever he comes near her, she feels faint. She has to find her way back to Andrey. She has deceived him even though she didn't give herself to another. She tries to recall their best times, but finds the doors barred. Andrey returns. He speaks of the future. Her love hangs over an abyss on the thin thread of his plans. "You have saved me, Maria." From what? She wants only to save herself. Sleepless nights. A mire spreads out before her, a sea of yellow, that unbearable color. When her mother knits, the yellow of her wool hurts as the sun did when she was blind. "Mother, I can't stand the sight of that wool." "Yours is a hard heritage, my child." Vassily comes back. He sends Mademoiselle Larue away. They wade through the snow until the house is out of sight. "I know too much about you, Mura." What does he know? Does he know that she still does not bear the marks of a woman? Seventeen years old. Doesn't blood flow in her veins? She was mistaken; she hasn't yet succeeded in routing fear—the fear of being discovered. He doesn't kiss her. On the way back, he has to support her. And then, by chance, she finds herself alone with Andrey. They kiss. Her tongue touches his lips, her breasts are pressed against his chest. He is startled. She wants to love him, but her body will not respond. He speaks of their engagement; she pretends to have a headache. In the night she dreams that she tells Andrey everything, and he challenges Vassily to a duel. Two men are dueling, but it is Vassily and her father. Her father lies in his blood, like the horse they had shot. She leans over her father—his blood is yellow. She writes to Andrey in Kiev: "Come, I must see you. Your bride," and doesn't know why.

Vassily arrives unannounced. Her mother is knitting just as her aunts once knitted. The yellow wool, Olga behind Vassily. "Look what I've brought for you!" In his hand, a bird cage, a round bird cage. At sight of the parrot in it, she feels a stabbing pain in her neck. Yellow breast, yellow feathers. The parrot is licking the bars of the cage with his ugly black tongue. "Why did you bring him?" "You wanted a parrot." Behind him, Olga: "You wanted a parrot." Just like a parrot. "Why do you bring me something that frightens me?" He laughs. "You are a child, Mura." Olga: "You are a child, Mura." The parrot screeches. Maria screams: "Put the wool away, Mother!" She senses her mother's arms around her shoulders, weak arms; still, they catch her. Her mother's face is sad and gray like the light in a chapel. Vassily leans over her. Or is it the parrot sitting on her chest? She wakes up in bed. From far off she can hear the voice of the doctor.

And then she is sitting at the window of her room. The veils of the moon are caught in the branches of trees that seem to have moved away from each other. They rise up out of the silver mist, like pallid water inundating the land. She hasn't seen Andrey or Vassily again. Mademoiselle Larue got rid of them both. "Mura is ill." Mademoiselle Larue says that her father called it an epileptic seizure. Tomorrow he will probably use the word "insane," at first cautiously—the way he did it with the aunts. She has to pull herself together. Her heart and her body speak two different languages; the one doesn't understand the other, and they talk themselves into a rage. They hate each other and themselves, because the one cannot understand the other or because they cannot make themselves understood. She has to step between the two and pass judgment on them. She has to decide for one or the other.

CHAPTER 6

I

The Catholic feast of Christmas came and went, a new year began; but the O'Rourke and Vyrubov families still did not celebrate the engagement of their children, Andrey Antonovich and Maria Nikolaevna. Maria recovered slowly from her strange illness. She asked Andrey to be patient; impatiently he granted her wish.

Spring began to announce itself. It was already warm at noon; the icicles on the gutters began to drip, but in the afternoon they froze again, and the sun paled like an invalid who had tried to do too much. Here and there the ice cracked under the skater's feet. A warm wind flew through the trees as a young bird, trying its wings, flutters startled back to its nest.

In March, a high fever felled Andrey's father. At first everyone thought he had caught cold; but inflammation of the lungs set in, and the doctors feared for his life. Andrey rarely left the house. He wrote Maria long letters and hurried to meet the mailman, waiting for an answer. He slept in the room of his father's valet, which was next to the sickroom. For hours he sat silently at his father's bedside. Contrary to the advice of his doctors, the old man lay flat, on a hard cushion.

Only now did Andrey grow conscious of how much he loved his father. It was difficult to picture another man's life, especially one's procreator's. The man in bed, forty years older than Andrey, was very thin, as if he would always suffer from the cold, but he had probably never been cold. His eyes were as frigid as an icebound lake, yet human beings and animals had gone to him. His hands were narrow and seemingly boneless, yet he had stood outside in the bitter cold and chopped wood. He had been considered an ascetic, yet Andrey had never seen him anything but gay. Gaily he had denied himself the joys of life. The Vyrubovs came from Poland. Anton Fyodorovich had wanted to become a priest, yet his piety was never on display; and if he was sometimes zealous, then it was because he felt the responsibility of being a member of a minority group in a Greek Orthodox world. He used to like to say that man possessed one quality around which all the others circled, one attribute that God had given him in all certainty, in which the Divine Will was clearly evident. Virtue and vice stood side by side, little stones around this larger one, shone upon or overshadowed by it, enhanced or devaluated. In the case of Anton Fyodorovich Vyrubov, this great stone was a man's sense of responsibility. He felt responsible for his religion, and therefore lived according to it; for his fortune, which he administered in a strictly orderly fashion; for his servants, which was why he loved them. Since the business of dying had set in, he felt responsible for that. He was not one of those religious people who fear the heaven they praise. He didn't want to hear of false hopes, because death might not appear hopeless to a Christian. The dead, he said, were relieved of responsibility, but it would be making matters too simple if the dying were to behave as if they were already dead. He advised Andrey to sell the house in the Lipki district after his marriage, for neither heir nor furniture profited by a false feeling of veneration. If he showed any traces of anxiety, it was only because he feared he might depart this life without receiving extreme unction. The Dominican father, Louis de Villemorin, a Frenchman and an old friend of the Count's, moved into a guestroom close to the sick man.

On a rainy April morning, on which the Count's condition had improved rather surprisingly and Dr. Nadyishdin began to feel a little more hopeful, Andrey at last received a letter from Otrada. But it was signed by Count Nikolay Vladimirovich O'Rourke, and read as follows:

My dear Andrey Antonovich,
Certain regrettable events in my house make it necessary for you to come to Otrada as soon as possible. What I have to tell you is not suitable to be entrusted to a letter, however circumstantial.
I know it will be difficult for you to leave the sickbed of your father, my dear friend, Anton Fyodorovich, for whose speedy recovery I pray

fervently to our Holy Mother. However, I could not forgive myself if I continued to leave you uninformed of a situation that has arisen without any fault on your part, and which it will be my sincere desire to help you to bear with manly dignity.

The heartfelt manner in which the Count's sentiments were expressed startled Andrey even more than the contents of the letter. He left for Otrada the same day.

2

How does one know that a locked door, which doesn't look any different from a door that is closed yet not locked, is locked? How does one know that someone, who even if she were at home would not be there to greet one, is gone?

Maria was not there. Andrey knew it when he entered the library, where a sinister darkness had enveloped the dark furniture. "Mura is gone." The words with which the Count received him struck him like a blow he had been expecting, yet struck him none the less violently. "She has run away like a whipped servant," the Count went on. It was quite evident that he feared to appear a coward in Andrey's eyes—that was why he spoke with brutality of what was on his mind, without consideration for himself or his visitor. "I would have to lie. Vassily Tarnovsky did not abduct her; she ran away with the help of the servants. She always did get along with them. To him. Without his help. Every stableboy in Poltava knows that the Countess O'Rourke has run away."

What he said after that Andrey could not understand. Something about Christmas shopping in Kiev. "For the first time I let myself be persuaded, and she took advantage of me and deceived me." And Mademoiselle Larue . . . "An anonymous letter. Here. A cocotte." Young Tarnovsky's visits; who could tell whom he had bribed? "A wastrel. His family's reputation isn't much better than he is."

The Count talked on and on. Andrey couldn't stop him. He was clinging to the wish to set the clock back to his ignorance. His presentiments had been warning signals overlooked. Maria lived, although she had died, a ghost of flesh and blood. Of whom was the Count speaking, and why to him? The man opposite became a cloud of stone, unreal, for he spoke what was incomprehensible as if it could be comprehended. He spoke, over and over again, as a man robbed of his senses would speak at a grave of himself, instead of about the dead he was lamenting.

"It isn't possible," Andrey said at last. A mistake, momentary confusion. No letter of farewell? Impossible. Perhaps she was wandering around somewhere in the neighborhood, lost. The thought that she might have gone insane calmed him. Insanity could be healed. Love and forbearance could cure insanity. Vassily Tarnovsky and Maria—impossible! "We must find her. We must bring her back."

The Count laughed. He was sitting stiffly erect, as if he had had a stroke while seated; he laughed motionlessly, a paralyzed laugh, and his laughter seemed to make him sit up even straighter. It was not bitter laughter. He was laughing at Andrey, who believed you could recall out of the ether a conversation that had faded away, or recapture a lost hour.

"I didn't ask you to come, Andrey Antonovich, because I intended to excuse Maria. You are here to listen to my own vindication." Again a veil descended between Andrey and the man of stone. The Count became one with the picture of the Czar behind him; the voice came out of the frame. The Czar was speaking. "I have given her my permission to marry Vassily Tarnovsky." Maria was in Charkov, at an aunt of Tarnovsky's, had been there for four days now. The flight had taken place in the night from Sunday to Monday. And the justification: "There was nothing else I could do." Had he been afraid she might commit suicide? No. Mura wasn't one to commit suicide. This, too, a reproach, as if only the noble took their lives. The name of O'Rourke was at stake, the family honor. "I sent the police after her, or I imagine she would already be with him, his mistress."

"You couldn't have done that," Andrey said. "She doesn't know what she's doing."

"Come to your senses, Andrey Antonovich. I understand your grief, but come to your senses!" The epileptic seizure. No, it had not been an epileptic seizure. All an act. "When I threw out that French cocotte—that's when it happened." Mura had thrown herself on the ground, gnashed her teeth, behaved like a woman possessed. "All an act. She has seen her mother in such condition, but she couldn't fool the doctor."

Andrey, for no reason he could grasp, thought of Shitomir. The same feeling of impotence. Was there no appeal against evil? Was evil the supreme court of justice, inappellable? He didn't ask himself if he wanted to forgive Maria or not; he wanted only to understand her. Only she could explain. He had to see her.

"You can't do it, Nikolay Vladimirovich," he said. "For Mura's sake . . ."

"Your father would understand me. The ancestors of the O'Rourkes were kings. I am the Knight Marshal of this province, and responsible to His Majesty. My son has become a revolutionary; I can't sit back and watch my daughter become a whore. What is to become of Russia if our sons become anarchists and our daughters prostitutes? I had to prevent it."

The Czar. The Czar had stepped out of the picture to put a stop to it. To what? "Mura is gone." Andrey raised his hands to his temples. "Mura is gone." Vassily Tarnovsky was nothing but a name, as if the enemy had made himself invisible, like a legendary hero under an invisible cloak. "Mura is gone." He couldn't bring her back, but that was no reason she had to be destroyed. The Count could not be speaking of Maria.

Andrey remained seated when the Count rose. It was as if he rose yet remained seated at the same time, as if a visible body were emerging from an invisible one. The man who walked over to Andrey now and laid his hands on Andrey's shoulders was visible, but the invisible one went on sitting behind him, and Andrey wasn't sure which one was speaking.

"When Anton's condition improves—and pray God it may," said the Count, "please announce my visit to him. It is my duty to beg his forgiveness in the name of my family. The doors of my house are always open to you, Andrey Antonovich."

No living creature could speak like that, thought Andrey. If Nikolay Vladimirovich was dead, then so was Maria; and he who heard the dead speak was dead, too.

Evening had taken the house in its embrace. The Count did not turn on any lights as he accompanied Andrey to the library door.

The passages were unlit. Andrey had to feel his way. He was grateful for the darkness; he hoped to meet no one. It was a disgrace to have been so mistreated. His pain was still dull, a merciful shock. Only at their graves did one realize that the dead were dead; pain became violent only after accustomedness had spread its gentle veil over it. Cold walls, a wooden door, a corner pillar.

A ray of light fell on the floor in front of him, as if a silver knife had cut through the dark.

Olga stretched out a hand to him, "My poor Andrey," and sobbing, she threw her arms around his neck. He was overcome by anger. She had obviously lain in wait for him. He did not step out of the dark. "Why did she do this to you?" she cried. "I don't need pity," he said. "She loves no one. She doesn't love Vassily either." "You're glad she is gone." "I wanted her to be happy," she said. "Poor little Mura . . ."

He wanted to push her from him, but the tears were raining down her cheeks. He could feel them on his face. Her hard little breasts were pressed against his chest; her hair was playing about his ears. She threw back her head, and her lips almost touched his mouth. It had to be coincidence. Only a short while ago Mura had told him that Olga had become engaged to Prince Katerinovich. Then Olga said, "Why? Why Mura and not me?" and began to speak of her love for him; that she had loved him since childhood, that she had become engaged only out of grief, revenge, and jealousy, that Mura had never been worthy of him, and he loved her, Olga, too, only he was bewitched and didn't know it.

He tore himself away and ran through the dark corridors. For a moment he thought of the wife of Potiphar, and that he was Joseph, the overseer of Potiphar's house; and that Maria was innocent because she had lived in this house; and that Olga would betray Katerinovich, as Maria had betrayed him. He stood in front of the door. The spring night was laden with warm scent; the horses were whinnying; his carriage drove up, the candles dancing in their glass cages. The eagles over the portal receded into the darkness. It was as if every stone in the street were being driven into Andrey Vyrubov's heart.

3

Three days later, on a Sunday, Count Anton Fyodorovich Vyrubov died.

Because he had never deceived anyone in his life, it had been impossible to deceive him. His son's face had told everything. "What will you do now?" he asked, and was proud because Andrey had no intention of fighting a duel. Then, as Andrey didn't answer, he began to speak of Sergey. He read his son's thoughts. "Sergey is not bitter," he said. "I admire him for that. He is wrong, but I admire him." In a low, strained voice, he warned Andrey of taking any rash steps. There were already too many rebels who were rebelling against nothing but their own misfortune. He almost became angry when Andrey told him of long talks with Father de Villemorin. "Louis is here to hear my last confession, not to fish for souls. Disappointment is a poor counselor, my son. The Church is no refuge. True humility walks with its head high. We have too many merry sinners and sad priests." He took his son's trembling hand into his own steady one. "We became friends too late, but probably we were always friends. It would be a good thing if I could remain with you, but it is not necessary. I am not afraid for you." On the last night, he mentioned Maria. "You will never stop asking yourself who she is. You may never find out. *'Tout comprendre rend très indulgent,'* Madame de Staël used to say, but I always felt it was a heathenish sentence. One cannot understand everything, and one should be lenient without understanding." A few hours later, he fell into a coma. Next morning, at dawn, he recognized Andrey once more. He called Father de Villemorin over to the bed, gestured in the direction of Andrey, but what he wanted to say was never revealed. The only words that could be clearly heard were, "He was a good son."

Sunday, at twelve noon, Count Anton Fyodorovich died. The church bells tolled. In his room nothing could be heard but the sobbing of the servant girls. The sun shone gaily through the window, which Anton Vyrubov had never permitted to be curtained. The foolish flies of spring buzzed cheerfully. One settled down on the dead man's chin. His eyes were still open—light blue, and as if amused over the impertinent game of the insect.

CHAPTER 7

I

Charkov, April 14, 1894. Tomorrow Maria is to be married.

The house of Vassily's aunt on the Moscovskaya is buzzing with activity. Messenger boys, mailmen, friends of Vassily, all kinds of women. Maria is admired, a little fleetingly and condescendingly. Baroness Gribayedova, Vassily's aunt, a widow, is like an ancient weasel. She calls Maria her "little pigeon." Her old eyes have forgotten how to smile. Vassily comes twice a day, kisses her, sings his favorite song: "Oh, distant steppes, oh, savage plains." When she tells him he can't see her bridal dress, he laughs at her superstition. While she is trying it on, he leans back in an armchair, smoking, pulls at the hem, kisses her on the shoulder. "My Botticelli angel!" He smells of vodka, tobacco, every now and then of strong perfume, a woman's perfume. She waits for a letter from Otrada. "Your father has given his permission. What more can you ask?" She writes to Andrey, tears up the letter. She interviews maids, and chooses Rosa, a Hungarian.

At last she is alone. It is twilight. The Charkov River tumbles by noisily. The shadows of the houses become longer and more narrow, until they lie across the city like fingers. What is happening in Otrada? Her mother is writing a letter to her in bed; Alexander is taking a music lesson; Zoa is listening at the door; Olga is embroidering; her father is pacing up and down in the library. She sees him as he looked when she pretended to have the fit. Suddenly she is frightened. Had it been an act? Had it been real? The anonymous letter, her father calling her in, the dismissal of Denise. It was then that her mother's seizures had occurred to her: teeth clenched, teeth bared, eyes rolled up, fists, falling down spastically. Suddenly she felt an unbearable pain in her jaw and wasn't able to open her mouth. She wanted to cry out for help, but a barbed wire lay around her throat. Her nails like steel in her palms, blood on her fingers. But she got her way—Denise stayed until her flight. Still, it is possible that she is ill. Perhaps it began just like that with her mother.

Poor Mama. After her wedding she will write to her mother and have the letter smuggled into Otrada. Is her mother suffering? Her mother knows that Mura, at least, had succeeded in defying Terrible O'Rourke. She would have become Vassily's mistress. She is sorry that she was prevented from disgracing the name of O'Rourke.

On the bridge across the Charkov River, the gas lanterns are lit, cyclops' eyes in the fog. The letter to Andrey remains unwritten. He isn't suffering, because he is just as incapable of suffering as of love. His eternal plans! Vassily makes no plans. They will travel. Later, perhaps, a house in Charkov or Kiev. There is time for all that. One thing troubles her—she still has not begun to bleed. What if it happens tomorrow? What if it never happens? She has to go to a doctor, secretly. Andrey did not desire her even when she was affianced to him; Vassily is marrying her to possess her. How cleverly she behaved in Yuri's *dacha!* How clever of her not to decide on flight until Vassily had given his word! The only thing she is afraid of now is the wedding. Strange people. Even worse than that, a strange church. It is difficult to depend on God's knowing why one is acting as one does. Since her flight, she hasn't gone to church. If Andrey has cursed her, she ought to pray that his curse will not be fulfilled. She doesn't fear her father's curse. God is deaf when addressed by those who are terrible.

She gets up and goes to look for the old Baroness. Vassily should not have left her alone.

2

It was past midnight. The gypsies were playing. Maria, in a pink chiffon dress, was sitting beside Vassily. She had taken off her wedding dress at his aunt's. Vassily's parents lived near Charkov, but he had quarreled with them recently. To this supper in the Grand Hotel he hadn't even invited his aunt.

Again and again Maria looked at the clock that hung over the door between the restaurant and the hotel lobby. The only guest she knew from the past was Peter. Vassily's brother was sitting at the other end of the table. Pale, with feverish eyes, he was watching Maria. A fat merchant was constantly ordering more champagne. "I'm paying for everything," he cried, then would look embarrassed; but with the next bottle he was boasting again. A blonde woman, with a deep décolleté, sat beside a Polish guardsman. "Julia Terletzkaya," Vassily had introduced her, "the jewel of Charkov." The jewel of Charkov was wearing imitation jewelry. A little man with a goatee was being addressed as "Monsieur le Consul." He was French. The eyes of two brothers, the Counts Maklakov, met across the bosom of a voluptuous Polish woman. There was a high government official with his wife; they spoke to no one and looked at the others disapprovingly, like customs officers surrounded by smuggled goods. A German Baroness von Blottheim sat on Vassily's right; tiny nose, high cheekbones, dark, silent, out of sorts.

When would the feast be over? Didn't the married couple usually retire long before this? Maria thought of the peasant weddings she had attended in her childhood.

Vassily had rented a room in the hotel. She hadn't seen it yet. The light brown, heavily carved furniture in the private room they were in reminded Maria of a station restaurant. You could hear voices and the clatter of plates and silver from next door. The smell of cheap food penetrated the room through a swinging door, milk glass with a flower pattern. The waiters' jackets looked like castoffs. At a quarter to one, she would ask Vassily if they couldn't leave quietly. At a quarter to one, she gave herself another five minutes. Then another five. One was a round figure, and would be just the right time. She touched his hand; shame held her back. Peter Tarnovsky was about to recite a poem. Everyone was laughing, although the poem was sad. She felt sorry for Peter, but she was laughing, too. With strangers you had to laugh because you could never tell what they were laughing at.

Vassily had drunk vodka, champagne, champagne with vodka. He looked at Maria with glassy eyes as if astounded to find her at his side. Every now and then he raised his glass and drank to her. "Your health, Countess Tarnovska." He said it like a carnival joke, as if they were pretending to be man and wife for an evening. "Why don't you say something?" She said nothing.

"Now let's go to the Versailles," the fat merchant cried. "I'm paying for everything."

"I like it here," Vassily protested. "Gypsies . . . a czardas!"

He rose and went over to Julia Terletzkaya. They danced as if they had always danced together. The little Consul clapped the rhythm. The Baroness Blottheim leaned across Vassily's empty chair and addressed Maria. She spoke Russian fluently, with a German accent. "What were you thinking of to marry such a beast, my dear?" she said.

Maria looked at the German woman, horrified.

"You're right," said the Baroness. "It's really much stranger that he should have married you. Who knows, maybe he's hungry for a virgin. And of royal blood, we have been told. If I were you, I would disappear quietly. You're not going to get him into bed tonight. He's got one of his bad days. But cheer up, he has good ones, too."

The blood shot to Maria's head. She was seventeen; the woman in the black dress and the snow-white décolleté like pure glass was over thirty. Maria needed help. She looked for Vassily. *"Ritka buza, ritka arpa, ritka rozs,"* sang the gypsies. Everyone was singing; only Peter, hurt, was silent.

"I'm telling you this for your own good," the German woman went on. "It doesn't do to treat men too well. The masters of creation are stupid dogs who don't understand anything but the whip. They like to be flogged. You know it's much easier to let oneself be tortured than to try to improve." Two fine bitter lines at the corners of her mouth betrayed her age. "I happen to know this fellow at any rate—I ought to. I have a child by him. Would you like to see a picture of her? The image of Vassily."

Maria grasped her champagne glass. She felt she had to pour fire into herself or she would congeal into a pillar of ice. Vassily was dancing, one hand at the nape of his neck, stamping his feet. The little Consul was running along beside the couple, clapping down at their feet as if to egg them on. The government official and his wife watched him with astounded eyes. "I'm paying for everything," cried the merchant, wet a banknote with his tongue and smacked it on the forehead of the gypsy leader. It sounded like a slap.

At last Vassily came back. His cheeks were red, his high collar was damp; but he walked upright, like a drunkard trying hard to walk particularly straight. "What sort of lies has Christiane been telling you?" he asked.

Maria jumped up, held up her skirt, and ran toward the exit. The laughter of the wedding guests followed her.

Only one light was burning in the lobby of the hotel, above the desk. Dusty palms stood in green vases; bronze virgins held dark lamps aloft; run-down splendor in a hostel. It was ice-cold.

"Your key is upstairs, madame," the desk clerk called out after her. "Number eighteen."

The passage was badly lit, too; new electricity, still a bit shaky. Dirty boots stood in front of room doors, in an orderly row or tossed out by drunkards; bachelors' shoes, shoes of married couples, pathetic children's shoes—portraits without faces. Maria stumbled over them.

In Room Eighteen it was light. Rosa was standing next to a silk lamp, a bisque figurine with voluptuous breasts. "May I help you, madame?"

"No," said Maria. "Please go."

The door opened behind her. For a moment the gypsy music from the restaurant grew louder. "Help madame to undress," said Vassily.

Maria made a gesture of refusal. "My hair," she said, and sat down in front of the mirror on the dressing table.

"What's your name?" Vassily asked the girl.

"Rosa, your Honor." She curtsied, and Vassily pinched her cheek.

Rosa undid the young bride's hair. Maria could see Vassily in the mirror. He had sat down and was lighting a papirossa. Hairpins piled up on the table. Vassily was looking at the maid's ample hips. Maria's hair crackled under the comb. She thought of her birthday. She saw her father's eyes.

"You may go," she said abruptly.

"I shall call you when we need you, Rosa." Vassily smiled. "What is your room number?"

The girl told him; the two exchanged glances; she curtsied again and left.

"Why did you run away?" Vassily asked.

"Are you the father of the Baroness Blottheim's child?"

"She is jealous of Julia Terletzkaya."

"Are you the father of her child?"

"Undress, for heaven's sake. You bore me."

"Don't you want to put out the lights?"

"They don't bother me."

She began to put out the lamps. With each light she put out another illusion. The illusion of her matureness and her escape and her freedom and her triumph. The only thing she did not want to put out was the illusion of her love. She longed for Vassily's arms no less than before this evening; no less. In the pain he would cause her, all pain would be submerged.

Only one light was still burning. With her back turned to Vassily, she began to undress. When her back was naked, she slipped on her nightgown. Vassily didn't move. It was as still as if the room were floating above the hotel. Suddenly she felt the urge to pray. Since childhood she had always prayed at night, in various languages, as she had been taught to pray by various governesses. She had never been quite sure which language God understood best. Now she kneeled down beside the bed and prayed: "Now I lay me down to sleep. I pray Thee Lord my soul to keep. If I should die before I wake . . ." Desperately she clung to the childhood prayer.

She felt Vassily's hand on her shoulder, pushing her onto the bed. "What on earth are you putting on an act like that for?"

"I've always prayed at home."

"Well, you're not at home any more." He looked down at her. "Now you listen to me. You bore me. You've been a bore all evening, and I hate boredom like the plague. I am not drunk. I could drink ten times as much and not be drunk. I'm just sick of your affectations, that's all. I was mad about you, and you caught me. I'm not saying I regret it—at any rate, not yet. But innocent little Mura is over and done with. She bores me." He was clinging to the bedpost. "You've kept me waiting too long. I want to sleep with you, but not until it suits me . . . when it suits me," he repeated. "And there's something I hate even more than boredom, and that's anything ridiculous. I am going to the Versailles. I am going to bed with Julia Terletzkaya, or with your maid, or with Blottheim. She won't say no, I assure you. In the meantime you can pray or cry or think. When you've thought things over and have more sense, I'll come back."

He opened the door, and she could hear the gypsies again. She ran to the door, locked it, wanted to walk back to the bed, but her feet gave way under her. A warmth streamed through her body as if a fire were breaking out in her. Blood flowed down her knees. She sank to the floor.

When Vassily came home in the gray of dawn, the doorman had to open his room door for him. Maria was still unconscious. Vassily behaved like a man shaken out of a drunken transport, awake but not yet in control of his senses. Panic-stricken, he called in everyone from whom he could possibly expect help.

When Maria regained consciousness, her Hungarian maid, the chambermaid, and Julia Terletzkaya and the Baroness Blottheim were standing around her bed. The manager of the hotel and a fat woman in a flannel dressing gown were whispering in the background. Vassily was kneeling beside the bed, upbraiding himself, imploring her not to die. She opened her eyes and closed them again. The German Baroness and the blonde "jewel" were still in their evening gowns, although the morning sun was streaming in at the window. Two graces at a Greek grave: Maria was reminded of a Gobelin tapestry in Otrada. The spectral vision left her only when the doctor came and she was alone with him.

Dr. Mayerberg soon calmed her. Nothing unusual had happened. The excitement of the wedding had hastened an event that was long overdue anyway. He ordered bed rest for a few days, a little more composure, and everything would turn out all right. He offered to speak to the young groom. Maria, already feeling calmer, now clung to his hands, begging him to speak to Vassily but not to betray what had happened to her so late, not for anything in the world!

The pity she had seen in the doctor's eyes when she had said this she now saw on every face. Julia Terletzkaya sat at her bedside and told her that she had been Vassily's mistress until only a few weeks ago. Poor Maria Nikolaevna, who didn't know that there were certain men who were marvelously cut out for bed, and just because of that, so much less cut out for the marriage bed. The Baroness, who rather fancied herself as Hera in the Choice of Paris, brought Maria flowers and spoke about Vassily's daughter, Natasha, who was six. She was sorry, she said, that she had upset the marriage feast, but wasn't experience the best gift a mature woman had to offer? Maria would not be happy with Vassily; still, she thought the unhappiness of a seventeen-year-old girl preferable to the peace of mind of a thirty-five-year-old woman. Other women came to see her. Vassily introduced them so that Maria should not be bored. A beautiful pair of twins, Poles, very quiet, with an anemic sensuality. And the young wife of a senile old prince who wanted to see "the miracle, Maria Tarnovska."

Maria asked herself why she didn't tell her chattering condolers to get out, but she preferred to be deceived than to be alone. She also felt a bitter sort of affinity toward her unbidden guests. All of them loved Vassily; each one had been deceived by him, any one of them would have married him. They had been his mistresses and didn't bear his name; she bore his name and was a virgin. He had cheated her of her wedding night, but now he was bound like a dog on a chain to his uneasy conscience. She could choose the hour of her happiness.

He took her by surprise. He had said good-by with a tender kiss, as on every other evening, and had gone to town. On this particular night he came back a little earlier, kissed her awake, lay down beside her, and took her before she could come to her senses. Then he kissed her again and fell asleep. He smelled of sex, tobacco, and vodka. She had felt nothing, not even pain. Freezing, lonely, robbed of her power, she lay at his side.

A few days later they traveled to St. Petersburg. She was glad to leave Charkov and didn't ask why St. Petersburg was the goal of their first journey together. Without telling her about it, he had taken an apartment, an elegant aparment in a *palais* inhabited by only one other person, a deaf countess; ten rooms in the Sergevskaya, near the Tauric Gardens, not far from the Nevski Prospect, the sick and hectic heart of the city. In a fit of determination Maria had dismissed her Hungarian maid; a pretty Ukrainian girl also lasted only a few days. Finally she hired Katya, an elderly little woman with the face of a white Negro.

Maria lived only for show, but not because she wanted to impress others. Vassily was just as much at home in the capital as in Kiev or Charkov. The life of the other ladies was just like hers: they gave parties, visited, went to the theater and concerts, and remained alone when their men spent the rest of the night in restaurants or night clubs. The women didn't seem to be unhappy. Maria began to believe that a smile was not the expression of a happy heart, that, on the contrary, the heart warmed itself gradually at the smile. Sh pretended to be gay when she felt like crying, and content when she was filled with rebellion. She ordered the most expensive dresses without giving a thought to whether she could afford them. She rented a troika, although Vassily already had one. She told her extravagant cook to serve whatever she pleased.

She waited in vain for happiness in Vassily's arms. He came to her almost every night. Sometimes, when she was sitting at tea, he would take her in his arms, without a word, and carry her into the bedroom, or he would pull her down on the divan. Once, on an excursion to Petershof, he stopped the troika, led her into the woods that sloped down to the sluggishly flowing Sbayelka, and made love to her on the grass, which was still damp from the rainy nights of the Estonian plateau. But what she had experienced in the dormitory in boarding school, and in Yuri Tolstoy's *dacha,* did not take place again.

At first she believed it was his violence that made it impossible for her to find fulfillment. It would not have depressed her—in fact, it would have filled her with false pride—to know that his fulfillment hurried past and ahead of her, as the conductor of an orchestra, making a mistake in the score, drives the orchestra to the finale while the instruments are still playing the overture. But he never seemed to notice this uneven orchestral race. Later, she even thought she could see a cool satisfaction in his eyes as they looked down at her motionless body. Now he had noticed the haste with which she was trying to follow him; still he did not stop. The agony of her vain efforts seemed to excite him. His Botticelli angel, he called her, but he said it like a connoisseur evaluating a painting; and once, when he became conscious of the fact that she didn't even notice his climax in her, he told her it was new to him and highly entertaining to copulate with an angel. He taught her sensual gestures and play, but the more indifference she displayed in fulfilling his wishes, the more she seemed to arouse his passion. She ceased thinking that he was a clumsy or selfish lover. Because the sight of his body aroused her just as it always had done and the strings broke only when they were supposed to respond at highest pitch; because she received his body blissfully, without however being able to bring about her own ecstasy; because the more fulfillment failed her, the more she yearned for it, she began to seek all blame within herself.

4

The city of tears and morasses—that was what they called St. Petersburg, and Maria could understand both. A smell of mold, smoke, and salt from the sea hung all day over the heartless buildings of the artificial metropolis. Almost two million people made their homes here, yet no one felt at home. The presence of the Czar weighed heavily on the visionary statue of Peter the Great.

> Ere on the golden weave of heaven
> Hath passed the sluggish dark of night,
> Scarce separate from the tide of even,
> Dawn's glow already is in flight.

Pushkin had sung the city's praises, but its beauty lived only in the poet's fantasy. Here splendor was a laborious duty, piety a stern regimen, amusement a secret vice. The morass defended itself against the city that it supported. Sometimes, in the morning, it seemed to Maria as if St. Petersburg had gone under in the damp fog; beneath a twilit sea lay Russia, alien, unattainable. In June it rained without cease. The people under their shining umbrellas were like black islands. July was ushered in by unbearable heat, but the sun remained hidden. The sky was a scorched yellow field between miserly rooftops. One didn't live with the city; one could consider oneself fortunate if one survived one's existence in it.

Maria was in a state of irritation. She looked for a scapegoat: the city, the weather, the light nights, the servants, Vassily, her body. One of her new friends—in St. Petersburg, where no one had any intention of tarrying, one made friends as on a steamer, quickly, merrily, forgetfully—had told her that Vassily's illegitimate child was staying with her grandmother in St. Petersburg, and that Vassily often visited the little girl. Maria suspected that Christiane von Blottheim came to St. Petersburg every now and then, and one afternoon in July she confronted Vassily with the fact. With the complacent candor she had once found so charming, he admitted that little Natasha was in St. Petersburg. "Since you can't seem to get pregnant, you can't very well forbid me the pleasure my daughter can give me," and it was no concern of hers whether Blottheim was in town or not. "Look, I can have plenty of young mistresses. Why should I warm up an old one?" He

154

talked himself into a fine rage, used his favorite phrase, "You bore me," and began to compare the love artistry of the Baroness with Maria's clumsy efforts.

That evening Maria again had to be hostess to half a dozen of his friends. One of them, old Grand Duke Alexander Dmitrievich, whose face looked like the window of a souvenir shop for vices, was whispering with Vassily. She heard something to the effect that they were going to amuse themselves vastly at the Grand Duke's *palais* later that evening. The Grand Duke waited until Vassily had kissed Maria on the forehead and was ready to leave with him. It was eleven o'clock.

Maria's decision to follow Vassily was born in a moment, but she had carried her bitterness for many long months. Not only was she sick and tired of being alone, of putting up with Katya's compassionate looks, of vainly stretching out her hand for another hand in her bed. And it was not only curiosity to find out at last where and how Vassily spent his nights that impelled her. She was hungry for life, and had been fed on crumbs. The hunger for life in her revolted like hunger for bread.

She told Katya to bring her an evening dress, one that Vassily had never seen—a reddish purple with a deep décolleté. Red silk underwear, red stockings, red shoes. There were clothes women bought only in misery or rebellion. Never had she thought she would wear any of these things. She put on a tiara of rubies that a jeweler had sent her on approval, and wound a red chiffon scarf around her neck.

The coachman had to be awakened out of his sleep. She urged him on. The three horses trotted faster and faster, past the sleeping buildings of the Austrian Embassy, across two or three bridges, past the dark Champs des Mars, gray barracks and hostile monuments. The night was sultry. It seemed to Maria Tarnovska as if the carriage would drive on and on, until in the end wheels, horses, and she herself would sink into the morass.

The *palais* of the Grand Duke Alexander Dmitrievich, on the Bolshaya Neva, near the Eremitage, was brilliantly lit. Gypsy music could be heard through the open windows. Maria rang; she told the lackey who she was, and that she wished to see His Excellency; then she didn't wait, but ran up the stairs, threw open the door, and found herself standing in a large oval salon.

A strange disappointment gripped her, because she saw what she had expected to see but had secretly hoped not to find after all. The salon in semidarkness; on low divans, men and women, their clothing in disarray; a woman in the embrace of two or three men at a time; men with their arms around two women; half-naked women; pairs kissing; perfume, gypsy music from the next room, broken pieces of glass on the floor, obscene laughter, the voice of a woman like the screech of a wild bird. In the center of the room, the Grand Duke, dressed as severely as at her house, a circus manager in his arena, a hideous *arrangeur*. He was standing with his back to the door and didn't notice Maria until the couples scattered and a few women fled into the next room.

"Where is Vassily?" said Maria, but as she said it, her anger passed, her hunger was stilled. She looked around her like a lioness fed to repletion, seeing her tamer as nothing but a disgusting piece of flesh. Lionesses were stupid. They could maul their trainers to death, yet they let themselves be driven in a circle by his whip, let him force them to do ridiculous dog tricks and chase them through burning hoops. Clever lionesses mauled their trainers even when they weren't hungry. Vassily had told her that he hated what was ridiculous even more than what was boring. There was nothing more ridiculous than unused power.

"Where is Vassily?" she asked again, but her question was neither urgent nor incensed. "What a pity that you never invite me to your parties, your Excellency. At last I know that it isn't always dull as ditchwater in St. Petersburg."

"You look marvelous, Countess," the Grand Duke replied, still astonished, already controlled. "I didn't dare to hope . . . May I bring you a glass of champagne?"

"Later. Wouldn't you like to show me your house? I have often admired it from the outside."

The lioness leading the trainer on a leash, she thought. Gypsies were playing in the next room; a couple were dancing as if too weary to stop. In the next salon, they startled a couple; the scantily clad woman fled, the man who had been holding her on his lap remained seated, staring idiotically into space. All the rooms were furnished in the style of Katharine I, the swaggering peasant girl from Lithuania. Classic bronze statues and vases stood everywhere; on the walls, dark oil paintings on which the great men of Russian history eked out their petrified lives. Dynasties and sex, history and abyss, museum and orgy. Where was Vassily? Alexander Dmitrievich hadn't denied that he was in the *palais*. He wouldn't show her the bedrooms. Why not,

Her jealousy was as dead as the dead heroes. The later Vassily turned up, the greater, and therefore more desirable, his guilt. The yearning for revenge overcame her like a voluptuous excitement, with no person or thing for its goal. She could have punished anyone else in his place, any scapegoat.

"The library," said the Grand Duke. One could see he was relieved that the tour was ended.

It was a magnificent room, with bookshelves to the ceiling, pure rococo; a Boucher and a Fragonard hung on the walls. In the subdued light Maria had not noticed the man who now rose from a divan, where he had been lying dozing or reading. "Captain Baron Vladimir Stahl," the Grand Duke introduced him. "We call him 'doctor' because, although he doesn't have the degree, he should have." He begged the "doctor" to take Maria under his wing for a while. Maria, amused by the Grand Duke's flight, sat down.

The man reminded her of a poplar. He was tall and slender; his body grew younger at the top, ending in a pointed crown. He seemed to have awakened from a dream, and not to know whether or not he was still dreaming. With sunken cheeks below high cheekbones, eyes so deeply set that they made the bones of his skull seem naked, he looked ailing; yet the sight of him did not arouse one's pity. An evil face. Whether pain had hardened it was not important. His gaze seemed to be feeling the woman in the red dress, yet there was nothing obscene in his eyes. They were only examining the young thing like a doctor making a diagnosis so as to be able to talk about the interesting case later.

"Did Tarnovsky bring you here?" he asked after a few polite phrases.

"On the contrary," she said, irritated. "I came to look for him."

"Don't hold it against him. He's young, although not nearly as young as you. Alexander Dmitrievich is a seducer. He likes to prove to himself that others are no better than he. More often than not, he succeeds."

"And why are you here, Baron?"

He laughed. "What an honest question! I never miss any of His Excellency's parties. And then I lie here in the library and read or sleep. It comforts me to find out that I don't despise human beings for nothing."

"Then you are like the Grand Duke."

"Not entirely. It stimulates him to ruin people; it calms me to know that I can't improve them."

"All people are not like the Grand Duke's guests."

"Because he doesn't invite everyone. These books—most of them deal with the Devil's struggle for the soul of man. Naïve poets! The Devil doesn't struggle for anything. The soul of man struggles in front of the gates of Hell, craving entry. The Devil is the maître d'hôtel of an overcrowded restaurant."

The longer Vladimir Stahl spoke, the less she believed him. There couldn't be another house like this in all St. Petersburg. She should have created a scandal, screamed, hammered against locked doors. Why was she waiting so patiently for the arms of a whore—and if it wasn't a whore, so much the worse—to release the man she had married? She had feared the ridiculous and had become ridiculous. She longed for Otrada, the despised Otrada. Or was it not Otrada? The brook beside which she had sat with Andrey. The grass across which she had run to meet him. The sleigh in which she had held his hand. Her lips formed the word "Andrey." For a moment she thought she had actually said it aloud.

"You are not listening," said Baron Stahl. "And you are quite right."

A lackey entered. "Your carriage," he said. "The Count is waiting."

She went down the stairs, her hand on the banister. Outside, the night, St. Petersburg's fleeting guest, had yielded to the dawn. Thin rays of sun fell like dew on the rooftops.

5

Vassily wanted to hold her fast; she tore herself away, ran through their apartment, into her bedroom, and locked the door.

He knocked, softly at first, as if he couldn't grasp that she had locked him out. She didn't answer. Weeping, she had thrown herself on the bed. She wept for her youth, for her mistakes, for her weakness, for her love. She wept because she wasn't sure that she wouldn't open the door. Then she sat up and listened. His knocking had become more urgent. "Mura, be sensible. . . . I beg of you. Mura, you misunderstand." She didn't answer, but she didn't cry any more. What she had seen in Alexander Dmitrievich's *palais* came to life, more real than reality. It was not Vassily's first visit. There was not only one Palais Alexander Dmitrievich in St. Petersburg. Perhaps that was why she had had to move to this damp city. "Mura, forgive me!" She didn't move. He began to curse. He had cursed on the bearskin in Yuri's *dacha,* like a cab driver, or a soldier. She listened to him tensely, attentively; she didn't want to miss a word. No love whispers could have filled her with a sweeter passion than his obscenities. She had wept out of impotence; he was cursing because he was impotent. She got up and began to undress. As it fell to the floor, her dress rustled. Could he hear it? She took her shoes in her hand and let them drop to the ground with a thud. He wasn't cursing any longer; he was whimpering like an animal. She stood in front of the mirror in her red underwear, in her long red stockings. He liked to untie the bows and undo the hooks of her bodice. Slowly she untied the bows and undid the hooks. She looked at the door. The handle was rattling up and down. For a while she watched his grotesque efforts. The handle was like the thirsty tongue of a panting dog. She could have told him to go to bed, that the door was going to stay locked, but he might derive hope from her angriest word. So she said nothing. Naked, she stood in front of the mirror and did not recognize herself. In the last months, her body had blossomed; she hadn't noticed it. "Mura, I am dying!" Too late. Slowly she stroked her breasts, her hips, her stomach. Never had she felt such warmth in Vassily's arms. She had felt only his power; now she felt hers. She had wanted to make him happy—and he had kissed her on the forehead and gone to the Palais Alexander Dmitrievich. Or to the Baroness Blottheim. Or to some other woman. She was tempted to peep through the keyhole and see him whining in front of her door, but she didn't do it. He threatened her. Now he was pounding against the wood with his fists; the door creaked in its hinges. In a minute he would be groaning and sniveling again. She lay down on her bed, naked. She wanted to call out to him, "Go on—snivel! Threaten me! Whimper! Hammer on the door!" But she was too afraid that he might stop sniveling, threatening, whimpering, hammering. His voice, the creaking of the door, his declarations of love, his curses, and his self-reproach were the musical accompaniment to the increasingly vehement pulsation of her blood.

At the very moment when she reached the apex of sensual delight, it became silent. Maria smiled as if in the arms of a godlike lover.

Every night, for fourteen days, Maria locks the door of her bedroom. Not a word about the evening in the house of the Grand Duke, no reproaches. During the day she seems to be carefree, gay, even flirtatious. Vassily buys her the ruby tiara she wore that night. She thanks him casually. When they are out, she acts like a young wife in love; in the troika that brings them home, she lets him embrace her, then she locks the door. At last, one night, she leaves it open. He makes love to her tenderly, cautiously; the tears roll down his cheeks. She feels nothing. At breakfast she behaves as if nothing happened.

He doesn't leave her alone any more. At the opera, at parties, on excursions, she can feel him watching her constantly. When she is conversing with other men, he breaks in on them, irritated. He comes home unexpectedly. Once he gets into a violent argument with Baron Nebrasov, a harmless man. Only the tact of their hostess prevents a duel. "You bore me," she tells him, and she uses the phrase more and more often. Boredom is revenge and provocation. The best way to force a man to constant pursuit is to convince him that one is bored with him. She learns fast. Vladimir Stahl comes to call. She arranges things so that she is alone in the Tsergiyevskaya when he arrives. He offers his assistance. "I don't need any help, Baron." Every day he sends her orchids. She forgets to thank him, but she doesn't forget to tell Vassily. Sometimes Vassily grasps her so hard that she screams, but she smiles again immediately, as if he can't possibly hurt her.

The mail brings a letter from Olga. "You will be pleased to hear that I am engaged." Prince Katerinovich. She remembers him—twenty years or more older than Olga. Half the province of Poltava belongs to Katerinovich. She can see the hand of Terrible O'Rourke behind it; sends a congratulatory telegram. She thinks of Andrey. She hasn't written to him yet. Her guilt accompanies her like a shadow, not disturbing, yet ever present. Not a word about Andrey in Olga's letter. "I hope you will be as happy as I am," she writes to her sister.

"I am bored," she says, and Vassily doesn't know what to do. Grand Duke Dmitrievich is not the only one who knows how to give amusing parties. In the house of Count Berezovsky, the guests sit in front of peepholes drilled into the walls of the bedrooms. The Count sends for whores from Paris, peasant girls from the Caucasus, dusky maidens from Martinique. "Are you enjoying yourself, Mura?" Yes, she is enjoying herself. After evenings like that, she pretends to have a headache and locks her door. In the Eremitage the gentlemen are enjoying themselves with gypsies. Vassily wants to go home. "I'm having a wonderful time." They are the last to leave. The sun is shining bright. Maria Tarnovska yawns. "I want to sleep, Vassily."

Peter Tarnovsky arrives from Charkov. Patiently she listens to him recite his poems for hours on end. "You are so changed, Mura." Under the touch of her hand, he trembles. From day to day he looks paler. "Peter is in love with you, Mura," says Vassily. "You say that about everybody," she replies. "Everybody is in love with you." She laughs. Peter comes unexpectedly. He has on his traveling suit; his carriage is waiting. "I am running away from you, Mura." She lets him go.

Everybody is talking about the aloof beauty of the Countess Tarnovska, who wades through the morass of St. Petersburg on dry feet. You can see her in the house of Grand Duke Dmitrievich; she sits in the library and lets "Doctor" Stahl massage her neck. On the following evening she receives the Grand Duke in her own house, everything so wooden and shapeless, the Czar would be proud of his subjects. When she rides through the Summer Garden in Baron Stahl's carriage, Alexis Bozevsky follows her on horseback. He is a Polish aristocrat, "the handsomest officer in His Imperial Majesty's Guard." There is talk of a duel between Stahl and Bozevsky. She doesn't even know the lieutenant.

That she cannot find happiness in Vassily's arms doesn't bother her any longer. Sometimes she lies beside his sleeping body, thinking. Who is she? She doesn't know. Her soul has separated itself from her body. Who is he? An empty glass that she has taken for a costly vase. Wind on his shoulders, moonbeams up his sleeves! Not all vanity is attractive. Those who are vain write interesting commentaries on their uninteresting personalities. Success with women is the success of the unsuccessful. Julia Terletzkaya, the Baroness Blottheim—she finds Vassily's conquests ridiculous. Ridiculous and boring. Vassily is strong only as long as no one stronger is nearby. Biting dogs, once tamed, retrieve their whips. Stahl asks her if she still loves her husband. She says yes, and she is not lying. There are women who love their dogs —until they find a man.

In September, Vassily tells her that he has to go to Kiev on important business. She knows nothing about it. Kiev. Does that mean

Otrada, Olga, Andrey? She finds the departure from St. Petersburg difficult. The city no longer teeters on a swamp; it stands fast, like the objects after her blindness.

On the way to Kiev, she feels sick. What she suspects becomes certainty. For the first time since she began seeing again, a feeling overwhelms her with tremendous power. She is expecting a child.

CHAPTER 8

I

Three fifteen—that was the hour granted Andrey Antonovich Vyrubov by the Master General of the Dominican Order.

Andrey had arrived in Rome the day before. Now it was a few minutes after two. The noonday sun was broiling over the city. The roll-shades of the shops and bookstores, in which devotional articles were sold, had been let down. On the corner of the Via Santa Caterina de Siena, a beggar was sleeping in the shadow of a doorway. In the glaring sunlight the elephant obelisk on the Piazza della Minerva looked like a heathenish monument from Africa before the church and seat of the Dominican Order. The walls of the only Gothic church in Rome were baked rust-brown. A cab drove by, its hood up; the trotting hoofs of the horse were the only sound in the midday stillness.

Inside the church it was cold. No pews, no choir stall, no triptych, no choir railing. In the gray light, the sarcophagi stood in gray petrifaction. On the right, the tombs of Paul IV, the terrible Neapolitan who had dipped his arm "up to the elbows in blood"; of Urban VII, dead after twelve days of rule, just as the Irish archbishop Malachias had prophesied; of Clement VIII, the first unworthy Pope; of Thomas de Torquemada, the Grand Inquisitor. On the left, the chapel of warlike Pius V; Benedict XIII of Avignon, whose scribe had spoken of the "corrupt" condition of the Church; of Aldobrandini, who had been in the service of Sixtus V, the Builder, in Poland. In front of the altar of the Medicis, Clement VII and Leo X; but towering over them all, the statue of Saint Catherine of Siena, who had nursed the sick, comforted the afflicted—patron saint of the Dominican Order, with crucifix, lily, book, and ring in her crest.

Andrey knelt. He did not pray; he was thinking, hands folded. Why, after his long talk with Father de Villemorin, had he chosen the Dominican Order? Father Villemorin, himself a Dominican, had cautioned him. There were less strict orders, which were not burdened with the Medicis and the Inquisition. But wasn't it just this seemingly stubborn discipline that had attracted Andrey and in the end prompted his decision? The world was only a half, with half measures. Philosophy did not yet dare to negate the existence of God; religions no longer dared to affirm his bodily existence. The Church did not deviate from its laws, yet closed one eye when they were broken. "Render therefore to Caesar the things that are Caesar's, to God the things that are God's." Christ had spoken only of the coins of the Herodians; He had not divided the world into half God's, half Caesar's. But now it had been divided; was therefore halved. Atheism still came disguised with the mask of science, but the Church was already taking part in the carnival. Today carnival, tomorrow Ash Wednesday, and then what? Where would mankind turn its confused vision; from what source would the thirsty drink; by whom could the sick be healed; according to what law would the blunderer act? Halfway morals demanded a severity redoubled. How foolish he had been to look for human error, omission, and crime in the history of the Dominicans! Why should the Church forgive only her enemies; why should she expel her straying zealots? In the magnificent coldness of the church Andrey could sense that institution's humility in the face of the Lord, before whose judgment seat popes and inquisitors had to answer. Stone sarcophagi hid the earthly remains, not the bliss of heaven; stone file cases concealed charge and defense. The day seeped in through narrow windows. Anteroom of the court, yet sanctuary. It had been Andrey's intention to pray for strength before his talk with the Master General, but suddenly he felt that he needed no strength. It was all just as simple as the construction of Santa Maria sopra Minerva in the midst of the confusion that was Rome. Faith was the recognition of what was meaningful. As he looked back now, it seemed to Andrey that all paths had converged onto this one path, as if there had been nothing, not the smallest occurrence, that lacked significance. Those who were happy and those who were miserable, all were in God's hands; but only those who were happy knew it.

With a feeling of joy, he entered the courtyard of the monastery by a side door. Flower beds basked in the summer sun; bees hummed as they settled on the blossoms. Under the arcades it was shady. Fading frescoes, depicting scenes from the history of the Order, still showed on the weather-beaten crumbling walls. Pages of renown, over-evaluated moments, memorials of the shameful years of dissolute princes and cruel servants of God. Outside, everywhere, imperfection and falseness: falsification of the past, halfway hopes. The present, too, was imperfect and false: here, joy over a victory, the recognition of error, the presence of God through the absence of the lie.

A Dominican friar came up to him; asked him if he was the Russian traveler whom Father Louis de Villemorin had written about. When Andrey said that he was, the friar led him to a narrow stair-case, up two stories, and handed him over to another friar, who opened a heavy oaken door. Andrey found himself in the study of the Master General.

2

The Master General, in the white habit of his Order, was an old man of about seventy, very small, with a face like a dried fruit. Andrey had expected to find a powerful man; and before this shriveled old man he, too, shrank, as happens sometimes when those who are strong and healthy are confronted with someone frail. The sick were ahead of their time. His own young body was suddenly a vain boast; the old man's smallness reduced Andrey in size. Nor did he feel more at ease when he looked down, because then he could see the hands of the Master General, and they reminded him of two dead sparrows. Body and hands had died long ago; if he was alive, it was because he possessed a strength that was not of this world.

He asked Andrey to sit down in a high Renaissance chair; he spoke of Father de Villemorin, whom he knew personally, but did not mention the purpose of Andrey's visit. He asked about conditions in Russia, let fall a remark about the difficult stand of the Roman

Catholic Church in that country, and spoke of the vain efforts to establish the Dominican Order there. And he said all this with amiable indifference, as if he could have dismissed his interested but slightly irksome visitor at any time. Andrey began to wonder if Father de Villemorin had told the Master General the true reason for his visit. Just as the man's small stature had confused him, he was surprised now that the Master General was not scrutinizing him, but only glancing at him now and then out of his wan eyes. Andrey wondered if his appearance could be so much against him that the Master General had decided to reject him without a hearing. Through a gap in the curtains a ray of sunshine fell into the high and exceptionally large room. Andrey could see himself going out into the afternoon with nothing settled.

"And you want to join our Order, is that right?" said the Master General.

Not a word of Andrey's, no pause, no gesture had evoked the question. Andrey, who had been waiting a good half hour for it, was so taken aback when it finally came that he couldn't answer at once.

"The reasons leading to your taking this step," said the Master General, "seem to me highly nebulous, if I have been correctly informed. The Church does not lack religious. The nunneries are filled with women who decided to espouse Jesus Christ only when some young man or other didn't want to espouse them. Our Lord is not there to fill the rueful gaps left by our earthly joys."

That was not the reason, Andrey assured him, certainly not the main reason. He had tested himself and found that it was, if anything, the other way around: the event to which the Master General was alluding had been his own fault; unintentionally, he had brought it upon himself. He was not at all sure that he could have made the girl happy of whom Father de Villemorin had evidently written, or that he could have been happy with her. He had envisioned an almost cloistered life for himself with this burgeoning young woman, and had probably frightened her with just these plans and been the cause of her flight from him. He had no intention of denying his disappointment, he said. Then he took courage and went on: "After all, many ways lie open to us for overcoming disappointment. I can see only one. That is why I am here, Reverend Master General."

"It is because of disappointment, nevertheless," said the Master

General. "Perhaps you think that your renunciation of earthly love will make an impression on her. You would not be the first man to enter a monastery out of vanity."

"I said that this was not the main reason."

The dead birds on the arm of the chair moved; the Master General touched the letter that lay before him. "Your bitterness is no better reason," he said. "We recognize passive rebellion as little as active revolt. I can remember a school friend, a rich man, who found the world so distasteful that he bought himself an island in the Mediterranean, where until his death twenty years later he saw no one but the few people who brought him food and books. He declared that he lived only to pray, and although this may have been true, I can't say that it touched me deeply. For this man was an enemy of mankind, and I don't know, therefore, whom he included in his prayers besides himself. 'This quiet island,' he used to write, but I think it must have been quite noisy with the clamor of his self-pity. Whoever flees from himself, flees from God." He looked up at a painting that hung on the wall beside Andrey. "Saint Benedict spoke of 'the evil of bitterness.' The Church is not an island on which to burn one's bitterness like refuse in the back yard of one's house."

"I think I am free of bitterness," said Andrey. "If not, I would wish to be."

"Faith alone does not justify the priesthood. It is as different from the vocation of spreading faith to others as the faith in a doctor differs from his ability to heal the sick. 'If anyone desires to do His will, he will know of the teaching, whether it is from God, or whether I speak on my own authority.'"

The Inquisition, thought Andrey. Hadn't he seen a picture of Cardinal Carafa on the crumbling walls of the cloister garden? He had hoped to be received with open arms, and was encountering mistrust and rejection.

As he was thinking this, his gaze fell on the clock that hung behind the Master General. Ten minutes past four. He had been sitting opposite the old man for almost an hour, but the parchment-yellow face, with its wrinkles and black teeth, showed not a trace of weariness or boredom. Andrey went on looking at the clock, and as he followed the regular motion of the pendulum, a supernatural strength seemed to flow from its narrow case into him. The Grand Inquisitor was not rejecting him; he was being tried.

"Reverend Master General, you want to know why I am here."

The Master General nodded.

Andrey began to speak, and he found himself expressing things that had not been clear to him until now. The Master General was to forgive him, he said, but he had to mention again the girl who was now the Countess Tarnovska. The wish that had led him here was connected with his experience with her, but not so superficially as it might have seemed even to his father's friend, Father de Villemorin. He had encountered the mysterious reality of the *corpus diabolicum* in the person of Maria O'Rourke all the more flagrantly because in her Satan had seized upon a fine and lovable creature, someone destined for happiness; had entered into her and gradually taken total possession of her. Since he had become convinced of the possibility of a demoniacal possession, the *possessio* of an individual, he had also become convinced of the suprapossession, the *circumsessio;* and it was just because of this that pantheism seemed to him to be heresy, because God lived above all things; the Devil, however, in them.

At this point Andrey paused, because he was suddenly aware of holding forth wildly with religious terms, as could happen only too easily in the zeal of a new knowledge. He apologized and protested that he felt neither hatred nor jealousy for the girl. He was deeply convinced that what was good had to be borne painstakingly, whereas evil reproduced itself like an infectious disease. The question whether he hated evil more than he loved good had occupied him; still, he felt that he was on the right path, for if he hated evil more than he loved good, he would probably have joined the revolutionaries. And it had struck him like a revelation that what was apparently great was paltry, and what was seemingly paltry was great; that the revolution wasn't capable of robbing the fires of Hell of a single soul.

He paused again. He had said too much, he went on, and probably expressed hasty opinions. He had nothing to add but that he had found peace in prayer and was filled with the grace of God.

The Master General had listened with his eyes half closed, as if he were dropping off to sleep; but evidently not a word had escaped him. "Are you aware, my son"—he used the appellation for the first time—"what sacrifices the priesthood demands? Obedience, poverty, and chastity are not symbols in the life of the Order. You spoke of Satan. Symbolism is one of the Devil's craftiest inventions. Symbol means that one sign stands for another, but the truth is as unequivocal as the cross. All symbols are at best ambiguous. I recommend that you read Paul's epistle to the Corinthians, in which he demands that 'those who have wives be as if they had none; and those who buy as though not possessing; and those who use this world as though not using it.' Here even the best Christian of them all formulates an 'as though.' With it, Paul took into account the impossibility of living as a perfect Christian in an imperfect world. Outside the Order, the words of Christ become conveniently symbolic. When you take your vows, you renounce every possibility of an 'as though.' But since we Dominicans go out into the world, since very few of us remain continuously behind monastery walls, since big cities and assemblages of people are the fields on which we encamp, we are confronted constantly with this 'as though.' We try to steer the ship of divine realism through a sea of worldly symbolism."

He rose. Upright, he looked even smaller and frailer. Andrey was therefore all the more surprised to see the old man move quickly and firmly. He walked over to the window and drew up the shade. The warmth of the summer afternoon, with its scent of flowers, humming bees, and sensual memories of other summer afternoons, streamed hungrily into the room. He gestured to Andrey to join him, and said, "Do you see that wall? Do you notice anything?"

"A walled-up door, if I am not mistaken."

"You are not mistaken. It is the walled-up door of the Inquisition. Behind it is a staircase that used to lead to the courtroom, and that is walled up, too. Sinners were brought before the Grand Inquisitor through that door. The Inquisition is walled up for all time. I am not telling you this to make the Order seem more excellent to you. The door over there represents the end of our worldly power. We have truly become an Order of beggars, not so much in the actual sense, but rather in that we can no longer enforce faith; we must beg for it. Obedience, poverty, and chastity are accompanied by powerlessness in a world that is governed by rebellion, gold, sensuality, and the greed for power." He looked at Andrey. "You are rich, you bear an illustrious name, and you seem to be equipped with outer virtues. Can you do what you want? Don't you promise yourself too much from the discipline of the Order, which can protect but not save you from temptation? Aren't you hoping for a perfection that, even in our family circle, you can find only within yourself, and shall find only if it is God's will? Don't you perhaps have a romantic idea of a priesthood that is always radical, never romantic? And above all, are you turning toward God or only away from the world? What you just told me was honestly spoken, yet it has not convinced me. Besides *possessio* and *circumsessio* we also have *obsessio,* and it is an *obsessio* to see the Devil everywhere. Many like you have stood before me. One was jilted by his sweetheart, another betrayed by his brother, the third revolted by his own debauchery, the fourth wanted to atone for his lack of love. I warned each one of them of taking the great step. But every now and then someone comes along who has heard the call of the Lord. Him I invite according to the words of Luke: 'And he sent his servant at supper time to tell those invited to come, for everything is now ready.' "

He walked slowly over to the door. "Brother Giacomo will give you all the necessary papers to familiarize you with the Order. Read them carefully, without thinking for a moment that any of it is meant symbolically. Then, if you haven't changed your mind, come back to Rome. Brother Giacomo will enter you."

"I have no intention of leaving Rome again," said Andrey.

The old man nodded.

3

Andrey remained in Rome. He stayed at a small but elegant hotel where he had stopped on his travels as a student. He spent part of his days writing letters. He had sold the house in Lipki, but the settling of his father's estate turned out to be very complicated. It was larger than he had anticipated and was invested in various ways. His mother's fortune, which included investments that bore interest, had gone to his father on her death; now, however, it had to be divided with distant relatives. His father's lawyer in Kiev, Dr. Steiner, came to Rome. It worried him to see with what indifference the young heir listened to his suggestions. But for that, Andrey lived outwardly the life of any wealthy young aristocrat who had come to Rome for a prolonged visit. Duke Ruspoli invited him to a party at his country estate on the sea-shore; from then on, the invitations poured in. Andrey accepted them all.

The refuse flowed under the *palazzi* of the Eternal City just as the filth swept by beneath the beautiful *palazzi* of Venice. The courtesans of the nobility resided in villas on the Monte Pincio; the visit of Cléo de Mérode, the mistress of the Belgian King, was celebrated like a state visit; distinguished ladies handed a handsome gypsy leader from bed to bed. The bordellos flourished as in the days of Pompeii. Women who were apparently living model family lives offered themselves to Andrey, and couldn't understand when he refused them. They told him about the wild adventures of their husbands. One story that was being repeated in every salon concerned two homosexuals, both members of the nobility, who had been living together for years. One day they had driven with a conspicuous entourage to the church of Santa Maria in Araceali, where, at the foot of the Capella Santa Elena, they had vowed to be faithful to each other until death. Only a priest had been missing at this ecclesiastical farce. At the wedding feast that followed it, at the *palazzo* of this peculiar couple, one of the two had worn a wedding dress made by the most expensive *couturier,* and Roman society had been vastly entertained until dawn. The murder of a demimonde, almost forgotten, was suddenly revived and provided spicy conversation, because someone thought he had seen, in the vicinity of Rome, the young Count who had undoubtedly killed the woman in a drunken brawl and afterward escaped to South America with the tacit co-operation of government officials. More or less harmless events such as these took place before the gates of the Vatican. To Andrey it was no coincidence. The Devil had shifted the battlefield into enemy territory.

That it was not difficult for him to resist temptation perplexed him. It was possible that he had already taken his vows in spirit, and only his body still remained outside cloister walls. But it might also be because the experiences of the last month had deadened his sensibilities; that he was therefore in a condition more akin to unconsciousness than holiness. Was he fleeing responsibility? Possibly. But it was also possible for impotent responsibility to be equivalent to complicity. He who fled from responsibility for what was barbarous fled from his share of the guilt. But was it really a choice between rebellion and priesthood? Was it his encounter with the Devil in Maria O'Rourke, or was it only Maria? One could not mistrust oneself enough.

In the society in which he lived, vice caricatured itself; easy to recognize, easy to deny. But what about the innocent joys? He found himself enjoying idleness, a long sleep, good wine, walks on a mild evening, the opera, a romantic dream. Again and again he went back to the books Father Giacomo had given him. He read the rules of the

Orders of Saints Basil, Augustine, Benedict, Francis, Ignatius; and although some things could not possibly be valid any longer, he preferred to accept one rule too many than one too few, as a measure of his own readiness. What had the Master General meant when he had said that the best among the applicants had heard the call of the Lord? In his most oppressed moments it seemed to Andrey that the hard discipline of monasticism attracted him only because, without it, he was not even capable of living the "as though" life of which Paul had spoken; but in his happiest moments he found that there were no external reasons for his desire to dedicate his life to the priesthood. The idea had not left him for months—that was call and reason enough.

His doubts weighed heaviest upon him when he met acquaintances from Russia. Czar Alexander III was on his deathbed. The sick drunkard had retired to Livadia in the Crimea. Twenty-six-year-old Crown Prince Nicholas Alexandrovich was watching at his bedside. There was talk to the effect that the Emperor had made him swear never to swerve from the principles of absolute monarchy, but the Russians Andrey met in Rome spoke of the dawning of a new freedom under Nicholas II. There was even talk of a political amnesty, which was supposed to lie ready and signed in the desk of the successor to the throne. The dawn of freedom in Russia, thought Andrey, and he would not be there to see it. There was no Dominican cloister in Russia; only God knew if he would ever see his homeland again.

In September, when the days suddenly became cooler and rain showers swept across the squares like messengers on horseback, when the Tiber was intermittently swathed in transparent veils, Prince Ivan Petrovich Trubetzkoy arrived in Rome. He was a few years older than Andrey, but they had always been quite friendly, and the Prince had followed Andrey in Sonya Petrovna's affections.

"My dear Andrey," said Trubetzkoy as they sat opposite each other in the hotel lobby. "I have good news for you. The evening before I left, I met Maria Tarnovska at a party. By the way, she was more beautiful than ever, although a little pale and weary. She raved about you all evening. Her marriage to Vassily Tarnovsky is so unhappy, all Kiev is talking about it. They say Vassily behaved scandalously in St. Petersburg. Although she is wooed by everybody, one hears only the best about Mura. I would be surprised if she doesn't regret the way she treated you long ago. If I were you, I would return to Kiev tomorrow. Unhappy wives are a gift of God, especially if they are married to someone else. It's not too late. They say that Peter Tarnovsky is courting her. If you don't turn up soon, she may listen to him. Take my advice, and you'll be the most envied man in Kiev."

That night Andrey did not sleep. Voices he had not heard for a long time whispered promises. New voices, speaking out of old books. The white and black angels crossed swords over his bed.

The next morning he entered Santa Maria sopra Minerva for the second time.

CHAPTER 9

I

The villa Vassily had rented in Kiev lay in a part of the city called Lipki, not far from the house where the Vyrubovs had lived. It belonged to strange people and harbored strange memories. Maria had the dark family portraits removed. They stood in the passageway looking reproachful. A fine old house, but run-down like all rented villas. Maria hated to think that she was going to give birth to her child here. Vassily said he had no intention of ending his days in Kiev, and anyway, he couldn't afford a house of his own—not until his father's death. She would just have to put up with it. One didn't talk to women about such trivial things as money and the future.

Since Maria's pregnancy, Vassily had become the man he had been before the evening at the Grand Duke's house. He slept until noon, took singing lessons, left Maria alone at night. The doctor had warned her not to endanger her delicate health and the life of her child. Vassily knew that she denied herself to him because she couldn't help it. He had tortured her and had been tamed only when she had tortured him. In the dark, when all you could hear was the whispering of the wind, and every now and then the light from a carriage lantern wavered across the ceiling of their bedroom, her imagination came to life. Once he had raged when a lackey had walked into her boudoir. She lay back and thought how she would ring for the lackey when she was taking a bath, and order him to hold her bathrobe; she would drink with Vassily, get undressed by the fireplace, then lock her bedroom; she would not give herself to him until he had grown too weak to make her happy. The punishments she thought up for him excited her to such an extent that she could hardly withstand the urge to awaken the man sleeping at her side. At moments like this she hated him as she had never hated him before. He was humiliating her, because she lay there in her sensual satisfaction, and he knew nothing of her dreams. She was punishing him, and he slept.

One winter evening Vassily made no move to leave the house. They dined at a small table in front of the fireplace. Vassily drank, and the more he drank, the more foul-mouthed he became. He looked at her across the candles with a half-tender, half-scornful expression. "Oh, by the way," he said, as if he had suddenly thought of something negligible, "do you know what's happened to Andrey?"

Her heart seemed to stop beating. The empty house, the stillness, the silence of their friends. Andrey was dead. He had killed himself because of her.

"I met Trubetzkoy," Vassily went on. "He's just back from Rome. Andrey has become a friar. A Dominican, something like that. A man becomes a monk because of my wife."

Maria laid her hands on her stomach. She did that always now when overcome by feeling, as if she had to protect the life growing inside her. "When?" she asked.

"While we were amusing ourselves in St. Petersburg. I wouldn't worry about him. In your condition, that might be harmful. Behind monastery walls, our little saint will be safe from all temptation."

"He didn't become a priest because of me."

"That would be too bad. I like to see men ruining their lives for something I can have just like that. Peter, for instance. I think he's drinking himself to death. When did you see him last?"

"Yesterday."

"They tell me he steals into the house at night. A good thing I can trust my wife. At any rate, as long as the doctors are watching over her."

During the last months she had banished all thoughts of Andrey to the depths of her soul, as one puts away the picture of somebody one has treated unjustly. Their play by the river; his hand holding hers; their first kiss; their flight from Mademoiselle Larue; midday dinner with Olga watching them; the Spanish bird cage; his last, unsuspecting visit. Evil gifts of her conscience. The dead were long-suffering; ghosts returned to their graves; but this dead man would not tolerate it that one forgot him.

"I received a letter yesterday from Vladimir Stahl," said Vassily. "He is coming to see us. You certainly attract the scum of the earth."

"You are jealous."

"Of Stahl? The 'doctor' is impotent. He lives from one morphine injection to the next."

"That is a lie, just like everything else you say."

"I told him he would be welcome. I think it would be a good thing for him to see you in your present condition."

"Do you know that I hate you?"

"Of course I know it. We hate each other. It prevents us from being bored. Nothing binds two people who are married more closely than hatred."

"Why did you want a child by me?"

"Did I say I did? I wouldn't mind having a daughter . . . but I don't like little boys."

"You hate me because I am pregnant."

"On the contrary. I shall see to it that you are constantly pregnant."

"You are afraid of me."

"Because you are like me, I consider you capable of everything base."

"And I am. Don't you think I know about your affair with Olga Kralberg? I shall deceive you, with one, two, ten men. I shall be constantly pregnant, but you will never know if it is your child or not. I succeeded in disgracing my father's name, but I never made him look ridiculous. I shall disgrace you and make you look ridiculous at the same time."

Vassily was leaning forward over the table, both thumbs pressed against the top, his fingers underneath it.

She was seized with the irresistible compulsion to drive him mad. It was as if her power over him grew in exact proportion to the loss of his self-control. She told him what she thought of him, and some things she had never thought before. The filth she poured over him included everything that may be contained in filth piled up for a long time: bitterness and forgotten accounts, excrement and mendacious love letters, self-pity and broken playthings, threads left dangling and righteousness insulted.

He let her go on. Satisfaction showed in his face. She was caught in her own web, because in her efforts to excite him, she only excited herself more and more. When she finally stopped, exhausted, he tipped over the table; china, glasses, candles fell to the floor, smashed, and a candle that didn't go out as it fell set fire to the carpet.

He didn't get up. He watched her jump up and trample out the flames with her feet, as if he wanted to prove to her how false her rage had been since she had come to her senses so quickly and been able to put out the fire. Then he went over to her, took her by the hips, lifted her up, carried her through the room, and threw her on the bed. She tried to fend him off, said something about the child, but he smothered her screams with kisses that were full of hatred.

2

Expectant mothers long for the mother who gave them birth; the cycle of life would have it that way. Maria's longing to see her mother had become so strong that she made new plans daily as to how to approach her without her father finding out about it. Then the opportunity came of itself. One day—it was the beginning of February 1895, and she was in the sixth month of her pregnancy—Edward O'Rourke stopped in Kiev on his way to Otrada.

Nothing had changed his love for his niece. He filled the salon with his presence; told stories about Ireland, wonderful tales of freedom and elves; didn't seem to care whether Vassily was paying attention to him or not, and looked at Maria with his red-rimmed eyes as if to say that she need not say anything at all. Conspiracy was in his blood, and he liked nothing better than to conspire against his brother. He drove to Otrada and stayed longer than he had planned. He was waiting for Nicholas to go to a meeting of all Russian knight marshals in Moscow. When he did, Edward at once bundled his sister-in-law into a sled and drove her to Kiev.

It was a dreary February day. Steely raindrops, like rifle shot, were digging black holes into snow piles. Maria felt so miserable that she had stayed in bed. She was in bed when she heard her uncle's voice echoing through the house, announcing the arrival of Katharina O'Rourke.

Later, when Katharina was sitting at her daughter's bedside—Edward, after boasting about the success of his ruse, had left the two women alone—she remembered that it had once been the other way around. Maria had sat at her bedside. Now Maria was lying bedded on cushions, her cheeks red with excitement, while Katharina sat on a chair, small, gray, insignificant, a wet sparrow on a telegraph wire. She hadn't taken off her hat, and although Schrantz, Kiev's best tailor, had made her suit, she looked as poor and provincial as most women who never left their homes.

For a while they lied to each other as best they could. Katharina said that her health was much improved, that she enjoyed her young sons, and Maxim Katerinovich, her new son-in-law; that Sonya had written, and even Anna. Maria told about her social successes in St. Petersburg, her new clothes, the ease of her pregnancy. But Katharina did not mention Maria's father, and Maria did not mention her husband. They were trying to deceive time, as if so very much couldn't possibly have happened in so short a time. But time would not be deceived; it did not adhere to its own measure. When it began to grow dark, they began to light the candles of truth, and they lit one candle at the other as one did in church. Gradually it grew bright with truth. Katharina O'Rourke sat on Maria's bed; she took her daughter in her arms; the little hat on her head tipped to one side. Maria rested her head on her mother's shoulder and sobbed, and they were happy because until now both had wept over themselves without realizing that another was weeping for them too.

And that was how Edward found the two women, and he too had tears in his eyes, because he couldn't bear to see women cry. He said that was one of the reasons he had never married. When a woman got married, she let herself go and wept "bucketsful." But since the red giant always tended toward bravado when anything touched him, he declared that in difficult times a mother's place was at her daughter's side, and he was going to see to it—how, that was his business—that Mura's mother would be with her when her time came.

The end of April, the beginning of May, that was all he needed to know. "Have a guestroom ready, Mura. I know how to manage your father. God knows, it won't be for the first time."

The little creature in Maria Tarnovska seemed to change her. She thought she was protecting her unborn child because she didn't know that unborn children protected their mothers.

She needed warmth and hoped that it could be found in human beings. At last she had her own friends. She lived at Vassily's side as if he were not present. Vladimir Stahl's sleigh stood at her front door whenever she wanted to drive out. Yuri Tolstoy, gross and boorish by nature, watched over her gently. Dr. Tshitshagov, the famous gynecologist, came to see her more often than was necessary, with the thinnest of excuses. Men who came to visit her with their wives came back without them. In her samovar, the tea never had a chance to get cold. She didn't have to use her teacups; men drank their tea out of glasses. From early afternoon until late in the evening, the sickly sweet smell of papirossi permeated her salon. If Vassily came home earlier than expected, he withdrew angrily to their bedroom.

She treated men with a sweet sternness, astonished at first that both seemed to attract them—the sweetness and the sternness. Vladimir Stahl had wanted to become a doctor and believed in the healing power of his hands. She let him massage her neck and shoulders, but once, when he wanted to kiss her neck, she struck him in the face. When Yuri became excessively jealous, she turned him out. He begged to be allowed to come again. She began to realize that there were times when the lords of creation would rather be dogs than lords; that they preferred to be tortured than to torture; that they experienced woman as the scourge with which God chose to punish them. Only when she played this game with Peter Tarnovsky did she feel she was playing with fire.

She had known him since childhood, but his courtship of her did not surprise her, because life in Kiev was boring, and in any society that was boring, late revelations were not uncommon. He was just twenty-one. His left arm was a little shorter than the right, from birth, and he had a habit of holding that shoulder high, and pressing his sick arm close, as if he were holding some secret object. He looked like an angel who had fallen and hurt himself in his fall. He wrote Maria ecstatic letters, sent her baskets of flowers not at all in keeping with his restricted means, read his sensitive poetry aloud to her; yet he could be stormy and impetuous too. Then he boasted of his brilliant mind and physical prowess, and was quarrelsome over trifles. He was unpopular and suffered because of it. Once or twice Maria let him kiss her when he was leaving, and laughed at him when he chose to misunderstand what she had meant as a family greeting. She ran her fingers through his hair; but told him never to show his face again when she found out he had boasted that she reciprocated his passion. When she did receive him again, it was only because his assurances that he would kill himself had sounded as sincere as the groom Ivan's assurances that he would die for her.

One evening, when she was alone, as usual, he turned up, teetering, lalling, obviously drunk. After a short while he began to curse Vassily.

"That my blood should be united with yours," he said, "yet not be my blood, is driving me mad. It is as if you were expecting a child from a man who raped you. Don't contradict—it couldn't have happened any other way."

He wouldn't let her say a word; he ran his fingers wildly through his hair, beat his fist against his forehead, threw his arms around her knees, and cried, "I shall kill him, Mura! I shall kill him." He was drunk, but he wasn't talking of murder because he was drunk. He would invite Vassily to go hunting with him, lure him into the woods, and shoot him. Or he would steal into the garden at night, make a lot of noise; Vassily would rush out, and in the dark he would shoot his brother down. They would suspect burglars. "And we would be free. Mura, I swear I would love his child as if it were my own. It shall never know that its father was a monster. It happened against your will, a devilish coincidence."

She took his head between her hands and spoke to him as one speaks to a sick child. To be sure, she was not happy with Vassily, but there was nothing to be done about that. "And you are wrong, I wanted a child." But all the time she was asking herself if she really wanted to calm him. Tomorrow he would have forgotten what he had said anyway; today she held Vassily's life in her hands. And the feeling of her own power streamed through her in hot waves of exultation.

He was kneeling at her feet, covering her hands with his kisses, her arms, her knees. Startled suddenly by his strength, which she could no longer control, she was trying to shake him off when Vassily came into the room. He grasped the kneeling youth by the neck, wouldn't let him rise; and with the flat of his hand he boxed his ears, not very hard, but rather as if he were chastising a naughty child. When Peter tried to rise, Vassily kicked him in the chest. Peter reeled back, sprang to his feet, and struck his brother in the face so violently that the blood spurted from Vassily's nose. Now they were standing face to face, full of hatred and indecision, as if trying to think of a way to humiliate each other. Vassily was fiery red; Peter's withered hand formed a fist.

Maria watched it all. Vassily's obscenities left her cold. He was licking the blood from his lips; involuntarily she wet hers. Peter's eyes narrowed; involuntarily hers did, too. For a moment she wanted to egg them on like wild animals, indifferent as to who might win.

"Go to the devil, you miserable cripple," said Vassily.

" I could beat you to death," said Peter.

Maria laid her hands on her stomach. "The child," she whispered, and fled to her room.

4

It is the end of April, April weather. The rain beats heavily against the pane, as if out of breath. The wind soughs, and sweeps fallen blossoms ahead of it, the white rain of spring. The sun shines rashly, deceiving itself. The sky is transparent blue and leaden gray, not yet awake but already spent, all in one hour. The trees are alive as never before, and as they never will be again that year. They gesticulate with their arms as if trying in vain to make themselves understood.

Through the high window of her bedroom Maria Tarnovska can see the sky and the treetops. For days now she has seen nothing else. Four days before, her labor pains had started, but it must have been a mistake, because a few hours later they stopped. Since then, she has not left her bed.

Everything seems as unreal as the changeable sky. It cannot be true that Vassily is gone, four days now. "A man is only in the way at a time like this. You are in good hands." Fled from the birth of his child as from a sickness. Shook hands with the doctor in the doorway; threw his luggage on the box. "I'll send the coachman back; he'll come for me." The coachman did not come back. She managed to send Uncle Edward a telegram. The old magician did not disappoint her.

Katharina O'Rourke comes at noon and leaves in the evening. Next morning she is there again, at noon she leaves. Swept in, swept out. How often does Dr. Tshitshagov call? She does not ask for him and he is there. She asks for him and he doesn't come. She thinks she sees Peter leaning over her bed. She asks her maid about it. "No. Count Peter has not been here for weeks." She can hear Vladimir Stahl's voice, whispering from far off. "I want to see him." "Baron von Stahl only brought some flowers." The room is a bower of flowers, as if she were lying in state. She orders all the flowers removed. Suddenly the room seems empty; she orders the flowers brought back. Dr. Tshitshagov gives her a sleeping draught. She is afraid of sleep, because, asleep, she experiences the birth. Once she dreams that Vassily and Peter, Vladimir and Yuri, the Grand Duke and the doctor, and forgotten men from St. Petersburg are standing around her bed as the child slips out of her. They are waiting for the birth so that they can take possession of the mother.

At noon on the eighteenth of April, the labor pains set in again, but she is no longer afraid, as if she already has it all behind her. She dares not die, because Vassily will give the child away. It is going to be a boy, and she has to protect him. Dr. Tshitshagov asks if she is in great pain. She grits her teeth and tries to smile. The house is like a beehive. Whispers become noise. She wants to ask after Vassily, but she controls herself. Her mother is sitting at the window. "You don't look well, Mama." "Don't worry about me. Think of yourself." She worries about her mother. "Do I hear Uncle Edward?" "He just came." She has to think of the day he led her down to the library. It is going to be a boy, and she will give him all her love. The love that one withdraws from people turns into hatred.

They bring in hot water, towels, linen, a tiny bathtub. A coming and going as at a railway station. An unknown traveler is expected. He will be welcomed, and forgotten. Arrival and departure count, birth and death; what lies in between doesn't count. Dr. Tshitshagov is standing with his back to her, sterilizing his instruments, a tall, slender, dark man. From the back you can see his bald head, meticulously hidden by a tonsure. Maria is overcome by a feeling of repugnance. She wants to cry out that he should leave the room. He too stood beside her bed in the dream; he too waited for her body to void the child and be free to receive love. She has to have another doctor, with no face. "Don't hesitate to cry out, Maria Nikolaevna, if you are in pain." She shakes her head. The midwife busies herself with Maria, encourages her—a plump little woman with red cheeks, a kerchief on her head. She looks like the peasant dolls that fit one into the other, big midwife, little midwife, smaller midwife, smallest midwife.

Only seconds without pain between the pains now. The evening sun falls into the room, outlining the distorted shapes of windows on the wall. Clouds move across the sky; the rhomboid cast by the sun disappears. And then it is there again, as if drawn by a spectral hand, visible one moment, gone the next. She stares fixedly at the wall. When Tioka is born, the sun will be shining. The child will be a boy, and she will call him Tioka.

5

A voice in the salon announced Vassily's return. He was singing, "Oh, distant steppes, oh, savage plains," his favorite song, which once had delighted her.

She had him called to her. He kissed her on the forehead as if he had never been gone. He scarcely glanced at the child in the cradle, and met her reproaches with one of his theories. Life was complicated enough, he said, stretching out on the sofa; one had to steer clear of things that were disturbing, unpleasant, or difficult. His frivolity no longer amused her; it was as faded as an old dance card. "Disturbing, unpleasant, difficult"—did he mean the child? He evaded the answer to that. At any rate, he had no intention of sitting at home and rocking a cradle. And he found life in Kiev boring and provincial. Life didn't have to make much sense, but its senselessness should at least be amusing. He spoke of their moving to Milan.

During the last weeks she had read almost every book in the house: Lermontov's *A Hero of Our Times*, Gontcharov's *Oblomov*, Turgenev's *A Hamlet from the District of Shtshigrovo*, Pushkin's *Eugene Onegin* again, and, above all, George Sand's novel *Indiana*, which all Russia was talking about. Vassily was Petshorin, Lermontov's "superfluous man." All men were superfluous. Dead souls. If she did not fly from them, her soul would atrophy, too. Over and over again she read what Petshorin had said of himself: "Although I am incomparably more valuable, interesting, and earnest than all of you, I am condemned to be unhappy, and you therefore shall also suffer, through

me, for I at least must make you feel my superiority, my power."
Vassily! Vassily, who thought he was valuable, interesting, perhaps
even to be taken more seriously than other people, and was therefore
a tormentor, a "hero of our times." Superfluous and dead. Like
Petshorin or Oblomov. "My life began with its extinguishment." Of
what further concern was this superfluous, dead man to her? At best,
she had met no one who was alive. Men—they were satiated slaveowners, just as George Sand described them. They had freed the
slaves, but kept women in their bondage. The pious believed that
animals had no souls, but only Russian men believed that women
had no souls. The divine George Sand knew better. The souls of
men were dead, as a punishment for the fact that only they had been
allowed to live. Now the unused souls of the women were coming to
life, alive in bodies that until now had belonged to the men. George
Sand, dressed like a man, living with Sandeau, Musset, Chopin.
Vassily's travel plans? Lermontov's sad hero: "His soul ruined, his
fantasy restless, his heart insatiable, as accustomed to trouble as to
pleasure, a man for whom all things are too little and life grows
constantly more desolate, so that nothing is left him but to travel."
Why did she go on living with him? Because the serfs too had
remained in Otrada with her father. It was difficult to grow accustomed to freedom. Or did she remain with him because she would
not deprive him of his punishment? ". . . and you therefore shall
also suffer, through me, for I at least must make you feel my superiority, my power." Her soul could recover only with his misery.

6

At the beginning of May, Vassily told her that his teacher was sure
he had the makings of a great singer. He wanted to go to Milan,
therefore, where a Professor Giovannari had instructed many a future
star in the art of *bel canto*. "I have spoken to Dr. Tshitshagov. You
can travel in two weeks, at the latest. I've just been to see my parents,
because of Peter. He is ready for an asylum. They are willing to take
the child."

Maria protested, wept, threatened. Kiev was boring, he was right,
but Matilda, the nurse, could come to Milan with them. "I refuse to
travel with a wailing infant," he said, and nothing would make him
change his mind.

Vladimir Stahl was the only one she trusted. As soon as she was able to leave the house, she went to see him. He had rented a roomy furnished apartment in the Tsuvoroskaya, not far from Lavra, the monastery of Kiev. It was a gloomy apartment, impersonal, with marks on the walls left by pictures that had been removed long ago, with forlorn furniture that looked as if it were mourning for long-lost brothers. An unpleasant odor like that of old medicine permeated the rooms. Maria remembered what she had been told about Stahl. A medical student who had not been able to finish his studies because he had written fraudulent prescriptions; captain of the guard, expelled because of cowardice in a duel; the husband of a rich woman who had been unfaithful to him with his friends and servants. Possibly a drug addict. A ruined man—her adviser.

They sat in the library. A few magnificent volumes and some books of Stahl's on the empty shelves, like corpses left on a battlefield. After a lean, bony servant with a sick face, who looked like his master —a ridiculous shadow—had brought in the samovar, Maria talked about Vassily's plans. "You are my fatherly friend, Vladimir Mihailovich," she said when she had done. "What shall I do?"

"Whatever I advise you to do, you will never leave Tarnovsky."

"Why?"

"Because you love him."

"What makes you say that?"

"You call me your fatherly friend."

"Does that offend you?"

He tried to smile, but smiling was an art, and, like every art, a cautious game within limits. Vladimir Stahl could not smile; he could only laugh, because everyone could laugh. His smile leaped beyond the limits of laughter and developed into a grin. He grinned with ugly horse teeth.

"Since I saw you for the first time in the Grand Duke's house, I have been on fire," he said. "Do you think I am here by chance, in this repulsive city that smells of incense just as this horrible apartment smells like a laboratory? I have left my house, my family, my friends, because I can breathe only when I am near you."

"I need a friend," she said, "not a lover."

"You will always have only lovers."

"Until now all I had was friends."

"That is what you think. Your friends are nothing but patient lovers. You belong to the type of woman in whom every man senses an enemy."

"I came to you for advice."

He pretended not to hear her, or perhaps he really wasn't listening. His eyes were upon her, filled with desire, yet livid; he spoke intensely, with exertion, like a clock that was threatening to run down. "You have heard people speak of lovable women," he said. "They deserve love, but no one loves them. Men love hateable women; they love the enemy. The strong ones love them, because in them they sense an adversary who is their equal; the weak ones love them because they hope to gain strength by a conquest of the enemy. One wants to be loved by one's enemies, Maria Nikolaevna; one is curious only about one's enemies. To see a hateable woman in the ecstasy of love— what satisfaction! And what ravishing disappointment when she does not immediately become lovable. And on top of that—vanity. Don't you know that actually women want only to please women, and men to please men? What magical strength he must have that the enemy's lap does not refuse him! To be envied—there is no stronger human urge."

"That is nonsense, Vladimir Mihailovich," she interrupted him although she was flattered to think that the older man was so much interested in her. "You are describing a witch of the Middle Ages."

"The witches have not died out, we have only stopped burning them." In every war, he went on, you found aggressor and attacked "To storm, to win, to conquer, to succumb, to possess—the whole vocabulary of love has been taken from the vocabulary of war." But a certain readiness for war was an integral part of the women who were attacked, too. She was the ideal enemy, he declared, because she was not only hateable, she could also hate. "Why did you come to me? Why didn't you go to your mother? Why don't you have single woman friend? Because you hate and want to be hated."

He poured tea. His hand was trembling. He went over to the book case, his steps unsteady, and stood leaning against the shelves. Their conversation seemed to have excited and tired him. The clock was running down.

"I wanted to hear from you whether I should stay in Kiev with my child," she said.

"Do you know Krylov's fable of the cat and the nightingale? The cat was holding the bird in its claws. 'I could eat you,' the cat said 'but I am not going to eat you as long as I like your song.' But the nightingale, in its deadly fear, could only cheep hoarsely. 'Is that your lovely song?' the cat sneered. 'Since you can't sing any better than that, I might just as well enjoy your meat,' and the cat ate up the nightingale. 'Let me discreetly tell you that/ a bird can't sing in claws of cat.' Your soul, Maria Nikolaevna, cannot sing a song when it finds itself in a cat's claws."

"So I am to leave him?" she asked.

His gaze was fixed rigidly on the door. Suddenly he excused himself and left her alone.

A ruined life, an old man, a sick man, but he had voiced her thoughts, even if he had intended it differently. She had to free herself of Vassily. But she could not free herself of him if she remained behind in Kiev. Peter, Yuri, Vladimir Stahl were not lovers Vassily feared. "And therefore you too shall suffer, through me. . . ." Through her he had to suffer. His jealousy had outlived his love. The man who would free her soul would destroy Vassily. Tioka! The little red crying bundle that lay in the cradle with a body incomplete and an old man's face and old man's hands. She had to leave her child because she had to destroy his father.

When Stahl came back, he was changed: his body was firm, his eyes shone, his voice was light and youthful. "Pardon me, Maria Nikolaevna," he said, "but I had to get rid of a visitor."

She rose. "I must go."

He grasped her hand. "What a lot of foolish nonsense I talked. I should have told you that it would make no difference at all if you went with Tarnovsky or not. If you go to Milan, I shall be there. I won't give up until I have freed you from him. I—no one else." He spoke fast. The months of her pregnancy had been torture. "Tarnovsky is having an affair with Olga Kralberg. She is worthy of him." He accused Vassily of unfaithfulness and implored Maria to become his mistress. "I know ways that can lead you to paradise," he said. "None of these idiots know them, only I do. Only I can free your soul from your body."

He wanted to take her in his arms. She pushed him away. A fatherly friend, she had called him. What more did he want? Peter's infatuation, Yuri's tenderness, Dr. Tshitshagov's politeness, Vladimir Stahl's intelligence—she needed them all, but she needed none of them.

Trembling, the "doctor" accompanied her to the door.

Six months went by. From Milan they moved to Rome, from there to Naples, and back to Florence and Milan. They had no home. They lived in grand or mediocre hotels, according to the money Vassily received from Russia. Matilda Skopin, the baby's nurse, wrote simple letters that were difficult to decipher. Often the letters followed them for weeks from city to city.

Vassily had given up all hope of becoming a great singer. In the days of his courtship of Maria, he had called himself a dilettante, a man of halfway measures, but since he had only half meant what he said, he couldn't accept the truth with good grace and sought acknowledgment in the most characteristic domain of the dilettante—society. On the way home from a party, depleted by his own gaiety, he would grow taciturn. Only with Maria did he no longer try to make his inner man match his external being. Now and then, in Rome and Milan, the blonde Austrian, Olga Kralberg, turned up. She had more tact than Vassily. At first she avoided meeting Maria; but Vassily invited her to join them, appeared in public with both women, denied nothing. Maria, bored and lonely in a foreign land, did not protest.

In October they were in Milan again. Professor Giovannari, who had no objection to the fees of his lay pupils, was planning an opera performance with them, in which he had given Vassily a small but choice part. Vassily's fluctuating self-confidence soared suddenly to a mood of fierce joy. On that day, Maria had gone to see the "Last Supper," and had wandered along the Via Carlo Alberto in the direction of the Hotel Cavour. It was a soft, Lombardy afternoon. The sky laid a cautious hand over the rooftops. The new electric lights in the old candelabra on the Cathedral Square had flared up too early as if anxious to test their youthful powers. In the side streets, though lamplighters were still moving from lamp to lamp, so that a dark borderline was drawn between square and streets, a ditch between yesterday and tomorrow. Maria stopped in front of shop windows. They glowed from out the walls of age-old *palazzi* like radiant sore that would soon erode the old stone. She would have liked to buy everything she saw, for her delight in buying had always grown in proportion to her misery, but she was aware of the fact that she had no money and was dependent on a man from whom she wanted to ask nothing. She was feeling more homesick than ever.

The desk clerk handed her a telegram. It was addressed to Vassily. She did not dare to open it. It was almost six. Vassily was at a rehearsal; later, they were going to a party being given by Prince Boncompagni. Maria rang for the maid and began to undress. Telegrams rarely brought good news, but something exceptionally bad seemed to emanate from this one. She thought of Tioka, and her motherly instincts, which had lain in a sick sleep, were suddenly roused. With her hair down, she darted away from the mirror and opened the telegram. It read: "Peter hanged himself. Come at once. Father."

Vassily came in. He hurried past her, humming a tune, then turned suddenly and took the paper out of her hand.

One look at Vassily sufficed to send the maid flying from the room. Whether overwhelmed by pain or remorse, or whether he just feared being torn out of the pleasure course of an idle life by the death of his brother, Vassily was one of those people who could find a scapegoat faster than his own guilt. He shouted, "You murdered him!" grabbed Maria by the hand, accused her of having corresponded with Peter and driven him to despair, called her a hardened liar, cursed the day he had met her. She tried to calm him. The telegram, she said, told nothing of the reason for Peter's suicide. But her sensibleness only made Vassily more senseless. When she remonstrated that the only thing she could be accused of was that she hadn't given in to the lovesick boy, he began to rage. She had had an affair with Peter, just as she had had affairs with Yuri and Vladimir Stahl; she had been a whore from the day of their marriage. He doubted if Tioka was his child; the boy might very well be the child of one of her lovers, perhaps the dead man's. His brother had died only because she had betrayed him with another. Maria, now getting more and more excited herself, reminded him of his own words: he had gone to see his parents to tell them that Peter was insane. Beside himself with rage, Vassily denied that he had ever said anything of the sort, but if he had said anything about insanity, then he could only have meant his brother's love for Mura. He shouted so loudly that some of the hotel guests collected in the corridor, and the desk clerk came up and knocked at the door to find out what was wrong.

Vassily had just sent him away and calmed down a little, as happens sometimes when an outsider interrupts a violent scene, when Olga Kralberg appeared. Vassily repeated his accusations. Surprisingly, the beautiful young woman took Maria's side. She did it in true feminine fashion in that she cast no doubt on the fact that Peter had in all probability taken his life because of Mura—this, however, was not Mura's fault. "Thank heaven for Mura's chastity," she said, "and for the fact, too, that any man would commit suicide for her. A dangerous angel—what more could you ask for?" She sat down beside Maria and tried to embrace her.

Maria withdrew from the woman. Peter dead. Because she was young, death seemed to be an agreement to which everyone bowed, although it did not exist. She could envision dying, but not death. She could see Peter dangling lifeless from a rope, his tongue hanging out, as in the drawings of hanged criminals she had seen in Italian newspapers. She was sure that he was still hanging in a window frame or a barn door; that they were waiting until she came so that she might see him with his tongue hanging out, his eyes bulging, his neck swollen. And she forgot how often she had seen him this last year, and could remember him only as he had been in their shared childhood, in Otrada, long before Vassily. He had worn a sailor suit— a dark blue one in winter, a white one in summer—with a wide collar. On the black silk ribbon of his round sailor's cap the word "Implacable" stood between two gold anchors, the name of an English vessel. The black ribbon fluttered in the wind. Peter ran across the grass, fell down, hurt his knee. In the winter he had complained that his knees were cold, and she had laughed at him because he had asked why he couldn't have fur on his knees. He had shivered, and he had been clumsy and ashamed of his short arm. Even then he had been doomed to die. His whole life had been nothing but a parole of twenty-two years. All people were doomed to die, although there was no such thing as death, with shorter or longer periods of probation; but they died regardless of whether they had broken parole or not. Twenty-two years old, and now he was hanging in a window frame or a barn door, in his sailor suit, with his round sailor hat on his head, the ribbon fluttering in the wind—"Implacable." Vassily was right: she should have given in to him and prolonged his period of probation. It didn't matter to whom one denied and to whom one gave oneself; there was no point in keeping anything secret or in waiting for a love that never came. In spite of all, she did not feel guilty, for whoever was condemned to die had to die, and cemeteries were only little cities within big ones. She heard Vassily's sobs. Now that he was assured of his mistress' compassion, he rather fancied himself in the role of the bereaved brother. She saw him as through a veil, with Olga Kralberg comforting him, and it suddenly occurred to her that the news had horrified but relieved her. When she had opened the telegram, she had feared for her child, only for her child. Now they would have to go back to Russia, tonight, tomorrow morning at the latest. Sixty-six hours to Charkov. In sixty-six hours she would hold Tioka in her arms, hear him cry, laugh, feel his tiny fists on her face, and she would never part from him again. She saw Vassily jump to his feet, come over to her, stand in front of her, but she started up only when the flat of his hand struck her full force in the face.

Only then did she realize that she had been smiling.

8

The Tarnovsky country residence, which Maria saw for the first time on that October afternoon, lay a few miles east of Charkov. It was called "the citadel" in the neighborhood, respectfully, yet also rather as if it were a ruin. A Tarnovsky who had lived in France for a long time had built it. With its stone walls, round towers, pinnacles, and arched windows, it stood out strangely on the Russian plain. It was so neglected that its magnitude seemed hollow, its splendor frivolous, and its pride disgraceful. And the people living in it, clinging to the crumbling stone and appearances, also seemed hollow, frivolous, and disgraceful. Vassily's father, a man in his middle fifties, who affected the air of a man of the world banished to the provinces; his mother, who surrounded herself with tattered splendor and, with a stony expression, seemed constantly to be resenting something; his older sister, who wore her ugliness like a chastity girdle.

From the gate, where the Count was waiting for them with his major-domo—an old man with the sarcastic devotion of servants who work without pay—Maria and Vassily were led immediately to the room where the dead man was lying in state. It was a hall of exaggerated dimensions, with a balustrade entirely of stone, with flags and standards and suits of armor, and all of it standing singly, as if some of the knights had been sold and some of the flags had turned to dust. Black cloth had been hung across the narrow barred windows. They looked like mourning clothes hung up to dry. Peter was lying on a bier in the center of the empty room, in his student dress, which he had never worn. It was buttoned up high, to his chin, so that you could not see the welt around his neck, but his face was swollen, and since he had been lying there for some time, between candelabra, candles, and potted plants, an odor of death and fermentation issued forth from the corpse on the catafalque.

When Vassily and Maria walked up to the bier, those who had been holding watch stepped back; only the dead man's mother remained standing beside the body, motionless, without even glancing at her oldest son and daughter-in-law. Maria still could not grasp the fact that Peter was dead. His face was changed by death; it had taken on a peasant aspect. He looked like a wan boy who was blowing up his cheeks for fun. If he hadn't been so pale, his face would have looked rounder, jollier, and healthier than it had ever been in life. A dark-violet, heavily embroidered cloth had been spread across the body, but it wasn't long enough to cover the dead man's feet. His shoes showed from under it, as if Peter had just lain down for a short rest. The October rain drummed with hard fingers against the pane. A few women were mumbling.

Into this monotony of rain and prayer, the voice of a child could be heard crying shrilly. No one paid any attention to it, but Vassily seized Maria's hand because he was afraid she might leave the dead to go to her child. The painful pressure of his hand had the opposite effect: she tore herself loose and ran toward the sound.

A corridor, two or three doors, the child's room. Tioka was lying in his crib, howling heartbreakingly and reassuringly. It was the cry of an infant, of no consequence. It did not abate slowly like the weeping of an adult who would go on bewailing himself long after he had stopped crying. The moment Maria leaned over the bed, the crying ceased and made way for a broad smile, as if the child were trying to say he had only cried for fun. Maria took her son out of the crib, pressed him to her heart, caressed him, touched his little hands, his feet, his face; she assured herself that he was whole from top to toe.

At supper she heard that Peter had left no message of farewell, no explanation. No one seemed to hold Maria responsible. He had been "weary of life"—that was the way people put it when they could find no better reason than that life was annoying. No one had noticed anything wrong, but then most suicides gave no sign of their intention. They lived with death as with a companion for life, like man and wife who had lived with each other for years before their marriage, to whom the wedding was therefore only an empty ceremony.

They ate the frugal meal on costly china in a huge dining room. Maria sat between Vassily and her father-in-law, who watched her constantly with a half-complaisant, half-provocative smile, as if he wanted to say that she was much too good for his son and that he, a connoisseur of women, was the only one who understood her. All the others looked at her disapprovingly: Vassily still furious because she had run off to her child; his sister, because Maria was so modishly clad; a brother, a sister of Peter's mother, and the Countess herself, because they had at last found a scapegoat. They spoke of the funeral, which they had put off not only because of Vassily's absence, but also because the shadow of an un-Christian burial lay over the house. When Maria began to speak of the child, they all looked down at their plates. One did not speak of the living in a house of the dead.

Later, in the guestroom, where only two smoking oil lamps were burning, Vassily told her that Peter had hanged himself from the bar of the nursery window. Once it had been his and Peter's room.

9

When the funeral was over, Maria and Vassily left for Charkov. Vassily rented a house. It was his intention to stay there for a few months, partly because he wanted to discuss certain things with his father, partly to prevent being the loser in the new will that would now have to be drawn up. Until then, Tioka was to remain at "the citadel." What was to happen after that would be decided later.

In early November, Maria was stricken with a high fever. At first she thought it was just a cold resulting from the sudden change in temperature. In Italy, summer had made way reluctantly for autumn; here winter had burst in on them as if out of ambush. The house was situated on a hilltop overlooking the river Lopan, and was exposed to the icy winds that swept across the Tshernosyom, the black earth of the Charkov region. It rarely rained; no snow had fallen yet, but the wind carried ice within it like blackmail.

On the fourth day of her illness, her temperature rose to a hundred and five. She coughed; her mouth was so dry, she asked for water all the time. She passed slime and blood. Little red spots, like fleabites, appeared on her breasts. Vassily, terrified by illness—as by anything that threatened to endanger his comfortable existence—sent for Dr. Mayerberg in the middle of the night. He was the doctor who had comforted Maria on her wedding night. But this time the old man had nothing comforting to say. Maria had typhoid fever.

In spite of the contagiousness of the disease, there could be no thought of moving her to a hospital. The hospitals didn't like to take typhoid cases; it would also have been risky to expose Maria to the cold air outside. Vassily moved to the house of his parents, but not until he had seen to it that Maria would have the best of care. Matilda Skopin proceeded to Charkov. She took her turn at the sick woman's bedside with a nurse who had been sent by Professor Veressayev from the Charkov University Hospital. Vassily sent the coachman back to be on hand to go for the doctor or medicine. He belonged to the type of people whom the Lord had imbued with fear in order that they might love.

10

Fever. A world of one's own imposed on the world, yet having no connection with the world. One's body immersed in boiling water, frozen in an ice cube, floating weightlessly above the cushions, sinking down into them as into a morass.

Maria asks for a mirror. Black, bleeding cankers on her tongue. The silver frame of the mirror winds its way like a snake around the glass. She will be blind, as after the measles. She cannot hold the mirror. Her fingers drum on the bedspread. The overseer in Otrada died of typhoid fever. Little Karina Shervayev died of it. What was the name of the jolly starosta who died of typhoid fever? "Dr. Mayerberg, I am going to die, aren't I?" "You are young, Maria Nikolaevna." Peter died because of her. The young died.

Profound darkness, and lightning-bright clarity. What she sees in her fever she forgets; what she thinks goes under in it. Only Andrey is ever present. She counts the days on which she does not think of him. Eighteen, three hundred and four, ninety-nine. She adds up her guilt; the figures read like a debt. Where is Andrey? Would he come if she sent for him? Would he forgive her if he came? "I have atoned sufficiently." She asks, he answers. She confides in the doctor. What she has to say about the Dominican must sound like feverish fantasies to the old man.

A child crying. Have they brought Tioka? "Take the child away!" "There is no child here, Countess." Vassily didn't want a child. He will abandon Tioka. She clings to the hands of his nurse. "You must save Tioka, Matilda." "Tioka is well, Countess." As long as she is alive. If she dies, Matilda will not be able to protect Tioka. She cannot die until she has spoken to Andrey. Andrey is sitting beside the bed. "I assure you, Maria, the child is safe." Dr. Mayerberg will have to persuade Vassily to call Andrey. She has to convince the doctor that she is sane.

When she passes her hand through her hair, it comes away full of hair. The cushion is covered with hair. She will be bald. She will lie on her bier bald. Vassily will turn away. He hates everything ugly. Her shoes will show from under the cloth. In her fear of death she screams, tears the thermometer out of the nurse's hand. One hundred and five. One hundred and five point two. If it goes any higher, she will die. There is a black line—the limit of life; death housed in quicksilver, a frog hopping up a ladder. Bells pealing, louder and louder. Who can kill Death? Her mother's hands are too weak. Anna and Sonya are in an asylum. Edward has gone back to Ireland. Vassily has fled. Has Andrey put a curse on her? "Even a murderer may have a last wish, Dr. Mayerberg. Call Andrey!" "I will speak to the Count." She looks after him as he leaves; she wants to read from his walk whether he is going to Vassily.

Strong hands are lifting her out of bed. The bed is bloody. They lay her in a cold bath. The fever comes back, higher than ever. Her father is wielding a whip. She is on horseback with Ivan. His thighs are pressed against her hips from behind. Her father is driving the horse in a circle, faster and faster. Now Vladimir Stahl is cracking the whip. "I know ways that can lead you to paradise."

Two doctors now, conversing in whispers. She can hear every sound. "Are you sure, Doctor?" And Dr. Mayerberg: "No doubt about it. She is pregnant. I would say in the second month." But she bled. No. That was long ago, on her wedding night. "I shall see to it that you are constantly pregnant." A dead woman was going to give birth to a child.

In the cold bath, the fever goes down. "Listen to me, Matilda. Can you hear me?" "I can hear you, Countess." "I have a friend, Andrey Vyrubov. He is a Dominican friar. The Count knows where you can reach him. You must send him a telegram. He must come. My life depends on it." "Certainly, Countess." Nothing is certain. No one believes her. "I swear to you, Matilda, I am in full command of my senses."

She is beside herself. "The bells should stop ringing." The nurse lays cold compresses on her forehead. If there is a God in heaven, he will not let her die before Andrey comes. Through the open door she can hear the doctors. "You should speak to Count Tarnovsky," the professor is saying. "Only a miracle can save her. Vyrubov's presence might be that miracle."

The pain becomes unendurable. She doesn't have the strength to call her nurse. It is dark, and the bells are still ringing.

CHAPTER 10

I

The prior of St. Jacob's Cloister in Paris, where Andrey had taken his vows, was holding a telegram in his hand. "A telegram from Russia," he said. "From Charkov. It is eight days old. A letter preceded it. The telegram is from Count Tarnovsky. Do you know him?"

Andrey said that he did.

"You know that you are not permitted to receive letters?"

Andrey knew.

"The telegram has been forwarded from Rome. It says that Count Tarnovsky's wife is dying. Only your presence, my son, can save her."

He was watching Andrey with his shortsighted eyes. They lay imbedded in a cushion of fat, yet they lacked all good humor; two little pieces of coal. They belied the words "my son." He had said them as a superior officer might say "lieutenant."

Maria was dying. Andrey repeated the thought in his mind. The telegram was one week old; the Church knew no haste. Maria had died for him when the gates of St. Jacob had closed behind him; yet, as happens in the cases where people have meant much to one, he had remained aware of her presence. He could not believe that she was dead.

The Prior offered him a chair. It was an unusual gesture. Behind the jovial exterior of a Balzacian Monk Amador, Prior Jean Senequier hid a hard, unfriendly personality. His decisions were as rare as they were feared. He wanted to see the instruction of Saint Basil—"Any word which is not in accordance with the purpose of God is useless"— obeyed, as he obeyed it.

"I am sure you have not failed to notice," he said, "that the Right Reverend Master General has chosen you for a special mission. It would be too early for you to know about it now. Let it suffice to say that the founding of a Dominican monastery in Russia has been a wish close to the Master General's heart for a long time. There are beginnings: the parish of St. Katharina in St. Petersburg takes care of thirty thousand souls, mainly Poles; there is the little parish of the Catholic Cemetery founded by Father Dominic Lucaszuwicz; and the Polish and French Catholic churches in Moscow. Beginnings, but for ten years now, no progress. The Right Reverend Master General would like you to undertake an informative journey through Russia."

"I would be the first of the younger brothers to leave the monastery."

"Am I to understand that to be an arrogant or a humble statement?"

"As a sign of doubt, Father Prior."

" 'We have gifts differing according to the grace given us, such as ministry, in ministering,' St. Paul wrote to the Romans. The Right Reverend Master General may dispensate even the youngest priest from certain regulations."

Andrey's gaze was drawn to the letter and telegram on the table in front of the Prior; he therefore wasn't looking the Prior in the eye.

"Who is the Countess Tarnovska?" asked the Prior.

"A young woman to whom I was once engaged."

"So it is she."

It no longer surprised Andrey that his superiors knew about his life.

Perhaps they expected too much of him. The inflexible discipline of the cloister knew of no exceptions; still, he had always felt the hand of the Master General over him. Why had just he been chosen for this mission?

"Are you afraid of your encounter with the Countess Tarnovska?"

"I am afraid of encountering the world."

"That will not be spared you."

"Later I would be better prepared for it."

"The decision does not lie with you."

"I know."

"The Right Reverend Master General wants you to start your journey through Russia in Charkov."

The Master General wants to put me to the test, thought Andrey. It was hard for him to suppress a feeling of bitterness. God tolerated temptation so that man might struggle with it in freedom, but it should not open up before one like a trap.

"Do you think the Countess Tarnovska has a special reason for asking you to come?" the Prior inquired.

"I imagine that she wants to ask my forgiveness, although there is no reason for that. I forgave her long ago."

"Are you sure?"

Andrey nodded.

"He who has forgiven has nothing to fear," said the Prior.

"May I say something?"

"That is for you to decide, my son."

"If the Countess Tarnovska has found her way to the Church on her deathbed, then any priest could do for her what I could."

"I said nothing about the Countess Tarnovska having found her way to the Church. The doctors write that they have come to the end of their resources. Their resources are soon ended. They hope to see the Countess' will to live revive through her meeting with you. To nurse the sick and comfort the dying are part of the noblest duties of our Order. The Countess is expecting her second child. I imagine that this was the point that moved the Right Reverend Master General to make his decision."

A sudden wave of heat swept through Andrey. Maria's second child. He had known nothing about the first. Never before had it been made so clear to him how high was the wall separating the monastery from the outside world. Had Maria found happiness? Why did she lack the will to live? For seventeen months now he had occupied himself very little with the joys and suffering of the human creature. Why should Maria be the first suffering human to cross his path? Why did he have to practice mercy where temptation lay waiting?

"I shall go wherever the Order sends me," he said.

"That is a superfluous statement," said the Prior. "I have been watching you, my son. As far as I know, you have obeyed the law faithfully from your first day here, but you seem to cling to it as if you would otherwise fall into an abyss. If truth could take the place of chaos, we would have everlasting bliss already on this earth. But truth stands firm within chaos. Because we do not fear chaos, we also do not fear the world. John à St. Thoma walked among those stricken with the plague. St. Hyacinthe went to live with the heathen. Charles Louis Richard was shot when he tried to resist the prejudices of the Revolution. The world is full of plagues, heathens, and prejudice. In time you shall meet all three. The Countess Tarnovska, by the way, has typhoid fever. You will have the opportunity to prove that, outfitted with the grace of God, you do not fear contagion."

"It is not contagion that I fear, Father Prior."

"The whole world is contagious, my son." He rose. "You leave today. On your trip you can study the Right Reverend Master General's instructions. You will not be coming back here from Russia. Further orders await you in Santa Maria sopra Minerva." A smile, the first Andrey had ever seen on the Prior's lips, was playing about his unnaturally small mouth. "The Right Reverend Master General was so kind as to ask my advice before making his decision. I wrote and told him that I trusted you. My knowledge of human nature is not very great, but I hope you won't disappoint me."

2

Andrey's heart was beating hard as he entered the house above the Lopan. It had been raining for days; he was wet through. The old nurse helped him out of his coat. It was not easy to grow accustomed to the awe inspired by his habit.

"The Countess is expecting you, your Honor," said Matilda. She was not at all sure of the ecclesiastical forms of address. "She is better, God be praised."

Maria was sitting up in bed. She had on a high-buttoned bed jacket.

Her head was covered with a silk scarf, which was fastened under her chin. Her face was so thin, so pale, that Andrey had difficulty recognizing her.

"I won't shake hands with you," she said.

It was still. Even the rain fell softly against the pane, barely making its presence known, a shy guest. The woman in bed and the Dominican priest looked at each other as if each was expecting the other to speak the first words, and was giving the other time to find them.

"I nearly died," she said, as if in apology.

"I am glad you no longer need me," he told her.

Now his heart was beating more quietly. Since he was no longer the same, she was not, either.

"I still need you," she said, "but I am surprised that you came."

"I am traveling on a mission for my Order," he said. "That was why I received permission to see you."

He could read disappointment in her face, and wasn't sure whether he had mentioned his mission on purpose or not.

"When they told me you were coming, I began to feel better right away," she said. She was toying with her scarf. "I had no one to talk to. My mother is too old and too preoccupied with her own ailments."

One day she had been gone, he thought, and he had sat in Nikolay O'Rourke's library. There was no stranger creature on earth than the creature one had been once. And still one could not pretend that nothing had happened. It would have been kinder if he had been the first to mention it, but this was a kindness they didn't teach you in a cloister.

"I have been through hell, Andrey," she said. "Not my illness." She talked about her wedding. One could believe that Hell had swallowed her up on the day she had fled from Otrada. She didn't say it, but she spoke about her marriage as a purgatory in which all her sins had been washed away. Vassily, Vassily's mistresses, Vassily's orgiastic way of life. All a terrible mistake, all a tribute to Andrey.

It was hot in the room. The tiles on the stove were glowing. When he said nothing, she began to speak of Tioka. He listened. Truth had its own vocabulary. The dictionary of truth stood small and thin beside the fat dictionary of mendacity, but light radiated from it. He encouraged her to speak on.

198

"I begged you to come because I was sure that after my death you would have taken the child," she said.

"I couldn't have done that."

"You could have taken him to my mother. No, not to Otrada. You would have found some other solution."

"Perhaps."

"And now I am expecting another child. Will Vassily tear me away from it, too?"

He knew that she was expecting a child, but to hear it from her own lips was hard. In Otrada they had often spoken of the children they would have. She had experienced not only suffering; he had to be cautious. When you met someone out of your past, you became a little the person you had been then.

"Do you want me to speak to Vassily?" he asked.

"It would be useless. He is jealous of you."

Now she is lying, he thought. The word "jealousy" was a bridge to the past. Vassily's jealousy was to flatter him, and flattery was to undermine the ground on which he stood.

"I always meant to write to you," she said. "All through my illness, I feared nothing more than that I might die without having explained to you what happened. But I couldn't write. At first I was ashamed of my happiness, then of my misery. Now you are here, and I still can't talk about it."

"There is no need to," he said.

Did she really need help? It was easy to lend a hand to someone who needed help—but what then? Was it truly God's will that the heart should lie between brain and belly? Was he still afraid of her?

"I am guilty," she said. "You entered a monastery because of me."

Suddenly anger overwhelmed him. She wanted to beg his forgiveness and was ruled by vanity.

"If I entered a monastery because of you," he said, "I would be grateful to you. But it was not because of you."

"Then why was it?"

"Not because of you."

It was still again, only the rain beating more impatiently against the window. Her cheeks had reddened. Her face was small, but its beauty was all the more pronounced, as if everything superfluous had been wiped away, leaving only the purity of her features. He recognized her. He had to avoid remembrances. The wish to experience the past was stronger than the longing for the future. Everyone loved the impossible.

"Am I to blame for my misfortune?" she asked. "Only you can tell me."

"I don't know enough about you."

"Sometimes I don't behave as I want to."

"Sometimes all people don't behave as they want to."

"Sometimes I am obsessed by the compulsion to cause pain."

She drew the bedclothes over her shoulders as if she were cold. She was begging for compassion. He couldn't give it to her because he had the feeling that she was yearning, not for compassion, but for his compassion.

"I am very unhappy, Andrey," she said.

"You are not yet twenty," he told her.

"I am very old."

"That's what one thinks when one is twenty."

"We would have been happy together."

"No, we would not have been happy together."

"Why?"

"I have become happy, and that is proof that we would not have been happy together."

"I don't believe you," she said.

She looked at him challengingly, and seemed a little astonished, as if she had only just discovered that he was wearing the habit of his Order. Her eyes, clear and blue, as if never dimmed by fever, undid the cingulum, took off his cowl, his scapular, not lasciviously—a hand untying a carnival mask.

"You can't be more than a novice," she said. "You haven't become one with the cloister yet." He was young and handsome, she went on, he would not be able to renounce life. "You are strong, and that is why I love you." The words flowed from her lips as if she, the stronger, the speaker, were saying them in his name too. "You didn't whine like the rest; you didn't choose flight into death." He had become a priest because he had wanted to get over it, but one could be a good Christian without burying oneself alive. She could still remember every word he had said. "Vassily, he is the world you hated. No, don't tell me that you have stopped loving me. I know better. stole these years from you, and I have atoned for it." Arrogantly, sh confessed. "I shall give you everything I took from you." Thousands before him had put their vows aside after a longer period in the priesthood. She spoke with increasing vivacity, like someone speaking louder and louder because he can hear no echo.

He let her talk, and would have let her go on even if she had said more. Suddenly he understood why their conversation was like the meeting of two people who pass each other by—friends once, strangers now—a friendly greeting, yet both busy with their own preoccupation. Later they would think, I should have stopped, asked questions, answered questions, we should have looked up at the sky together. Where did the other come from? Where was he going? Perhaps he was waiting for a gesture, perhaps he needed it. Too late. He understood why their conversation had been so hollow, but her he did not understand. If she had received him naked, if she had offered herself . . . This woman, sick and pregnant, thought that it sufficed to confess her defeat, and he would throw his soul overboard and follow her. Power was the Devil's original gift. Whoever possessed it was possessed by it. Was Maria possessed? Or was the Devil still perched on the other side of the bed to alienate her soul from him? Was she evil personified, or the personified example of his mission? "You will never stop asking yourself who she is," his father had said.

She lay back in her cushions, eyes closed, lips parted, as if expecting kiss or verdict.

Andrey was overcome by a feeling of shame. "I don't love you any more," he wanted to cry, as one cried out "I love you." He distrusted himself, unsure whether he had triumphed over himself or only over her. In five or ten years, the love he was praying for would have liberated him from the love he was fleeing.

"You are not yet twenty," he said, "and you have Tioka. Soon you will have a second child. Don't let yourself be parted from them. They will go on ahead of you. Misfortune is like a lowered torch with the flame burning upward. Happiness is a boast. I was boasting when I said I was happy. Forgive me. I should have spoken of peace. I shall pray that you may find it, as I have found it."

She sat up, her lips narrowed. "You damnable monk!" she said, and tore the silk scarf from her head.

She was bald. Her face was no longer beautiful. It was the face of sick child, a pitiful street urchin. She was no longer beautiful nor evil, not seductive nor repulsive—she was only bald.

"I curse the day I asked you to come," she said, the tears choking her. The rain prickled against the pane; an angry rain. He rose.

"Your hair will grow again," he said, and passed his hand gently across her head.

3

Andrey traveled through Russia for four weeks. Since there were no Dominican cloisters, he stayed in monasteries of other Orders. He visited Moscow, Poltava, Yekaterinoslav, and Kiev. In Kiev, he stood in front of the house of his childhood. A general lived there now; his children were having a snowball fight in the garden. Old houses knew no loyalty.

Shortly before Christmas he arrived in St. Petersburg, his last stop. He was received at the Alexander Nevskilavra Cloister. For four days he worked on his report, tearing up what he had written the day before. Perhaps the Master General hadn't done such a good thing in sending a Russian to Russia. Andrey was taken by that patriotic sickness that saw all things as through a magnifying glass. A peasant's tale on the train; the numbers of beggars on the Kressnaya Square in Moscow; a Greek Orthodox priest lying in the snow, cooling off his drunkenness; the uncared-for graves in a cemetery; laughter, hunger, birth, death, gluttony—everything seemed to have importance, which he countered with skepticism. He reduced twenty pages to ten; in the end there were only three. At last he was satisfied.

That evening he took his letter to the post office at the Warsaw Station, in the south of the city. The streets lay under a thick covering of snow. The sleighs glided across them as soundlessly as if they were being drawn by fleet, light-footed deer. Voices singing in harmony issued from the churches. Andrey stood still because he thought he could hear organ music.

After not having thought of her for days, he thought again of Maria. Why hadn't he wanted to think of her? People knew so little about love that they believed all evil disappeared when one turned away from evil. God hated evil and loved the sinner. Was this the borderline that the foot of man might not overstep? The way to truth was full of mantraps, yet just those who did not dare to walk it stumbled. He was ashamed of his feeling of triumph after his visit to Maria. One thanked God for having been spared in a thunderstorm

202

but should one not rather think of those who were still out in it? Had Maria really stretched out her hand to him to seduce him or perhaps, after all, so that he might grasp it and save her? He who demanded that the beggar's hand be clean never helped a beggar. The doctor who was afraid of contagion was a wretch; he who was afraid of having to suffer with his fellow men couldn't help them. Hadn't she said that she was obsessed with the compulsion to inflict pain? If she had to inflict pain, then she suffered pain, was therefore sick. Why did she want to inflict pain? She had always thirsted for passion; perhaps there was a mysterious connection between pain and passion. A virgin received the first evidence of love with pain; painful jealousy united two lovers more strongly; people spoke of the sweetness of reconciliation when what they meant was the bitterness of the quarrel. One destroyed the personality of the other person in the name of harmony. Had Maria answered for him the riddle of pure and sexual love? Was pure love nothing more than love without pain, and sexual life nothing but love sullied by pain? But if this were so, then sexual love was unconditionally impure. Or was it purified when it freed itself from the giving and receiving of pain?

Occupied with these thoughts, Andrey reached the Fontaka and was about to cross the Ismailov Bridge when he heard someone calling his name. A young man in a fur-lined overcoat, a fur cap on his head, caught up with him. By the light of a lamp, Andrey recognized Nikolay O'Rourke.

"If I believed in miracles," he cried, "then I would believe this to be a miracle. What luck to meet you, Andrey Antonovich!"

They shook hands, but Nikolay didn't say why he found their meeting so fortunate. "You can't surprise me," he said, "because I've just come from Kiev where they told me all about you."

"Then you know about Maria's illness."

"I heard about it only after her recovery."

"Did you visit her?"

"Charkov is dangerous territory for me. I have to be careful. Twenty-four hours in Kiev, and only because I had to. The police happily make up for their lack of consideration by their stupidity."

"Are you still a conspirator, Nikolay Nikolaevich?"

"You ask me that as if you wanted to know if I still sold grain. Is it really two years since I visited you? What excited us both then must seem negligible to you today."

"I'm afraid since I've been in Russia it doesn't strike me as at all negligible."

"How long are you staying?"

"I am leaving the day after tomorrow."

Nikolay took his arm. His handsome face, more like Maria's than ever, darkened. "Come with me. I want to exploit this miracle as long as it lasts."

They crossed the bridge. It was snowing, big white flakes. As was often the case in St. Petersburg at this time of the year, it was only a few degrees below freezing. There was something warm and comforting about the picture the city presented at eventide, with the sleighs gliding by as if life were being played out on a white carpet in a nursery, as if all life were a miniature imitation of life.

"Sergey is in St. Petersburg," Nikolay said quickly. "I was on my way to him. He is in a hostel, only a few streets away. It was going to be a hopeless undertaking, a last effort; now, since you can undertake it in my place, it doesn't look so hopeless to me any more." He leaned closer to Andrey. "The Czar is to be assassinated. Not that I am against it. Since the young monarch gave his blessing to the murder of the strikers at Yaroslav, all hope for an improvement is lost. He has made it quite clear that he intends to be just as autocratic as his unforgettable father. Unforgettable is right! The doom that hangs over Czar Nicholas takes its prescribed course. But that's just the point. Certain plans, which I can't discuss, need more time. An assassination, even were it to succeed, would throw the revolution back years. There are moments when an act of terror can be the worst enemy of revolution." He wouldn't let Andrey go, led him into a dark side street. "I don't ask you to agree with me. I am not a good Christian. It's all the same to me why the good thing happens. If you want to prevent the assassination because the life of the Czar means something to you, if you want to prevent it because Sergey will most likely die because of it, it's all the same to me. Just talk to him! Convince him. That's all that matters."

He stopped in front of a narrow two-story house, the door of which stood open in spite of the cold. A horrible smell, as if coming from a goat stall, issued from it.

"You'll find Sergey in the cellar," said Nikolay. "It's called the 'Etappe.'" He looked up. "Upstairs are 'Siberia' and the 'Bagno.' That's where the criminals live, if you want to call it that." He took a small purse with some coins in it out of his pocket. "Give him that. He doesn't have a kopek."

4

As Andrey descended the cellar stairs to the 'Etappe,' the stench became unbearable. It was as if he were wading through excrement. To the right and left of him people were sitting on the steps. Their heads had fallen forward between their knees; others slept with their heads on the stone floor. Snow, dragged in on dirty soles, had melted and was running down the sleeping men's necks.

On one of the last steps, Andrey stopped. A wooden door, once the door of a stall, stood open, and he could see the entire cellar. In the steam from wet clothing and the smoke of a petroleum lamp, Andrey could not find his friend. Dozens of cots, wooden boards on posts, stood lengthwise and crosswise. On each cot lay two or three people, men and women. Many had squeezed in under these ramshackle beds; all you could see were legs, heads, arms, like unburied bodies. Here and there a table; men bent over paper, writing. At Andrey's feet, a man on a low stool. With nimble fingers he was taking the fur lining out of a coat, and sewing the coat together again. Half a dozen people, among them two dirty women, had formed a semicircle around him and were egging him on with jokes, nudging, cursing. His needle flew faster and faster. At the other end of the room, two women were tugging at a howling child. A blond boy sat cross-legged on the floor. He was rocking an empty brandy bottle in his arms, singing it to sleep with a lullaby. Except for the people around the tailor, no one was paying attention to anyone else. Each drank, cursed, sang, or snored away his misery. Here misery was like a cratered landscape—torn-away islands, seemingly close, actually separated by abysses.

A fat man, with an apron stiff with dirt, came up to Andrey. "What do you want, Brother? To beg? You've come to the wrong place."

"I am looking for a friend."

"You won't find him here."

"His name is Sergey Burintzev."

"Nobody asks for anyone by name here. Only the police. Are you working for the police, Brother?"

The word "police" caused the people around the tailor to prick up their ears. They moved closer to each other. The tailor's hands were still. A woman shoved the fur under a chair.

"Is this the only room in the cellar?" Andrey asked, stepping closer.

An old woman barred his way. She was holding a pair of torn children's shoes in her hand. A smell of vodka streamed out of her toothless mouth.

"He has nothing to do with the police," she said. "He wants to teach us to pray." The laughter of the others encouraged her. "Do you know why we don't pray, Brother?"

"Why, little mother?"

"Because there is no God."

One of the men stepped forward. Lean, pale, with kindly eyes, long silky hair, and a short beard, he looked like Christ on a lithograph. "Right!" he said, and an ugly laugh distorted his beautiful face. "She's right. And what is the conclusion? If I go into a shop today and say I am the servant of His Excellency Count so-and-so, he has sent me, and they are please to give me a bottle of vodka and some white bread and a sausage that long, and they're please to write down what it costs, and my master, His Excellency Count so-and-so will pay for everything, and then, gentlemen, there is no Count so-and-so, he doesn't exist—what is the conclusion? The conclusion is that I only dressed up as a servant, and that I am a swindler, and that I wanted to get bread and sausage and vodka out of the merchant, and the conclusion is that the bill will never be paid. But, friends, you are much too stupid to understand what I am trying to say, and the conclusion of that is—I must explain it to you. This man here, now, is such a messenger dressed up as the servant of a master who does not exist, and that's why his bill will never be paid; and you have given away all sorts of things for a salvation you're never going to see—bread, perhaps, or prayer. And what is the conclusion? That you would do well to grab this false servant by the collar and throw him down the stairs—that is to say, up the stairs, for there is nothing lower than this place here; unfortunately, therefore, no one can be thrown down from it."

The speaker received unanimous applause. The people sitting on the stairs applauded, the writers at the tables got up, a few heads looked out from under the cots, even some of those snoring stirred in their sleep. Only the boy with the brandy bottle went on singing his lullaby.

"Brother, get out!" said the man with the apron.

At that moment, two strong arms made way for the body behind them, and Sergey Burintzev stood before Andrey. He had been in one of the next rooms, and the noise had brought him here. He stretched out his hand to Andrey, led him through the room, and pushed open a wooden door. No one stopped him. The tailor picked up the coat again, the men went on writing, the sleepers lay back and snored.

Andrey and Sergey sat down on the wooden board that served Sergey as a bed. "Nikolay told me about you," said Sergey. "I wasn't surprised."

He asked Andrey about his Order and why he was in Russia, but seemed to only half listen to Andrey's replies. "I met Nikolay. He told me where to find you," Andrey said.

They looked at each other, filled now with sincere curiosity. Sergey had changed very little. He was smooth-shaven; his short hair above his too-wide forehead was tidily brushed; he had on a threadbare but clean shirt. Andrey smiled, and because he felt he had to explain why he was smiling, he said, "You look just as strange here as I do, perhaps stranger."

Sergey nodded. "The tailor next door works all night to change the coats that thieves bring him; next day he sells them to a shady dealer. The men who are writing are copying plays, fifty kopeks an act. The children don't belong to the women; they borrow them for twenty-five kopeks apiece. When it is dark, that woman over there sleeps with anyone who comes near her, sometimes ten a night. They would be people for you. The only thing one could save is their souls, and I'm not interested in that."

"I know you too well."

"Our rulers degrade man to the status of an animal; then when he behaves like an animal, they say, 'Look, he is an animal, and deserves nothing better.' Thus the victim becomes a justification for his own disaster. Do you know what happened at the coronation festival?"

"I heard something about it."

"Three hundred thousand people assembled, because they had been told every visitor would receive a mug with the Emperor's coat of arms on it, and a ruble. Coat of arms and a ruble! Three hundred thousand animals. When they began to hand out the mugs, three thousand men, women, and children were pushed into a ditch and trampled on. The papers admitted to one thousand five hundred and twenty-seven dead. There were three thousand. The Czar? They didn't want to upset him.

That night he went to the ball at the French Embassy. Everyone there knew what had happened; no one dared mention it to him. Three thousand dead. And they danced. And why the consideration? Nothing was to dim our Little Father's joy."

"May I speak openly here?"

Sergey looked about him. "We know the informers. The others won't hear. These animals aren't interested in anything any more."

Andrey repeated what Nikolay had told him. "What good would it do to murder the Czar?" he said in conclusion. "The three thousand dead would not be resurrected."

"It is a question of the resurrection of Russia, Andrey."

"Resurrection by murder?"

"Someone has to ignite the powder keg."

"And create new chaos?"

Sergey looked about him. "Would you call this order?"

"It is the human chaos in which divine order originates."

"I would be satisfied with human order."

"There is no such thing. For thousands of years, humans have been fighting chaos, but their own ideas on order are so chaotic that they only sink down further into chaos."

"In a minute you'll be talking about love, and that's hopeless, because everyone sees something different under that heading. Christian love has nothing in common with the love of which I speak. The postulate of Christian love is an expiatory death."

"The expiatory death of Christ. Religion demands no expiatory death."

"But it demands tolerance. The Church has misunderstood Christ. When He came, the world had ceased to need a new religion long ago. Buddhism, Shinto, Jainism, Brahmans, and Jews had already recognized everything that Christians preach today as their dogma. But Christ was the great translator. He was a political man. By that I mean he wanted to change conditions. And what did the Church do? The Church took the love he had translated into action and translated it back into an incomprehensible love. *In principio erat verbum, et verbum erat apud deum, et deus erat verbum.* But for you, the word is no longer according to God, the word has become God, the ultimate thing. Christ suffered so that you might become intolerant of suffering, but you have interpreted it as if suffering were the ultimate thing. For you it is always Good Friday, and you pay only lip service to Easter."

"You are right," said Andrey. "Everyone understands something else under love."

"The inquisitors were probably also convinced they were acting out of love."

"They were probably just as sure they were right as you are. The Inquisition was the tragedy of man convinced he was right. Absolute assurance leads to inquisition."

"Aren't you absolutely sure you are right?"

"I am sure that only love can lead us out of chaos."

"The comfortable path of religion on which one can travel without ever getting anywhere."

"What you say—that is chaos, where people act like a drowning man who won't grasp the rope thrown him because he thinks that's too simple a form of salvation. The storm should abate, or at least a steamship should pick him up. So he drowns."

"Are you throwing me a rope?"

"I didn't come to convert you. I came to convince you that political murder is murder, too."

"Love thy mass murderer as thyself."

"No. Fight him in the framework of order."

"And where has order led us?"

"I don't know. Because until now, one condition of disorder has relieved another."

"The Czar has been condemned to death. That is the future order."

"Condemned by whom?"

"By our tribunal."

"Who appointed it?"

"The people who are mute."

"And why must you be the executioner?"

"We drew lots."

"So you draw lots for who is to be a murderer."

"The mind determines the deed. The hand that carries it out is unimportant." He touched Andrey's arm. "I'm glad I saw you, but I think you should leave. There will be inquiries. It won't be difficult to find the Dominican who visited the murderer in the hostel."

A head appeared from under Sergey's bed as if bodiless, the unkempt head of a vagabond. "Will you stop talking!" said the head. "Your place is down here."

Sergey turned to Andrey. "He's right. I'm supposed to lie underneath half the night. On the floor costs only five kopeks."

Andrey gave him the purse. "From Nikolay."

Sergey laughed. "Stay down there, little father. I'll pay your five kopeks."

A hand, outstretched for the money, and the head disappeared under the bed again. Then Andrey saw a young man come in and walk over to Sergey; but when he saw the Dominican, he stopped abruptly in astonishment.

"Don't worry," said Sergey, "you can speak in front of him."

"Alexander Ilyich has been arrested." The young man spoke hesitantly. "In the editorial offices of the *Rabotskeye Dyelo,* just as the first edition was coming out."

Sergey jumped to his feet.

"I am to tell you that our plans have been changed." Now the youth was whispering. "You have to get out as fast as you can."

"How could it have happened?"

"As it always happens."

"Betrayed?"

The young man shrugged.

Sergey looked at Andrey. Suddenly he had grown thinner and older "God is on the side of the strong battalions," he said. "Alexander Ilyich Ulyanov was our great hope."

"Who is Ulyanov?"

"We call him Lenin." He smiled bitterly. "He is the great translator."

The three stood in the middle of the cellar. "Lights out!" the whore on the next bed cried. She took off her shirt. The men who were transcribing plays looked up; one of the sleepers spoke aloud in his dream. The unkempt head looked out from under the bed again. The man with the apron appeared in the doorway. "Lights out!" he cried Oil lamps went out here and there; only two were still burning.

"Now it is all over," said Sergey. "Well prayed, Andrey!"

Andrey kissed his friend on both cheeks; then he groped his wa through the dark room.

CHAPTER 11

I

To everyone who knew Maria Tarnovska, it seemed that in June of the year 1896, after the birth of her daughter, Tania—a difficult birth, complicated by blood poisoning—her life changed radically.

Vassily's father had died a few weeks before of internal hemorrhages, after being thrown from his horse. He left only a small estate in cash, but Vassily proceeded to convert everything else into cash also, and to spend every ruble of it as pleasantly as possible. He rented a small *palais* in Lubyanskaya Square in Moscow, and bought a *dacha* in Kossino, not far from the city, on White Lake. His parties soon won for him the approbation of a society that could never be so accustomed to luxury that it was not hungry to be entertained even more luxuriously. The birth of a daughter had put him into a rare good mood. He saw a good omen in it. At last fate was beginning to take his wishes into account. He had Tioka brought from Charkov, partly to placate Maria, partly so that the boy might amuse his little sister, perhaps also because he no longer felt that his peace was threatened. He permitted Maria to engage a personal maid, and she hired an efficient, self-effacing Swiss woman, Elise Perrier.

Vassily made many new friends, and Maria lost none of her old ones. Three or four months after her recuperation, the precaution of her doctors, who had insisted that her head be completely shaved, turned out to be correct—her thick, dark blond hair was again her crowning glory. She was more beautiful than ever, said Vladimir Stahl, who had moved to Moscow; said Yuri Tolstoy, who spent their first summer with them in Kossino. The banker Maximov and their neighbor, Count Sheremetyev, also admired her beauty. Tioka, straw blond and blue-eyed, grew healthy and—so it seemed to his mother—extraordinarily intelligent, while Tania, who was the image of her father, kept the whole household in a state of suspense.

Maria's life was like the portrait of a painter of society women, rendering only a flattering semblance and betraying nothing of what is going on inside. The luxury that Vassily was now able to offer his wife had freed him from any feeling of guilt and, with that, of all consideration. He didn't try to hide the fact any longer that he was bored with Maria, and since he had always fled boredom like the plague, he now fled from her. Anything they had to say to each other never went beyond trivialities; she never found out anything about Vassily's plans unless a third person was present. Like a naughty child, he had his "no"-days; that was what he called them himself. He came to Maria's bedroom when his mistress happened to be away, or so drunk that he could find the bed only. His conception of marriage as a mixture of hygiene and bordello challenged Maria to fight back, but the indifference of her adversary lamed her. If she refused Vassily, he yawned his acceptance of her refusal; when she tried to arouse his jealousy, the most she got out of him was a reprimand; when she tried to practice the arts of love with him, he told her that whores were better at it. She no longer had any power that she might have misused.

The more she felt humiliated, the more often she thought of how Andrey had humiliated her. What she had dared to say to him suddenly seemed absolute madness. She didn't know whether she had seriously intended to tempt Andrey to betray the Church, or whether she had acted like her father, who used to drive the length and breadth of his estates only to convince himself of the extent of his power. Or had she let herself be driven by a sensuousness that had reached its apex during her conversation with Andrey, as during the wanton confessions of her childhood? Was confession like a mirror from which an enchantment issued forth when she stood before it naked? Was Andrey a colossal hypocrite, or was he as chaste as he pretended to be? Hypocrites and purists had the same effect on her— she had to destroy them as a child does its doll when it wants to see what is inside.

Her defeat absorbed her more than her motives. That Peter had been capable of killing himself because of her sometimes filled her with satisfaction, but then, right away, she would ask herself if she wasn't loved only by men who suffered for her. Perhaps she was loved only by the dead. She didn't care whether Vassily still meant something to her or not, since she could never be happy in the arms of another until she had subjugated Vassily. She could recover only through his misery.

2

One night, in Kossino, Vassily told her that he was going to fight a duel next morning. Their guests had left. It was a hot July night. The stars were little candles in the sky; the land was swathed in black velvet; a sweetness lay in the air as on nights in which one loved or died. They were sitting beside the water. He told her that he would die. He spoke in short, terse sentences, like a hero bidding his wife farewell: heroic lines that were supposed to pacify and at the same time show that the hero was a hero.

She sensed that he was afraid, and that made her happy. She had thought he was indolent, and although she knew that attributes went in pairs—parsimony with cowardice, gentleness with courage, ambition with envy—she had never thought that indolence and cravenness went together. Vassily didn't go to war, and in duels few fell. He was afraid.

At first it never occurred to her that he might be dueling because of her. Not until he told her, reluctantly, that his opponent was Yuri Tolstoy did she recall that Yuri had not been in Kossino for a long time. She reflected whether she should tell Vassily that she had not deceived him. What was more ridiculous: a man who had been deceived, or a man who fought a duel in a mistaken cause?

"I shall speak to him," she said. "You don't have to fight him."

He said, "My honor is at stake."

She didn't believe in his honor; still less in that an idiotic duel could restore it. Yet a pleasant feeling of excitement had crept in upon her. The conventions in which George Sand had ceased to believe had their good points—a man had to fight a duel over his wife even when he didn't love her. Perhaps Yuri, even if he didn't kill Vassily, might injure him. He wouldn't be suffering through her, but at least because of her.

"I must get up early," he said.

"Pistols?"

"Pistols."

213

They walked toward the house. He put his arm around her hips. While people lay dreaming, candles glowed in the sky, crickets chirped, the water lapped at the shore. She caught herself envisioning herself in widow's weeds at his grave. His death would rob her of victory, but it wasn't really important whether one had been victorious over the dead or not. Her excitement grew. Now she could recall quite clearly how rarely he had given her complete satisfaction. When he had lured her to Yuri's *dacha,* before their marriage; when she had locked her door after the evening at the Grand Duke's palace; when he had carried her into her bedroom after the quarrel over Andrey; once, after Peter's death. Without his co-operation, against his will. A miserable record. And always when he had been humiliated. Through her thin summer dress she could feel that his hand was cold. Like a dead man's. He was trembling. Perhaps Death was a whore who taught the dying the meaning of passion. Tonight they would love each other. Next morning she would dismiss him from her bed, perhaps to his death.

3

Six o'clock. The morning heralded a hot day. The sky was innocent of the past night, innocent of the coming day. The twittering of the birds seemed intended to awaken the bushes. Maria stood at the window. A carriage drew up, closed, wintry. Two men got out of it— Count Sheremetyev and a hussar. She thought she recognized Count Alexis Bozevsky, "the handsomest officer in His Imperial Majesty's Guard," as they called him in St. Petersburg, where he had often ridden behind her carriage. Sheremetyev entered the house and came out again almost immediately with Vassily. The black carriage, the men in their black frock coats, black gloves, black patent-leather shoes, top hats, brought back her childhood. In a black carriage, dressed ceremoniously like this, Terrible O'Rourke had driven twice a month to the cemetery to visit his wife, the dead Princess. Maria was filled with mistrust. It was a hoax; the men were dressed-up actors. The duel would never take place; Yuri and Vassily would celebrate the farce with *blini,* caviar, and champagne. She had wanted to make Vassily look ridiculous, and she was the one who was being made to look ridiculous. He would never know that she had been happy only with death.

She tied a scarf around her head, left the house, followed the carriage tracks. It was cool; the bushes were white with dust. She took a side path. Her scarf caught in some branches. A bearded head hung among the branches. She stopped, stood still. It was the head of a coachman, sitting high up on the box; that was why he looked as if his head were hanging in the branches. She ducked. A branch snapped. She sat down under one of the bushes.

Between two white birches, she could see the entire clearing. Eight men in two groups. Sheremetyev, Vassily, the officer, and Dr. Purishkyevich, the village doctor. She had seen him last when Tioka had had a sore throat. He was in costume, too. The other group—Yuri, Count Sierakovsky, two men she didn't know. The three men with Yuri wore pearl-gray overcoats with black velvet collars. The groups approached each other. Vassily and Yuri's heads bent over a flat box, their top hats almost touching. Maria nearly choked as she tried to restrain her laughter. Were all men as grotesque as this when they thought no woman was watching them? A chivalresque duel? Dressed up like the attendants at a funeral parlor, clowns in frock coats. How stupid they must be to take themselves so seriously!

One of the men led Yuri and Vassily out of the shade of the trees into the clearing. He paced off the distance between the two men. Maria thought she had never seen a more ridiculous little man. He was thin as a rail and tiny; his top hat slid off his forehead—as he paced off the distance, he had to adjust it twice—a little boy dressed up in his father's clothes. Did little steps count the same as big ones? Then they would stand facing each other at very close range. From where she lay hidden, she could not see Vassily's face. Yuri's was calm. The Lord had blessed him with stupidity. He would aim calmly and hit the mark surely. He had not wanted to duel Vassily, but she was grateful to him. If only she could see Vassily. When he dissolved inside her, without any concern for her, there was triumph in his eyes; his teeth glittered, his chest expanded. What had he done that any rutting stallion could not have done better? He was proud of his sex. Only men were proud of their sex. Women knew there could be no sex without the other. To see his face mortified and recall his face victorious; then, when he was lying over her again, to recall his face mortified.

Yuri hefted the pistol in his hand. A dancing bear with a pistol in his paw. The others stood aside. Dr. Purishkyevich. "A-a-a— open your mouth, Tioka. A-a-a— that's a good boy!" Again, repressed laughter shook her. A light wind had sprung up; it rustled in the leaves as on a keyboard. The heads of both coachmen hung in the trees. If they had known that the Countess was watching them, they too would have laughed.

"Gentlemen, are you ready?" the little man asked, shoving his top hat into position.

To Maria it was as if she were standing in front of a picture, the sun behind her so that her shadow fell on the picture, her head gigantic. She was the only one who was living, the others were diminutive figures in a painting. It was not a painting; it was a caricature.

"One!" the little man counted, and the two men put their left hands behind their backs and lifted the right with the pistol. They were pretending to be grown up.

Otrada, thought Maria, and could smell the estate—an early spring day, dust, modest blossoms, the smell of laundry, hammering from the smithy, one of the maids singing. Andrey had stood at her side. They had shot a horse.

"Two!" the little man counted.

Why had she thought that only one of the two men would die? Both of them would. The horse had lain there with stupid eyes wide open; the blood had trickled out of its forehead between the eyes. Her knees were trembling; a voluptuous feeling crept from her knees up her thighs to the pit of her stomach.

"Three!"

One single sound, like the plop of a stone in water, and a little flame of light shot out of each pistol. Both men, standing upright, let the hand that held the pistol sink. Not a drop of blood. Maria was seized with the same disappointment as when the vitality of the man in her body ran out inside her and she herself felt nothing. Ecstasy deceived, an ending that lay somewhere beyond her reach; death without grandeur; unquenched thirst at a table of carousers; fury with no object; humus, the organic portion, abused; a humiliating flickering. . . . All of a sudden the clearing was filled with motion, the wood with voices. The heads of the coachmen disappeared from the trees. Maria got up.

At the breakfast table, which had been set in the garden, Count Sheremetyev sat on her left, Count Bozevsky on her right. Vassily was in high spirits. He had changed. In a light suit he looked very young beside the wintry figure of the village doctor and Sheremetyev and the tiny man who had conducted the duel, a Baron Protopopov. And there were two other men, whom Vassily must have picked up on the way home. The two duelists had parted on a conciliatory note. Vassily, smiling, said that he should have invited Yuri. Like a comedian, who after a successful premier can't hear enough about his performance, he constantly brought the conversation around to it. Maria was ashamed as one can be ashamed only for others. Vassily's seconds knew that mostly cowards liked to talk about the dangers they had escaped. When she looked at Vassily, he looked at his guests, as if her presence was an embarrassment to him; and their guests could sense it.

Alexis Bozevsky said very little. Maria got the impression that he too was ashamed, but she couldn't tell whether it was because of Vassily's bombast, or because of the farce of the duel, or because the woman for whom the duel had been fought was present. Once he leaned forward and said to Maria, "The German philosopher Schopenhauer considers duels a foolish superstition, and knightly honor a childish obligation to fight like gladiators over trifles." She had never heard of Schopenhauer, but her shame united her with Bozevsky. If only he had said it aloud! She would have applauded; Vassily would have protested, insulted his guest. Bozevsky wouldn't shoot in the air like Yuri Tolstoy.

The guests got ready to leave. Vassily insisted on showing them the park. He didn't want to part from the witnesses of his heroism or his happiness. Or perhaps he didn't want to be alone with Maria. The little black group gyrated around Vassily, as if trying to avoid Maria. Neither Sheremetyev nor Dr. Purishkyevich loved Vassily. Did his friends blame her for the fact that Vassily had risked his life? They hurried past her. When she addressed Sheremetyev, he pretended not to hear.

Only Bozevsky was still on her side. He was a good two heads taller than she, and his beauty was provocative rather than attractive.

Men would naturally sense an adversary in such a man, and for a woman, too, his beauty was embarrassing, as if he had stolen something that was theirs by right, and they had thereby forfeited a possession. His exterior perfection, like all perfection, was not only embarrassing, it was enigmatic. A man who looked like that could only be totally ruined or totally chaste, infinitely vain or touchingly guileless, mirror or distortion of his appearance.

"Why don't you go with the others?" she asked.

"I would rather stay with you, Countess."

She laughed. "You at least don't think I have an infectious disease."

They passed a bed of strawberries, and she leaned down to pick one. As she straightened up again, she saw astonishment and pity in Bozevsky's eyes. She put the strawberry in his mouth; her fingers touched his lips. He took her hand and pressed it to his mouth.

"It was unbearable," he said.

"The duel or the breakfast?"

"Your humiliation."

"I don't care what these people think."

"I must tell you," he said hesitantly, "because Vassily allows you to appear ridiculous. . . ."

"I don't understand."

"And I don't understand you," he said. "Do you really think Vassily fought because of you?"

The morning sun was burning down on the orchard, but Maria's blood ran cold. "I want you to tell me the truth," she said.

"They fought over Olga Kralberg. Yuri has fallen in love with her. He wants to marry her. One night the two got into a brawl with Vassily in the Strelna." He stretched out a hand toward Maria.

Don't faint, she was telling herself. Fainting was as old-fashioned as dueling. George Sand would not have fainted. Don't make a scene; don't make a fool of yourself. What had Peter said? "He raped you. It couldn't have happened otherwise." Last night—it couldn't have happened otherwise.

5

She didn't mention a word to the effect that she knew of Vassily's deceit. With almost ascetic devotion, like an artist living for the completion and perfection of his masterpiece, she lived for her hatred.

Alexis Bozevsky rented a *dacha* in Kusskova and rode over to Kossino every day. When she saw him appear between the trees of the woodland path, her heart beat faster. He was not in uniform. His blond hair fluttered in the wind; his sunburned neck gleamed above his white shirt. She no longer wondered what his beauty could be hiding—there was nothing hidden in Alexis. She no longer looked for flaws—he couldn't possibly be equipped with further virtues, but she did begin to think that fate had sent her a superhuman creature. When he played the piano, Tioka, leaning against the instrument, listened to him; even Tania was silenced. The books he brought to Maria were difficult reading, but he never tired of explaining them. The servants became his natural allies. Vassily didn't dare forbid him to come. Alexis spoke of his love for her with a patient passion, as if he had possessed her long ago. He was not like Andrey, who had seemed bodiless, nor like Vassily, who had no soul. He was like no one else.

She did not mistrust his love; she mistrusted her own. Hadn't her love for Alexis grown out of her hatred for Vassily? Wasn't it blossoming out of evil ground? Shouldn't she rather protect him from her love? How could she love anyone without causing him pain and without receiving suffering in return?

At the beginning of August, Vassily gave one of the parties he had enjoyed giving ever since the duel. As if he were grateful to the weapons that had spared him, as if he wanted to make up for the dexterity he had lacked then, he bought pistols, revolvers, rifles, ammunition. By day he shot at targets and wine bottles, at night at candles.

That night there were twelve guests, among them Alexis, Count Sheremetyev, Vladimir Stahl, the banker Maximov, old Count Gregorievsky, with his young American wife, who had apparently taken Olga Kralberg's place in Vassily's affections. The night was warm; the air heavy with the scent of acacias. The gypsies Vladimir had sent to Moscow for were playing. Eleanor Gregorievskaya had concocted a new drink, a cocktail called "mint julep," out of ice-cooled vodka and mint. The candles were burning in bottles on the park wall.

Vassily handed Maria a Flobert rifle. "I don't want to shoot," she said.

"Don't be silly, or I'll put an apple on your head and play William Tell." He was drunk.

Eleanor Gregorievskaya, at Maria's side, was shooting with a Browning. The sound of glass breaking; one candle went out.

Alexis was standing behind Maria. "I'll put my hand over your ears," he said, and did so. Under his hands, her body awoke as if she had felt them long ago; on her ears, her breasts, her knees, her body. To hear nothing, to see nothing! She wished he had covered her eyes. "Not so hard," she said. The tender pressure of his hands lessened. "The third candle from the left!" Vassily cried. "I love you," Alexis whispered. She pressed the trigger, felt a blow against her shoulder, and thought she had hurt herself. It was only the recoil of the rifle. Everyone applauded. The candle had gone out, third from the right. That's the way to snuff out the life of a man, she thought. Ears shut, eyes closed. Ten or twelve candles were already out; ten or twelve men dead in the dark. Ten or twelve were still flickering. "I love you," whispered Alexis. "Put your hands over my ears." She narrowed her eyes; she could feel the pressure of her gritted teeth. Sheremetyev was chasing the gypsies in a circle. They didn't stop playing. A second candle, a third, a fourth. Eleanor Gregorievskaya was shooting, so were Stahl, Maximov. A bullet ricocheted against the wall. Alexandra Maximova screamed. The gypsies played louder. Two men were dancing the tarantella.

Suddenly Vassily was at her side, in his hand an apple. He grasped her arm and dragged her across the lawn. "Now I'm going to shoot the apple off your head!" They were standing among the broken bottles. He forced her to her knees, stood the apple on her head, ran back to the others. She sat down. The grass was covered with shards. Her knees were cut. The apple had fallen from her head. She took one of the candles out of its bottle, held it over her head; the hot wax dripped down her fingers. Vassily would shoot. He wouldn't hit the candle, he would hit her. She would die and he would go to prison. A hot feeling of bliss surged through her. Candles burning to her right and left. She was on her bier. The candles began to rotate like Catherine wheels at a fair.

She was sitting in the light and could not see the others. She could hear laughter, voices quarreling. She let her candle sink to the ground. Alexis had wrested the rifle from Vassily. The two men were struggling. There was applause. Among the laughing voices she could hear Eleanor Gregorievskaya's. Then Alexis was standing in front of her. He helped her to rise.

As the dawn rose out of the water, the gypsies were still playing. Most of the guests were still there. Vassily was asleep on the grass among the shards.

Two hours later she woke up. It was seven. She rang for Elise. The girl, fully dressed, in black as usual, drew open the curtains. "Open the windows," said Maria.

It smelled freshly of dew on the meadows. The green of the trees was bright. Birds were twittering gaily. The cool silver of the sun broke through the dark firs. Maria ran to the window. She wanted to be kind to the maid and asked, "Aren't you homesick for Switzerland, Elise?"

"Oh yes, Countess."

"I am homesick, too. Do you think I should leave here? In Switzerland perhaps . . ."

"Homesickness for Switzerland and Russia are two very different things, Countess."

"What do you mean by that, Elise?"

"I long for the mountains, the forests, and the villages . . ."

"And I?"

"You long for peace, Countess."

Maria got dressed and went downstairs. The door to the salon stood open, but the room smelled of yesterday's wine. One of the gypsies, with his boots on, was asleep on the sofa. No one else was up.

She took the wooded path on which Alexis usually appeared. He came from Kusskovo, and it occurred to her that Kusskovo was not far from Ismailevo, the royal estate she had visited with the girls from school. She thought of the shortsighted teacher, her first kiss. White and yellow butterflies accompanied her. Foolish flies were buzzing as if they were going to live forever. Sunshine fell through the branches, and the autumn leaves at her feet came to life. She thought of Otrada, but she was not homesick.

On a clearing, not far from the house, she stood still suddenly, as if reality were towering in front of her. Here Vassily had had targets put up for his morning sport, five or six of them, standing in a row like soldiers in black and white uniforms, and to Maria it seemed strange that one was supposed to shoot at them. They looked more like a firing squad themselves, ready to shoot down a condemned man. On a rack, rifles, pistols, and ammunition were spread out, and she was suddenly filled with the urge to shoot at the black and white soldiers and topple them one after the other so that they could not shoot anyone any more. As she raised the rifle to her shoulders, two hands covered her ears. A hallucination, she thought, and turned around.

"Up so early?" said Alexis.

"Haven't you been in bed at all?"

"As you can see—I have ridden over from Kusskovo. I was worried." He laughed. "Justifiably."

She turned to face the target again and raised the rifle to her shoulder once more.

"This is foolish," he said.

"No, it's not."

He put his hand over the mouth of the weapon. "And now repeat what I say. 'I love you, Alexis.'"

"Take your hand away."

"'I love you, Alexis,'" he said, stressing each word.

Her finger was on the trigger. She took aim. She could see the target through his fingers, which were spread in front of the barrel. "I know you love me," he said.

All men believed that she loved them. The urge to press the trigger grew more and more violent. Her finger wavered between guard and trigger. Every one of his fingers was a lasciviously erect penis, every one greedy for her. All she had to do was press the trigger, and their proud manhood would be abjectly deflated. The lives of five men. Her body was on fire.

"Take your hand away," she said.

He pressed the palm of his hand flat against the mouth of the weapon.

He didn't think she would shoot. He knew that she loved him, so he didn't believe she would shoot. If she put down the rifle now, he would kiss her and his face would be like Vassily's. She closed her right eye. Between Alexis' fingers the black spots on the target came closer. She pressed the trigger.

Alexis screamed and turned deathly pale. She thought she had killed him and began to scream, too. "Be quiet," he said, and covered her mouth with his hand. His blood ran down her cheeks, into her mouth. It tasted sweet. She pressed his hand to her mouth and kissed it. His palm was like a warm cushion. Her tongue ran lovingly, hungrily, across his hand.

He swayed only for a moment, then he leaned over her, forced her to the ground, and covered her bloody face with kisses. The grass stood high. It smelled of hay and blood. The sun's rays danced over the clearing. They made love in the sun, under the cloudless sky, shamelessly, wildly, exhaustingly; two animals tearing each other apart. And the grass began to bleed.

7

Winter came; they returned to Moscow. To Maria it seemed as if the house in Kossino, park, woods, and clearing, had sunk into the waters of the lake. She had become the mistress of Alexis Bozevsky. In the summer she had ridden to Kusskovo every afternoon. When Vassily had gone to Moscow, she had crept out of the house at night. They had made love in Alexis' house, in the woods, in the clearing. They had challenged their fate and returned again and again to the meadow where the targets stood. They hadn't feared discovery, they had longed for it.

Now he was in Moscow. Night fell early. The *izvozchiki* on the street corner knew her: a veiled woman who drove across the Varvarsk Square, past the All Saints Church, to her lover. At the door he was waiting for her and took her in his arms. They spoke very little. Sometimes she wondered if he found happiness in her arms, for his eyes remained wide open, looking at her as if he expected her happiness to flutter up out of her eyes like a bird out of its nest; only then was he ready for flight, and they flew off together. When she asked him if he was happy, he looked at her, perplexed—didn't she know that he knew no other happiness but hers? She couldn't remember ever having lain in Vassily's arms, and when, like all lovers, they spoke of the first time, she said, "The blood on the grass was my virginal blood." Although he was only the second man in her life, she was sure that she would never find happiness again in the arms of another. She realized that she had been ill, but she realized also that she was not yet healed. She was like the sick who trust only one doctor, seek restoration at only one source, are dependent on one medicine only. Her love for Alexis blotted out not only her marriage but her childhood as well. She no longer dreamed of Otrada, Ivan, Terrible O'Rourke; she no longer heard the pitter-patter of the twins in a sleeping house. She no longer thought of Andrey.

In the mutiny of her body, her soul gradually grew calm. Now they spoke often and at great length, and after every conversation she was prouder, as if she had exchanged arrogance for pride. She was proud of her lover's beauty, of his passion and discretion, of his knowledge of Russian, French, English, and Italian poets; of his wealth and the love his servants bore him, of the indifference with which he spoke of the possibility that they might be found out. He didn't brag that she deceived her husband with him; he didn't speak disparagingly of Vassily, as Peter had done; he didn't retreat before him, either, like Andrey; in their contempt of Vassily, they were also united. Her love flew so high, it was as if she had left herself below on the ground. Under the wings of her soul, her conscience became smaller and smaller and, in the end, invisible. Her love was without pain.

Sometimes, however, she asked herself if she would love Alexis as much if Vassily had died or disappeared or evaporated into thin air like a jinni. She found herself, in Alexis' bed, thinking of Vassily; wanting to imagine him standing beside the bed. Her lust rose to almost unbearable heights at the very idea.

Vassily's misery completed her happiness. He could not be indifferent to Alexis, as he had been to Andrey, Yuri, Peter, Vladimir Stahl. In Milan he had accused her of being a whore, but he had probably never believed that she would deceive him. The society in which she moved protected the unfaithfulness of men and the virtue of women. His jealousy was vanity, and not until Alexis had he had a rival who was his equal. The change in him had begun when they were still in the country; in Moscow it became complete. If she mentioned Alexis' name, he raged. If she invited Alexis, he didn't dare forbid him the house; but he got drunk, boasted, retired in a fury, or attacked completely innocent persons. He told how a brother of Alexis had shot himself because of his gambling debts, although he knew very well that the man had been only a distant relative. When he felt Alexis watching him, he kissed Maria's neck. Now, with what had once been his lost to him, he put on a show of possession. He almost never left the house any more in the evening, but when he did go out, the coachman would bring him home shamefully drunk. When they were alone, Maria would guide the conversation toward Alexis, because she had to speak his name and see how it affected Vassily. When will the wild animal in him break out, she would think as she looked him in the eye. He knew better than to accuse her. When he stormed, she waited patiently for him to go down on his knees and beg her to forgive him. If he accused her, she only nodded. She spoke to Alexis in whispers, even when she had nothing to say; she wanted Vassily to know that she despised him. She made no more excuses. When he tried to approach her, she told him, "Go to Eleanor." "Do you want to fight a duel over Olga?" she asked. "Unfortunate women who have to be satisfied with a ruin," she mocked him. When he stood before her naked, she turned away and pretended she could not keep her eyes open for sleepiness. He bellowed at her, threw himself on her, struggled with her. She shook him off as if he were a leech. He wailed, begged, wept; she laughed at him. She recalled Krylov's fable. "A bird can't sing in claws of cat." All this bird could still do was peep.

8

Parties, balls, theater, ballet, gypsies, séances—winter in Moscow. In the three royal theaters—the Grand, the Little, the New—they gave operas by Moussorgsky, plays by Gogol, Tchaikovsky's *Swan Lake* and *Nutcracker*. A young stage director, Alexeyev Stanislavsky, offered his audiences something to think about. Concerts were held, balls arranged at the English Club and at the Peer's Club on the Bolshaya Dmitroska. St. Petersburg had been a city of parvenus who circled around imperial favors like moths. To hell with the Czar! Civil servants, officers, industrialists were busybodies who didn't count. Little Mother Moscow was another story. Here you didn't have to do a thing to be considered distinguished. If you fell, you went under in glory. What did it matter if you could see the lackey's naked knees through his threadbare hose—he stayed with his master. What did it matter if you left the Jar or the Strelna owing the bill—another bottle of champagne, spiked with vodka, plenty of vodka! *Tshto russkomu sdorrovo, nemzu smert* (Enough to kill a stranger does a Russian good). A good century was coming to an end; might the earth lie lightly on it. Rooms in the hotel between the Eremitage and Cloister Vyssoko Petrovsky were called "holy rooms." The most volup-

tuous prostitutes in Moscow, painted, with feathered hats and Cul de
Paris, looking frazzled, paraded up and down in front of them. A man
could go to the Svatye Nomera with a whore, a lady, or both. The
church bells rang for matins; the whores made off with the sleeping
man's wallet. It was empty anyway. The pockets of the merchants were
full, but who envied them? Their daughters drove through Sokolniki
Park in open sleighs, hands in muffs, marriage brokers at their
sides—were they any better than prostitutes? If a man had a good
name, all he had to do was go to the svacha to get a girl with a fortune.
Then it could start all over again: her father could enjoy seeing his
noble son-in-law throwing his money out the window. Evenings in
the palaces of the *nouveaux riches*—why not? It didn't make them
more distinguished, but no one was the poorer for it. One of the
palaces on the outskirts of town, where the dogs howled, had a
chapel where Black Masses were held, with naked women dancing
around the altar. You had to have seen it. The dear Lord in heaven
couldn't get too upset about Little Mother Moscow. She had four
hundred and fifty churches, twenty-five cloisters, and eight hundred
charity institutions. A good century was dying; let its death throes
be merry. "Milk! Milk! Who will buy milk?" the peasants cried in
the streets, but who heard them? The shades of the windows
were down until noon, the curtains drawn. The mail was delivered
in the morning and brought nothing but bills. In the afternoon one
drank tea at one of the dressmaker's on the Bolsh-Nikitskaya Boulevard.
"There is only one ruble in Moscow, darling, and that's being loaned
from hand to hand." In the evening everyone wanted to go to the
séances being held by Professor Delphinius in the Hotel Metropole.

9

One of the most distinguished houses that winter, not far from the
boarding school where Maria had spent two years of her life, was
that of the former Captain of the Guard, Baron Vladimir Stahl.
Maria, who knew that the "doctor" had spent a small fortune because
of her, believed it more than ever, for now she felt that every tribute
was intended for her. Of course, the Baron could not have furnished
his palace so extravagantly if he had not sent for his wife to join him.
She was an imposing blonde woman of middle-class origin, the
daughter of a German industrialist and millionaire, and it was said

226

that she had obeyed her husband because she hoped to find in the aristocratic society of Moscow the recognition she had been denied in bureaucratic circles in St. Petersburg.

One evening, one sleigh after the other drove up the ramp of Stahl's palace, which, with its Greek columns and gables, stood aggressively, yet at the same time rather lost, in the heart of Russia's second capital. Captain Stahl was giving a ball. Delphinius, the German soothsayer, raiser of ghosts, and prestidigitator, was going to treat the guests to a look into the future.

Maria was wearing a red dress with a train. The dress left her shoulders bare, was narrow at the waist, covered with Valencienne lace from the waist down, and from the waist up with thousands of tiny red sequins, glittering like thousands of rubies—the latest innovation. When she entered the ballroom, even those who were dancing turned to look at her, and the thirty gypsies, men and women, seemed for a moment to play more softly.

Vladimir Stahl, hectic red spots in his cheeks, looking more ailing than ever, asked her to dance. "You look happy, Maria Nikolaevna," he said.

"I am happy, Vladimir Mihailovich," she told him. "Do you object?"

"Do you really know what happiness is?"

"I never ask any more."

Her eyes sought Alexis and found him with the sure aim of loving eyes. A dozen beautiful women were trying to attract his attention, but he was paying no attention to them; he had eyes only for Maria.

"There is only one happiness," said Stahl. "Freedom."

"I feel free."

"Your freedom is deceptive."

"And what do you mean by that?" She was smiling at Alexis. Stahl's philosophizing was ancient history.

"Were you ever at the market on Trubnaya Square?" he asked. "There you will always find a few fools who buy doves from the bird dealers—or let us say, they buy the birds their freedom. The cages are opened, the stupid populace applauds, and everybody looks after the fluttering feathered creatures. Unfortunately, the bird dealers are sly; they have their hustlers, who catch the pigeons again a few hours later. The illusion of freedom is over. Bozevsky opened the door, my little pigeon, but Vassily will soon catch you again."

"How do you know that Bozevsky and I . . ." she asked, taken aback.

"I have begun to hate Bozevsky more than Vassily."

"You love fables," said Maria. "But I am not going to let you spoil my mood."

But her mood was spoiled. She danced with Grand Duke Constantine Ivanovich, who could talk of nothing but his race horses; with Isyaslav Uvarov, the Prince from Kiev, whose wife, Sonya Petrovna, had died recently in childbirth; with young Count Shtcherbatov, of whom it was whispered that he was in touch with the revolutionaries. Her longing for Alexis accompanied her like a faithful servant, stretched out its hand to her, annoyed her, was ever-present, called and uncalled for. She hated people who knew her secret, but she hated those who didn't even more. Who had said that only men were proud of their possessions? Weren't the women who couldn't abide secrecy, who wanted to possess what they owned openly, proud too?

At last, when everyone was crowding around Professor Delphinius in the game room, she managed to get close to Alexis. She touched his hand. "I want to kiss your throat," he whispered in her ear. "I want you to kiss my breasts," she whispered in his.

The bearded seer, in tails, decorated with the medals of obscure kingdoms, looked up. The light from the candles in the candelabra standing on a card table at his side fluttered across his face, which looked happy, only to be laced suddenly with shiny tears.

"Haven't we met before, Countess Tarnovska?" he asked.

"I don't know." She also didn't know how he happened to know her name. She held out her hand to him. The ladies and gentlemen around the oracle stepped aside, as if what had been amusing had suddenly been transformed into something serious. Around the green table, it was still. The stillness was interrupted by Vladimir Stahl.

"Don't say anything, Professor," he cried. "Don't tell the Countess anything."

Delphinius was still holding Maria's hand in his, which was ice-cold.

"I want to hear what he has to say to my wife," cried Vassily.

Only now did she notice that he was standing behind her. He smelled of vodka. Perhaps he had heard what she had whispered to Alexis a moment ago. She wasn't afraid; she hoped he had. Why had she deceived him if he didn't find out about it? Wouldn't it be easier for her if he found out by chance what she was going to have to tell him in the end anyway?

Delphinius seemed to have heard neither Stahl nor Vassily. He let Maria's hand go as one drops a stone, leaned back, and closed his eyes. If he was a fraud, then he was a grandiose fraud. He mumbled words, staccato, singly, like a man in his sleep speaking about nothing.

"Speak clearer!" cried Vassily.

His outcry seemed to penetrate Delphinius' dream, because he began to speak louder, but still in unconnected words. "Beloved . . . officer . . . revolver . . . the child . . . prison . . . shots . . . officer . . . water . . . tulips . . . duel . . . prison . . . the park . . . the lover."

"I want to know who my wife's lover is!" cried Vassily.

Stahl tried to calm him. A group had formed around Vassily, men and women surrounding him with their chatter. Maria fled into the ballroom.

"Let us dance," said Alexis.

Her body did not belong to her, but it did not belong to him either; it was swaying between him and her, and she had a vision of herself naked, as naked and bald as in her illness. The roots of her hair hurt as they had done then. The motions of the dance were a relentless duty. She wanted to dance out of the ballroom, but she had to keep turning in a circle.

Men and women had come out of the dining room. Instead of mingling with the dancers, they remained standing in the doorway, Vassily between them as if surrounded by a bodyguard. Maria began to laugh, senselessly. Alexis said nothing. Maria's throat began to ache with her laughter. As she danced past Vassily, he threw his glass on the floor. She knew he was coming toward her, but the dance had separated them. Now she was facing him again. Across one of her naked shoulders she saw him grab Vladimir Stahl by the chest. Vassily was screaming, "Give me a revolver, Stahl! I'll kill the dog! I'm going to kill my wife's lover!" The melody the gypsies were playing broke off on a high note; they let their violins fall to their sides; only the cymbalist played on, a few more notes, like the tinkling of the glass a while before. Vassily shook off the men who were trying to hold him back. Everyone had stopped dancing. The men still had their arms around their partners' waists; the ladies were clinging to their men. Alexis and Maria were standing like the rest, his arm protectively around her, she seeking protection at his breast. Vassily walked up to them, making way for himself with both hands, although he had the whole center of the room to himself. "Lights out!" he yelled. "Lights out!" No one understood what he meant. "I want to play blindman's buff," he yelled. "Blindman's buff with the hussar! Bing, bang, blindman's buff."

At last everyone understood. Blindman's buff, the name borrowed from the English, the most senseless duel of all. Two men shooting at each other in a darkened room; shooting as vases, plates, mirrors, windows were shattered, shooting and waiting and shooting again, until the answer was silence and one man wasn't shooting any more.

"Blindman's buff! Blindman's buff with the hussar!" Vassily was screaming, turning in a circle, hand outstretched as if aiming a revolver. "Lights out! Blindman's buff!"

The couples stepped back against the wall. The room grew larger. To Maria it seemed as if the walls were moving back. They had been dikes, stemming a torrent; now the water steamed out across the parquet floor. The people were swept away by it; gold, green, red dresses swam on the water, uniforms and white cravats, heads bobbed up and sank down again. She could hear the rushing of the torrent. It grew dark; she went under. When she opened her eyes, she saw a scorpion with pointed sting approaching her naked arm. Then her vision cleared. It was not a scorpion; it was a needle, a hypodermic needle. Behind it, diminuted, as in the wrong end of opera glasses, she saw people. She tried to find Alexis and Vassily, but she could recognize only Vladimir Stahl, leaning over her with the hypodermic needle.

10

Little Mother had her scandal, a scandal that excited all Moscow. All Moscow comprised a hundred people, perhaps two or three hundred. These hundred or two hundred or three hundred had their own laws. Since they were not the laws of the people, nor of the land, and since they were not to be found in any book or pandect or judgment, the few who believed in them had to repeat them continuously so that they themselves might believe them. Vladimir Stahl had said once to Maria that no one had as yet come up with a law that could forgo punishment, but since high society could hang no one, nor put them behind bars, nor even rob them of their fortune, it had invented exclusion. This, however, could be felt as a punishment only if the society's members were sufficiently convinced of the importance of their membership. That society was therefore constantly gyrating in a circle of its own was no coincidence, much less vain sport. Since they could imprison no one, they could also not pursue the deserter; on the contrary, the deserters, once they had escaped, and to society's great astonishment, went right on living happily. It was therefore paramount, before all else, to prevent those who remained behind from finding this out. That was why a wall of gossip, evil talk, veiled threats, and a false sense of importance had to be erected around the vacuum. No law without punishment, Vladimir Stahl had philosophized, but also no law without weapons. Society had no stick, no rifle, no guillotine; its only weapon was scandal.

Maria Tarnovska learned what this weapon meant. When her sleigh glided through the Alexander Gardens, the ladies in theirs turned their heads away. The frame of the mirror in which she had once stuck her invitations remained empty. The seamstresses asked her to come for a fitting in the morning, when she would meet no one. When she sent the coachman into a restaurant to order a table, he came back with a red face. Even in the kitchen, that distorted mirror of the salons, all conversation ceased at sight of her. The scandal, which was the chief topic of conversation in all houses, villas, and palaces of the Byely Gorod, seemed to be fanned solely by women. The men, on the other hand, not only Vladimir Stahl, showered Maria with attention. Friends and acquaintances laid their admiration at her feet. Why, she wondered. Was it because, since they had found out that she shared her bed with Alexis Bozevsky, they were waiting around her bed, as they had done during her pregnancy? Were they putting themselves hopefully in the role of Bozevsky, or with self-torture in that of Vassily? Did they want to be received or deceived?

It became more and more apparent to her that they wanted to be deceived, as if all of them bore an invisible guilt they hoped to atone for in a self-chosen slavery. Vassily's behavior could be explained in no other way. He had been brought home raving and insensibly drunk. When he woke up next morning, Maria was still sleeping under the influence of the morphine the "doctor" had given her. But she need not have dreaded her first meeting with Vassily. He seemed to have forgotten what had happened, never left her side, showered her with valuable presents. The house was a bower of flowers.

He was there when she needed him, made himself scarce when she wanted to be alone. If he ever mentioned the scandal, then only to declare his own guilt. If Maria spoke of any insult she had suffered, he behaved as if he had been insulted. He put aside not only his personality but even his wishes.

Without forbidding Maria to see Alexis again, he found a way of preventing their meeting. Maria, who was pining for Alexis, found out from Stahl that he and Vassily had met. It had been around Christmas; Stahl himself had arranged it. When Maria reproached him for having reconciled the two to destroy her love affair with Alexis, Stahl assured her that to save her position in society was his whole endeavor. Shortly after that, Vassily himself told her that he had met Bozevsky at Stahl's house. Alexis had sworn that there had been nothing between him and Maria. Just like himself, Alexis wanted nothing but to prove Maria's innocence and clear her name. That would of course take time. Moscow society would not easily relinquish a scandal of such proportions. Vassily suggested that they spend a year in Rome and Paris—with the children, of course. Before she could reply, he told her, "It has all been arranged with Bozevsky. On Tatiana Day, he is going to invite us to the opera and dinner at the Eremitage, a farewell dinner that will demonstrate how mistaken I was, and the injustice of Moscow."

Moscow—a hundred people, perhaps two or three hundred. For them she had to sacrifice her happiness.

II

January twelfth, Tatiana Day, founding festival of the university, the opening event of the carnival. Students crowding from the university at the Alexander Gardens to the Theater Square. *Gaudeamus igitur*. Dominoes, young men dressed up as peasant women, bandanas around their heads. Rickety baby carriages filled with bottles of vodka. Enormous swaying figures on stilts with paper heads, gypsies, students dressed as gypsies. It has been snowing for days. The horses sink up to their knees in snow. The snow shovels on the rooftops are tied to the chimneys. A man dressed like a witch is riding on a roof with a broom between his legs. Students singing the Marseillaise, the police watching grimly; it is carnival time. Students dressed like policemen dragging a convict in paper chains through the snow. Trappers

232

bayaderes, grandees. Sausages boiling in huge copper cauldrons. Snow sliding off the roofs, people climbing merrily out of the avalanches. A couple of naked boys bathing in the icy Moskva. They demand vodka. Already at noon a few vodka corpses sprawl in front of the Grand Theater.

Opera at the Grand Theater. Mink, chinchilla, ermine, diamond tiaras, black pearl tiaras, ruby necklaces. Count Alexis Bozevsky has taken three boxes. In the middle one, Maria between Alexis and Vassily, on her head a little crown of diamonds. A fusillade of opera glasses. In St. Petersburg she visited the waxworks. Maria Stuart with a head, Maria Stuart without a head. Aren't the O'Rourkes related to Maria Stuart? She is made of wax, a wax figure. The State Theater in Kiev, Mademoiselle Larue, the Frenchman; that was the evening she met Vassily. Did wax figures have hearts? Her knee touches Alexis'. She will never see him again. If she has a heart, it will break. In the intermission everyone crowds into her box. Greetings are exchanged between those seated in the orchestra and in other boxes. Hesitant greetings at first, as if a rigid harness is still holding back the horses' heads. Slowly the reins are loosened, heads are freed; they greet. Victory over scandal. She doesn't care. Vassily looks at her; Alexis is staring at the stage. Her hero has bowed in submission; he is a traitor. She is not going to Italy to please Vassily but to spite Alexis. When the house is darkened after the second intermission, and it is still, and the curtain has not yet gone up, one can hear the howling of students outside. *Gaudeamus igitur, juvenes dum sumus.* She is twenty-one.

Across the Neglinny Proyesd to the Eremitage. Five sleighs. Alexis has gone on ahead to receive his guests. Maria is seated between Stahl and Vassily. The "doctor" is cold; his teeth are chattering. Of course, throughout the entire performance, no injection. She hates the puppeteer. Students throw themselves in front of the sleigh; the horses rear. A gypsy woman runs after them, wants to tell their fortune. Maria knows everything already. Delphinius. The gypsy falls face-down in the snow. Under the fur robe, Vassily is holding her hand. Andrey held her hand under the fur robe. The memory glorifies Otrada. Alexis has left her alone with Vassily shivering, with Vassily humbled.

The Eremitage. She sees herself in the mirror. Never has she been more beautiful. She spent the whole day making herself beautiful.

That is how Alexis will remember her. It is the last picture that counts, the picture that endures. Alexis is standing in front of the velvet draperies in gala uniform, kissing Vassily on both cheeks. His blood flowed over her lips. The clearing in Kossino, the bed with the carved angels, the gold-framed mirror in which their bodies were reflected. The last picture is not the only one that counts.

Alexis offers his apologies. Tatiana Day has brought a peculiar crowd to the Eremitage; can't be helped. The table runs lengthwise along a wall. You stare at everyone; everyone stares at you, a zoo. She has to remember to take home the masks lying on the table, for Tioka. Masks, snappers, colored balls, paper trumpets, flowers, confetti. The table is set for fourteen, Alexis opposite her, Stahl and old Gregorievsky to her right and left. Ruins right and left. Banker Maximov's glasses dangle from a silk ribbon. Baroness Stahl finds everything "lovely." Sheremetyev is pale. Now Alexis is looking at her. He raises his glass. "Ave, Maria!" Stahl leans forward. "Has it ever happened to you that you couldn't go on with a quotation because another stubbornly intruded itself?" "What do you mean?" "Ave, Maria—*morituri te salutant*."

Everyone is talking about their departure next day. "Moscow will be empty without you, Countess." Moscow. The stairs to his bedroom. She walked up them with Alexis, their arms around each other. "I shall miss you," says Eleanor Gregorievskaya. An adversary conquered is no longer an adversary. Everyone is laughing. Maria looks where everybody else is looking—a student has climbed up one of the palms and is scratching his behind, playing monkey. On the stage a theology student is standing in front of the gypsies, conducting with both hands. "I feel trapped," says Stahl. A very young man in tails is dangling his patent-leather-shod feet in the pool. Vassily is drinking constantly. She calls out to him, "Please don't drink so much." He tosses his champagne glass behind him. It breaks against a mirror. Silence. Vassily laughs, declaims, "'Then did he fling his chalice/ Into the surging main./ He watched it sink and vanish—/ And never drank again.'" She turns to Stahl. "What do you mean, trapped?"

The waiters smile as if petrified; they feel responsible for Tatiana Day. Half-naked girls pop out of artificial grottoes, chased by students, disappear. "Today anything goes. God knows where they picked them up." A fish jumps out of the pool, flip-flops across the dark red carpet in a grotesque death agony. Two men, flat on their stomachs can't catch it. "We should leave," says Stahl. "I don't like Alexis." Alexis' eyes won't let her go. He drinks a toast to her, to Vassily; he is drinking too much. "If it were not such a sad occasion, what a wonderful evening!" Baroness Stahl declares ecstatically in broken Russian. Tomorrow at this time . . . Suddenly Maria feels that Alexis is suffering just as much as she is. He is suffering; he has not betrayed her. If only she can speak to him once more, put her arms around his neck. He has saved her without asking if she wants to be saved or not. Heroes don't concern themselves with the downfall of others.

Again Vassily throws his glass to the floor. His face is red. "I am King of Thule!" he cries. Alexis raises his glass to speak. Silence.

"You are the King of Thule, Tarnovsky," he says. "But I am Knight Olaf, who was condemned to death for daring to love the King's daughter. At the last banquet, the King said, 'Take heed, Olaf, for headsman stands at the door.' Whereupon Olaf rose for the last toast." Alexis rises and recites, in English:

"'I bless the joys that I have had
And the joys that I have missed;
I bless the eyes that have smiled on me
And the lips that I have kissed.'"

He turns to face Maria:

"'To thy red lips that I have kissed
I raise this cup of wine,
I bless the radiant loveliness
That made my life divine,
And I bless the hour that brings me death
For the hour that thou wert mine!'"

Vassily jumps to his feet. Maximov and Sheremetyev are already at his side. From behind, a drunken student throws his arms around him. The half-naked girls suddenly reappear from the grotto. "The sleighs are waiting," Gregorievsky cries. Waiters surround Alexis. Eleanor Gregorievskaya kisses Maria on both cheeks. "Bon voyage, darling."

Maria doesn't know how she got out of the room. The night is icy, the stars frozen in the sky. Cold smoke issues from the nostrils of the horses. Sleigh bells jingle impatiently. Stahl helps Maria into her sleigh. "Bon voyage, Maria Nikolaevna!" She turns around. Alexis is coming toward her from the lighted doorway. With every step, he seems to grow bigger and bigger, as if he were going to outgrow men, horses, sleighs. No coat; bareheaded. He bows low over her hand, kisses it, doesn't let go. "It is all over," he says. The sound of a shot. The horses rear, plunge to one side. Beside the second sleigh, Vassily, a pistol in his hand. He is laughing. The drivers are cursing.

Alexis collapses beside her sleigh. Blood spurts from his throat. She is at his side, leaning over him. Blood. Blood as before. Her fur is bloody; her hand is bloody. Stahl tears his silk scarf from his throat, binds it around Alexis' neck. His hand, too, is bloody. The snow is bleeding. Blood is flowing from Alexis' mouth.

CHAPTER 12

I

In September Andrey had undertaken a second journey through Russia. Now it was January, and he knew what duties the Master General had in mind for him. The present was knocking with tough fingers at the door of the Order. To barricade oneself behind it was hopeless; one had to find out who was outside. Paul had gone to Cyprus, Antioch, Beroea, and Thessaly. In Jerusalem they had reproached him for consorting with heathens. But how was one to convert the heathen without consorting with him?

Throughout his entire journey Andrey had been filled with doubt. He had been in cities and villages, in cloisters, hostels, factories, and prisons. Young Count Andrey Antonovich Vyrubov had known next to nothing of misery. The revolutionaries claimed that a hundred million of Russia's one hundred and twenty-six million inhabitants lived in deprivation and degradation, and it was true. In Georgia, men and women worked seventeen hours a day; they slept, half starved, under the open sky or in holes in the ground. The workers earned si to eight rubles a month. Often a quarter of their pay was deducted for penalties; often they received no money at all, only some insufficient nourishment. Ten people slept in one room—father, mother, three children in one bed. In one village, where a census was being taken, the peasants thought the kingdom of the anti-Christ was come, that was why the people of the earth were being counted. Singing "Hallelujah," they began to bury one another alive. "I am very pleased with the conduct of my troops," the Czar told the Governor of Yaroslav when the latter had ordered the strikers shot down. The same peasants who had revolted against the Czar streamed into the cities to set fire to the houses of the Jews, because they thought the Jews were going to depose the Czar and pronounce the Kingdom of David. Confusion, misery, superstition, gluttony, hunger, ostentation, incest, drunkenness, and hatred that begot hatred—Andrey had met nothing else.

It was not divine justice he doubted. The strategy of a single battle was incomprehensible to the common man—how could he expect to understand God's eternal strategy? Andrey doubted the mission of the Church, or, more specifically, its power to fulfill it. He listened to inflammatory speeches and had to admit that the agitators were expressing his views. The Church had been conspiring with the powerful of this earth for too long. God had only one face, the Devil many. And the Devil was not above pretending to be fighting himself. If mankind strove to free itself from his yoke, quick as a flash, he knew how to replace one devilish dominion with another. God seemed to be standing beside the sickbed of the world with empty hands, and quackery was in flower. Every time Andrey preached in a village, he left it in despair. He had no panaceas, no miracles to offer. Why should slaves believe that he was speaking in the name of the Lord when he had to proclaim tolerance for the slaveowner? Why should they believe that he was providing for God's acres and not for the acres of the slaveowner? Was it just a case of proclaiming love—should one not also ask oneself to whom one was proclaiming it? He who owned nothing could give nothing away; the outstretched hand turned into a fist. He who appealed to the clemency of beggars mocked them. Love thy neighbor meant nothing more now than solidarity against the outsider. The hands of the clock turned relentlessly; the calendar leaves fell without cease. It was too late to send out missions to the poor; not too late, perhaps, for a mission to the rich.

In December Andrey had dared to put his thoughts on paper in a report to the Master General. In early January—he had been in Tula at the time—he had been handed a sealed letter. The orders in it filled him with fresh hope. It was the wish of the Master General, the letter said, that Father Andrey Vyrubov betake himself, free of all monastic regulations and mindful only of the word of Christ, into the big cities, in order to impress first and foremost the rich and the powerful, to admonish them and, if necessary, warn them, to preach contemplation and conversion, and, if necessary, demand them. "That, my dear son," said the letter, "was the duty I had in mind for you from the start." The Master General closed with the words of Paul in his second epistle to the Corinthians: "We are troubled on every side, yet not disturbed, we are perplexed, but not in despair; persecuted, but not forsaken; cast down, but not destroyed. . . . For our present light affliction, which is for a moment, prepares for us an eternal weight of glory that is beyond all measure; while we look not at the things that are seen, but at the things that are not seen; for the things that are seen are temporal; but the things that are not seen are eternal."

2

Andrey began his mission in the province of Poltava, which was so familiar to him. He had written to Count O'Rourke, who had answered at once. The Roman Catholic aristocracy of the province would assemble in Otrada to hear the Dominican preach.

A peasant had picked up Andrey. Now he was walking through the snowy park. It was not yet late in the afternoon, yet already almost dark. The ravens squatted in the snow, a little darker than the dusk. It wasn't snowing any more. When Andrey looked about him, he could see his footsteps in the snow, the only tracks far and wide. He felt as if he were approaching a house from which all life had passed, but perhaps he was mistaking the past, which was dead, with the people who were still living. Perhaps others had walked through the snow and the wind had scattered their footprints. Every step forward was a track left behind. Nothing experienced was so unreal as when one had experienced it. He thought of Maria. No happiness was as great as one believed it to be, no unhappiness was either. One should keep only one's memories, as if what happened had no consequence, as if memories were children that didn't grow.

As he approached the house, he noticed that there was no sleigh standing in front of it. A servant he didn't know answered the door and led him to the library.

When he saw the Count, Andrey asked himself how old Nikolay O'Rourke might be. Sixty-four or sixty-five? He looked older than seventy. He had grown old suddenly. You could tell, as with most men, by his neck, which rose thin and wrinkled from his collar, the throat of an old man.

The Count excused himself for not having notified Andrey. "You will understand, of course, that I cannot receive guests now." Now? The Count was astounded to hear that Andrey knew nothing of what had taken place at the Eremitage. Hesitantly he began to talk about it, growing more and more eloquent, until his sunken cheeks were red with excitement. "Tarnovsky gave himself up to the police and was arrested. Bozevsky's condition is serious, but not hopeless. The bullet entered his throat from the side and came out under the chin. Mura stayed with him. I had the children brought to Otrada." With unsure hands, he stroked his beard, which was not as well groomed as formerly. "Give me an explanation for it all, Andrey," he said. "Give me an explanation."

"For what?"

"So much is incomprehensible. I tried to seek the guilt in myself. But Mura and Olga grew up together. Olga, my pride and joy; Mura, my shame."

"I don't know if you are guilty, Count O'Rourke. It is easier to rule over a thousand peasants than to rear one child. Our daily responsibilities are the superhuman ones. Because we produce children, we think we know them, but they fall unknown from God's hand. The same upbringing? It wouldn't mean anything even if we were not speaking of two different creatures of God. Because you don't know if you said something once to the one that you did not say to the other; whether the one didn't happen to see something the other did not notice; whether the one didn't experience something at the wrong time, the other at a propitious moment. The same environment, the same upbringing—but the same love?"

"I tried to feel the same love for all my children."

"Did you succeed?"

"Are you accusing me?"

"It was you who asked."

239

The Count nodded. "What drives Mura to ruin the people with whom she comes in contact? Or does she attract those who are ruined? You know what I think of Tarnovsky, but Bozevsky . . ."

"Do you know him?"

"I have heard only good things about him, the best."

"I can't answer your question. Even if Mura were possessed of the Devil, she would not be his possession. Since the death of our Savior, no one is. The Devil lays siege to a soul, but the soul does not belong to him. But the Devil still owns what we call 'world.' The world is therefore not ruined by man, but man is ruined by the world. The world grows no worse with the arrival of a newborn babe, but the newborn babe grows more evil with every breath that inhales the world. The larger the world is in a man, the larger is Satan's portion of him. But Satan is dependent on man, and for just that reason is not divine. Through man he hands the world down to man; and the more world he owns, the more evil he is able to pass on to man. Maria is one of those unfortunates whose worldliness seems to be inexhaustible."

The Count was looking at him with disappointment, and a certain disapproval was clearly discernible in his old eyes. In all probability he did not understand Andrey. Andrey asked himself if he had done the right thing to come first to Poltava. People despised what they knew and didn't want to believe that anything familiar could be their match. Their distrust of themselves was so great that they trusted no one with whom they had been associated for any length of time.

"You are not very tolerant," said the Count.

"Tolerance is indifference. We tolerate what we don't want to change."

He regretted having spoken so vehemently, as if defending himself. He had not yet learned to be sparing with words; his enthusiasm made him overzealous. Would he have passed judgment so hastily upon any other woman? What was the meaning of what was visible? He was not even sure whether he hadn't felt a certain satisfaction over what Count O'Rourke had told him. Had he put himself, with more passion than aversion, in the role of the two men?

"So you have no hope for Mura?" the Count asked.

"I didn't say that. It is possible for everyone to liberate himself from his own sinfulness, but for nearly everyone the price is too high."

"What do you call the price?"

"The surrender of one's identity. Man is more proud of his per sonality than of anything else, which is why so many people are ready to exchange their health, their purse, their family life with that of another, but never their personality. They aspire to a personality because they believe it sets them apart more than anything else from the world. Actually he rates highest who has absorbed within himself more of this world than his neighbor. And the greatest personality of all—that is to say, he who is identical with this world—is the Devil."

"Are you trying to say that Mura's only salvation is the cloister?"

Andrey smiled. "The cloister is neither the only nor the safest place to relieve oneself of one's personality."

It had grown dark, as on the day when Count O'Rourke had asked young Andrey Antonovich Vyrubov to come to Otrada. The cold seeped in through cracks in the windows. The Count paced up and down the room, his back bent, moving between the furnishings like a blind man. Every time he struck against a piece of furniture, it gave forth a creaking sound. To Andrey, he seemed even more strange than at the beginning of their conversation, for now he wore his arrogance like the habit of a stranger. Was he really so deeply wounded? Could the deeds of one human being be the punishment of another?

"I know what you think of me," said the Count. "Perhaps you are right, and my conscience is stirring in me only because on a few nights I felt the hand of death upon me. Just the same, I should like to help Mura. Tell me how I can do it."

"Do what you can to reunite her with her children."

"So that she may infect them, too?"

"Mothers do not infect their children."

"I am not so sure about that."

"It is worth trying. The only love that is assuredly unworldly is the love of parents for their children. And this cannot be said with assurance even of the opposite; children often love only the world in their parents."

"And you say that as a priest?"

"We try to be *patres*."

The Count was clinging to the back of his chair. "I did my duty." He waited for Andrey to answer, then went on. "You forget that Mura left her children to me of her own free will. She stayed with her lover."

"Would you receive her?"

The Count straightened. Now Andrey recognized him, and knew at once what the answer would be. "In Otrada? Impossible!" But when

Andrey turned to leave, the old man asked him at least to spend the night in Otrada. They could speak about the matters that had brought Andrey here, he said, almost pleadingly. The next day they would visit Count Savinsky on his estate. The Count was anxious to meet Andrey.

In the end, Andrey accepted the invitation because he remembered the cause for which he had come, or perhaps because he wanted to see Maria's children.

3

A few days later, Andrey was in a small town, Mirgorod, on the Kiev-Poltava line. It had been his intention to travel to Kiev, but snowdrifts had paralyzed the railways. The rules of his Order forbade him to spend the night at an inn without a compelling reason, so he asked the man who ran the station restaurant if he might sleep on one of the benches.

He had been sitting in the taproom for hours—the station restaurant was little more than that—small, black with smoke, with yellowed timetables on the walls, and a picture of the Czar who was no longer living. You couldn't see the tracks. The building itself looked as if it had been swept there. Every now and then the wind blew across the invisible tracks, a wind from nowhere, whistling maliciously and senselessly ahead of itself. When it died down, you could see the tracks it had plowed in the snow, senseless tracks; and the hairs of the cat—crouching on the seat that ran around the stove—stood on end, as if she sensed an enemy. Then she went back to sleep. She was afraid of howling dogs, but the wind was too powerful to fear. Andrey pressed his forehead against the pane, on which the frost had etched tulips and ferns. The frost drew flower pictures of a warmer clime. Andrey's forehead was hot; he had a fever.

The door opened; the wind blew snow into the room. Andrey thought his host's beard was of ice, but when the man sat down beside Andrey, he saw that the beard didn't melt. He was a gigantic man. Everything about him was gigantic: his big hands—like paws—his beard, the bulbous nose of a drinker, and his blue eyes. The eyes were young, as if they had forgotten to age with the rest of him. Andrey couldn't imagine what had taken the man outdoors in weather like this. When he asked him, the man replied that he had gone out to talk to the wolves—in the loneliness here he had formed the habit

This was nonsense, of course, because wolves didn't talk; besides, there weren't any around here. The man got up, shook the snow from his fur and boots, got a bottle of vodka from the bar, and came back to Andrey.

"You may have to stay here for days, Brother," he said. "Once we didn't have a train go by for twenty-one days."

"How do you live?" asked Andrey. "Does anyone ever come here? How do you pass the time?" He questioned the man because he wanted to show he was grateful.

Without asking if Andrey would like a drink, the man poured a glass of vodka for Andrey; for himself he filled a waterglass full. "When I get bored," he said, "I lie."

"To whom do you lie?"

"To myself, of course. Who else?"

"And what do you tell yourself?"

"Ha! If I were to tell you! I have a thousand lies. Of course, I have my favorites. When I'm going to sleep, I tell myself one of my favorites. I know them by heart. I'm not curious about how they're going to end, because I know how they're going to end. So, slowly I lie myself to sleep. One of my favorite lies is my visit to our Little Father, the Czar. I used to make up the whole audience, with medals and music. Then I found myself falling asleep on the steps of Zarskoye Selo. Now I often fall asleep in the train to St. Petersburg."

"Those aren't lies," said Andrey. "You just tell yourself stories."

"No, no. You're wrong. If they were stories, I wouldn't believe them. They're lies, and that's why I believe them. If I can find someone to listen to me, I tell them. I have the reputation of being the biggest liar in the neighborhood, Brother."

"The greatest storyteller."

The man shook his head angrily. "You'd better believe me. I am a liar. Of course there's always a little kernel of truth in my stories. For instance, the one about my wife . . ."

"You are married?"

"My wife is dead. It was on a night like this. The snow was piled up to the cross on the windows, and the wind was howling." He paused, listening, as if the wind might do him the favor of demonstrating how it could howl. "Only the girl and I were in the house, and my wife, of course. She was in bed coughing. She had a horrible cough. Then yakkity-yak, and she was dead. There she lay in her bed for seven days. We washed her down with snow, because she stank to high heaven. When the people could get through to us again, I told them I had poisoned her. The doctor came, the gendarmes came, they interrogated me, and they opened her up. The girl they took with them to the city, but of course they had to let her go because she hadn't had anything to do with it. There was nothing to it anyway, because I hadn't harmed a hair of my wife's head and there wasn't any poison in the house. As I just told you—yakkity-yak, and she was dead."

"You made it all up."

"That's just the point—I didn't. I had promised to marry the girl; she was expecting my child; and I'd have liked to murder my wife. I'd been giving it a lot of thought—how to do it, I mean. It was one of my favorite dreams; one of the stories I lied myself to sleep with. But I didn't have any poison and even less courage."

"And then you had a guilty conscience, and that's why you made a false confession."

"Nonsense, Brother! Why should I have had a guilty conscience when God was so obliging as to take her to Him? I just didn't want to let them ruin my beautiful lie. What we lie, Brother, that's what we really want. Everybody lies, but they won't put up with it that the next man lies. Everybody's envious of his neighbor's lie—can you follow me? If everyone was to believe his neighbor's lie, then nobody would be expelled from Paradise. It's the doubters who make the liars unhappy—you follow me? And they make themselves unhappy at the same time, because every doubter is at the same time a liar made unhappy by the next doubter who comes along. Now take yourself. I could see it in your face that you didn't believe me when I told you I'd been out to talk to the wolves, or that once we'd been snowed in for twenty-one days. Just tell me, what would it have cost you to believe me? Then you would have been good for one or two lies with me, and we could have amused ourselves the whole night long with our lies."

Andrey was finding it difficult to follow the man's chatter because the fever he had felt coming on all day was shaking him. He felt cold and saw everything with a double clarity: the cat's hairs, the man's beard, his blue eyes, the ciphers on the timetables. But he wasn't at all sure that he was actually seeing what he saw so clearly. For instance the girl came in of whom the man had just spoken, but after she had whispered something to the man, and left, Andrey wasn't sure that he had actually seen her. The glass of vodka would have done him good, but instead he asked for some tea. With a sigh the man walked over to the samovar that was standing on the counter, and brought Andrey a glass of tea. Only a few seconds had passed, but to Andrey it seemed as if the man had left him long ago and only just got back.

"So you want to stick to the truth?" the man asked.

Andrey nodded. He felt miserable.

"You know what the truth is, Brother?" the man asked. "You don't. If you were to tell me a true story now, it would be dull, and it wouldn't be true. Because you'd sprinkle lies into the truth like raisins into raisin bread, and in the end you'd be just as big a liar as I, sprinkling a bit of truth into my raisin bread of lies. My oldest brother —he emigrated to America; that is to say, he ran away when they wanted to make a soldier of him—he wrote that he was doing well, better all the time, and in the end he wrote that he was living in a sky-scraper in New York, and was filthy rich, and to prove it, he sent me a few dollars. Of course I didn't believe a word he said, but I kept the dollars because I don't believe in making anybody unhappy. Then one day an American came through here, a grain dealer. He used to come over every evening from Mirgorod. We had a pretty girl here at the time. And you know the way things happen—we got to talking about my brother, and what do you suppose I found out?"

"That he was a poor man."

The man laughed. "Just the opposite! Every word he had written was true!"

"So?" asked Andrey, although the tea hadn't helped, and his head was aching.

"I told the American that I was the rich man's brother. He laughed at me. Because my brother, who had written me the truth, had told the American that he had a brother in Russia who owned a big hotel in Moscow, or St. Petersburg—I can't remember which. He was a truth-loving man, my brother was, God rest his soul; he just chose to deny his poor brother." He looked at Andrey. "You aren't feeling well, are you?"

"I think I have a fever."

"There's a good bed upstairs."

Andrey thanked the man, who shrugged his shoulders, finished his glass of vodka, took the bottle back to the bar, turned the oil lamp down. "At least let me give you a blanket," he said. "God couldn't possibly resent that."

4

Andrey wakes up. The girl is moving around in the room. Could it be morning? Outside it is pitch-black; only the oil lamp is still burning on the counter. The girl busies herself with the bottles. Andrey doesn't move. Is it the girl or is he dreaming? A cold sweat breaks out on his forehead. The night before he had a fever. His teeth are chattering. Can she hear it? He closes his eyes. A big ugly hand is tossing colored stones into the air, where they remain suspended. When he opens his eyes, the girl ducks under the counter, playfully, like a child hiding. Then her head pops up again above the counter. It isn't the girl; it's Maria. Her head is bald. He can see her naked shoulders. The head rises higher and higher above the counter. He can see her naked breasts. He wants to turn away; instead, he stares at the counter. He is the Dominican friar Andrey Antonovich Vyrubov. Father Andrey. Who is Father Andrey? He doesn't know any Father Andrey. Maria in a rain of colored stones; she is naked. He wants to get up, flee into the cold. The snow has swept away the tracks. She comes toward him, without stepping. The wall behind her approaches; the counter comes closer. He stretches out his hand to her and the wall recedes. And then he knows what happened. They were married in the chapel of Otrada. He got senselessly drunk at the wedding; he couldn't embrace her. She will marry the man who runs the restaurant, and he will murder her. But it isn't too late. He raises himself, supports himself on his elbows. She takes a blanket off the counter. The blanket. Now he remembers. But this blanket is transparent. She holds it against her body; he can still see her breasts, her thighs, her knees. She waves the blanket from side to side like a dancer. Hadn't she been bald? Now her hair falls to her shoulders. He starts to tear at his belt. Why undress? He is naked. The bottles behind the counter move toward him; the timetables move. He is in the taproom of the Mirgorod station. Father Andrey. His head falls back on the bench with a thud. It's the servant girl, not Maria. But he doesn't know if she is still in the room. She puts out the light. He shivers. Why can't he hear her steps moving away? She has sat down on the bench

246

beside him. He had better lie motionless and pretend to be asleep. A woman's hand caressing his body. It is a delusion; it is not the servant girl. His body is on fire. He is in Charkov. Isn't she sick? Isn't she lying in bed? Why is he lying in bed, and she sitting beside him? He is Father Andrey Antonovich Vyrubov; he has taken the vow of chastity. He can feel her warm breath in his ears, her breasts against his body. He cries out to all good angels; presses his back against the hard mattress. The mattress is like a wall. He is fighting with his back to the wall. He can feel the taste of her lips, recognizes it. If he doesn't move now, he is lost. He sits up and pushes Maria away with all the strength he can command, grasps into a void. A door creaks. The great bliss of victory overwhelms him. He is Father Andrey, lying on a hard bench in a taproom in Mirgorod. The contours of the window stand out against the dark.

CHAPTER 13

I

For a year, Maria traveled with Alexis from country to country, from city to city, from doctor to doctor. The seasons passed by like alien landscapes. Hope journeyed on ahead of them, settled down, disappeared when they arrived.

Yalta, Paris, Brussels, Genoa, Vienna. Alexis entered the hotels they stayed at, mummified; left his room only to go to the doctor; crept away when it was over, like a thief. From his lower lip to where his neck began, his head was bandaged. He spoke with great difficulty; the water he drank had to be given to him drop by drop by Maria or Elise Perrier. "Don't move your head," the doctors said. "Don't move your head," they repeated, the pompous ones, the pacifiers, the ones who knew the answers to everything, and the frightening ones. They

247

unwound the white bandage, the yellowed gauze; they cleaned the wound, a blue hole; they put on new bandages. In their hands Alexis' head grew smaller and smaller, a thing that was wrapped, unwrapped, rewrapped. And then there were the charlatans, the lamplighters of the hopeless; they helped the traveler to deceive himself; they boiled herbs in hotel rooms, laid on magnets, murmured formulas.

He never complained. His selflessness, which was one of the reasons she loved him, expressed itself in its strangest guise, in which virtue was most closely akin to egoism. He seemed to realize that at this point, she would find his mistrust the most difficult thing to bear. The sick proclaimed their mistrust of the healthy by telling them they felt superfluous. Never did he suggest that she leave him, that he was less than he had been before, that her young blood must be thirsting for physical love. Was it pride? He accepted her love as if he were sure of it. He never forgot that it was easier to live with a dying man than with a beggar. With cheerful lies he repaid what he received from her in the form of merciful lies. He let her suffer with him, but did not torture her. He uplifted her in that he did not humble her.

Although very little news reached them, Maria knew what was being said about her in Russia. Her husband was in jail; she had abandoned her children; she was traveling in Europe with her lover. But her conscience did not plague her. She hated Vassily; her children were safe; she loved Alexis. She slept beside him; their bodies didn't touch. "You mustn't move your head," she said, and started out of her sleep because she dreamed that he had moved his head. He feared the sleepless nights. When evening approached, she turned the clocks back; not one told the right time any more. "No, it's only six," she said when it was eight. Every night his eyes expressed the hazard that lay ahead. Slowly he turned his head to face her, his cheek sank into the cushion; his blond hair fell across his forehead like a golden frame for the dark picture of his agonized face. He lay thus, facing her, watching her as if he had to watch over her sleeplessness, like a fearful master lying awake himself in his anxiety that his watchman might fall asleep.

Since their first kiss, an invisible bond of pain had united her with love. Now, lying beside the suffering man, her love had grown painless. Still, she felt that she was not acting unselfishly. The beautiful and mysterious obligation to do the right thing would be gone when Alexis died. She clung to him as if he were her savior, not she his.

Sometimes she admitted to herself that it would be better for Alexis to return to his family, that he might live longer in a sanatorium, and die more peacefully. But between her and the abyss lay nothing but his constantly shrinking head, nothing but the hopeless child he had become. If fate took Alexis from her, then she was doomed to destroy herself and others. Her children? Her heart ached for her children, but they did not protect her. The thought of returning to Vassily sent cold chills down her spine. Vassily or any other man—the same contest of strength, the same fury of destruction. Alexis must not die.

She had succeeded in quieting her conscience, but her nerves became threadbare. She fell asleep only when Alexis had fallen asleep, and slept only as long as he did, three or four hours. Because she did not want to show her irritation, and because the exertion it took to make herself look attractive, to smile, to lie, exhausted her, she often fled from his sight. The dialogue with herself drove her around in eternal circles. Like a starving man who sees a piece of bread in every stone, she saw in every stranger someone to talk to. She confided her most secret sorrows to Elise Perrier, and heard her own words come back to her like a hollow echo. In a Viennese park, she told an old woman the story of her life, but by the time she was through, the old woman was no longer sitting beside her. Two or three times Katharina O'Rourke sent her secret messages, reporting on Tania or Tioka. Her mother had to write in secret, like the aunts in their asylum. Her mother was a blade of grass over which swept the wind of Otrada. Only one of Maria's old friends showered her with letters—Vladimir Stahl; but she despised herself for answering him, one outcast to another. She found herself talking aloud to herself, and ran back to the hotel afraid that Alexis might have moved his head and died; or because she felt safe only at the source of her misery. Now she could visualize death, but the daily business of dying had become something so ordinary that the dying of death seemed inconceivable.

She prayed a great deal, without faith. There was a God who had created the world and those who peopled it, with their manias and their poverty and their need, perhaps too with their joys and forgetfulness and foolishness; but the earth with all its people was a spinning top for children, spinning on and on, and He who had started it gyrating was no longer alive. The earth went on spinning, the top of a dead God.

They were staying at the Kurhaus Stefanie in Baden-Baden. The name of this station of hope was Professor Hannocker, an old man who had retired to the German spa but still occasionally saw patients. Alexis' condition had deteriorated visibly, but he tried to calm Maria, encourage her, urged her not to despair. His spirit was alive, and he often entertained her with stories and recollections, even with plans for the future. She didn't know whether he ever slept any more.

It was a wet, cold February. The fog buried its fangs like a hungry animal in the shrubbery of the Kurpark, into the bed of the river Oos, into streets and alleys and valleys. The naked branches of the trees fought with the fog like Laocoön and his sons with the snakes. In the evening one could hear the stringed instruments of the orchestra in the salon, and the laughter of guests in the lobby.

On the day after her arrival Maria received, from an anonymous source, a newspaper from Moscow, the *Russkiye Vedomosty*. She often received anonymous mail. Sometimes it sanctimoniously exhorted her to contemplation, or reproached her for her wickedness. The hand-writings were all alike: the script of people who lived the life of another. On this day, a reporter asked to be allowed to speak to her, a certain Dr. Hugo Friedlieber, from Vienna. He corroborated what she had read in the paper: Count Vassily Vassilyevich Tarnovsky had been acquitted by a court in Gomel of the charge of attempted murder, and been set free. He had acted, so it said, with justified indignation over his wife's unfaithfulness and the provocatory behavior of her lover. "I imagine," said Dr. Friedlieber, whom she had refused an interview, "that Count Tarnovsky will now demand custody of the children. That shouldn't come as a surprise to you, Countess."

She had spoken to the journalist in the writing room of the hotel, but she did not go back to Alexis. The news had upset her; she didn't want him to see her disturbed. She couldn't stay in the lobby. It was full of Russian guests who had come to the Kurhaus for the Roman baths and the gambling; a steamship, motionless, frozen fast in an icy harbor. On arriving, she had seen, through a glass door, the Grand Duchess Katharina Leopoldovna; now the whole hotel knew that Maria Nikolaevna Tarnovska and her lover were staying there.

She paced up and down the corridor in front of the rooms. Maria

Nikolaevna Tarnovska, née Countess O'Rourke. She said the name aloud to herself, contemptuously, the way people spoke of her now; lasciviously, like the men; indignantly, like the women; spoke the name like a prosecutor, a priest, a hangman. Attempted murder; justified indignation. What about Julia Terletzkaya, Olga Kralberg, Eleanor Gregorievskaya? Who were the sanctimonious judges, the bribed witnesses, who had dared to acquit Vassily? Up and down she paced, past the doors of rooms, listening if one was opening, watching the end of the corridor where the elevator door might open. She had to hide, and Vassily would demand custody of the children. Tania, whom he had conceived in anger; Tioka, whom he had not wanted to sire. The evening in the Eremitage: "Moscow will be empty without you, Countess"—and since then she had done nothing but love. Her body had been silenced, and she had been happy that it had remained silent. She had changed bandages, set clocks back, thought up white lies. And for that she now had to fear a door opening, the elevator stopping at their floor. Punishment was not meted out for sins. One should have asked the God who was dead to forgive one's good deeds. And Alexis' suffering, which only his eyes betrayed. Like the tactile sense of the blind, they had to function doubly—they saw and they spoke.

> Preferable 'tis to live
> A lowly slave in upper regions
> Than exist in waters Stygian
> As phantom king or hero brave
> Whose feats are sung by Homer.

Heine, his favorite poet. Why was Alexis being punished? With which of Vassily's mistresses would Tania and Tioka live? They would understand each other, Vassily and Terrible O'Rourke. Naturally, you can keep your children! Adultery, manslaughter, justified indignation. She had to return to Russia and prevent the kidnaping. Up and down went the elevator. Behind the door, voices grew louder. Russian voices? The carpet swallowed up the sound of her steps; the corridor became longer and longer. Vladimir Stahl. He would come if she called him; he would hurry to her with deceptive, egoistic hopes. What did it matter? He was a human being like herself. He had forged prescriptions and behaved like a coward. He was a drug addict. What did it matter?

A door opened, Alexis' room. Professor Hannocker, an important man, they said. A big, dirty, bearded man, like a muzhik. How did he find Alexis? What was the verdict?

The wound had eaten its way deep into the bone, the professor explained. Impossible to operate. How long would he live? The professor shrugged. "Keep him as motionless as possible, and he will live longer." Other doctors? "Let's be honest, Countess. You could have saved yourself this trip to Baden-Baden." He nodded, bowed. Mistresses did not die from sorrow.

Her eyes filled with tears. She had always been able to cry only in rage. Manslaughter, justified indignation, acquittal. They are your children, Count Tarnovsky. An adulteress.

Alexis' death. What would she do with the dead man; how would she bury him; to whom could she turn; how was she to live from now on? She wanted to cry out for help. The doors would open, the elevator would stop, the Grand Duchess Katharina Leopoldovna would step out. But the doors remained close; the corridor was still.

3

In the carriage that was taking her to the station Baden-Oos, the feeling that she had made a mistake grew in her until she was in despair. Were there any insinuations more dire than those experienced in loneliness? Help from Vladimir Stahl. Hadn't he been waiting for this hour?

Stahl had evidently given himself an injection on the train, for he was in high spirits; still, it seemed to her that he had deteriorated. He couldn't sit up straight in the low carriage, and she wondered if he would ever be able to hold himself erect again. She had sought asylum and fled to a ruin.

It was an unusually mild late February evening. The fog had grown lighter, but not lifted. It grew light from the top down: first the sky, then the rooftops, then the street. From the hills of the Schwarzwald came the aroma of firs. The Kurhaus, both castles, and the Casino were illuminated.

"What inappropriate surroundings to die in," said Stahl. He looked at her from the side. "You don't look well, Mura. A wasted year."

"You are a monster."

"You are a child. Only youth treats the years so lightly."

"I wasn't pursuing pleasure," she said.

"But that is what you should have been doing. You know that Alexis must die, so you are deceiving him and yourself."

"His will to live . . ."

"Is pure illusion. His body longs for death, but his soul forces him to the suffering you call the will to live. By the way, why don't they give him morphine?"

"I told you that he isn't allowed to move his head. If they gave him morphine, he wouldn't know what he was doing."

"Does he complain much?"

"Alexis doesn't complain."

"Of course. A real man from top to toe. And a high moral sense. People mistake the cowardice with which a man endures suffering for morality. Whoever isn't prepared to suffer is considered immoral."

"Be still," she said. "You don't understand."

The carriage rumbled across large cobblestones. "Why do you love him?" asked Stahl.

"I don't know. And I don't want to know. He taught me to feel. But that doesn't mean anything to you."

"And he lets you suffer with him. He doesn't have an infectious disease; but believe me, every disease is infectious. The dying poison the living. Dying is painful, bue easy. The whole burden of the lie is yours. For Alexis, destruction means peace; you will have to fight on. By the way, I consider you just as incapable of loving as myself. Even the love between man and woman requires a certain benignity of which you don't know the meaning. When you can't torture someone else, you torture yourself. I have always been suspicious of members of the nursing profession, as I am of good friends. *Donec eris felix, multos numerabis amicos: tempora si fuerint nubila, solus eris.'* Ovid knew nothing about the human race. Those who are fortunate have no friends; those who are unfortunate don't, either, but at least one can always find mourners. At the bedside of the dying, people feel no envy. The death of the other gives them a feeling of superiority—they think fortune has favored them."

"I wish you would turn around and go right back," said Maria. "I forgot that you have brought me nothing but misfortune."

Stahl smiled—that is to say, he laughed, because he couldn't smile. "Now, there's gratitude for you! I came to help you. I am no mourner.

Let the dead rest; I want to save the living. I know an excellent lawyer, Dr. Prilukov, sly as a fox. He will handle your divorce. By the way, do you have money?"

"I don't know."

"Didn't you ever bother to find out?"

"Alexis is rich."

"That's not going to do you much good. Never mind. Don't worry about it."

The outlines of the hotel appeared. Now the gas lanterns stood quite close together, and the Augustaplatz looked like a ballroom.

4

She told Alexis that Stahl happened to be in Baden-Baden for the cure. He received the Baron reluctantly, almost inimically. Stahl sat down beside the bed of the sick man. Only one lamp was burning. It drew a shadow circle on the ceiling.

"What are they saying in Moscow?" Alexis asked.

"Don't worry about that. You have been forgotten. Andrey Makarov has just been cashiered out of the Navy for gambling debts. Right now, that's making the rounds."

Maria was watching Stahl tensely, ready to interrupt him at any moment. She should have discussed Vassily with him, the children, the possibility of a return trip to Russia for her, to attend to legal matters; but she should not have let him see Alexis. She had, of course, familiarized Stahl with the entire list of forbidden subjects, the roster of lies attached to the beds of the sick like a fever chart—but how did she know she could depend on him?

Suddenly Alexis interrupted his visitor's chatter. "You are as good as a doctor, Vladimir Mihailovich. Don't you think I am doomed to die of this wound?"

"You don't have to die, my friend," said Stahl. "Your doctors are fools. They treat you as if you were paralyzed—in fact, they paralyze you, a method that is quite passé. The quicker you learn to move around again, the better."

Maria's nerves were a thousand fingers drumming a senseless rhythm.

"But the pain," said Alexis. "It is impossible."

"Naturally, the pain," said Stahl. "We must free you from that. You just said I was as good as a doctor. I was a doctor once. They refused me a diploma because my colleagues sensed that I was an enemy of pain. Pain, the watchdog of the organism. Ridiculous! Pain is the signpost of the charlatan. Without pain the patient would be saved and the doctor lost."

"I can't tell you how I hate the doctors," said Alexis.

Why did he trust Stahl, Maria wondered in her despair. Had he, like herself, needed a stranger?

"Everybody who has had any experience with doctors hates them," said Stahl. "Suffering, my dear Alexis, is unnecessary. Our charlatans glorify suffering; our doctors, philosophers, theologians. Christianity is one monstrous glorification of suffering. If you want to see heaven, you must get there via the cross. It is a plot of those in bondage against those who are free. Happiness is nothing but freedom from pain. You should know that better than anyone else. Those who are not free have branded happiness as frivolity. In our whole lives we know only a few painless moments, and that is valid for the healthy as well as for the sick. And they want to rob us of these, too."

"I think Vladimir Mihailovich has tired you enough," said Maria. But for the first time, Alexis was not paying attention to her. He had eyes only for the big black bird sitting at his bedside.

"Can you free me?" he asked.

"I can do much more than that. As soon as I have you free of pain, try to move your head." He took a little leather etui out of his bag.

"I forbid you to do it!" Maria cried, leaning over the sick man. "Don't let him tell you anything, Alexis. He is a quack!"

"You have consulted many quacks," said Stahl.

Alexis sat up, supporting himself on his elbows so that he might see Stahl better. The bandage, like a heavy burden, seemed to be dragging his whole face down.

Stahl sterilized the needle, held the hypodermic up to the light. "There is nothing sublime or grandiose about suffering," he said. "The dying only cause others suffering because they believe they may then suffer less."

"I won't allow it, Alexis," Maria said. "He is a drug addict."

"As you wish," said Stahl, and started to put the hypodermic needle away again.

Alexis stretched out his hand. He lost his self-control; his pride went under; his lies crumbled like cloth that had hung for a long time and turned to dust at the first touch. He implored Stahl to free him of pain just for one night. Then he turned to Maria, beseeching her, as if she had not nursed him for a year but tortured him; as if he had borne his pain for her sake; as if she were standing between his freedom and bondage. "One night . . . for just one night," he begged, as if she had never stood watch, as if he had had to stand watch for her.

Why couldn't she overcome her pity? Was it that she couldn't lie any longer now that he had stopped lying? That the longing for peace and liberation was overwhelming her, too? Or was it only the incredible weariness that overcame one, deathlike, after the death of a beloved?

Stahl pushed up Alexis' sleeve and gave him the injection.

The effect came fast. Alexis fell back, and a transformation, contrary to nature and therefore all the more miraculous, began. It was as if what had been destroyed were being restored. Cells were being put together again, furrows smoothed out, scars made invisible. Yet Maria was not startled, because it was not a new face she saw—it was the new face that disappeared behind the earlier, familiar, beloved one.

"Let him rest," said Stahl. "We'll try it later." He didn't say what they would try later.

Alexis slept. Stahl sat beside the bed and watched him. Maria had sunk down in the armchair under the lamp. It was as if everything around her were being transformed, too; as if the night were shining through the drawn curtains as the sun usually shone through them; as if Vladimir Stahl were made of paper, a black drawing; as if the salon orchestra were playing the same melody over and over again, the rattle of train wheels; as if Alexis were a wax figure with the painless face of a wax figure, the face of a boy, or of a dead man. His mouth was half open. Every now and then his tongue moved across his lips. He was wetting them—a dead man who was thirsty. He mumbled something that sounded like "thirst." She got up. Stahl handed her a glass of sugar water. She let her hand glide under the cushion in an experienced motion, lifted his head, and held the glass to his lips.

Then her eyes widened, like someone who couldn't believe what she saw, yet, under some mysterious compulsion, must observe it more closely.

The bandage around Alexis' neck had grown damp. Water, half pink, half pus-yellow, was seeping through the gauze, through absorbent cotton and muslin. Had she spilled the water? But if she had spilled it, why was it the color of blood and pus? He drank thirstily, and the more he drank, the wetter the bandage became. Suddenly, as if out of ambush, the realization overwhelmed her—he couldn't swallow. The liquid was coming out of his gullet; the water was running through the wound, washing it out from within, taking along its sediment, and leaving his head through the opening in his throat. She screamed: "The doctor! The doctor!"

Stahl grasped her wrist. "The doctor can't do anything." He bent over the bed.

She tugged at his shoulders; he shook her off. He seemed to know that Alexis had his eyes fixed on one spot; now Stahl, moving back and forth, tried to project and fix himself in the sick man's line of vision. Then, with what seemed to Maria superhuman forcefulness, he spoke to Alexis, commanding him to move his head. And Alexis began to move his head, a little to the right, a little to the left; at first, as if out of habit, slowly. Then his eyes came to life, mirroring his ecstasy. He began to move his head faster. He seemed to be saying no, stubbornly, angrily, joyfully—no, no, no! He shook his head. And a gurgling sound came from his throat; the rose-red, pus-yellow water dripped from bandage to pillow.

Maria covered her face with her hands. Like someone fighting for breath, she fought for her will but could not find it. It was as if she had exhaled it with her last breath. The palm of her hand, pressed to her eyes, was a black mirror. She wanted to defend herself, but she had become one with Alexis. Blood was running over her tongue, chin, throat. The desperate wish to free herself from pain overpowered her so forcibly that she cried, "Free me! I can't stand it any longer. I can't suffer any more."

She saw Stahl turn toward her, felt him push up her sleeve, felt the needle in her arm, his thumb pressing hard on one of her veins; then a deep stillness fell upon her, and everything around her submitted to its solemnity. Alexis lay still, eyes closed. The music from the hotel lobby was muted. Stahl was walking on velvet feet. What had dragged her down now carried her aloft. Her soul slipped away from its duties. And she felt infinite gratitude. She was grateful to the magician for her painlessness and freedom; she even saw herself touchingly with the eyes of the sick man.

She let Stahl take her by the hand and lead her into the next room; let him undress her like a child that one was putting to bed; let

257

him touch her naked body. She experienced her insensibility as an unearthly feeling; above her self floated a second self, and it covered her with benign hands. Freed from pain, she had been freed also from ecstasy. She lay on the bed and didn't know who she was; he took her, and she didn't know who he was.

When she awoke, the sun was shining into the room. She wanted to go on sleeping. It was as if she were standing on the borderline between unreality and reality; she could still turn around and go back into unreality. But suddenly memory grasped her and pushed her across the borderline. She got up and threw her dressing gown across her shoulders.

Vladimir Stahl was sitting beside Alexis' bed, dressed, his long head sunk forward like a broken treetop. As in an exorcism, he was stammering incomprehensible words. The bed was covered with yellow gauze, bloody cotton, soaked bandage. Alexis had torn the bandage from his head. He was dead.

5

Maria Tarnovska says nothing. She orders Stahl to attend to all formalities for her: the professor, the coroner, the hotel management, the morgue. She insists that Stahl accompany her. He is at her side when she is asked to identify the dead man, his name, her relationship to him. "He is my lover." Is she married? Yes, two children. The burial to be provisional.

The sky above the cemetery is a cloudless blue, the air crystal-clear; spring in its cradle. They stand beside the grave. "His blood is upon you, Vladimir Mihailovich." On the way back into town, she stops the carriage at the Russian church. Its onion tower gleams golden. "You are coming with me, Vladimir Mihailovich." She kneels for a long time in front of the Madonna. "I prayed for hatred."

Telegrams to Alexis Bozevsky's family. Preparations for the removal of the body to Russia. Bills. Railway tickets. A last visit to Alexis' grave, the carriage filled with flowers. "You carry the wreath, Vladimir Mihailovich."

He speaks to her; she doesn't answer him. On the journey to Kiev, she locks herself in her compartment with Elise Perrier. In the dining car she tells Stahl, "I demand that you go on to Moscow."

Across the Russian border, snow and cold weather. Stahl hands her an envelope full of banknotes. She doesn't thank him; gives it to her maid. When he says good-by, she turns her head away.

She drives to the Grand Hotel. They regret, but they don't have a room. In the Hotel Continental she gives her name—no room. The same reply in the Hotel National, the Hotel de l'Europe. The Hotel François on the Fundukleyevskaya Boulevard takes her in. They haven't installed electric light yet; the gas lamps flicker wearily; the room is poorly heated. A pockmarked boy brings an earthenware hot-water bottle. Maria Tarnovska cannot sleep.

On the street, she meets acquaintances. They turn away. Kiev seems small, a village. She locks herself in her hotel room. In the dining room, traveling salesmen are telling dirty jokes. It is difficult for her to recall why she came to Kiev. "Your children, Countess." The children. All will be well.

She writes to her mother. No answer. She doesn't mourn Alexis. It is comfortable to die. Sometimes a tender warmth fills her being, but then Alexis is not dead. He is lying on her breast; she can hear his breathing. When she falls asleep, she dreams of Vladimir Stahl, sees him in rags, starving, covered with running sores. In the morning she wants to go on dreaming. Mourning is love; he who wants to live has to hate. A letter from her mother. Tioka is in Otrada, but Tania is gone. "Vassily came and took her away with him." Took her, like a thing. And nobody stopped him. "Your father has put aside an allowance for you." Five hundred rubles a month. "Is that a lot?" she asks Elise Perrier. "For me it is a lot, Countess."

If Vassily finds out that she is in Kiev, he will kidnap Tioka, too. She hires a carriage to drive to Otrada. The thought of Terrible O'Rourke. The carriage drives up to the door; she sends it away.

One night she gets up, dresses, asks the doorman the way to the nearest apothecary. The shop is closed. Another one. Closed. The third one opens for her. The apothecary, in felt slippers, is an old man with kindly eyes. He speaks with a foreign accent. He reminds her of Dr. Frithof, the eye specialist. A good omen. She embarks on complicated explanations. Somebody is sick at the hotel, in unbearable pain, doesn't want to call in a doctor. At last she says the word "morphine." No surprise. Morphine is sold without prescription, like cough drops or headache powders. Vladimir Stahl's great secret! She has to laugh. "Do you know how to give yourself an injection?" the apothecary asks. He hasn't believed a word she said. "I would advise you to dissolve the gray powder over a flame until it is a crystal liquid." He wraps the hypodermic needle up carefully. She runs back to the hotel as if she were expecting a beloved.

Next day she sends Elise Perrier to Otrada. This time she demands her child. She orders a third room. Without fear of meeting people she knows, she hurries to the Kreshtshatick Boulevard. The sun is shining; the ice is brilliant; shop windows, church towers are glittering; sleigh bells jingle merrily. "How old is the child?" they ask at the toyshop. She has to stop to think. "Four years. A boy." Two salesmen bring the boxes to her waiting sleigh. The hotel room is transformed into a paradise of toys. She can't stop looking at the clock. Three clocks, all telling the same time. She no longer has to deceive time. Alexis had to die because he tried to deceive time. For thirteen months she took all suffering upon herself; for one night without suffering he left her. Tioka is four. What is the name of the lawyer Stahl mentioned? He would bring Tania back. For Vassily, Tioka was a toy with which Tania might amuse herself; now Tania should be a toy for Tioka.

It is six. Elise left at ten in the morning. Dusk descends on the Fundukleyevskaya Boulevard. Tioka might catch cold. For thirteen months she hasn't given a thought to the chance that he might catch cold. She will give them another hour, then she will take a sleigh to Otrada.

The door flies open. Tioka comes running to her. She doesn't know afterward how long she held him in her arms. It is as if he returned to her womb, as if his heart were beating once more inside her body. Elise Perrier stands in the doorway. Her smile is like the light music that in the south sometimes accompanies the burial of a child.

6

Dr. Donat Dmitrievich Prilukov's office, in the heart of the Kitaigorod of Moscow, was impressive. It comprised an entire floor, and consisted of a suite of large rooms where junior counselors, chancery clerks, and secretaries rushed busily in and out. A telephone hung beside every desk. Their ringing, and the sound of their handles being cranked, interrupted business conversations. For Maria, who had already waited a quarter of an hour, it was a new world. She had known only a society that spent money; here she discovered a world that made money. She had only known people to whom things happened; here she saw people who made things happen.

She experienced the same fascination of strange things when she took a seat opposite the lawyer. On the walls of the spacious corner office, there were photographs of grateful clients, diplomas, attestations. The room was overcrowded with screens, file cases, potted palms, but the desk was comparatively empty. Except for a bronze desk set and a marble ash tray decorated with monkeys playing, nothing stood on it but a family photograph of a blonde woman with two children. The man behind the desk was slim yet broadly built, an unusually tall man, completely bald, and, contrary to the current fashion, clean-shaven. Bushy dark eyebrows shaded his deep-set eyes; big, very even teeth seemed to rupture his little mouth.

Maria explained her problem. She wanted her marriage to Vassily Vassilyevich Tarnovsky annulled, and her daughter, Tania, returned to her. Prilukov listened like a man hearing a story he had known for a long time. He watched her as if only the movement of her lips interested him, but his gaze was inquiring rather than sensual, that of an art connoisseur rather than a ladies' man. Under his gaze she became conscious of the fact that her youth had proved to be stronger than her misfortune. Her white skin, her blue eyes, her lower lip protruding a little, her figure had apparently lost none of their charm.

"I don't like divorce cases," he said when she had finished. "As you know"—she didn't know—"I am a trial lawyer. And I am interested mainly in political cases. In civil law cases, a lawyer faces one or more individuals; in a criminal case, he has the pleasure of facing the entire administration of justice. I like what is difficult. If I take your case, it will be because I am attracted by the miscarriage of justice Tarnovsky's acquittal certainly was. There's a corruption of the court there, no doubt about it, because the public prosecutor should have lodged a plea of nullity. That the case was brought to court in the little town of Gomel, where Tarnovsky obviously has family connections, stamps the whole affair as a judiciary farce."

"I am not interested in going into the past," she said.

He took the receiver of the telephone off the hook, gave some legal advice over the instrument. She had the feeling it was something that could have waited.

"Leave everything to me," he said, picking up the thread again. "If we want to get your child back, we have to clear you. If we want to clear you, we have to slander Tarnovsky. It will be costly and take a long time, but we shall of course win both cases."

"I don't know if I have so much money."

"I imagine you don't have any money. But don't worry about that. By the way, who is looking after your son?"

"My maid."

"Is she reliable?"

"Absolutely."

"I don't consider it out of the question that Tarnovsky might try to abduct little Tioka."

Her heart beat fast. "He never liked the child."

"That wouldn't matter. I imagine that Tarnovsky is still in love with you. He will try to strike where it hurts most."

He accompanied her to the door. At one of the arched windows, he stopped and pointed to an automobile standing in front of the building. "A Panhard-Levassor, one of those devilish little motorcars. I'm pleading an important case tomorrow. It might interest you. Shall I have my chauffeur call for you?"

7

For the first time since Alexis' death, she spent a quiet night. Next day, when she was driving to the courthouse on Krassnaya Square, she felt as if she had been floating above the ground since the death of her lover, a lost soul seeking other lost souls. Love for the dead man and love for her child had carried her aloft, hatred pulled her back to earth; in love she could no longer feel at home, in hate, not yet. She was not alive, but she was not dead either, like someone who was being operated on under a strong anesthetic, and knew he should be feeling pain, but felt none. She could have bled to death without crying for help. Now she felt, not that a healing process had begun—there was no such thing as healing—but as if she might regain the strength to cry out and show her wounds.

The "important case" Prilukov had mentioned was being tried in the three-cornered courthouse at the Arsenal. Maria had often driven past it with a feeling of horror during her boarding school days. She experienced the same fascination as in Prilukov's office. He was defending three young men, anarchists. They had tried to assassinate the top-ranking Public Prosecutor of Moscow and had wounded him fatally—an act of revenge, because the man had sent one of their comrades to the scaffold. The case had been going on for ten days; today the defense was summing up.

Maria looked at the three wretched figures in the dock—they were young, blond peasant lads with innocent faces, worn down by their long confinement—and at the same time, she tried to put herself in the place of the judge. She envied the old man, envied the jury— peasants, *meshtchanine,* and a retired army officer with one arm—who had the power to give these miserable creatures their lives, banish them to Siberia, or execute them. Prilukov's junior counselor had explained to her that formerly accused men had often been sentenced to a hundred lashes of the whip; now one resorted to the more humane execution of the guillotine. While the judge lost himself in a long- winded legal argument, she looked at the people in the courtroom— ladies, lawyers, peasants, relatives of the anarchists, a few dandified men of the world, officers; the early Romans had probably watched Christians in the arena like this.

Not until Donat Prilukov rose to speak did Maria remember that she was the defense lawyer's guest, that he was her lawyer and pro- tector too, so she really had to hope for a favorable outcome to the proceedings. Prilukov's persuasiveness was overwhelming. He spread his arms like protective wings over the accused; held forth like a Shakespearean actor in the Imperial Grand Theater; changed his voice and spoke unctuously like a parson in the pulpit; pulled mercy, fury, heartrending tones, indignation, and sentimentality out of his top hat like a magician; shrank, grew to towering heights, and seemed to be in as much control of his muscular body as of his voice. Every now and then Maria caught a sentence that sounded familiar—"injus- tice," "hunger," "arbitrary police action," "misery," "power"—words from Andrey's vocabulary. Andrey . . . How much did he know about her and what did he think of it? She didn't dwell long on the thought, for it became increasingly clear to her that defense counsel Prilukov had turned to face her, and was addressing her above the heads of the accused, police officers, and reporters. Once, in the middle of a portentous sentence, his little mouth smiled. He was smiling at her triumphantly, seeking affirmation of his triumph. But all Maria could think of was that he was the type of ugly man whose ugliness grew more and more fascinating and was transformed in the end into animalistic beauty. She saw a vision—Vassily was in the dock. And her lawyer, in charge of her case, avenger in her name, her devotee, was the public prosecutor. It couldn't possibly end differently: they would sentence Vassily to a hundred lashes of the whip. She told herself that if these three peasant lads were acquitted, Vassily would be convicted. Now, like the majority of those present, she was on the side of the accused. Prilukov was bringing his speech for the defense to its conclusion. It was evening. Gaslight fell sickly green over the courtroom, as if accused, secretaries, onlookers, jury were languid fish in an aquarium. The jury withdrew.

In the poorly lit passage, which smelled of wine and sweat, Prilukov came up to her. As he bent over her hand, a plain little blonde woman touched his arm, smiled, and kissed him on both cheeks.

"I saw your picture in Dr. Prilukov's office," said Maria.

"Wasn't my husband wonderful?" said the woman.

Prilukov interrupted her. "The jury will be out until midnight, at least. We can take the Countess back to her hotel."

She wouldn't hear of it. In the cab, despair again took the place of excitement. The homelessness of the hotel room; Tioka in danger; sleepless nights; Tioka's questioning eyes; packed trunks; the specters of poverty and morphine. She belonged neither to those who did nothing nor to those who lived actively. She could still hear the lawyer's voice; and his speech for the defense—in which he had pled more for her than for the accused—seemed a despicable farce. In every man there was a portion of Vladimir Stahl. Perhaps there had been a portion of Vladimir Stahl in Alexis, too, and only his death had saved her from seeing it. Hadn't she sworn to live only for her hatred? Why did one possess power if not to abuse it?

CHAPTER 14

I

The Dominican cloister in Vienna was situated on a quiet street, but the noise of the celebrating city penetrated its stony walls. The night sky was bright with stars, Milky Way, rainbows and fountains of fireworks. It was the night of the thirty-first of December.

Andrey had been in Vienna for four weeks, on orders of the Master General, to stand by the Prior there in the settlement of certain grievances. It was almost two years since he had visited Count O'Rourke in Otrada. They had been rich years—too rich, it sometimes seemed to Andrey. He was not yet thirty, but many already looked upon him as the secret ambassador of the Master General. They praised his diplomatic ability, his integrity, his knowledge of human nature, and his quiet air of authority. There were some who envied him, but they were in the minority. Andrey, however, often asked himself what he had achieved. Had he really achieved anything at all? His sermons in aristocratic circles, among the higher bureaucracy, and in financial circles were quoted, several times even mentioned in the press; but he didn't know whether he had ever helped a single human creature, or saved one soul. The results of his missions were recognized in Rome, but with every mission there grew in him the fear that he was becoming a chargé d'affaires for the Church, "affaires" meaning trouble. Although he did not make the decisions, his recommendations seemed to meet with such approval in Rome that the Master General acceded to them every time. Responsibility rested heavily upon the Dominican.

In Vienna he had attached himself to an old priest, Father Joseph. The lean, quiet man reminded Andrey of his father. Father Joseph was paralyzed in both legs. He was in charge of the cloister library, and managed his activities from a wheelchair, cleverly and lucidly. He was one of those people whose wisdom remained all the purer because it was not burdened with the lees of experience. Andrey liked to visit him after vespers, and his visits seemed to please the old man.

"Turn of the century," said the old priest on this evening. "What are they celebrating—the end of an era or the beginning of a new one?"

"It looks as if they were expecting miracles from the calendar," Andrey said.

The old man in the wheelchair pointed to the open Bible on his knees. "I was reading the twenty-fourth chapter in Matthew," he said. " 'For you shall hear of wars and rumors of wars. Take care that you do not be alarmed, for these things must come to pass, but the end is not yet. For nation will rise against nation, and kingdom against kingdom; and there will be pestilences and famines and earthquakes in various places. But all these things are the beginnings of sorrow. . . . And then many will fall away, and will betray one another, and will hate one another. And many false prophets will arise and lead men astray. And because iniquity will abound, the charity of the many will grow cold.' "

"Do you think our Lord was speaking of the twentieth century?" Andrey asked.

"It certainly sounds like a description of our times." The boom of a cannon shot echoed against the walls. "I don't envy you the twentieth century," said Father Joseph.

"The old have always looked back with nostalgia," said Andrey, "and forward with anxiety. And they have always worried about the young."

"That doesn't prove that their anxieties were ever unjustified. Repetition seems to be soothing; actually it is deceiving. It is like the attacks of a sickness that become more and more familiar to the sufferer; in the end it kills him just the same."

"I know it isn't easy for the aged ones to give up the steering wheel," Andrey was smiling, "but is this not the divine law of the seasons?"

"It is not the law of the seasons that winter follow summer. The new century will dispose of autumn, Father Andrey; later on, o summer as well. Nothing will remain but spring and winter. Th twentieth century will do away with the time for maturity and harvest. The young people won't grow up, they will grow senile. Unable to progress to maturity, they will step forward into a state of decay. And the old people? Unable to harvest the ripe fruit of autumn, they will grasp the unripe fruit of spring. I can see the confusion of the seasons coming."

Andrey looked out into the bare garden, across which the lights of the fireworks flickered. The streets must have been full of merry-makers now; friends kissed each other; those who didn't know each other kissed each other too, even enemies did. They toasted each other in homes, restaurants, cabarets. Men were doubly male and women doubly female as they celebrated the fact that they were alive. The fireworks display shone brightly above the cemeteries. A new century was beginning even for the dead.

"Forget your dark thoughts, Father Joseph," said Andrey, rolling the wheelchair to the window.

"My thoughts are not dark," the old man said stubbornly. "I stopped mourning the torn-off leaves of the calendar long ago, or believing that the new were any cleaner. It is young men like you whom I pity. Read Matthew. 'For as in the days before the flood they were eating and drinking, marrying and giving in marriage until the day when Noe entered the ark, and they did not understand until the flood came and swept them all away; even so will be the coming of the Son of Man.'"

"But you are speaking of the calendar, Father Joseph. Of what importance is a new century within eternity?"

The man in the wheelchair laughed dryly. "What will eternity mean within the new century? Don't you see how the power of the Devil is spreading?" He looked up at the sky. "A harmless festival. But those false stars up there—are they not a symbol? We shoot stars up into the sky and bring down the stars. You will see young people growing up so thirsty for knowledge that they will drink the salt water of the sea, which increases thirst until it becomes unbearable. To live in Paradise means to understand everything and know nothing; to live in Hell means to know everything and understand nothing."

"Why do you think we are losing faith?"

"Because we falsify it. They don't dare yet to negate the physical presence of Christ, but they are replacing God with philosophy. The

Son of God would therefore be the son of a philosophy. It explains evil without fighting it."

The noise of the city came closer, but Andrey, whose thoughts were fluctuating between the warnings of the old man and his own fantasies, felt no curiosity for what was going on in the streets. Since the night in the taproom in Mirgorod, which he liked to call to himself the night of temptation, all connection between him and the past seemed to have been severed. Had he become arrogant since temptation could no longer touch him? How about the others, the tempted and the tempters? For the first time, the image of Maria Tarnovska rose up before him again. Where was she? Had she forgotten him? Had she cried out to him and had he not heard her?

"You are far away, Father Andrey," said Father Joseph.

"I was listening to you. It may be because of my youth, but I can't share your fears. When you look back, you find centuries of stormy progress followed by eras of complete stagnation. Compare progress in the days of the Egyptians, Babylonians, Greeks, and Romans with the stagnation of the Middle Ages."

"And what do you deduce from that?" asked the old man.

"Why shouldn't this also be applicable to love? We live in a time of apparent progress, and at the same time in the Middle Ages of love. Love is like a retarded child in a family of many children, all growing, all developing; only one child remains small, can scarcely speak, and seems to be stupid. But one day this child begins to grow and grows a head taller than any of the others. Attributes that developed while it was mute become evident; it catches up with the others, surpasses them. What is natural happens like a miracle." He laid a hand on the shoulder of the old man. "The people don't know what they are celebrating, but are you so sure they have no reason to celebrate?"

"You will live to see the one form of progress, or the other," said Father Joseph. The bursts of fire were mirrored on his features.

2

Six months later, in the first summer of the new century, Andrey found a message at Santa Maria sopra Minerva from Yuri Tolstoy asking Andrey to meet him on St. Peter's Square.

Andrey had to smile when he saw Yuri coming toward him under the arcades. He hadn't seen Yuri—who in Kiev had belonged to his circle of friends—for a long time, but he had hardly changed at all. He still looked like a dancing bear, was dressed much too warmly; anyone could have guessed at once where he came from. In these alien surroundings, the aristocrat was a muzhik. Yuri was on his honeymoon. After Olga Kralberg left him, he had married a cousin.

It was a hot July day. They walked up and down in the shade of the arcades, between English tourists, nuns, guides, and priests. Andrey wondered why Yuri had wanted to see him, for they had nothing to say to each other, and Yuri spoke only of their mutual friends—as was usual with friends who had nothing to say to each other. Suddenly he stopped and stood still. "Did you know that Maria Tarnovska was in Rome?"

When Andrey said no, Yuri began to talk about Maria. "Her marriage has just been annulled by the Vatican. I don't know any details, but I know she lost the custody of her daughter. If Vassily wanted to, he could take little Tioka away from her, too. That is why— among other reasons—she prefers not to return to Russia." He began to walk on.

"Will she marry Alexis Bozevsky?" Andrey asked.

Yuri laughed. "I quite forget that you live behind cloister walls."

"Cloister walls? That is exaggerated."

"Just the same, you don't seem to know what's going on in the world. Alexis has been dead for a year and a half. And what has happened to Mura since then . . ." After Alexis' death she had returned to her homeland, he went on, but had stayed only a few weeks—just long enough to start proceedings for the annullment of her marriage. "She couldn't possibly stay in Russia, you understand? The scandal over the death of poor Alexis had scarcely died down when all of Moscow began to talk about the suicide of Vladimir Stahl." He chattered on in the same prattling tone, but quite obviously determined not to let himself be interrupted. "You know, once the world has a scapegoat, he's to blame for everything. Mura hadn't seen Stahl for at least half a year when he took poison. Unfortunately, they found letters, a very one-sided correspondence. He must have been writing to her for some time, letters she didn't answer; but Stahl—apparently off his head—went right on writing to her. Only he didn't send the letters off; he kept them in a drawer. They say there must have been about three hundred of them. Before he took his life, in Kiev, he

269

ordered that all the letters be given to Maria Tarnovska, including the last one. They say, of course, that he killed himself because of her. In reality, drug addiction very often ends in suicide."

"And now she is in Rome?" Andrey asked.

"That's just it. My wife and I saw her. Fortunately, she didn't notice us. It was night. She was teetering along a wall; she looked terrible. I think she was drunk. But I hear she's staying at the Grand Hotel. Nobody knows where she gets the money. If old O'Rourke is giving her five thousand rubles a year, that's putting it high. I think she had a short love affair with Ivan Trubetzkoy, but I guess he was smart enough to . . ."

"I must leave you now," Andrey interrupted him. "Where does the honeymoon take you from here?"

Yuri Tolstoy leaned against a column and mopped his brow. Instead of answering Andrey's question, he scrutinized the Dominican with a seriousness that was not like his usual superficial self.

"I looked you up, Andrey," he said, "to talk to you about Mura. Things are going badly for her, worse than you think. At some time or other she must have come under Stahl's influence; she is a drug addict, too. She has fled from God knows how many hotels. Her mother has paid her debts more than once, because otherwise the police would have stepped in. All her jewelry has been stolen, so she says. . . . You must help her."

"I don't know you as the good Samaritan, Yuri."

"I'm no good Samaritan, or I'd do something about it myself. But if you had seen her . . . Andrey, you are a priest." He took Andrey's arm and started to walk again, heavily. "It's like a superstition. I was madly in love with Mura once, all of us in Kiev were—Stahl and Peter Tarnovsky, and probably Vassily, too. She was expecting Tioka and was untouchable, believe me; in spite of that, any one of us would have died for her, or killed the other. We were obsessed. Since then Vassily has killed a man; Peter and Stahl are dead. I seem to have escaped her, miraculously. Perhaps I had the good fortune that she didn't return my love, but did she love any of the others? Perhaps all of me wasn't lost to her. I don't know; thinking isn't one of my strong points. But when I saw her the other night, I had the feeling that I must do something for her. After all, she does have a soul—or don't you think so?"

"I wish you bon voyage and God's blessing on your marriage," said Andrey. "Good-by, Yuri."

He could feel Yuri's disapproving eyes on his back. Not until he was sure that the tourist couldn't catch up with him any more did he begin to walk more slowly. Yuri thought he was a coward. Perhaps Yuri was right. Had he snatched a single soul from the Devil since he had put on the habit of Christ? The saving of a soul. For Yuri it was as simple as that. When Jesus drove the Devil out of the man possessed in Gerasa, the man said to him, "What have I to do with thee, Jesus, Son of the most high God? I adjure thee by God, do not torment me!" The man had worn "no clothes . . . and lived in the tombs, not in a house." He had lodged with death, like Maria. And like Maria he had feared the Devil less than salvation. "Do not torment me!" Although he knew that Jesus was the Son of God come to save him. And then Jesus had put the Devil to flight. But that had been the love of Christ. He, Father Andrey Antonovich Vyrubov was not capable of that. He would pray that Michael, the leader of the heavenly host, send one of his angels to Maria; but he could not be that angel. When doctors were anxious about their own children, or about their mothers or their wives, they called in another doctor, a stranger. The good angels had to be strange angels. Did he still fear temptation? Only God knew that. But didn't it say, "and lead me not into temptation," and wasn't the prayer recommended by Matthew senseless if one walked into temptation with one's eyes wide open? Appeasing thoughts; the question as to who had sent Yuri remained unanswered. Devil or archangel? Andrey tried to tell himself that the Master General's trust imposed duties on him that were more important than the fate of Maria Tarnovska. Was anything more important than a human soul?

The noon of midsummer brooded over the Piazza della Minerva as it had done when Andrey had first entered the church. Six years. What had he accomplished in those six years?

3

In September Andrey found himself in Russia again. Plans for the foundation of a Dominican monastery had been fairly advanced when a very subtle, and therefore all the more effective, intrigue of the

Orthodox Church had again impeded them. Andrey was to meet with representatives of the Orthodox Church to find out, before anything else, if the opposition really came from the Holy Synod. He had already conferred with the head of the Roman Catholic Church in Russia, the Archbishop of Mohilev, who resided in St. Petersburg. It was then he had found out that Sergey Burintzev had been arrested in Orel and would probably be condemned to death. With the permission of the Archbishop, Andrey proceeded to Orel.

Although he arrived on a glorious autumn day, the city made a dismal impression. From the station, the Moscovskaya ran for miles through a miserable section of the town. Men, women, and children in rags crouched in front of dilapidated wooden huts; the senile aged lay alongside the canal; from the houses and shops came the smell of dank clothing and foul flesh. The dirty water of the River Orlik ran past the neglected houses of the inner city. The few public buildings, palaces, and clubs of the aristocracy looked as if they had a guilty conscience.

After Andrey had tried in vain to find out more about Sergey's fate, or get permission to see him, he decided to throw the weight of his name on the scale. An hour later he was told that the Governor of Orel, Gregory Ivanovich Naumov, would receive him.

The Governor's palace, situated next to the Peter Paul Cathedral, which was finished only a few decades ago, looked as if it were above any such thing as a guilty conscience—above conscience, therefore, that existed only when it was guilty. With its snow-white walls, marble steps, gigantic paintings, and enormous candelabra, with its soldiers, guards, and lackeys, it somehow gave the ostentatious impression of an Oriental government palace. Andrey would not have been surprised to see Bedouins, camel drivers, beggars, and lepers outside its high arched windows, but all he saw was a park with an English lawn being watered by a gardener.

"Welcome," the Governor said, stretching out his arms in greeting. "Do you know that I knew your father very well? I still own a French engraving he gave me. You must see it. May I give you a glass of tea?"

Andrey at once began to explain the reason for his visit. He described his friendship with Sergey, and mentioned casually that his father had been very fond of Sergey. Whether Burintzev was guilty or not he couldn't say, but he was of the opinion that there were certain people who simply could not do certain things. That Sergey might have been seduced—perhaps; but that he should seduce others—never. He pretended to know nothing about the seriousness of the accusations against Sergey, and casually expressed his wish to see the arrested man; it was probably only a very understandable error of officialdom that had prevented his visiting Burintzev before now. He spoke on and on, spoke in the end only because he hoped the Governor would at last interrupt him with an encouraging word. But Gregory Ivanovich Naumov said nothing, like those who have learned to wait quietly until the other man was caught in his own web. He was a man of about sixty, with ice-cold blue eyes and a blond mustache, browned a little at the edges from the smoke of papirossi. His hair was thick and blond, and grown lighter with age, so that it was difficult to tell blond and white hairs apart. He was the type of man whom rich widows called handsome.

"I am surprised," he said when Andrey, ashamed of his own loquaciousness, stopped dead in the middle of a sentence. "Very surprised. Your friend Burintzev is not only a member of the Revolutionary Executive Committee; he is one of the leaders. That is—in case you don't know—the organization that had the Chief of Police Indeykin beaten to death with a crowbar. Do you know who was to be the next victim of these bandits?"

"Nobody would give me any sort of information."

"I was to be their next victim, my dear Andrey Antonovich. The bomb that was to put an end to my superfluous existence was found in your friend's suitcase."

"Has Burintzev confessed?"

"We haven't considered confessions important for a long time. At the trial the defendants revoke them and declare they were obtained under duress."

"So Burintzev is accused of the illegal possession of explosives."

"Are you serious?"

"Well, he can't be accused of an assassination that didn't take place."

The Governor held Andrey's glass under the tap of the samovar. "We have fifty-nine governors in Russia. We can't sit back and watch all fifty-nine being murdered."

"Does Burintzev have a lawyer?"

"I am sure the court will give him one."

"Someone who will serve the interests of the state, no doubt."

The Governor lit a papirossa. With the same deliberation with which he had listened to Andrey before, he didn't let himself be ruffled now. "I am not at all sure, Andrey Antonovich, that a lawyer appointed by the court will defend your friend. These anarchists, nihilists, revolutionaries, or whatever they call themselves, are backed by considerable financial resources. Foreign money, in part; money contributed by those who envy us, and by our enemies who want to overthrow the Pobyedonosszev regime with the help of the rebels. But that wouldn't be the worst. The worst are the so-called liberals, who dream of a parliament, or even a constitution, men who call themselves Russians but secretly sympathize with the nihilists. The Moscow lawyers Prilukov and Mlodetzky belong to this group. In St. Petersburg we have Zykler. You won't find any bombs in their suitcases, but they carry a whole arsenal of bombs in their heads. It wouldn't surprise me if one of them took on your friend's case."

Andrey tried to remember the names. For weeks it had tortured him that he had let Maria down. Sergey he would not let down.

"When will the trial take place?" he asked.

Gregory Naumov shrugged. "In a few weeks, months, years."

"Then the prosecution can't be so sure of its case."

"On the contrary. But Burintzev—even if he did want to get rid of my humble self—isn't important enough. For once, we want to put all the leaders of the organization on trial at the same time. At any rate, in the province of Orel. One man always arouses sympathy, that's human nature. Sympathy for the accused stands in opposite proportion to their number."

Love, thought Andrey. He had to try to love even the Governor of Orel. He didn't succeed. The thought that this man could keep Sergey behind bars for years, until the number of the accused had reached the desired round figure, caused the blood to rush to his head. If they were looking for assassins in order to be able to stage a show, then the bomb might very well have been smuggled into Sergey's luggage.

"If I understand you correctly, Gregory Ivanovich," he said, "you are less concerned with Burintzev the individual than with the effect of the court proceedings on the general public. But as far as that is concerned, I would say you are in an extremely advantageous position As Governor of Orel you are faced, not with just another anarchist but with the man who tried to kill you."

274

Gregory Naumov laughed. "You are a Dominican, Andrey Antonovich. You should have become a Jesuit. I know what you are driving at. The Governor pardons his murderer—what a gesture! The assassin has his life given back to him by his victim. Good newspaper material; fine for sermons and schoolbooks. And, you see, that's just why Burintzev must die. If I could pardon him without anyone finding out, it wouldn't bother me. But just as, in bowling, the ball never hits all nine pins but achieves the desired effect by knocking down one that topples all the others, I would drag others down with me if I fell. The 'All nine!' of the revolutionaries is the death of His Majesty the Czar. I stand in front of him. . . ."

"You are comparing yourself to a piece of wood," Andrey interrupted him. "Are you trying to say that the revolution is the rolling ball?"

"I am saying that the hand that throws it has to be stopped in time, and not by holding onto it. That is much too tedious. It has to be chopped off. Liberalism is nothing more than the effort to meet the revolution halfway, and to such an extent that what one is defending is no longer worth defending. What you demand from me is to let mercy precede justice; but that is a paradox, because there is nothing more merciful than justice. I hope that you have come to see me as a man of the Church and a friend of the assassin, without any sympathy for his ideas. But you must realize that we may be guardians, not only of the fate of those who rule Russia, but perhaps of the whole world as well. Not only the sun, but darkness also rises in the East, my dear Andrey Antonovich."

A not unfriendly but final gesture indicated to Andrey that the interview was ended.

"I have undertaken a long journey," said Andrey. "Am I to leave Orel without seeing Burintzev?"

"He is in the prison hospital," said the Governor. "You can't see him now." He accompanied Andrey to the anteroom. "Oh, I wanted to show you the engraving, didn't I? As far as I know, it was once owned by the L'Ardennois family."

Andrey shook his head.

CHAPTER 15

I

Her father's telegram reaches Maria in Rome. Her mother is dying; she wishes to see her daughter. When Maria arrives in Kiev with Tioka and Elise Perrier, another telegram is waiting for her. Katharina O'Rourke is dead. Maria's father lets her decide whether or not to attend the funeral.

It is the end of September, late summer weather. The trees have not yet dropped their leaves. A cool magnificence lies over the earth in this hour of struggle between nature and death. Nature is indulging in a grandiose self-deception. Only the birds know better. They are flocking south, fugitives preserving life. Maria is not afraid of the people in Otrada. She wants to see her mother; the dead woman is to know that she is there. She fears the memories of childhood, the longing for evil that, once past, is no longer evil. She orders the carriage to get them to the funeral just in time, and to take them away again immediately afterward.

For months now she hasn't given herself any more morphine injections. A doctor in Rome advised her to try the newest cure—cocaine. The same effect, simple and harmless. But today she takes no drug. Early in the morning, she sits down in front of the mirror. She makes herself beautiful seldom now, and only for Tioka. Her cheeks are hollow, her eyes lack luster. Today she wants to be beautiful. They will stare at her: her father, Olga, her brothers. How old are they now? Alexander, twenty-one; Zoa, nineteen. She isn't sure. She sends for her tailor, Schrantz. Would he please do something with her black dress, quickly? Schrantz is sorry, but the Countess already owes

276

him twenty-five thousand rubles. With Elise, Maria works all night on the dress.

The great hall of the house in Otrada is full of people. Maria recognizes no one; no one recognizes her. She clings to Tioka's hand. A servant leads her into the salon. Her father comes toward her, hesitates, then kisses her on both cheeks. She would like to throw her arms around his neck, but she controls herself. Then the others dare to embrace her. Alexander is wearing glasses, his face covered with pimples; from top to toe he is the head of his class. Zoa is small, nimble, a jack-in-the-box. Olga is smiling through her tears, both very apropos—smile and tears. She takes Maria by the hand, introduces her husband. Prince Katerinovich is about fifty, stooped; he walks as if on tracks and afraid of slipping off them. Didn't they send for Katherina O'Rourke's sisters? Maria notices their astonished expressions. Anna and Sonya, both are dead. Six months ago Anna died; a week later, Sonya. Now they are pattering through heavenly regions, in step, their heads wagging. Only their steps cannot be heard in heavenly regions. Did they summon their sister? The dead fear loneliness.

The family sits mutely under the paintings of their Irish ancestors, the first Christian King of Connaught, the Bishop of Danzig, the martyr Cornelius O'Rourke, 1578. Tioka clings to his grandfather; the Count puts his arm around the boy's shoulders. Patriarch and grandson, a picture. Maria can feel no sorrow. Anger is the antidote for grief. Her mother didn't die of epilepsy; she froze to death. Where will they bury her? Beside the Princess? Will her father go twice a month to her mother's grave? He always does the right thing. On the first and third Tuesday, to the grave of his first wife; on the second and fourth, to Katharina's grave. Prince Katerinovich is holding Olga's hand; Alexander and Zoa are sitting side by side; then patriarch and child, ancestral portraits under ancestral portraits. She had to become what she had become—because they made her wear dark glasses, because she pulled Zoa out of the stream, because Anna Dobroyubova left her alone, because Andrey spoke of Shitomir, because her father flogged the groom.

They drive to the cemetery. In the first carriage, her father, Prince Katerinovich, Olga, Maria. At the open grave, she stands beside her father. The autumn wind moves gently in her veil. If the wind were to raise all veils, it would reveal that no one is crying. Veils were invented to hide indifference. She pulls her veil away from her face; the tears are rolling down her cheeks. Olga makes a horrified gesture. The cemetery is black with people standing between the graves, all the way to the wall. In black, the staff, the peasants, the *starosti*— country gentry, *semsky natshalniks*—old people, former *dvorovyes* and *kreposturyes*. Which one of them knew her mother? They are making their reverences to death, not to the dead. From the rise of ground where she is standing, she can see the mausoleum of the Princess. They are burying Katharina O'Rourke in a provisional grave. She ordered that her body be taken to Kiev, to be interred in the vault of her family, the Seletzkys. Maria had been told this on the way to the burial. Her gray, docile mother. Her last act of will had been her first. In death she struck a blow. She had not wanted to go to her final rest in Otrada. Like pregnant women, the dead tend toward their mothers. Maria, too, will arrange to be buried beside her mother.

They return to Otrada. Maria does not enter the house again. Her father, Olga, her brothers kiss her on both cheeks. She does not want to embrace anyone. Night is falling. Elise Perrier is looking out the window. "Be glad that this is not your home," Maria says. "I am glad, Countess." The lights in the carriage dance as if they were far away. Maria takes her snuffbox out of her bag. Tioka has fallen asleep, his head on her shoulder. In the bliss of her intoxication she has the feeling that she has saved her child from Otrada.

She wants to leave Kiev for fear Vassily might come and abduct her son. "Pay the bill," she tells Elise. "We don't have any money, Countess." Maria laughs. "Did you take your salary, Elise?" "We have no money, Countess." Maria doesn't open the envelopes with the weekly bills. "They will throw us out into the street, Countess." Maria laughs. In moments of clarity, she tries to think of someone from whom she could borrow: a gentleman she doesn't know, in a carriage passing by; an old headwaiter in a restaurant; a teller in the bank—he would only have to put his hand in the till. Absurd ideas. She doesn't follow up any of them. She writes to Uncle Edward. He sends her money. She opens some of the bills at random, buys cocaine for herself, toys for Tioka. There isn't enough left to leave Kiev. When they walk, she holds Tioka fast by the hand. Her cocaine dreams are not always blissful. She sees ghosts. All doors have to remain open. The dead stand behind closed doors, erect, waiting. Alexis, yellow gauze around his neck; Peter in his student uniform; Vladimir Stahl, a hypodermic needle in his hand. One night the door between salon and bedroom falls to. She is afraid of waking Tioka; she doesn't dare to call Elise; she doesn't dare to open the door behind which Alexis stands, yellow gauze around his neck. In the morning Elise finds her frozen to the spot, bathed in sweat, staring at the door.

She asks herself why, of all the dead, she fears Alexis most. He had been good, and she had been good to him. Because he had been good, he had not been permitted to live; and because she had been good to him, he had left her. Every day she burns one of Vladimir Stahl's letters. There are still two hundred and fourteen left. When the last one is burned, a miracle will take place.

On a rainy October day, Elise Perrier comes back from town in a state of excitement. She has seen Vassily Tarnovsky. Maria lies awake all night. Next morning she summons all her strength and sends a telegram to Donat Prilukov.

2

Donat Prilukov arrived in Kiev two days later. It was afternoon, but Maria was in bed. She had slept very little that night. She asked him to wait. For only a few hours at a time could she still look as she had looked before Alexis' death.

"I am relieved," he said. "Your telegram sounded desperate."

"I am desperate, Dr. Prilukov."

"Financial worries?"

"I have sixty rubles left."

"Leave everything to me."

"Vassily is in Kiev. I am sure he has come to take Tioka from me."

"I can manage our smart Count."

She described her life since she had left Moscow, not completely, but not deceitfully, either. Mainly she talked about the insults she had had to endure socially. "You may think all this is ridiculous, but it is the only society I know."

"I don't know if you have noticed, my dear Maria Nikolaevna"—he called her by name without asking her permission—"what a change the word 'society' has undergone lately. *Obshtshestvo*. Until the middle of the last century, it stood for a coterie of more or less rich aristocrats who formed a tight little circle around Little Father, the Czar. *Matushka Russya,* our Little Mother Russia, had to subordinate herself to Little Father, *Batyushka Gossudar;* just as the mother, in our patriarchal system, must subordinate herself to the father. Then the circle began to expand, and gradually *obshtshestvo* began to mean—as it does in all civilized countries—public opinion, that is to say, the opposite of a privileged society. The smaller circle quite logically tries to prevent being swallowed up by the larger one. It is the tendency of every privileged caste to build the walls highest at the very moment when they are no longer capable of protection. The rats boarding the sinking ship. The sooner you recognize that you are not being banished from the living to the dead but that, on the contrary, specters are pushing you out among the living, the better it will be for you." He was pacing up and down with long strides. "Until all that becomes obvious, you must go abroad."

She became aware of the ambiguity of her feelings. The strength emanating from this man was a physical strength in an almost scientific sense—a magnitude emanating from a body that could change speed and direction of other bodies. In the proximity of Donat Prilukov she felt safe, but she feared that he might become indispensable to her and destroy her personality. Meanwhile she could not ask of what stuff the lifebelt he had thrown out to her was made.

"Abroad?" she said. "I have just told you that I can't even pay my bill here."

"Leave all that to me," he said. He was looking out the window. "We are going to have a miserable winter. You are going to leave for the Riviera tomorrow."

"From hotel to hotel . . . I moved with Alexis Bozevsky far too often from hotel to hotel."

She leaned back, and spoke, not sure any more if she was speaking under compulsion or in despair, whether she wanted to startle the man with her confession, or arouse his pity. Since the only man she had ever loved had left her—she explained—she believed in nothing; only her love for her child was keeping her alive. It was not her conscience that was torturing her: she hated the dead who had left no other heritage but guilt; but she had sunk deeper and deeper—wasn't that how people put it? Morphine and cocaine were her only support, but the intoxication they brought with them was no salvation any more. The dead pursued her, stood behind closed doors. "I am not fit for anything. Or I am capable of everything. I think I am going out of my mind."

"Let me take care of the dead," said Prilukov.

She thought the words strange. They made her laugh. At last Prilukov sat down. That was agreeable; his presence no longer filled the whole room.

"You must have guessed long ago that, as far as I am concerned, you are not only a client, Maria Nikolaevna. I wouldn't have hurried here otherwise. I am a busy man. Your telegram had to come. You are probably thinking that I am taking advantage of the situation, but six months from now, you will see things quite differently."

"Are you proposing that I become your mistress?"

"If that is the way you want to put it, although I must say, only my honesty forces me to admit it. What I intend to do for you, I intend to do in any case. I suggest that you leave tomorrow for Nice, and stay at the Hotel Négresco. You will find an account in your name at the Crédit Lyonnaise. My friend Dr. Fournier will look after your health." He looked at the clock, but he spoke not in terms of hours, but of months. "As soon as my time permits—right now I am representing General Rhil in an important inheritance case—I shall visit you in Nice. By that time you should be perfectly capable of making your own decisions. Whether you want to stay in Nice or rent a house—we can leave all that to the future."

"So you are ready to leave something to the future?" said Maria. "You seem to be taking everything else upon your shoulders."

"My shoulders are broad."

She wanted to say all sorts of things—that she was not a mistress, never had been; that he was forgetting his wife and children, but she was not forgetting them; that perhaps love was ruthless, but that she could not make love without love; that society had ostracized her, but that a Countess O'Rourke remained a member of society even when ostracized. She had taken cocaine and her sensibilities were sharpened, so that all contours seemed keen-edged, even if she couldn't quite tell whether they outlined man or thing. While she was thinking what to answer, Prilukov had risen again, as if he had come to change her life only between trains. Strangely, though, it was just this businesslike haste, this unseemly objectivity, that drove any argument from Maria's mind. A man who anticipated her yes so dispassionately would accept her no with the same lack of emotion.

"Thank you, Dr. Prilukov," she said. "I think you know very well that only a miracle could make you mean more to me six months from now than a very kind friend; and if you don't mean more to me than that, I shall not become your mistress."

"Let that be my affair, Maria Nikolaevna," he said, his little mouth turning up in a smile that showed his large teeth. "All great minds try to make the world more distinct by bisecting it. Religion divides it into devil and angel; Machiavelli speaks of those who go under and those who survive; Lao-tse, of those who reflect and those who act; Marx writes of the satiated and the starving. I am satisfied to differentiate between the man who gambles and the man who won't. I happen to be a gambler."

3

If there was anything that irritated Maria during the next six months, it was the feeling that she was like the hand of a clock, following its prescribed course, subordinate to the will of invisible works. Numbers and hands told the hour, faced owner and reader of time; but without the hidden wheels, if only a winding wheel, spring, or anchor were missing, they were nothing better than the lifeless drawing of a child.

The journey had taken place with the precision of a clock. The rooms in the Hotel Négresco had been reserved; the account in the name of the Countess Maria Nikolaevna Tarnovska replenished itself; Dr. Fournier appeared without having to be called. That Prilukov had chosen Nice was also no coincidence. In France a law had recently been enacted restricting the sale of narcotics. Maria could do nothing but obey Dr. Fournier. She did so unwillingly and slyly; she soon found a doctor who from time to time was able to procure what she wanted. She paid ten to twenty times the official price; bribed employees at the hotel, the apothecary. But Prilukov had foreseen this too and, in a roundabout way, had made an ally of Elise Perrier, who hid hypodermic needles, spilled cocaine, broke bottles. Since Maria was incapable of managing her own finances, she had to obey Elise Perrier, too. The maid called Prilukov "our Lohengrin."

Maria began a new life in that, like all people who begin a new life, she went on living the old one. She met Count Sheremetyev; he did not

282

turn away. She met the banker Maximov; he did not turn away. She met Prince Trubetzkoy, who, of course, did not turn away. Perhaps society was so constituted that its laws were valid only within certain geographic borders; outside their confines, its members behaved like runaway convicts. Perhaps society was so constituted that it condemned to death those who flaunted its laws, yet if they managed to survive, took them in again. Maria dined in London House, which was supposed to be the most expensive restaurant in the world; at Néris she ordered the gypsies—who looked like devils and were dressed like lion tamers—to play Russian airs for her; she went to the Tiranty theater, took Tioka to matinees at the Théâtre Royal, strolled on the sunny Promenade des Anglais. She made the acquaintance of young, consumptive Russian girls, who had come to Nice to die; English aristocrats, who had their bathtubs filled with salt water; adventurers, whose last hope was the roulette wheel. Tioka was seven, and took up a great deal of her time. A Russian and a French tutor were teaching him. His quick grasp, his diligence and modesty, delighted Maria. Visions out of the past year rose up and enveloped her in noxious mists; the hotel in Rome from which she had fled through the back entrance, Tioka in her arms; Yuri Tolstoy, whom she had met one night and who had pretended not to see her; the one-eyed apothecary who had struck the cocaine out of her hands and chased her out into the street. Vladimir Stahl strode through her dreams, naked and ugly; Alexis walked through them, the yellow gauze around his neck; Andrey, a fishing rod in his hand. But memories, visions, and dreams began to pale. Sometimes their pallor startled her. Her body, blossoming again visibly, remained lifeless. Once a month it came to life, and then the only reminder of living was pain. Those were the days when she screamed for a narcotic, abused Elise Perrier, threw things, begged to be forgiven, cried without reason.

Autumn passed by; so did the winter season. Open carriages clip-clopped across the Place Masséna. People sunned themselves in front of hotels and coffeehouses; the gently splashing waves made a friendly sound. Spring came in, looking innocent. At the end of March Donat Prilukov arrived in Nice.

4

She lay beside the sleeping man. The insidious gray of morning crept through the curtains. Insidiously she watched Donat. When he was awake, you couldn't watch him. Physical bodies described certain undeviating movements, uniformly, at a uniform speed; but his body described all motion at once, irregularly and surprisingly. Now he was still.

A bald head, smooth as a knee. Had he lost his hair? Unthinkable! He had never had any. Where did his forehead begin? A beautiful forehead, beautiful when seen apart from his face—high, majestic, nobly wrought, a costly vase filled with ideas. His eyebrows. They sprang out at you like a hairy animal; they had a life of their own—monkeys lurking in the bush. Now his eyes were closed. That was the wrong expression; his eyes were not closed; he had only lowered his lids over them like thin curtains. Behind them Donat's little black eyes were wide open. It was quite possible that they could see through the curtains like malicious watchmen. His big, bony, slightly bent nose should have told her what sort of man he would be in bed: hard, insatiable, sure of himself; in complete harmony with his own personality. His mouth, open a little now, not too much, not too little, as if the man had command of it even in his sleep; too small for his face, too delicate, too red, the mouth of a liar. His teeth belied his mouth, horse teeth, their red gums visible with every strong wave of emotion.

Maria leaned back a little in order to see his face as a whole. As a whole, the face looked different than when taken in detail, like the pattern of a carpet in which, if one focused one's eye on it, one discovered a square here, a triangle there, a few stars. She lay back in her cushions.

His arrival. The hotel in a turmoil, as if a crown prince or an Indian potentate had arrived. Presents. For Elise Perrier and Tioka, too. But that wasn't it. "My train won't go," Tioka told him. That was it. Faith in the stranger. "We'll soon fix that." And he did. Tioka flew to him. It was even more difficult for children than for women to live without men. Gambler or nongambler? No. The world was divided into those who bribed and those who accepted bribes. Lawyer Donat Dmitrievich Prilukov might be above taking bribes, but to bribe was in his blood. Supper at L'Hirondelle. Only fifteen tables. You had to reserve a table two weeks in advance; a committee decided who would be accepted. For Donat the ruling didn't exist, and the waiters stopped paying attention to the grand dukes and lords. The gypsies at Néris—Donat knew all their songs. A little tipsy, filled with bravado, she asked them to play Vassily's song, "Oh, distant steppes, oh, savage plains." Donat said, "Leave all memories to me." He paid in Russian five-ruble gold pieces, twenty of them. In his suite, the champagne was standing on ice. He undressed her without kissing her. She let it happen, convinced for a long time that she would have to pay. She was grateful that he didn't speak a word of love. As he kissed her shoulder, she felt that they were kin, and that blood knows no incest.

Maria closed her eyes. She had moved, and Donat had turned in his sleep. She did not want to wake him. When he awoke, he would take her as he had taken her three times in the last few hours. He was forty-three, he had told her, boasting with middle age as one boasted of one's youth. The laws of nature? If she asked, he would answer, "Leave the laws of nature to me, Mura." Vassily. The helpless egoist whose love she had been able to enjoy only when his helplessness had been transformed into humbleness. A bad child, bearable only when punished. How often had she been happy with him? Three, four times. The nights had been nothing more than an event arising from the day. Alexis. Was she betraying the dead? That had been happiness, but happiness that ended in misery was no happiness. Who said that soul and body were one? They were jealous sisters. The soul robbed the body of what was the body's, and the body robbed the soul of what belonged to the soul. The body wanted its own love. Ivan Trubetzkoy. A fleeting episode, forgotten. Vladimir Stahl. A nightmare dispelled. Donat loved soullessly. The soul, a chaste rival, laid no chains on him. Consideration, unsureness, fear, surprise, shame, failure, the eternal virginity of man—he didn't know the meaning of them. As if he were saying, "Leave that to me, Mura." His body was as clever as his brain. He gave his passion full rein; they careened over the uneven ground, the axle creaked, the wheels sparked, but nothing broke; and at any moment the driver could make the horses stop and stand still. Only he who was sure of himself could be so bold. He took no consideration, yet he was considerate; he didn't wait for her ecstasy, but forced her to reach it with his.

Donat opened his eyes and stretched out his arms to her. His eyes were as awake as if they had truly only hidden behind a curtain.

5

Prilukov stayed in Nice. On his arrival he had told her that he intended to stay two weeks. He had to be in Moscow in the middle of

April to plead the case of six conspirators. During the first weeks, he spoke often about the case. One evening he declaimed his entire speech for the defense for her benefit; moved chairs out of the way, draped his cravat around his shoulders as if it had been a toga, and did it all so convincingly that furniture was transformed into jury, a pen into a crucifix, Maria into a judge. Shortly after that, he seemed to have forgotten all about the case. When she mentioned it, he asked her, with irritation, whether his company was too much for her. Anyway, the case wasn't important; anyone in his office could plead it. They went to Monte Carlo, where he played for high stakes and didn't seem to care when he lost. He answered Maria's questions about his wife and children with the same irritation as he replied to questions concerning his official duties. When he finally had to return to Moscow, at the end of May—opened and unopened letters, even unopened telegrams, had piled up on his desk—he made Maria swear by the welfare of her child that she would meet him in Vienna the beginning of September. Meanwhile she should continue to recuperate in Franzensbad, where he had ordered rooms for her in the British Hotel Bristol.

In Franzensbad, she recovered fully. She took mud baths, massages, drank the iron-rich waters, went for long walks and excursions with Tioka and Elise Perrier to Miramonti, Kammerbühl, and into the Eger valley. Her monthly pains, her outbursts of violence became rarer; her craving for morphine and cocaine was gone. Privation, sorrow, sickness had left no trace on the face of the twenty-four-year-old woman; they had only occupied the guest rooms of her youth; they had not been steady lodgers.

The summer was still at its height when Prilukov arrived in Franzensbad. He had not announced his coming. One afternoon he was there, his luggage consisting of one trunk. He drove into town with Tioka, spent hours with the boy in a toyshop, bought the child clothes he didn't need. Together they went to the hairdresser, and to the famous bakeshop, Uhl.

At supper Prilukov was distracted. When he spoke of the happiness of being together again, it sounded more like a leavetaking. In answer to her question about the reason for his unexpected arrival, he answered only that he had to see her again; but when she intimated that he might be jealous, he laughed like someone who didn't have to fear a rival. His plans? He pretended not to understand her question, and began to talk about autumn in Vienna. He lied without expecting to be believed. Proud of her familiarity with Franzensbad, she suggested that they go to this or that night club, but he looked at the clock and was in a hurry to get back to the hotel.

In her room, he kissed her with an impatience that strengthened rather than allayed her suspicions. It was not the impatience of a man who had waited too long, but rather the haste of a man who had no time to lose. When he had only half undressed her, she drew away from him, sat upright on her bed. "I want to know what is wrong," she said.

"Afterward."

"No. Now."

"Afterward."

The word was repulsive. Human beings desired one another like animals, but God had given them speech to hide their desires and to make what was intentional appear fortuitous.

"Now," she repeated.

"Do you want to reproach me with the fact that I can't live without you?"

"You didn't come with one trunk to live with me."

"The rest of my luggage is on its way."

"You are lying."

He began to pace up and down, his steps unsure, as if he were trying to avoid hidden trap doors. "I didn't want to tell you about it because it is unimportant. I don't want to cause you pain. My wife and children are in Karlsbad."

"Does that mean that you are going to shuttle back and forth between Franzensbad and Karlsbad?"

"They wouldn't have understood it if I had spent my holiday without them."

Anger swept like an icy wind across her soul. "And what do you tell your wife?"

"Nothing. A business conference."

"She must be used to that." She said it like an accomplice who had nothing against the conspiracy but only wanted to find out more about it.

"You met her," he said, "a gray mouse."

"Why did you marry her?"

"Every woman asks that. None of them can understand your marrying anyone else. And at the same time they reproach you for being unfaithful to your wife."

A philosopher of adultery. He thought he was insulting his wife and in reality was insulting her. The more unfavorably he spoke of his wife, the less Maria thought of herself.

"Why did a man like you marry a gray mouse?" she asked.

"In Nice you didn't ask questions."

"In Nice your wife was a thousand miles away."

"Why, why? She is the daughter of a famous lawyer. She understood me; she shared my interests, admired me."

Maria's glance fell on the mirror. The top part of her dress had dropped down across her hips. The flesh of her full breasts gleamed through her batiste chemise. She was reminded of a picture by a modern painter that she had seen not long ago. "Prostitute." Perhaps that had been the name of the picture; perhaps she had only imagined it. A prostitute and her guest. On pictures like that, the guest was always dressed. She could see Vassily before her, and a wild longing seized her for the man she hated more than all the rest. What was it? He was a Count Tarnovsky; they were cut of the same cloth. He was hateful, but he was real. Donat Prilukov was hateful and unreal. He threw his money around and was greedy for the adulation of waiters. He chose a meal like a gourmet, then devoured it like a glutton. He wanted to be a man of the world and married a gray mouse. He thought he couldn't live without the Countess Tarnovska, but instead of doing what Vassily or Yuri Tolstoy or Ivan Trubetzkoy would have done—travel a thousand miles and back to spend a night with her—he moved his family to the next spa. Was there anything more humiliating than convenience? How did he look at home? His suspenders hanging up, the newspaper at the table, felt slippers. Vassily had mistresses; this man couldn't have mistresses, only whores.

He sat down beside her on the bed and tried to put his arms around her. "I want you to understand. I shall leave her as soon as it is possible. She is sick."

Sometimes a picture out of the past cropped up in one's mind before one knew why. Charkov, she thought. The hotel room. Vassily's mistresses at her bedside. Julia Terletzkaya, the Baroness von Blottheim, the consumptive sisters. "What do you want?" the Baroness had said. "He married you." All men said that their wives were sick. Sick gray mice. The wives were sick, and the children needed a father. They could not be abandoned. Later! Afterward! Julia Terletzkaya had said, "In all comedies, those who have been deceived are made to look ridiculous."

Deceived husbands, deceived wives, *cocus*. But it wasn't true. Only mistresses were ridiculous—receivers of stolen minutes, dependent on other women whom they didn't even know and who remained part and parcel of the love they received, worms in an antique dresser. Mistresses were hopeless contestants against complacent habits; arrived too late, loved too late; tolerated tolerators, liars deceived, conspirators in a conspiracy against themselves. "Don't cry," the Baroness had told her. "You are the victor, Countess Tarnovska."

"For heaven's sake, Mura, try to understand," she heard Prilukov say. "I can't do with a scandal right now. The government, the landowners, the Church . . . My downfall would be a major triumph for them."

"You are a dirty muzhik," she said.

His face darkened. His hand twitched so violently that the slight movement was like a broad gesture. He bit his narrowed lips, and his mouth grew smaller, but he only said, "I earn my money by working."

"I don't care how you earn your money."

"My future, and with it yours . . ."

If he had struck her, she would have listened to him. Only dirty muzhiks let themselves be called dirty muzhiks. He who let himself be beaten deserved to be beaten.

"You don't think I would marry you?" she said. "Your mistress, perhaps, but Mrs. Prilukov?" She laughed. She couldn't think of anything funnier. "Mrs. Prilukov, née Countess O'Rourke, mother of Count Tioka Tarnovsky." She couldn't stop laughing.

He could understand her bitterness, he said. He was ready to forget her insults. Never again would she find anyone so considerate. He spoke of his love for her, which was unlike any love he had ever known. "I am forty-three and found love for the first time in your arms." He made desperate efforts to preserve his personality yet win her, to retain his mastery yet give in to her. He made promises that left reality far behind.

She listened to him and discovered that the great lover knew as little about the vocabulary of love as a poorly prepared schoolboy. Love knew no grammar. It expressed itself in stammered phraseology, as the blind write. Donat Dmitrievich Prilukov pled for his love as for a defendant; he collected proof, exonerating evidence, quoted witnesses, used alibis, all of it rounded out smoothly, and unconvincing.

She rose. She stood in front of the mirror and began to undress slowly. When he wanted to help her, she pushed him away. He watched her as if under a spell. Her dress fell to the floor, her petticoat, chemise, drawers. She sat down on the bed, her eyes on the mirror, and took off her stockings. She enjoyed every move she made, as if she were administering him a blow with every move. When she was naked, she walked up to the mirror and examined her face as if she had found some blemish on her chin. Then she went back to the bed and sat down.

"You may go home now," she said. "I am tired."

He went down on his knees, grasped her knees in his arms, couldn't believe that she wanted to send him away. He threatened to abandon her to her fate, to poverty and ruin; he laughed at her, stammered that his wife and children meant nothing to him, enumerated all he had done for her, reminded her of her own declarations of love.

She looked down at his bald head, which was trying to push its way between her knees, and laughed at the grotesque idea that she suddenly had three knees. She pressed his head between her knees so hard that he cried aloud in pain and his nails dug into her thighs. He didn't have to remind her of the nights in Nice; she remembered them. She also remembered how she had longed for him in hot summer nights, how she had lain awake and relived every hour spent with him, how she had forgotten who he was and remembered only that she had never known such passion in the arms of any other man. But the ecstasy that overwhelmed her as he cursed and twisted and turned to free his head was no less than in the moments of her fulfillment.

She loosened the pressure of her knees, took his head between her hands as if it had been the head of a wounded man, kissed him fleetingly on the mouth, and said, "Go to your gray mouse. I don't feel like making love to you today. If you like, you can come back tomorrow."

6

For four weeks, Prilukov shuttled back and forth—as Maria chose to put it—between Franzensbad and Karlsbad; two days here, three days there, three days here, one day there. Then he went back to Moscow, and she left for Vienna. He came to Vienna for a week, left, was back again a month later, had to go away again.

Why didn't she leave him? Because she had grown accustomed to a carefree life, because she was still haunted by the miserable memory of her years of wandering, because she feared she might become addicted to narcotics again, or because of the touching relationship between Donat and Tioka? All these things, but there was more to it than that. Maria Tarnovska began to sense the fact that she was an addict, not of morphine and cocaine, but of pain. Her addiction to give pain and to experience passion through pain became clear to her all of a sudden, without any visible reason. She was like someone who had been taking morphine for a long time because of a physical ailment, or sniffing cocaine for fun, and discovered suddenly that he couldn't live without the drug. And in that, too, her addiction was like an addiction to drugs, for she had until now considered beneficial what she had actually been doing only for the delight it gave her. She had been kind to Vassily, and he had deceived her; she had punished him, and he had come crawling to her on his knees. She had treated Vladimir Stahl like a friend, and he had taken advantage of her; she had chastised him, and he had become her slave. Now she realized that she had not only wanted to test her power and subject her victims to severity, ridicule, and mortification; she had above all wanted to satisfy herself. Thus the one being punished, ridiculed, and subjugated became indispensable. She humiliated Donat, but since she thought she could not live without his humiliation, she degraded herself to achieve the delight of his degradation. Not for any other man in the world would she have hidden in Franzensbad, as she did some days; or participated in the double life he led; or overlooked what divided them. She was like a policeman who had manacled himself to a transgressor and lost the key to the handcuffs.

Maria Tarnovska recognized her addiction at a favorable moment, like the cocaine addict who has become aware of his addiction just when he happens to possess an inexhaustible supply of the drug. All she had to do was mention that she would never have dreamed it possible that she would sleep with the son of a peasant whose ancestors had been serfs, or insinuate that his tie was vulgar or his shoes unsuitable, or jeer at the school to which he sent his half-grown daughters; and Donat, the great Donat Dmitrievich Prilukov of the Moscow courts, shrank like a whipped child. And it was not lost on her that, with every humiliation, the desire to seem more powerful in her eyes grew in the man. The bed, he thought, was his domain; in bed, muzhiks and grand dukes were alike, which might have been true; but he forgot that she was not his mistress—he was her lover. When she moaned in his arms, exulted, and dissolved, he felt his mastery over her, while she was enjoying the idea of copulating with a serf. Every time it took place, he thought he had broken down her resistance to him, and had no idea that she had resisted him only to inflame his passion.

Maria would have enjoyed her dark happiness with Prilukov to the end if she had not become increasingly aware of signs that he was trying to escape her, and might succeed. A telegram from Moscow, an interesting case—and he would suddenly declare that the acquittal of a man who had been unjustly accused of murder was more important than all their nights of love. He spoke of Moscow society, the nobility, and the court as a bunch of scoundrels, and prophesied with a gleam in his eyes that one day the Czar would sit in front of a church begging for alms, and he, Donat Dmitrievich Prilukov, would be able to say that he had helped put Little Father there. He called her a parasite, dependent on his mercy; without him she would have to go to the poorhouse or a bordello. On that first evening in Franzensbad, his feeling of guilt had come to her assistance, and later too, there were evenings on which he seemed to bend to her will as if he had none of his own. But the very next evening he was capable of stopping abruptly in the act of loving and refuse to continue until she had repeated some degrading words after him. He went down on his knees before her, like Vassily, Peter, and Vladimir Stahl, but as soon as he stood up again, it seemed incredible that he had ever groveled at her feet. He presented her with his meekness like a favor, but she had to woo the slave in him as a slave woos his master.

However close she came to the source of her lust, she never knew if she loved Donat in spite of this abrupt and unpredictable opposition or because of it. She was sure only of one thing: she had to break him. But when she tried to find out the origin of his beloved and hateful strength, she felt that it was to be sought only in a second life of his, which was closed to her. Tarnovsky, Tolstoy, Stahl, Trubetzkoy—all of them had had only one life. Prilukov's second life was his profession, was his conviction of his mission in life, was his pride in his ability to make money; it was the secret of those who acted. The origin of his strength was in his speaking powers. She had to rob him of them; she had to destroy his second life.

On a winter evening—Maria was staying at the Hotel Bristol in
Vienna; Prilukov was in Moscow—she was told that a Father Andrey
Vyrubov wanted to see her. She let him wait for almost an hour. When
she finally walked into her salon, Andrey and Tioka were absorbed in
such an exciting conversation, they hardly noticed her. Tioka left the
room reluctantly, and only after Andrey had promised to visit him
again.

Although she had taken time to prepare herself for the meeting, her
heart beat faster at the sight of Andrey. He was thirty-one years old.
His beauty was not perfect, like that of Alexis; but in his white habit,
he reminded her of the statues of young Roman senators that you saw
frequently in Italy. Figure and face were as if chiseled in stone, yet the
effect was not cold, not of a human being turned to stone, but rather of
stone made human.

"What a surprise," she said, after pouring tea for him from a
samovar she took with her everywhere.

"You will be even more surprised when I tell you what brings me
here," he said. "Do you remember Sergey Burintzev?"

"The anarchist? You told me about him once."

"Sergey is not an anarchist, but that's beside the point. He is implicated in an assassination that was being planned. Naumov, the
Governor of Orel, was to be the victim. They have been holding
Sergey in prison for years, for no justifiable reason. They call it legal
custody. Actually it is . . ." He had almost said "Inquisition." "The
case against Sergey, and ten so-called conspirators, is going to be tried
in the beginning of March. All eleven are to be defended by one lawyer,
a man called Schipov, whose duty it is to send all eleven to the scaffold,
if possible."

"And I am to persuade Prilukov to defend Sergey."

"How did you know?"

"I have not grown stupider. You would not have visited me if you
hadn't needed me."

He looked at her calmly. He had expected to find her changed. In a
pale violet silk dress, with a high, black lace Maria Stuart collar, she
looked young, and she was enchantingly beautiful. She had the same
way of pushing her lower lip forward a little, and of passing her middle

finger across her long dark blond lashes. He felt no embarrassment to be so near her, but was astonished to detect a trace of compassion for her.

"Why didn't you go to Prilukov directly?" she asked.

"The first time I was in Moscow, he wasn't there. The second time, he wouldn't see me. The other lawyers are too cowardly or too busy. And all of them want money."

"Prilukov wants money, too."

"You could talk to him."

"Don't you think this is a very strange request?"

"I don't think Prilukov practices law only for money. The revolutionaries admire him; the others do, too—of course, more because they fear him."

It did her good to hear Donat praised, although she wasn't sure if she was glad for Donat's sake, or because Andrey knew how strong her influence over the eminent lawyer was.

"I didn't mean that," she said. "I meant strange for the priest to come with his plea to Prilukov's mistress. Shouldn't you condemn my relationship to Prilukov?"

"Let us say you were not what you were," Andrey said, "but a thief. And I happened to know that you could help a sick man. Should I prevent the thief from doing a good deed? Wouldn't I do much better to help her atone for some of her guilt by doing good?"

"How ingenious!" she laughed. "But not ingenious enough. You can help the thief do her good deed without sanctioning her thievery, but I can do your good deed only because I am a sinner—that is to say, the kept woman of a married man."

"If you want me to tell you that I approve of your relationship to Prilukov, then all I can say is that I can't do it. Or do you want me to give you a lecture? I am not your confessor. Or would you like me to go down on my knees and beg you to speak to Prilukov on Sergey's behalf, which I suppose is what you really want. That I am ready to do. For Sergey it is a matter of life or death. Prilukov is probably the only man who could save him. I would have gone down on my knees to the Governor of Orel if it would have done any good, although I consider you only an unhappy sinner, whereas I think he is a godless villain."

She rose and walked over to the window. Evening had fallen upon the day and destroyed it. She drew the curtains to. His words had moved her. If he had told her only that she was a sinner, she would have laughed. "Unhappy sinner"—that was something else again. She remained standing at the window. The February rain was whipping across the Ringstrasse. The broad avenue was empty, and lighted street-cars were rattling along their thin tracks as if they were rushing survivors from the flood. Maria toyed with the hem of the curtains; her nails, touching the silk, gave off a crackling sound. She should not have received Andrey. "To regret nothing is the beginning of all wisdom." She had read the sentence in some book or other. In Andrey's presence she always had to walk back into the past, to the fork where she had taken the wrong turning. But how far back did the way go? Where was the fork in the road, and who could say if the other direction would have been the right one?

"Who told you I was unhappy?" she asked, turning to face him again. "I have everything I desire. It hurts me that I lost Tania, but I am happy that Prilukov was able to save Tioka for me. I live with a man whom even you admire. As for society, all the intelligent men I meet, from you to Prilukov, are convinced that it is disintegrating. You fled from it to a monastery, Prilukov defends their murderers, and I . . . I find them ridiculous. I admit, sometimes I am homesick, but that is all. Anyway, I am thinking of returning to Moscow."

Andrey rose. "I came to beg for your help," he said, "not to convince you that you are unhappy."

She walked over to him. "Why do you avoid me, Andrey? I know that you refused to visit me in Rome. I was unhappy then. It wasn't Christian of you. Your only excuse is that you were afraid of me."

"Perhaps I was, Maria."

"You are still the only one who calls me Maria."

He pretended not to notice the sudden warmth in her voice. "I am not afraid that I might succumb to the temptation of you; I fear only that you might be tempted to tempt me. There are many reasons for the separation between confessor and father confessor; one is that it is not only easier to confess to someone invisible, but it is also easier to forgive someone unknown. God forgives men, not because he knows them, but in spite of it. The more people know about each other, the less merciful they become. I pray for your remorse, but I am the last person who could bring it about."

"So you really came only because of Prilukov."

He nodded. It took self-control not to ask more questions. On his deathbed, his father had told him that he would never stop trying to fathom Maria. The longer he stayed, the less he would think of the real reason for his visit. Wasn't one supposed to strike out at the Devil wherever one came across him? It was quite possible that Maria was waiting for a word, a gesture, a sign of love. Disappointment might plunge her even more deeply into misfortune.

"Very well," she said. "I shall help you. I shall persuade Prilukov to defend Sergey Burintzev. You were right—if I want him to do it, he will. I am not doing it for Burintzev; I hate the riffraff Prilukov defends. I am not doing it for you, either, because you are an egoist and let me down when I needed you. I am doing it because it amuses me to think that you will confess today that you went to a sinner and asked her to beg her lover to save a poor soul from damnation."

Andrey left hurriedly. Maria was overcome by the need of crying. It had not been easy to lie.

8

In March the Countess Tarnovska is in Orel. She has insisted on hearing Prilukov plead the case of the conspirators. The city looks like an armed camp. Carriages and wagons are being stopped, and searched for weapons, dynamite, bombs. In the lobby of the Hotel Berlin, policemen sleep on cots. Reporters besiege Prilukov's suite on the second floor. Tioka plays lawyer. Once Maria catches him making small balls out of newspaper. He is playing assassin. In the lobby a man comes up to her, gray unkempt hair, horn-rimmed spectacles—doesn't she remember him? Baden-Baden. Dr. Hugo Friedlieber, *Neue Freie Presse,* Vienna. She shakes him off. The evening before the trial, she asks Prilukov what he is going to say in defense of the assassins. "I haven't prepared my speech," he tells her, but she knows he is lying. The unprepared speech is supposed to impress her. On the evening before the trial, she wants to take leave of him, but he goes up to her room with her. The hotel is deathly still; a nine o'clock curfew has been imposed on Orel. They make love until four in the morning. Prilukov is trying to prove to her that his strength is inexhaustible, superhuman. Next morning she sees him surrounded by journalists, politicians, curious spectators. He is in his element.

It has been raining for days. In the mist rising from the Oka, its bridges seem to be spanned in a void. Orel has only eighty thousand two hundred inhabitants. The one-story courthouse looks like a big peasant restaurant. When Maria gets out of her carriage, she can hear French, English, German. The little dot on the map has grown. Only officials, government employees, advocates, delegates from St. Petersburg, and journalists are permitted to attend the trial. Although she has no experience in court proceedings, even she can tell that the case is being tried with unseemly haste. The jury look like calves on the slaughter bench. The judge is a little old man. He is chewing his gums. When a witness is called, he moves the crucifix lying in front of him to one side, and back again. The jury follow his every motion and pay no attention to the witnesses. There are only nine defendants; two died in prison. Sergey Burintzev sits in front, the first man on the right. Maria has the feeling that he doesn't know where he is.

After the noon recess, the Crown witness is called, His Excellency *Vashe Vyssokoprevos'choditelstvo,* the Governor of Orel. A youth sitting at Maria's side, beautiful as an angel, turns to her. "My father." He introduces himself. "Nicholas Gregorievich Naumov." "Those people were going to kill your father," she says. "The world would have been none the poorer for it," he replies. After the Governor gives his testimony, the court rises, and the judge thanks the Governor in a voice filled with emotion.

They quite evidently want to terminate the trial today. During the speech for the prosecution, the judge keeps nodding his head as if he can't stop. Then it is Prilukov's turn. The rain drums against the window panes. Prilukov has to speak loudly to be understood; instead, he chooses to speak softly. The courtroom grows silent; nothing to be heard but his voice to the musical accompaniment of the rain. Maria thinks she knows every word. His pleas in Nice, in Franzensbad, in Vienna; the nights of love that followed them. Through his robe she sees him naked. Perhaps he really isn't human. Nicholas Naumov, more boy than youth, leans forward, his eyes glowing. He is murmuring something. "Baudelaire was also accused. *'Ainsi, abus de pouvoir et entraves apportées à la défense!'* " She doesn't understand.

Prilukov is saying that the charge is a structure of lies; the proof arbitrarily assembled; the confessions made under duress; the witnesses bribed and unreliable; the Czar the father of his people, but sabotaged by bureaucrats; the monarchy undermined by the petty police minds. "He is playing with fire," the junior counsel says to Maria. The judge is moving the crucifix back and forth, but the jurymen are not looking at the cross any more. Their calf eyes are beginning to gleam.

They aren't ready with the verdict until late that night; then it is unanimous. All of the nine accused are not guilty of attempted assassination. Four, among them Burintzev, receive three years penitentiary for the illegal possession of explosives. A crowd numbering hundreds, who waited outside in the rain, goes wild with enthusiasm, all for Prilukov. Only the soldiers' bayonets can disperse them.

Prilukov, who defied the court, now feels strong enough to defy society. In May, Maria moves to Moscow. Her villa lies near the Ssadovaya, is elegantly furnished. She has a butler, a cook, two maids, a gardener, a coachman. But her salon remains empty. For weeks she receives no visitors. She waits for invitations; none come. When she gives her name in a store, the salesgirls look at each other. Prilukov brings a few colleagues and clients to the house; as soon as their business with Prilukov is finished, they stay away. Two schools for aristocrats refuse to take Tioka Vassilyevich Tarnovsky. Tioka studies at home, asks questions, begins to understand, weeps. Only one of Prilukov's friends, a Dr. Mankovsky, remains faithful. He implores her to leave Prilukov. "Donat doesn't have much money. God knows how he is paying for all this." In bed she tells Prilukov, "I hear you are ruining yourself for me." He says Mankovsky is a liar, and gives her the address of a jeweler. All she has to do is mention his name, and he will open every safe for her. "And if I had no fortune, I can earn whatever I like."

Sometimes he looks old. He stays away from the villa for days. Neither Vassily nor Alexis nor Stahl ever worked. If work is ennobling, what, then, is the sense of nobility? Boredom hovers over her like a dark cloud. She hates Moscow as one hates all cities that have closed their doors to one. She hates its white walls, the onion towers of its churches, the miserable pavement, the bearded priests, the market on the Ssacharev Square, the Turks in their red fezzes. One day Mankovsky tells her hesitantly that Prilukov's wife is going to report her to the police. Mademoiselle Larue, a demimonde who had to flee Paris. So now she too is a demimonde. She decides to leave Moscow. If Donat loves her, he will follow her.

Spring, 1903. Her trunks are packed. Tioka is playing in the garden. He is accustomed to seeing his mother pack; he is used to playing alone. A piercing scream from the boy—Tioka is lying on the grass. A gigantic dog has knocked him down. Blood-red foam is flying from the animal's mouth. A rabid dog. Tioka's shirt is hanging from him in shreds; he is bleeding from the breast, from the shoulder. Why does she have to think of Vassily? Vassily robbed her of Tania. She picks up a large stone from the edge of a flower bed and begins to beat the animal on the back of its head. Blood runs over her hands. The dog lets Tioka go; its teeth sink into Maria's left arm. With her right, she strikes it on the snout. The dog screams; he doesn't howl, he doesn't whimper—he screams like a man. Vassily is dead. Maria takes Tioka in her arms. She must not cry. The maids come running. Maria's brain is working coolly. A short while ago she read the life story of the Brontë sisters. One of them was bitten by a mad dog and cauterized the wound with a glowing iron. "Heat a piece of iron," she orders the cook, "until it is red hot." The doctor? He will come too late. She carries Tioka into the kitchen; blood from her arm falls on his bleeding shoulder. "You must be brave." He obeys; he always does. "It doesn't hurt, Mama." The maids weep. She berates them, calls for hot water, washes Tioka's little chest, his narrow shoulders. She gives Elise a sign to cover Tioka's eyes. "It will all be over in a second, my darling." The iron trembles in her hand. "God help me. If there is you—help me!" The maids mumble prayers. She speaks to her hands as if they are human. They stop trembling. She cauterizes the wounds. The child roars with pain. "It is all over, my darling." Only then does she remember her wound. She is not one of the Brontë sisters; she is no heroine. Donat! It is Sunday. Donat is in the country with his family. "Let that be my worry, Mura. Leave everything to me." Her laughter startles the girls out of their prayers. Elise Perrier runs for the coachman; then the horses are tearing through the Sunday calm of the city. "Faster! Faster!" She drove the coachman on like that on her way to the Grand Duke's palace. Vassily is dead—a black, dead dog. In the Katherina Hospital, she finds a doctor.

For three weeks, tension keeps Maria on her feet, then she collapses. Elise Perrier has to hide what is left of the cocaine. Maria rages. Alexis is standing behind closed doors. Only when Prilukov comes does she do anything for her appearance. On Sundays he is at his *dacha* with his wife and children. He sends her a hundred red roses. She doesn't thank him. When he asks her if the flowers have arrived, she calls him a proletarian. "What are a hundred red roses?" She demands that he fill her whole room with flowers. A carriage filled with roses drives up in front of the house. She looks out of the window and is reminded of a hearse. She fills her boudoir with the flowers, forbids the servants to put them in vases. The roses wither; the floor is covered with their petals; the room smells like a cemetery. Although she finds happiness in Prilukov's arms, she conceals her desire from him. When he reaches his climax, she tells him that he reminds her of Vassily. That September, Prilukov has to plead the most important case of the year—General Rhil's entire fortune is at stake. She knows that Donat cannot leave Moscow, but she demands that he go with her. He refuses. She leaves for Paris with Tioka, Elise Perrier, and a young tutor called Zolotariev.

The Rhil case is adjourned. Prilukov follows her to Paris. He is jealous of Zolotariev—a blond student, barely twenty—and demands that she dismiss him. She does not dismiss him, buys him some new clothes, invites him to dine with her and Prilukov. Again unopened telegrams pile up on Prilukov's desk. They move on, from Paris to Berlin, Brussels, Rome, in pursuit of the fleeting seasons. She goes to pray in the church of Santa Maria sopra Minerva, hoping to meet Andrey. One night she dreams of an hourglass filled with gold, Donat's gold. Slowly the gold runs through the glass. In the summer he rents a house on the North Sea. A cold wind sweeps across the dunes. The newspapers report unrest in Russia. She watches Donat's restlessness—like the unrest of an animal liable to break out at any moment. In the morning he makes love to her on the dunes; in the afternoon behind drawn blinds; in the night, when he awakes as if from a nightmare. He accompanies her to Berlin and travels on to Moscow.

She cannot sleep without sleeping pills. Love does not satiate the body; through love the body becomes insatiable. She writes to Donat, three, four times daily, describes the hunger of her body in the crudest colors, hopes that the censor will open the letters. One night, after she seals a letter to Donat, she goes to Zolotariev's room. Without a word, she undresses, lies down beside him, watches every move the boy makes, is aware of every sound. When he tries to kiss her, she strikes him in the face. Back in her room, she describes every detail of the night in a letter to Donat. "I love you more than ever." For days she dozes, counting the hours until Donat's reply comes. Elise Perrier implores her to send the tutor back to Russia. In her rage, she puts out her burning cigarette on Elise Perrier's hand. Donat must have the letter by now. When she falls asleep, she dreams of the black dog. He has a tiny mouth, Donat's teeth.

It is a mild winter. The sky above Berlin is blue. Only in the windows of toyshops is there glittering paper snow. Electric trains drive through green tunnels. Tin soldiers wage war; the drawbridges of castles are down. "Where are we going to spend Christmas?" Tioka wants to know. Children know more about homesickness than adults. A few days before Christmas, a telegram awakens her. Donat, calling her to Moscow. She leaves the same evening.

9

When Maria arrived in Moscow on December 21, 1904, she had no idea that she had come to a country standing on the brink of revolution.

The Russo-Japanese War had been fought for almost eleven months, a conflict Russia thought it could win in a few weeks, whereupon the Czar would take over the "heritage of Genghis Khan," and "place himself at the head of the people of the Orient." Life in Russia went on. People spoke of the war as of an earthquake in a foreign land; one of nature's catastrophes, a sad business that concerned no one. But gradually the factories and workshops had begun to empty; a power greater even than that of the landowner took the young peasants away from the plow. The news grew sadder, and the obituary columns longer. In the jubilation of a war won, the needs of the starving might have gone under; but in the lamentations of a hopeless struggle, the cries of hunger also grew louder. One week before Maria's arrival in Moscow, four workers, members of the legal union of factory workers, had been dismissed from the Putilov Works in St. Petersburg. The board of directors had refused to reinstate them. Other men had left their machines—one hundred and fifty thousand workers were on strike. The unrest spread into the provinces, at last reached reluctant Moscow. When Maria drove to the Hotel Metropole, it took Prilukov's automobile a half hour to cross Theater Square. Thousands of demonstrators flooded it. Police and military were still waiting for orders to intervene.

Prilukov was busier than ever. He came to the hotel for an hour, then went back to his office; sometimes he woke Maria at midnight on his way home. He had dismissed Zolotariev at once, with a fat check; but as far as Maria was concerned, he had pretended not to believe that she could possibly have been unfaithful to him. He would have been jealous of the youngest or oldest aristocrat, but Zolotariev was a peasant son, like himself, and therefore harmless. When Maria, disappointed by Donat's indifference, wanted to talk about the young tutor, Prilukov waved the subject aside. "That isn't important." Neither she nor he nor their love seemed important any longer; his life went under in a universal fate.

One night in January, he wakened Maria out of her sleep. She had the feeling that an old man was standing in front of her. His face was as if drawn by a malicious caricaturist: everything ugly about him stood out sharply; everything attractive had been left out.

"The revolution can't be stopped any more," he said. "This morning one hundred and forty thousand people—workers, women, children— marched to the Winter Palace. Gapon was to hand his petition to the Czar."

"Who is Gapon?"

He looked at her incredulously. "Is it possible that you don't know? George Gapon is a young priest. He left the seminary only a short while ago to join the revolutionaries."

She thought of Andrey. She still could not form any sort of picture of the revolution. For her it was a mixture of riffraff, stench, con-spirators, jailbirds, and vileness; something that would pass; at best something that hotheads like Nikolay had joined. But now when Donat spoke of the young priest, George Gapon, it suddenly occurred to her that God might have a hand in the revolution, that priest and rebel had something in common, that perhaps there was only one God and not two—a God of the rich and a God of servants—as she had believed in her childhood.

"What a strange destiny," Prilukov went on. A few years ago, the police had arrested Gapon. He had declared himself willing to betray the workers and had become a government agent. "A spy among a race of informers." Extremely gifted, a brilliant speaker and dema-gogue. Minister of the Interior Plehve—"that God-forsaken bastard"— had thought he could outsmart history. He wanted to take the wind out of the sails of the revolution, so he had ordered agent Gapon to form a labor organization. "Naturally, only to deceive the starving." But Gapon had become familiar with the cause of the oppressed and had begun to side with them in earnest. "History travels with the wind that one wants to take out of its sails." Gapon, no informer any more but a leader of the workers, had set up a petition to the

Czar. Prilukov took a paper out of his pocket and read, " '*Gossudar!* We workers of St. Petersburg, our wives and children, our fathers and mothers, helpless old men and women, are come, *gossudar,* to beg justice and protection from you. Only two ways lie open to us— either to freedom and happiness, or to the grave.' " Prilukov laughed. So that was how they had chosen to go this morning—to the grave. The unsuspecting creatures had marched to the Winter Palace, carrying a picture of the Czar. "They also carried church banners and holy pictures. It was a festive procession. They were lured into a trap, with their church banners and holy pictures. A trumpet signal, and soldiers fired into the crowd. They haven't counted the dead yet, but they are speaking of thousands. They shot salvos after those who were fleeing. Now the bodies lie under the church banners." Gapon was saved by a miracle. "Here is his proclamation. The people haven't heard it yet. 'I, a priest, curse the officers and soldiers who at this very hour are slaughtering their innocent brothers, women and children.' " He stopped, as if he had suddenly noticed that Maria was not listening.

She had only been half listening. She knew that he wanted to speak solely about himself. Compassion with the starving? He worshiped abundance. Hatred of the aristocracy? If they knighted him, he would stop hating them. Enthusiasm for the revolutionaries? Only because he had them to thank for his fame. He did not have two faces like Janus; he had countless faces.

"In the night from the fourteenth to the fifteenth of July, 1789," he said, "Count Riancourt woke the sleeping King Louis XVI with his report of the storming of the Bastille. '*Mon dieu, c'est un révolte!*' the King stammered. '*Sire!*' answered Riancourt, '*c'est une révolution!*' Our sleeping Little Father thinks this is a revolt, *mais c'est une révolution*. Whether the revolution wins or chokes in its own blood, this Sunday will go down in history. Plehve, the bastard, has succeeded in doing what he wanted to prevent—Gapon's legal workers' movement is uniting with the various underground factions. They are marching together."

"And why do you have to tell me all this at two o'clock in the morning?" she asked.

"Because you must leave Russia as quickly as possible. I couldn't foresee all this. If the revolution is victorious, they will hang women like you from the chandeliers."

"You sound as if you liked the idea."

"If I did, I would not be urging you to go."

"The revolution will not be victorious."

"But its defeat means civil war. Moscow is no place for you right now."

"This means that you want to leave me alone again."

"Until the situation has cleared up." He sat down beside her. "You are a Countess O'Rourke, a Countess Tarnovsky, yet I trust you. I have money that belongs to the revolutionaries. If I were to leave Russia now, they would think I'd gone off with it. I don't mind cheating the rich, but I can't betray the poor."

Although Prilukov continued to urge her to leave, she could not make up her mind for several days. Reports in the censored newspapers belied his stories. A monstrous farce, he said, had taken place in Zarskoye Selo. Thirty-four innocent workers had been detained and brought to the palace, where Nicholas II had said a few fatherly words to the terrified men. Then they had been wined and dined; high-ranking officials had sat down at table with them; they had been filled up with champagne and vodka and food until they had thrown up on the laden tables. They had been sent back to St. Petersburg to proclaim a "peace pact" with His Majesty. But the workers had looked upon the whole thing as a betrayal, and beaten up the unauthorized delegates.

Prilukov seemed to be right and the newspapers wrong—the revolution spread. The St. Petersburg university had to be closed. In various parts of the country peasants set fire to their masters' palaces. Aristocratic families arrived at the hotel where Maria was staying after having fled from their servants. Powerful industrialists implored the government to make concessions before it was too late. Even the generals feared that the armies in the Far East might mutiny, and advised a reappraisal of policy. Intellectuals, doctors, engineers, writers, professors joined professional organizations. Lawyer Donat Dmitrievich Prilukov was elected chairman of the Lawyer's League. When Maria looked out of her window onto Theater Square, she could see excited crowds, people fighting for newspapers; suddenly hundreds streamed into the square, carrying banners and flags. In the night you heard the voices of men and women singing. Every now and then, a shot. Tioka woke up crying; Elise Perrier sat trembling and smiling beside his bed. On the seventeenth of February the snow lay piled high; no one was removing it any more. The doors of the shops were barred; the city looked like a snowed-in village; doormen fled into the entrances of their hotels; church bells rang as in times of stress. Moscow was drowning in snow. Extras were issued, framed in black. Not far from the Kremlin, the bomb of a rebel called Kalyayev had killed Grand Duke Sergey Alexandrovich.

Next day Prilukov brought Maria Tarnovska, Tioka, and Elise Perrier to the station in his sleigh. He looked thin; his eyes were red-rimmed; his collar lay limp around his neck. Maria didn't believe that he was sacrificing himself for the poor. She believed only that he was cheating the rich.

10

That evening, in the dining car, she sat opposite a man who had been watching her during her departure from Moscow. She was still accustomed to having men watch her, the ones she knew and those she didn't know, obsequiously, admiringly, provocatively. Elise Perrier had told her that the gentleman was traveling in the sleeping car with his small son. The two boys had met in the corridor and made friends.

"It didn't take our children long to find each other," said the man, bowing slightly. He introduced himself. Count Pavel Ergrafovich Kamarovsky. "You have no idea how much I have heard about you, Countess."

Maria started, and realized suddenly that she was afraid of people who recognized her name.

The man smiled, a tired smile. "Do you remember your schoolmate, the Countess Golitzin?"

She did. The anemic, bigoted girl who had never taken part in their games, who had kept her first bleeding a secret. "Emilia was my wife. She passed away two years ago."

His unctuous way of expressing himself didn't ring true, yet was somehow touching. Only now did she notice that he was in mourning. Two years after his wife's death? She tried to think of whom he reminded her. His small, delicate build, the narrow, quite handsome head with its neat goatee, his sad eyes; with all this, and contrasting with it strangely, triangular eyebrows, a mustache waxed and turned

305

up at the ends, and strikingly big ears. No, she couldn't think of whom he reminded her, but it was a memory that swept in from the distant past, perhaps out of her childhood.

The Count spoke about his dead wife, of little Granya, to whom he was now exclusively devoted. "You know, Countess, when an heir is born to a man in his near fifties . . ." He spoke about Tioka, and how quickly the two boys had made friends. He asked Maria if she had any more children. This pleased her. She was surprised to find herself talking to someone who knew nothing of the Countess Tarnovska's scandalous past. She had always been able to see herself with the eyes of other people, and now she soon felt at home in the role of the Countess Tarnovska traveling abroad with her child to escape from the unrest of the revolution, as so many ladies of society were doing these days.

"God knows, you are doing the right thing," Kamarovsky assured her. "Not that there is any doubt in my mind as to how this suicidal revolution is going to end. All comparisons with the West are misleading. Our people are not capable of ruling themselves. Every democratic concession we make only succeeds in washing the rabble up to the surface. The tragic thing is that our poor people are being driven to their own misfortune by irresponsible agitators. Believe me, I ought to know. Fifty thousand souls live on my estates. Not one of these God-fearing people ever dreamed of rebelling. And now they are being stirred up just when we are defending our rights in Japan."

Maria looked out at the snow-clad fields. The squares of the car's lighted windows flew by like sleighs drawn by invisible horses. What Kamarovsky was saying was doing her good. Like the stupid muzhiks, she had almost let herself be upset by Donat's powerful personality. He had taken advantage of her situation to cut the umbilical cord that bound her to her mother—Russia, and its society. It was soothing to hear her language spoken, although Kamarovsky's way of expressing himself was overly sanctimonious. He spoke like a priest who saw something good in everyone. He felt sorry for the souls led astray; he had understanding for the conflict in the hearts of the soldiers who had to fire on their own countrymen; he could put himself in the Czar's difficult position; he tried to do justice to all, and condemned only—but this, too, in carefully chosen words—

the intellectuals who had let themselves be bound in front of the revolutionary wagon.

He had barely finished his dinner when he excused himself. "Granya won't go to sleep if I don't give him his good-night kiss," he said, with a modest smile. "I have to be father and mother to him."

II

Maria felt it was not a coincidence that Count Kamarovsky stopped off at the Hotel Bristol, too. A few hours after his arrival, he sent her flowers; whenever she walked into the lobby, there he was, sitting in an armchair. Granya's governess, an old Englishwoman, appeared— whether Maria had sent for her or not—to take Tioka off to play with Granya, to go for a walk or a sleigh ride with them. Although Tioka rarely felt like playing with the spoiled, arrogant child, Maria told him to be friendly, partly because Tioka didn't know any other children in the strange city, partly because it touched her to see the orphaned child attach himself strongly to her. Children and servants always loved her; she knew how to handle them. But Granya's attraction to her was so impetuous that Tioka became jealous. Then too, the old enemy, boredom, was again with Maria. After such a long acquaintanceship, it might really have presented itself to her in a more agreeable form, but boredom was like old people whose characteristics became clearer with every passing day. So it came about that she accepted Kamarovsky's invitations gladly. They were shyly put, uttered hesitantly and in an utterly respectful fashion, and he reacted to her acceptance with boundless gratitude. They ate in the best restaurants, drank the finest wines and the best years of Veuve Cliquot, all of which took place with the most modest and casual discretion, so that Maria found it difficult not to compare it with Donat's vulgar ostentation. Donat, it seemed to her, sought affir- mation only of his own success with the money they squandered. He did not buy amusement for both of them, only self-confidence for himself; whereas every attention Kamarovsky paid her was ren- dered as if he were the impersonal bearer of tributes from far away. You could squander a lot of money and still spend it with a reluctant hand. Self-made money stuck to the fingers; it couldn't be thrown away easily. She had been permitted to take part in Donat's grandiose self-glorification; Kamarovsky seemed to desire only the barest participation in her pleasure. His conversation was impersonal. When he wasn't speaking of art and poetry, of pedagogy and politics, he talked of the immortality of the soul, of the reunion in the hereafter with the people one had loved, of the resurrection of the dead on Judgment Day. Sometimes it irritated Maria that he mentioned his dead wife so often, that he carried his mourning in front of him like a church banner. It irritated her even more when she saw his eyes fill with desire for her, even though he immediately looked down as if guilty. The care with which he avoided any conversation about her past aroused in her the suspicion that he had known all about her already in the dining car of the Moscow Express, and had been silent only for tactful or God knew what other reasons.

She heard from Prilukov rarely. The revolution had been quelled; but the Viennese papers, uncensored and obviously malicious, reported continued unrest, and the fateful defeat of the Imperial Russian Armies at Mukden and Tshushima. Instead of letters, Prilukov sent telegrams that were just like him, exaggerated or threatening, filled with jealousy or protestations of love, and always two or three, sometimes four or five, pages long. When Maria came back from an evening with Kamarovsky at the Sacher Hotel or Jockey Club, the desk clerk would hand her the folded paper with the red seal. Always the Count found some excuse to turn away, almost as if he had witnessed something obscene. One April evening Maria told him that she would not be able to see him the following day. Kamarovsky said nothing. As usual, he thanked her for the evening; as usual, he ceremoniously kissed her hand.

Not until she was lying in Prilukov's arms did she admit to herself how much she had missed him. Had the distance between them been deceiving? She had deprecated his good qualities in her mind and magnified his bad ones. The acoustics of love were so constituted that everything that had sounded loud when the loved one was absent—reproaches, comparisons, betrayal—were silenced when he was near; the eyesight of love was conditioned so strangely that one saw one's beloved less clearly the nearer he came.

Prilukov got up and walked over to the window. It was a cool spring night.

"I'm cold," she said, drawing the covers over her shoulders.

He came back to her and lay down on the bed. "I need air."

She stretched out her hand to him. "I won't let you go away again."

He laughed. "I can't go away again. I can't go back to Russia."

"The revolution?"

"No. Not the revolution. Anyway, it's not the immediate cause."

She sat up.

"All I have left is five hundred rubles."

"You're not serious."

"I'm deadly serious."

"But then you certainly must go back."

"You don't understand. Mura. I am a thief. I have stolen one hundred thousand rubles—or if you want to be exact, one hundred and eleven thousand four hundred and twenty rubles, if that means anything to you."

It didn't. The word "thief" didn't have any meaning, either. It was a ridiculous word; in connection with Donat, it couldn't have any meaning. Thieves were dirty creatures in ragged suits who drank in taverns and slept in shelters.

"What you are trying to say," she told him, "is that you have debts."

"I am trying to say that I have stolen, have been stealing for years. What we have been squandering was the money of the revolutionaries. Of course, I didn't have to give it back to them."

That was the old voice speaking. She recognized in it the inflexible arrogance that knew how to turn even theft into a noble action.

"I could have kept it," he went on. "There were no receipts, not a scrap of paper, only their faith in me. The revolution came too soon. They needed the money. I gave it to them, down to the last kopek."

"So?"

"Nothing, except that I didn't have it. So . . . I took the money from my clients. Robbed Peter to pay Paul—the established method of all swindlers. Of course, I could now proceed to kill myself. A Count Prilukov would put a bullet through his head. But suicides are born. And anyway, my life is too valuable. This is the great hour of the prosecution. I could say that I am being persecuted for political reasons, and I may do just that if it becomes necessary. Political persecution—that can be made to mean letting a thief go whom one would otherwise not let go. But it doesn't change anything; he remains a thief."

He lighted a cigarette. By the flickering light of the match, she saw his face for a moment, naked as his body; and for the first time, she had the feeling that it belonged to his body. There were no thief-bodies nor Count-bodies; there were only thief-faces and Count-faces. Perhaps he had always looked like a thief, only she hadn't noticed it. She could still feel the hardness and heat of his body in her body, and she was filled suddenly with a deep emotion at the thought that he had made love to her all evening and all night without betraying that he was a thief, a runaway thief. Had he thought she would reject him because he was a thief and had only five hundred rubles? The great hour of the prosecution? She was his prosecution, and her hour had come. He didn't dare to say that she had ruined him, that he had ruined himself for her. No defense, no accusation—only surrender. To her. A thief, a ruined man, no longer capable of anything but love. A boastful word, and she would say, "Be silent, thief!" A word about the great noble revolution, and she would say, "Thieves like you!" She didn't know how she would get money, but she would find a way and give it to him—not too little, not too much, so that he might never forget where it came from. And if he ever wanted to go away again to hold hollow speeches, or to his wife and children, she would chain him up and make him beg like a dog for a bone. She would stuff banknotes in his mouth as one fed a dog. Sometimes she would let him starve. To see him brought low, degraded, in spite of the brave show he was putting on; the certainty that he would never elude her again, never again show his hundred faces; the satisfaction to see her work done and his second self destroyed—she was filled with an ecstasy in which she almost reached the heights of love without having touched him. She threw her arms around his neck, pressed her body against his, lost herself in his arms as she whispered, "Thief, thief, thief . . ."

12

She acted according to the plan Prilukov had conceived, although she couldn't quite see what his purpose was. For the first time, she invited Kamarovsky to her apartment. He had sent her orchids. Punctually at eight, he appeared, in black, high stiff collar, a guest at a wake. The windows were open. Spring was behaving like a precocious child. The evening was wafting the mild May air into the room from the Ringstrasse; a frivolous promise. It was as if the trees were in love and were whispering sonnets to each other. Severa times during supper Kamarovsky kissed Maria's hand. He thanked her for her invitation, but his little speech of thanks sounded more like a toast for the manager at a feast celebrating the appointment of a purveyor to His Majesty. Mainly he spoke about Granya, and the absolutely miraculous effect Maria had had on the unfortunate orphaned boy.

"I bless the revolutionaries," Kamarovsky said over coffee. "They forced me to leave Moscow that day. Since then, there have been hours like this, during which the clouds of melancholy seem to withdraw. They have hung like a heavy burden over my life for two years."

There was a knock on the door; a page announced Dr. Prilukov. "An old friend," said Maria. "I must receive him for a moment." With a smile, she added, "I shall send him away again at once."

Like a play being staged for her alone, Maria watched what now happened. Prilukov remained standing in the doorway, feigning astonishment. He was holding a large sealed envelope in his hand. Then he came briskly into the room, bowed low before Maria, gave Kamarovsky a short nod. Maria asked him to sit down, but he thanked her, no, and stood there turning the envelope around and around in his hands nervously. Finally he gave it to her, bowing again. When she gave him her hand, he said softly, almost in a whisper, "I want you to know, Countess, that I appreciate the honor of your confidence."

When he had left, Kamarovsky frowned. "Who was that?"

"I just told you—an old friend."

"The lawyer Prilukov."

"The famous lawyer Prilukov."

"How do you happen to know him?"

"He arranged the annulment of my marriage."

Torturously and apologetically, Kamarovsky asked what Prilukov had meant by his parting words.

"There are ten thousand rubles in this envelope," said Maria, putting it aside as if it were an annoying object.

"Did you lend him money?"

Maria laughed. "Donat is a rich man. Of course not. He is lending me money."

Kamarovsky jumped up. Never before had he permitted himself such violent behavior in her presence. "You can't do that, Countess. You can't become a debtor to that man. He may be an old friend of yours, but in Russia he has a very bad reputation. He isn't the kind of man who would lend a beautiful woman ten thousand rubles without . . ." he hesitated, "demanding something in return."

"*Cher ami,*" she said, "there are moments when one simply cannot ask where the money comes from."

She glanced at the envelope. She knew that it contained nothing but a folded piece of newspaper. Her feelings for Donat had always fluctuated between admiration and contempt. It was fashionable just then to talk about Professor Lombroso, who had discovered the connection between genius and madness, madness and genius. Donat was a genius and a criminal; perhaps he was mad as well. He had foreseen every word Kamarovsky had said, every move he had made. Genius was foresight, forethought, forefeeling. Had she agreed to go through with this farce because she loved Donat; or because she couldn't pay the next hotel bill, and never wanted to flee with Tioka out the back doors of hotels again; or because she could only hold onto her power over Donat if she had money; or perhaps even because she wanted to punish this Philistine in mourning for his hypocritical behavior? What did it matter—the stage was set, the curtain had gone up, and she was on stage.

"You must never become a woman who does not ask herself where the money comes from," said the Count. "Oh, I am speaking like a moralist, I know," he went on, in a changed voice, "and I am really only a jealous egoist. I feel guilty too, my dear Mura. Will you let me confess something?" Like someone attending to a duty belatedly, he told her that for quite some time it had been no secret to him that Maria was in financial difficulties. Fate had not been kind to her, he knew, and perhaps she had not been entirely blameless. "No, don't say anything, my dear Mura. Not a word, please. The past weighs like a shadow on your soul; you must free yourself of it. I am not afraid of shadows; but when you give them names, they take shape, human shape; they come to life as ghosts." He knew men whom he did not want to name; about the ghost who had just left the room, he knew nothing, but the glances she had exchanged with the man had sufficed. "I thank the fate that let me be witness to this degrading meeting, the fate that permits me to save you from this last, disastrous step." With glowing eyes he begged her to promise him to give the envelope back unopened to "that man," and to accept his, Kamarovsky's help. "All of us need friends, Mura, friends whose selflessness is proof of the nobility of the human race, in whom we may have unerring confidence, and from whom we receive nothing but devotion." Whereupon he sat down to write a check for ten thousand rubles.

She looked at his narrow, black back, his bowed head with its distressing baldness poorly concealed under his thin hair, his sloping shoulders, and his throat—hairy, bristly, wrinkled, and red—which suddenly seemed to be the ugliest part of a man's body. For a moment she could think of nothing but the events of the last hour, this farce that reminded her of the impossible plots of rococo operas—idiotic excuses for scherzos, arias, duets. But then she suddenly felt sick with revulsion for Kamarovsky and Prilukov, for man, who was an animal with a tiny, disgusting head, a worm without heart or soul. Prilukov was only a criminal, not a genius. Genius and criminal differed in that the former foresaw, forethought, forefelt. Donat had foreseen that she would take Kamarovsky's money; but he had neither forethought nor forefelt that this widower in deep mourning and solicitous father was already thinking with his male animalism, just like every other man, and that he would present his bill with the interest figured out, and she would have to pay it. A violent desire to punish Donat seized her, and mixed with it, like vodka in champagne, a second yearning—she would punish Kamarovsky for his hypocrisy, his silence, his grief, and for the assurance with which he thought he could buy her. As she said to him, "My friend, my friend," her voice was trembling with excitement.

"Go to bed, *dushka*," Kamarovsky said. "I know how hard it has been for you. But before you fall asleep, remember that your martyrdom is over."

13

A few days later, Maria begged Prilukov to leave Vienna for one or two weeks. He agreed, because his money was gone, and because she swore to meet him in Strasbourg. A rich wine merchant called Gutweiler lived in that city. Prilukov had represented him once, successfully, in a difficult and not very clean affair. He would most likely know nothing about Prilukov's flight from Russia and would probably help him.

Maria sent Prilukov away not only because she wanted to punish him, or because she feared jealous scenes, but also because she believed the time had come to test him. She was not sure whether Donat had acted selflessly or not. Kamarovsky wanted to buy her; perhaps Donat wanted to sell her.

A week after his departure, Maria wrote him a letter, care of Richard Gutweiler, Strasbourg.

My beloved!

I wish I had never sent you away. Do you remember the fairy tale of the frog who was transformed into a beautiful prince through the love of a princess? Kamarovsky was never a beautiful prince, but through my "love" he has been transformed into a toad.

Last night I was in his apartment. He spoke as usual of the immortality of the soul, and wanted me to tell him if I thought he would find his beloved Emilia again in heaven. (There seemed to be no doubt in his mind that he would go to heaven.) After the waiter had removed the dishes, Kamarovsky sat down beside me and tried to kiss me. His lips were still dripping with words like Emilia, salvation, Paradise. I thought of our happiness, and let him have his way. You wouldn't have minded it anyway, would you? What was unavoidable would be quickly over, I hoped. Instead, he started to talk. First about Vassily, then about Alexis, finally about you. He said he wanted me to have everything that had ever made me happy. He promised to be an apt pupil; in his humility, he was willing to learn from the lowest man. I suppose he meant you. He wanted to know if I had enjoyed sleeping with Vassily and Olga Kralberg, which of course never happened, and if it was true that I had loved Alexis to death and had made love to him while he was dying, and if a plebeian like you had any specific powers. . . . I should know what he meant by that, said he. Don't think for a moment that he insinuated any of this subtly, or veiled it, or even expressed it with any refinement. I simply cannot repeat what he said in a letter, but he used words that may be customary in bordellos. And all the time, sitting very properly beside me, like someone come to condole.

Beloved, I did the wrong thing, as always. His effrontery so infuriated me that I began to invent anything that I thought might torture him. In my wildest dreams I have never seen the things I told him had taken place. He implored me to give in to him; he whined and wept. For two years now, ever since Emilia's death, he hadn't been able to touch a woman. Emilia, it seems, never really recovered from the difficult birth of her child, and the doctors forbade her ever to make love again. But his passionate blood drove him from bordello to bordello, from mistress to mistress. Because of his sinful life—eight years of it—Emilia had died. He beat his forehead with his fist, went down on his knees, confessed to me as if I had been his anemic wife. I have never seen anyone so completely changed in a matter of minutes. Only I, he cried, could save him. Why me, I wanted to know. Suddenly—I swear it happened in seconds—he was the sanctimonious little man again! He sat down beside me, took my hand, spoke to me like a doctor. Only he spoke about his own illness. He understood his complaint only too well; it had not begun by chance with Emilia's death. He had killed her, and only hell on earth could save him from eternal damnation! Was I supposed to be this hell on earth? You see, I tried to make a joke of it, but he replied in dead earnest that hell was what he expected of me. I was to tell him about my lovers; the cruder the colors in which I painted my happiness in their arms, the better it would be for his sinful soul. In due course he would find other ways in which I could torture him, although he had the feeling that I was perfectly capable of inventing them myself. And he said all this absolutely calmly, sitting there with his legs crossed, apparently quite sure that I would fill his prescription! Of course, he got around to speaking about money, very cleverly, avoiding anything that might hurt my feelings. Because he had sinned so heavily against Emilia—I never could stand the girl, and now if I hear her name mentioned again, I think I'll scream!—he could save his soul only by living a charitable life. If I would therefore look upon his fortune as my own, he felt he might still have a chance of seeing the Lord's face on Judgment Day. So his fortune is mine, on the condition that I never thank him, and accept everything I get casually and coldly. And if ever he should not be sufficiently generous, I am to punish him!

Don't ask me to write what he wanted me to do for him afterward, in his bedroom. I am exhausted. When your telegram arrives, telling me that your business in Strasbourg is halfway completed, I shall flee from Vienna as I did in the days when I could not pay my hotel bill.

I lie in your arms, beloved,

Your
M.

P.S. When you telegraph, use the name Adele for Kamarovsky. The telegram might fall into the wrong hands. When I was a child in Otrada, Olga, to my horror, used to play with a toad. She called it Adele.

No telegram came, but a week later Maria received a letter from Strasbourg, dated June 6.

Mura, my beloved!

I shall be brief, because my negotiations with G. take up all my time.

1. I have no money. Send me a hundred gold marks at once. (Wiener Kreditanstalt.) If I'm to get anywhere with G., I've got to look right.

2. Don't break with K. under any circumstances. *Quem Deus vult per-*

dere, prius dementat. We must not lose our heads now. Good fortune turns up in the strangest disguises. If K. were a normal man like myself, I would be torn by the furies of jealousy, drop everything, and tear straight off to you. That would be fatal because a) we still need K. and b) my negotiations in Strasbourg are off to a good start. What I need now is time.

3. If you run out of ideas, and K. insists on doing something for you, have him take out life insurance, naming you as beneficiary. For half a million francs, at the Wiener Anker Gesellschaft, if you can get him to go that high.

What does K. know about hell? I know what hell is—every hour without you.

Your

D.

On the day this letter arrived in Vienna, Maria wrote to Prilukov.

My only beloved!

It is a sensuous June night. I didn't know Vienna was a city of lilacs. Everything is saturated with their scent; it seems to follow you with every step you take. The chestnuts are in full bloom. At night I lie awake and long for you.

What a poetic introduction to a letter that must contain nothing but misery.

K. has asked me to marry him.

Common sense tells me to accept. My ten thousand rubles will soon be gone; you will never get enough money out of G. Vienna is beautiful, but I know myself. One day homesickness will drive me back to Russia. And you won't be able to follow me.

But the most important thing is Tioka. He is going to be ten and can't spend his whole childhood in hotel rooms. He is healthy but not strong, and I tremble for him. He is exceptionally intelligent. When he looks at me with his sad eyes, I think he knows everything: why his father left us, why his sister has disappeared, why we wander from city to city. One day he is going to hold me responsible, and he will hate me. I couldn't bear that. Sometimes I believe that every person has only a certain amount of love within himself. All the love I am capable of belongs to my child. I am jealous of him, as I have never been of any man. He grows more and more attached to Elise. She is a good soul, loyal and devoted, and, in her modest way, not so simple as one would believe. I am jealous of Elise, because Tioka is more open with her than with me. Children feel and hate restlessness. He finds rest only with Elise. And children seem to be faithful. Tioka asks after you daily. He has developed an inexplicable aversion to K. But that may be connected with his antipathy to Granya, that naughty, repulsive child, in whom his father's hideous characteristics are not yet concealed by hypocrisy. Granya has attached himself slavishly to me, which is one more reason for Tioka to be jealous.

You can see that I am trying to weigh pros and cons.

My hatred for K. grows by the hour. He is an animal that should be exterminated; this in spite of the fact that he showers me with attention. Yesterday a carriage all decorated with roses stood at the front entrance. I put on a new dress, and we drove, with the children of course, to the Parade of Flowers in the Prater. The entire Austrian nobility was present. K. introduced me to quite a few illustrious people. His name, he says, will protect me from all animosity; I shall enter Orel like a queen. That is where the Kamarovsky castle is. Last night he took a box at the theater. They are giving an operetta, *The Merry Widow,* a great success here. He had already seen the charming performance that afternoon with Tioka, Granya, and Elise, but like "the good angel" he is, didn't mind at all seeing it a second time. You know how music enchants me, and what childish pleasure I can take in the glitter of an evening at the theater in style. Just when the music of a waltz had put me in the most sentimental mood, and I was rather enjoying the cross fire of opera glasses and complimentary looks, all directed at me, just as in the days before the scandal, K. began to whisper the most incredible obscenities in my ear, a dream he had had the night before. Every day he "dreams" up something new, and your lively fantasy, my beloved, pales in comparison. Of course he made the whole thing up, and wanted me to make it come true for him right behind the curtains of our box! I told him he was a swine, and he sat beside me, good as gold, for the rest of the evening, a gentleman from top to toe. I simply cannot see myself living with this monster! But is there any way out?

Don't let me wait so long again for an answer.

Your

M.

P.S. I have begun to mention the life insurance. What do you plan to do with it? Can one take out a loan on it? K. said he would take out insurance on my name after our engagement.

Maria waited for days for an answer from Prilukov. She had written about Kamarovsky in such detail because she had to confide her misery to him; because she wanted to arouse his jealousy; because she couldn't believe that her relationship to Kamarovsky could leave Donat indifferent. The sufferings she inflicted upon Kamarovsky did not excite her; that she could not torment Donat tortured her. Kamarovsky was getting impatient, but she could not come to a decision. At last a letter came, not by mail; a traveler handed it in at the hotel. It was dated June 28, and had been written in Paris, at the Hotel Napoléon.

Mura, my beloved!

I can't entrust any more letters to the mails. The Public Prosecutor in Moscow has put out a warrant for my arrest. What hurts most is the triumph of my enemies. A warrant for my arrest—that means I would be arrested the moment I crossed the Russian border. Usually it is a prelude to an international warrant in all countries with which Russia has a treaty of extradition. Not that I am afraid. I can prove at any time that I am being persecuted as an enemy of the Czar's terror regime.

While I was negotiating with G., he found out the truth through a letter from Moscow. He paid me off cheaply, and that was that. Friends in Paris —people who are still grateful to me—are going to get me a passport under the name of Zeiler. I have already registered here under that name.

Can you understand it if I tell you that, in spite of all this, I am not unhappy? I feel that our love was never stronger. You know that I am the only man you can ever love; I know that I have never loved another woman. And I also feel like a man who is perhaps sick in body and soul, but whose brain is functioning all the more gloriously.

Get engaged to K. I swear that you will never have to marry him. Leave everything to me. The only important thing is that you keep me informed of every detail of your—and his!—life. Your letters will always reach me.

The thought that this monster holds you in his arms drives me mad. But K. is like an octopus with innumerable arms, and not one of them a real arm. When he comes near you, think of the happiness we have had, and shall have.

You don't have to send me any more money.

Your

P.

On the third of July, Maria decided to write a last letter to Monsieur Zeiler, Hotel Napoléon, Paris.

Beloved and detested one!

This is my last letter from Vienna. On the seventh of July, all of us are leaving for Venice. We shall be staying at the Grand Hotel des Bains on the Lido.

I have come to the end of my resources.

I shall marry K. Yes. That is what you have just read. I shall not only become engaged to him, I shall marry him.

K. has set the festivities for our engagement for Thursday, July 6. His most beautiful engagement present is to be the guest list. He has invited not only members of his family and his best friends from Russia, but also people he knows less intimately, thirty in all, and all at his expense. A grandiose plan, says he. News of the engagement will make the rounds in Russia; the guests, more or less bribed, will spread tidings of my "transformation"; when we return in a year as "a young married couple," the Countess Tarnovska will be forgotten. K. reminds me of the landowners who send the maid to the bath house before they go to bed with her! By the way, he asked me if I had friends I would like to see at the festivities. I have asked him to invite Uncle Edward, but not my father or Olga, both of whom he wanted included. He accepted my suggestion to invite Andrey. When I mentioned Ivan Trubetzkoy, he said, "I can't invite all your lovers." The name Dr. Donat Dmitrievich Prilukov was on my list. You were crossed out with the words, "Not that criminal!"

So you have been crossed out, Donat; a black line runs through your name like a mourning rim. In a way I am glad. Perhaps I have ruined your career and your family life, but you have ruined my soul. When I wrote to you about K., I was giving you a last chance. If you were not a plebeian . . . Now I understand: you only became a thief because you were a plebeian. If you were not a plebeian, you would have rushed to Vienna to free me of K. Or you would never have let me send you away. Instead of fleecing him of ten thousand rubles, you would have killed him. Vassily, who killed Alexis—the only man I ever loved, don't have any illusions about that; compared with you, Vassily is a Lohengrin. Elise used to call you "our Lohengrin." You are a Lohengrin for servants, Donat, a servants' entrance Lohengrin. I forgive you for cheating K. out of ten thousand rubles, because ten thousand rubles is less than a kopek to him; but I don't forgive you for making me your accomplice. For a kind word, or, if you will, for a sound chastisement, K. would have given me ten thousand rubles, and I would not have had to degrade myself with your disgusting farce. A black line has been drawn through your name, Donat, not only on the guest list.

That is why I shall marry K. And for Tioka's sake. And because I am at the end of my resources. I have had enough of your lies. Engagement, but not marriage? What are your plans? I don't want to know them. "Leave everything to me, Mura." What have you ever accomplished? You fixed Tioka's train—that's the only thing you ever accomplished. When the mad dog bit Tioka, you were with your family. When were you ever there? For a while I clung to your optimism. I hate optimists who boast with a fate over which they have no power. Optimists like you end in suicide. You lie to yourself and others. I shall marry K. because he is transparent. Repulsive, but transparent. I shall accept his hypocrisy at face value. He calls me his "virginal love." I shall show him how virginal I am. I shall transform his white days into white nights. He has told me that after Emilia's death it was only Granya who kept him from entering a monastery. Our marriage shall be his monastery. But don't draw any hope from that. I may hate him, but I hate you just as much.

Did I write "beloved and detested one?" Let me tell you something, Donat. Yesterday K. surprised me with a repulsive thing that is fashionable just now in Paris society. Men like K. make their "insatiable ladies" happy with it. I know now what you were to me, Donat—a Paris thing. I couldn't do without it. Now I hate it, and throw it away. Farewell, Donat.

M.

On the morning of their departure for Venice, Maria received a telegram from Paris.

ONE DOES NOT WRITE IN SUCH DETAIL ONLY TO SAY FAREWELL STOP POSSESS A FORTUNE STOP I AM THE MAN I ALWAYS WAS WHOM YOU ALWAYS LOVED STOP COMING TO LIBERATE YOU FROM ADELE.

14

Part of the terrace of the Grand Hotel des Bains had been set aside for the banquet. Maria knew that in her white dress she not only looked beautiful; she looked extremely young. Twenty-eight, and she felt old. A few hours ago she had received the news that Uncle Edward was dead. A heart attack; a beautiful death. That was what people said, as if it were a beautiful thing to depart without saying good-by. The crosses were shooting up around her like trees, many trees in many cities. The trees of her mother and Vladimir Stahl in Kiev, the aunts in Warsaw, Alexis in Moscow, Peter in Charkov, Uncle Edward in Dublin. Uncle Edward had been the last line of defense to which a defeated army withdrew.

She glanced at Kamarovsky. He was no longer in mourning, seemed in excellent spirits. Suddenly she knew of whom he had reminded her from that first moment in the dining car—Dr. Orlov, the eye specialist in Kiev. The little man with the goatee and the triangular eyebrows. The searching eye in the glass. "You guessed that one," he had said scornfully, and made her put on her dark glasses again. Saddle leather. Dr. Orlov's hands, the hands of her fiancé. Then the dark glasses had lain in the snow. Uncle Edward was dead. No line of defense. No news from Andrey. Had the Devil been riding her when she had invited the Dominican? Had she forgotten that he had sent Tioka stamps from Manchuria? Nursing the war sick and the wounded. But if he hadn't been in Manchuria, he wouldn't have come anyway. Perhaps he was dead. One more cross; one tree more. When one was twenty-eight, one should not be at home in cemeteries. Kiev, Warsaw, Moscow, Charkov, Dublin, perhaps Japan . . . She was at home in cemeteries.

Strange faces. Kamarovsky's closest relatives had not come. His old mother had sent her blessing in a telegram. Nearly all the guests bore illustrious names, but they were not the noblest bearers of the name. A Sheremetyev, but not the Sheremetyev; a Tolstoy, but not the Tolstoy; a Uvarov, but not the Uvarov. The Gotha Almanac with an inferior cast. Pavel wanted to protect her and was making her look ridiculous. When big parties were given at Otrada, lackeys were borrowed from neighboring estates. These were borrowed guests. Fat Count Branicka, who ate like a pig; Prince Dolgoruky, who was already drunk; Princess Godounov in a faded dress—borrowed lackeys. How Donat would have laughed! When one had lived with a man, it was hard not to see things through his eyes.

The Governor of Orel, Kamarovsky's best friend, had sent his son. Nicholas Gregorievich Naumov sat at the other end of the long table, staring at her as Peter had stared at her during her wedding feast in Charkov. Vaguely she recalled their first meeting. The courtroom in Orel, Sergey Burintzev, the crucifix in the judge's hand, Donat's speech for the defense, the Governor. "The world would have been none the poorer for it," the young man had said. She looked across at him: thank you for coming. An angel; blond, blue eyes. Mantegna's Saint George in the painting in the Accademia. She turned to Kamarovsky and asked him about Naumov. Not yet twenty-three, a student and already famous. Russia's foremost translator of Baudelaire. "His father is proud of him, and worried about him." The young man had mentioned Baudelaire in the courtroom. He did not respond to her smile. His eyes were now like a knife cutting through her conversation with Kamarovsky. She looked up at the sky. If you looked away from the hundreds of candles, you could see the sky. In Otrada she had wanted to see the moon. She should have stayed blind. She could feel Anna Dobroyubova's nails in her palms. Only the blind were led safely. It was as if she had exchanged her life for another, the life of a stranger; a threadbare dress for a glittering one; but the new dress did not belong to her, it hung loose and flapped against her body. In this strange dress they would jeer and throw stones at her. Toasts were drunk, gypsies played; she nodded her thanks, smiled, pressed Kamarovsky's cold hand, and knew that they would jeer and throw stones at her. Naumov's dinner partner spoke to him; he started and replied. Kamarovsky gave her a sign. She rose; the disguised lackeys moved into the ballroom.

"I must speak to you, Countess." Naumov was standing at her side. She remained behind. "What can I do for you?" he said.

She looked at him, surprised.

"You are unhappy," he said.

"How do you know that?"

"I am a poet."

"A mind reader, you mean." She laughed.

"Poets read only dark thoughts," he replied seriously.

Had she concealed her thoughts so poorly? Was she no longer capable of hiding them?

"You are too young to understand," she said.

"I am not too young," he replied, like a child being sent out of the room because it is not supposed to hear something it has already known for a long time. "In that respect, too, I am like Baudelaire. *'Je suis, comme le roi d'un pays pluvieux/ Riche, mais impuissant, jeune et pourtant très vieux.'* "

She could imagine him "king of a rainy country." Rich and powerless, young *et pourtant très vieux*.

"I cannot remember many of Baudelaire's poems," she said. "In one he writes of death riding through cemeteries like a prince across his estates."

"Yes. Death on a pale horse."

"What do you know about me?"

"I know that you are suffering, and that you were not born to suffer. You have lost faith. What do you believe in, Maria Nikolaevna?"

"What do you want to hear? That I believe in God or in my salvation?"

"You have to believe in fate."

He took her hand and pressed it passionately. She looked at him as if he were an apparition. Had she really seen him only once before, in the courthouse in Orel? She had seen him a thousand times. Mantegna's Saint George. Was everything around her a dream? Reality unbearable, fantasy therefore real? The gypsy music and the music of the waves. Laughing voices, the tinkle of glass, flickering candles, the moon, the light from the ballroom. Cocaine had had the same effect on her: sounds from behind walls, blurred lights, one figure alone illuminated, one voice only clear. She was not Pavel Kamarovsky's bride; she was not in Venice; the ridiculous guests were a painting. Saint George had stepped out of a frame and was speaking to her with the voice of a manly angel.

"You must believe that fate sent me," said Naumov. "I have come to save you." He had loved her, he said, since Orel, when he had been permitted to be near her for a few hours. "Still, I would not have dared to appear before you again." But when the terrible news of her engagement had reached Orel, he had implored his father to send him to Venice. He had traveled day and night, sleeplessly; he had wanted to urge the wheels of the train onward, and they had told him, "Hurry, hurry, you must save her." Didn't she know that she had called out to him, *"dans les nuits maudites, des chambres d'éternel deuil, de profundis"*? He was the herald of a higher power, sent to save her in her great need. "A higher will has commanded me to obey your orders, Maria Nikolaevna. Give me the order to take you in my arms and carry you through the air, and I shall do it. Order me to set fire to this festive house, and I shall do it. Order me to die at your feet, and I shall do it."

He was trembling, and seemed rooted to the ground like a tree through whose branches a storm was passing but which would stand fast against all storms. Had she really called him, wished him here with a supersensory power? It couldn't be anything else, because she had not betrayed her misery with a word or gesture all evening, yet this youth knew all about it. In the twelfth century, one of her ancestors, Tiernan O'Rourke, whose wife had been abducted by the King of Leicester, was saved in battle by an angel. Why shouldn't there be savior angels in the twentieth century?

"I have known Pavel since the day I was born," Naumov said, more quietly now. "He is old and ugly and wicked. He sullies you when he so much as looks at you. Marriage with him would be an abyss, Maria Nikolaevna. My youth shall be your shield. Say the word, and I shall challenge him to a duel. Say the word, and I shall kill him."

Behind her she could hear the threatening noise of the festivities; in front of her lay the threatening silence of the sea. "Would you die for me?" she had asked Ivan, the groom, and he had nodded happily. Power over life and death had been given to her, and she was going to marry a toad. She had not taken cocaine; she was not dreaming; she was not mad. The feeling of her power, which she had believed lost, was found again. She took Naumov by the hand and went with him into the ballroom.

15

Shortly after midnight, Maria discovers Elise Perrier standing in one of the doorways. Prilukov is waiting in the salon, she whispers, and is threatening to create a scandal. Maria runs down the corridor. Shoes outside the room doors stare at her, their mouths open, their tongues hanging out—ugly dogs. Where has this happened to her before? Charkov, her wedding night. Only hell experienced is truly hell.

Prilukov is standing in the balcony doorway, smoking a cigarette. She wrote him the place and date of her engagement, he says; her astonishment and pretended innocence are therefore hardly appropriate. His face is new to her. He looks like a man who wanted to commit suicide, but having escaped self-destruction, inflated himself with a false vitality. Money? He has more than enough. Where did he get it? That doesn't matter. Is his name still Zeiler? An irritating interlude. He begins to empty his pockets—banknotes, gold coins, a whole heap of them. He digs hastily in his waistcoat pockets—a few more kopeks, a single French franc. He turns his pockets inside out; they have vomited their contents, are empty stomachs. "I have come to free you. I promised I would and I keep my promises." Like a fakir climbing up his unsupported rope, Donat is climbing up his self-confidence. How does he intend to go about it? "Leave that to me." She begs him to leave Venice. To prevent a scandal in the middle of the night, she swears to return to him. When she finally succeeds in getting rid of him, she is exhausted.

Naumov stays in Venice. It cannot escape Kamarovsky, who knows that he does so because of her; yet he shows no signs of jealousy. Because Naumov is the son of the Governor of Orel? Or because he sees in Naumov's presence another possibility of torment to wrest his soul from damnation? Maria feels that he is only waiting for the opportunity to see her in Naumov's arms, the latest of his inexhaustible perversions. One evening he drives off to Venice with friends, leaving her on the Lido, alone with Naumov. She tries to persuade the youth to return to Russia. "I have brought misfortune upon every man who came in contact with me." She tells him about Alexis and describes his death. Growing pale, he puts his hand to his throat, tells her he

324

envies the dead man. He is capable of enduring every kind of suffering for her sake. He wants to prove his readiness to suffer for her—she should put out her burning cigarette on his breast. Feverishly he unbuttons his shirt and bares his chest. She presses a burning cigarette into his flesh. He covers her hand with kisses.

Prilukov—or Signor Zeiler from Vienna, as he now calls himself—has taken up quarters on the top floor of the Grand Hotel des Bains. He is afraid Kamarovsky might discover him and never leaves his room. Five, ten times a day, he sends messages to Maria. She is sure he has succeeded in making Elise his accomplice once more. The maid brings him food, drink, news. Maria finds out that Tioka creeps up to the imprisoned man's room and spends hours with him. Most of Tioka's toys find their way up there. Maria tries to reason with Tioka about it. For the first time, he lies to her. His vow not to betray Donat's hiding place is more sacred to him than his mother. That night she goes up to see Donat, determined with pleas or threats to persuade him to go away. He paces up and down his attic room, beats his head against the wall, and she remembers his office in Moscow, the high rooms, the humble employees. The idea that she is traveling with a captive tiger delights her. She forgets what she wrote to Donat. It isn't true that the torment of others gives her an orgiastic pleasure—not of all others. Pavel's torment is repulsive. She does not return to her room until dawn. Through Elise, she sends Donat caviar, *foie gras,* delicacies, packed in a box marked "dog food." For days she won't visit him, but writes him letters describing excursions with Kamarovsky and Naumov.

With every day her fury against Kamarovsky grows. He gives her no money. She is living in indescribable luxury, but can call nothing her own. He too seems to conspire with Elise. He gives the money to the maid. "She understands more about it, *dushka.*" She remembers that he told her to be cruel when he was miserly. Under her abuse he blossoms like a watered plant. She doesn't want to give him pleasure, stops abusing him. There is no way out. She buys a fifteen-carat diamond ring, a necklace, a tiara, at a jeweler's in the Merceria. Smiling, he pays for them. At night he locks the jewelry in his safe. "There are too many thieves around." She thinks of Donat, and the idea that she is feeding the future thief of her jewelry under Kamarovsky's very eyes gives her satisfaction.

The Count rarely tries to approach her now. "You know him—he goes limp when I wear a deep décolleté," she writes to Prilukov. Kamarovsky behaves like someone so sure of his property, he doesn't have to touch it. To boast of her as his in front of Naumov seems to satisfy him. His every word, his every gesture infuriates her. Tenderness and defiance, consent and opposition—all a challenge. She wants to do the opposite of everything he desires, but is afraid he will only love her the more for it. She is trapped. But is she trapped? Why doesn't she free herself? Only a third person can free her.

Sometimes she is overwhelmed by the realization of how grotesque her situation is: the wild animal in the attic; the dwarf with his portfolio; the youth reciting Baudelaire. The calendar claims it is August 1905, but that cannot be right. 1705, or 1605, or 1505. Rococo, baroque, the Renaissance. She stands in front of her mirror and begins to laugh, and like those who are in pain and cannot imagine what it would be like to be without pain, she cannot imagine how she is ever going to stop laughing. Elise comes running into the room, fully dressed—she always appears fully dressed, even in the night—and helps her mistress to bed. Maria is still laughing. Elise Perrier sits down beside her, holds her hand. Why doesn't she say anything? Why doesn't she call Pavel, or a doctor? Nurses know what to do with someone who has gone mad; they have their instructions for that. One can be mad and know it. All madmen know from time to time that they are mad. The dark rooms of madness open up before everyone now and then, but only the mad enter them. Consciousness goes away, comes back, goes away again. The dark rooms are tunnels; they have two ends. Terrible O'Rourke was right—Aunt Anna was mad. Her mother died before madness could take possession of her. Sir Brian-Murtha O'Rourke was executed in the Tower of London; half criminal, half madman. 1521. The mad have good memories. Vassily and the parrot. "Yours is a hard heritage, my child."

It is a sultry August; it hasn't rained for two weeks; the sand is saturated with sunshine. After a night of dancing under the stars, she decides she has to get rid of Donat. Only peace can save her from final destruction. Peace at Pavel's side? She refuses to think so far ahead. Men are like the mud on the country roads around Otrada in autumn after a long rain. When you step on them, you sink in deep. You have to step on them, nevertheless. Donat cannot follow her to Russia. She demands that Pavel take her back to Russia. "It is too soon, *dushka*." He doesn't think she is washed clean yet. Fortune, rank, power, family—and he trembles before the slick monster called society. "Why did I become engaged to you?" she asks. That night she stays with him. His body fails him; he talks all night. Next morning she has his promise.

Cautiously, she begins to prepare for her departure. Elise has to swear not to betray her plan to Prilukov. For the first time, she lies to Tioka and tells him nothing about their impending journey. On the night before her flight, Prilukov appears in her bedroom. Tioka went up to get a toy and say good-by. Prilukov sweeps a lamp off the table, roars that he will go to Kamarovsky, rages about his wife and children, his ruined life, weeps. She doesn't contradict him, because she is suddenly filled with compassion for him, and because it touches her to find that she can feel compassion. Still, she has to recapture the wild animal that has broken loose. She has to eradicate the past, the name Tarnovsky; she has to have peace for Tioka. Prilukov raves on. She tries to calm him. He tears out of the room, and comes back with two small vials. Nitrate and chloroform. "You must kill him. There is no other way." She swears that she will. Tomorrow, she thinks, she will throw the poison into the gutter. But Prilukov sees through her. "Swear by the life of Tioka to destroy him." She shivers. Never has she broken her word. The punishment for perjury is death. "Not Tioka!" "You love Tioka." "By my life," she whispers. "Your life isn't worth anything to you." She thinks of peace and freedom. To be able to forget Vassily's name. Security for Tioka. Prilukov makes her take the oath ceremoniously, hand on crucifix, like the judge in Orel.

16

The illusion of freedom. Kamarovsky has to stay with his mother at the castle. Maria occupies a suite at the Hotel Berlin, as she did with Prilukov. Naumov also returns to Orel and stays at his father's palace. The Governor is still in America, with Sergey Witte and Baron Rosen, delegates of the Czar. In Portsmouth, Russia's defeat in the Russo-Japanese War is being ratified.

Naumov plans a party in honor of Kamarovsky and Maria. The guests excuse themselves; at the last moment, it has to be canceled. Since the revolution, society is more than ever afraid of being undermined by concessions. Invisible channels connect the various salons; they reach from Kiev and St. Petersburg and Moscow to the provincial town of Orel. "You see, the name Kamarovsky does not protect you, Maria Nikolaevna," says Naumov. If she will leave Kamarovsky, they will go to Paris, the native city of poets.

His adoration makes life with Kamarovsky bearable. She dines with Naumov in the Governor's palace. He sits at her feet and reads aloud to her from his translation of *Les Fleurs du Mal*. *"Comme tu me plairais, ô nuit! sans ces étoiles/ Dont la lumière parle un language connu!/ Car je cherche le vide, et le noir, et le nu!"* Perhaps that is peace? Starless nights, a void, and nakedness. She lays her hand on his hair, passes her fingers across his lips. He jumps to his feet. He doesn't long for tenderness, he tells her. To save her he needs strength. Only slaves are strong. She can sense what he is about to say. Stammering like a boy, he boasts that she is not the first woman he has loved. When he was twelve, he made love to his governess. There was a thunderstorm, and he cried. To punish him, she whipped him, then took him into her bed until the storm was over. The Countess Dobrinskaya let him run naked in the snow, tied to her sled. Maria has to promise him she will do the same thing. "I am accursed," he cries, "a king in a rainy land." She doesn't know whether he is quoting Baudelaire or speaking about himself. "To be able to love, I must suffer. Pain gives my soul wings; torture uplifts my body to higher spheres. Sex is low, but pain ennobles it. Only he who can give pain or suffer it is godlike; only master and slave are gods." He has sensed that she is a master; with every pore in his body, with every fiber of his heart, he knew it on that first evening in Venice. Master and a soul damned, master and slave—both accursed, the chosen ones of suffering. For her he will bring down the stars from heaven and ask nothing in return—if only she will flog him.

Excited and filled with disgust, Maria leaves him. It is not the first time she experiences the two sensations paired. She throws herself on her bed and weeps. The similarity between Pavel and Nicholas, toad and angel—perhaps they know about each other. Pavel certainly knows about Nicholas' sickness. She thinks of the story of the magic deathman who had only to hate, and whomever he hated died. Thus, those died who were richer and more beautiful than the deathman, the younger and the more fortunate, until the town was empty and the magic deathman remained alone. He hadn't wanted to bring death to anyone; they simply fell under the scythe of his secret wishes. By the same magic, her secret wishes draw to her those who are accursed. She feels capable of flogging Nicholas to death, not because he desires it, but because he knows she can do it. Surely there are millions of men, of all races, in every country, of every rank, who would not fall under the scythe of her sick passion, but she is damned to love the others and to destroy them, to be loved and destroyed by them.

Almost daily she receives telegrams from Prilukov. He begs, threatens, demands, reminds her of her vow. She destroyed the vials of poison in Venice. The punishment for perjury is death. If Tioka is a little hoarse, has a sore throat, a slight stomach-ache, even to see him in a bad mood, puts Maria in a state of panic. Her fearfulness is contagious. The boy becomes more and more apprehensive, quieter, frailer. When Kamarovsky arrives with Granya, he hides. No one can find him. Maria confides in Elise Perrier. It is like the time of their wanderings. The Swiss woman is the only person she trusts. Nicholas Naumov is groveling at her feet; Donat Prilukov is threatening suicide; Pavel Kamarovsky reads every wish in her eyes; but she is alone with her maid. Does God punish one for breaking a vow, even when it is a vow to commit a crime? Does an innocent creature have to die because a guilty one committed perjury? Elise looks at her, horrified. Only a confused brain could ask such questions. But as usual, Elise does not dare to reply. Why doesn't the Countess turn to the Church? A strange priest? Never. Then why not Father Andrey? "I shall send him a telegram: 'Let me know if I should murder Kamarovsky,'" Maria says scornfully. And she laughs until Elise puts her to bed.

Count Kamarovsky's future wife is not received at the castle. She insists that they leave Orel. Kamarovsky's mother is ill; he has to spend Christmas with her. Without saying good-by to Nicholas, Maria leaves with Elise and Tioka. The only thing that can still calm her is the sound of wheels. She thinks of Vassily, Lermontov's sad hero: "His soul ruined, his fantasy restless, his heart insatiable, as accustomed to sorrow as to pleasure, a man for whom all things are too little and life grows constantly more desolate, so that nothing is left him but to travel." Travel is change; the hunger of those who are satiated; rest for the restless; home for the seekers; fulfillment for those who are empty; the hope of the next station.

In Kiev they have to interrupt their journey. The country has been seized by renewed unrest. In a single week, in a hundred and ten different places, thirty-five hundred Jews have been killed, ten thousand injured. To combat strikes, an organization has been formed consisting of officers and criminals, Tshorniye Sotni. The Black Hundred. The people are singing,

> "In his fright the Czar
> Issued a manifest:
> For the dead, freedom,
> For the living, arrest!"

Railway connections with the West have been disrupted by sabotage. Tioka is constantly fighting tears. They spend Christmas in a hotel. Tioka receives a card from Andrey, from the war front; it has been on its way to him for months. Maria is seized with the temptation to go to Otrada. The lonely house, Terrible O'Rourke . . . On January 2, she continues her journey.

Now she has sufficient means to hide. She confides to no one her address. She feels like a criminal in flight who succeeds in obliterating all traces. Spring she spends in Rome, summer in the Black Forest.

One day Tioka comes running into the room. "Uncle Donat is here! Uncle Donat is here!" "Of course I found you," Prilukov says. She is happy to see him; only he can free her of her vow. If he will do that, she will stay with him. She tells him everything that has happened to her since her engagement. They move on to Nice, Hyères, Paris. If Prilukov is afraid of the police, he doesn't show it. Whenever he speaks of the fact that he is a hunted man, he does so with a certain pride—a political fugitive who would be brought home one day in triumph. The world is divided into "enemies of Prilukov" and "admirers of Prilukov." He forgets that Maria knows all about him, and is suddenly nothing but a victim of the Czar. Often she believes him. Tioka blossoms out again. Uncle Donat sits on the floor with him by the hour; together they learn poems, spend half the day at the zoo. On a clear October day in Paris, while Maria is waiting for them to come home, policemen knock on the door. They are looking for the "former" lawyer, Dr. Donat Dmitrievich Prilukov. Elise takes a cab and drives quickly to the zoo, meets Prilukov, warns him. Without luggage, and with only a few francs in his pocket, he leaves. In his pocketbook, Maria finds ninety francs. She herself has only three hundred left. She telegraphs Kamarovsky. He replies at once that he is on his way.

She is more sure than ever that she loves Donat. He is a proletarian a thief, a murderer. One can fall prey to the Devil without loving him but she loves the Devil. The thought that Pavel will press his wet lips against her mouth and the saddle-leather smell of his hands fill her with revulsion. She is filled with revulsion at the thought that she sent for him. She blames Elise for advising her to do so; when the girl contradicts her, Maria slaps her face. Remorse is mingled with disgust. She can bear to be near Kamarovsky only if she takes cocaine.

As usual with Kamarovsky, the unexpected happens. He doesn't reproach her; he reproaches himself. He does not make love to her; he is a kindly father, worries about her, prepares to make every sacrifice for her. When she tells him about Prilukov, he asks her if she kept a diary of their intimacies. Two weeks later he turns up with another surprise. They are going to spend Christmas in Vienna. "Our good Naumov will bring Granya." Isn't he jealous of the beautiful young man, she wants to know? Smilingly, he replies that if she wants to give him a present, she should give in to the beautiful young man and let him, Kamarovsky, watch their love-making from some hiding place or other. Her own indignation appears to her as absurd as his demand. She promises to do what she has no intention of doing. For Christmas, she wants him to take out a life insurance for half a million francs, naming her as beneficiary. He agrees; but he still gives her no money, and he keeps the policy. That night she says to Elise Perrier, "Kamarovsky must die."

She travels to Vienna with Kamarovsky and Naumov, from there to Hyères. Although both men obey her, she treats them like disobedient dogs. She makes up a story to the effect that she met Prilukov in secret. Sometimes, in a cocaine delirium, she thinks she sees Donat. She runs after strange people, and stands waiting for hours outside a hotel. Naumov torments her with his jealousy, and repeats that heaven sent him to save her. She is sick of hearing it. At night she puts her shoes outside the door and demands that he lick them; in the morning he brings her her shoes and begs to be allowed to put them on. Her savior, her Saint George! She has no desire any longer to see herself; she doesn't know any more who she is. Elise Perrier combs her hair, dresses her; she hardly ever looks at herself in the mirror.

Kamarovsky speaks of marriage again. Apathetically, she agrees. In the autumn, in Vienna. In July they return to Venice.

She bathes alone on the Lido, very early in the morning, when there is no one on the beach. Suddenly she sees Donat behind her bath house. It is one of those moments in which she becomes aware of the tragic-comic aspects of the situation. That night she slips out of the hotel and drives to the pension where he is staying. He looks like a harassed monkey. Even before he takes her in his arms, he tells her that he intends to shoot Kamarovsky. He hands her a letter in which he confesses to the murder out of jealousy. "So that no suspicion falls on you in case I am arrested." But he is not going to be arrested, he assures her. "I have defended more than eighty murderers." He is as proud of the crime he is planning as of the acquittal of his innocent clients. She believes that he will do what he threatens to do, but not that he will escape justice. Later she shakes him out of his sleep. The effect of the cocaine is gone. His outrageous plan no longer seems the obvious solution. She implores him not to do it, hurries back to her hotel. It is six o'clock, a cloudless summer morning. In the night, the air cleansed itself; the bath houses seem to be stretching out of their morning sleep. The waves of an ebbing tide are withdrawing gradually from the sandy beach.

Dressed in black, Elise Perrier is waiting for her. She hasn't slept all night. Tioka is ill. His thin little body is shaking with fever. He doesn't recognize his mother; he is delirious. Maria rouses the hotel management. Doctors come; the hotel doctor, the doctor from the spa, a doctor from Venice. Scarlet fever, a severe case. Is his life in danger? "Very hard to say, Countess." Should she have him moved to a hospital? The doctors cannot agree about it. The hotel management demands it. Kamarovsky confers with the management, with the doctors. Doctors and hotel manager quarrel. Kamarovsky has Granya taken away, to Venice. Maria leans over the bed, jumps to her feet when the child's laborious breathing stops for a moment. "But you do have hope, Doctor, don't you?" "I don't know, Countess."

Vow, punishment, God, poison, revolver, Donat, Nicholas, salvation, cocaine, madness, Tioka, loneliness, insurance policy, punishment, vow, death, Tioka, Pavel . . . She scribbles a few lines on a piece of paper and sends Elise to Prilukov's pension with it. "I am ready to fulfill my vow." Elise comes back with his answer: "Be calm. I have a plan. Leave everything to me. Everything is going to be all right."

All night long, two doctors and a nurse, Elise and Maria, watch at Tioka's bedside. "This is the crisis," says the professor. Tioka is asleep. His face is red; he gesticulates in his sleep. At four o'clock the nurse takes his temperature. One of the doctors says gruffly that she can't possibly be right; there are no miracles. The boy's temperature is almost normal. Maria knows that there are miracles.

On the next night—Tioka is sleeping peacefully—she drives to Prilukov.

332

On August 17, 1907, the Countess Tarnovska, accompanied by her fiancé, Count Pavel Ergrafovich Kamarovsky, and the young translator of Baudelaire, Nicholas Gregorievich Naumov, her maid, Elise Perrier, and the two boys, Tioka and Granya, boards the train to Vienna. They take the Pontebba Express.

CHAPTER 16

I

Tired, disappointed, filled with doubt, Andrey returned from the Russo-Japanese War to Rome in the beginning of the year 1906.

It had been the will of the Master General, shortly after the commencement of hostilities, that Andrey go to the front with the Russian troops as nurse and priest. The wishes of the Master General coincided with his own. His rise in the Order—*magister studentium, baccalaureus,* and, before the customary time, *magister theologiae*—had been so rapid that he had been afraid of becoming more a man of the Order than a man of God. It had been the intention of the Order that he preach to the wealthy, the satiated, and the vain of this world, in the course of which he had almost forgotten the sufferings of the poor, the oppressed, and the lonely.

On the battlefields of the Far East, further confusion awaited him. He was a Russian, going out into the field with Russian troops; but although Japanese torpedo boats had attacked the harbor of Port Arthur on a dark winter's night, February 8, 1904, without any declaration of war, Andrey soon realized that, unlike most other wars, a wrong on the one side did not make for a right on the other. The policy of the Russian monarchy had forced the Japanese to wage war. Minister of the Interior Vjatslav Plehve, "the bastard," had proclaimed that this was to be a "minor, victorious war." But there were no "minor" wars, and no one could be sure about the outcome of this Russian roulette. The very circles to whom Andrey had preached contemplation, reform, and a return to the Church had started the war. Nicholas II, who called the Japanese *"macacos,"* was in the hands of ruthless speculators such as the lumber merchant and Secretary of State Besobrasov; foolish favorites like the Czarina's equerry, Count Gendrikov; arrogant officers like Admiral Alexeyev. The soldiers—peasant lads, still half serfs and illiterate—whom Andrey had encountered on the battlefields of Dalny, Liaoyang, and finally before Port Arthur, had no idea why they had to die; many didn't even know where they were. Andrey had preached peace to the warmongers; he could not bless their flags. He could not preach to those who were doomed to die, either. He nursed the wounded, wiped the sweat off the brows of those gasping for their last breath, spoke to the dying in their language. As in his youth in Shitomir, he was overwhelmed by the feeling of his own powerlessness. But in Shitomir he had had a choice between love and hatred; now he had to close his eyes to injustice and could do nothing but minister to its victims. Perhaps Little Father Czar had thought that people whose lives weren't worth living would be glad to give their lives. But a man didn't die more easily because his life wasn't worth living. One day Andrey stood by as, not far from Talienwan, hundreds of soldiers fell upon the cars of a freight train because they thought the weapons had arrived at last—weapons with which they could defend themselves against the superiority of the Japanese. But when the cars were opened, they contained nothing but church banners and holy pictures; that was all General Kuropatkin had requested. Was Andrey to tell the men that church banners alone didn't make for a successful campaign; and that machine guns would have been more humane than holy pictures? Another time, on the Yalu, news of the revolution in Russia spread to the soldiers. They were lying on the banks of the Yellow River, too tired to move or jubilate; they only raised their hands and waved to each other, and passed the news on that the warlord had been overthrown and the war was over. But Andrey had to tell them that the warlord had not been overthrown and the war was not over. He helped a few to get up and led them along the river's edge, and knew that he was leading them to their death. When the sun rose—a pale sun, with the face of a Japanese—the battlefield was littered with corpses, for death had discovered new weapons, which came tearing down the hillsides or crept out of holes in the ground. Andrey had stood amid the dead, target for Japanese sharpshooters, and in the midst of the senselessness of death, his own life had seemed senseless.

In the year and a half he had spent on the battlefields of the Russo-Japanese War, he had thought very little of the people who had once meant something to him. Wars were fought in the name of family, nation, even of mankind; but in war, man lost his identity. It may have been a heretical thought, but to Andrey it had seemed that the war was worse than Hell, for the souls burning in this witches' cauldron of the conflagration knew only of their own suffering. They didn't remember the sufferings of others; they didn't care about mother, brother, wife, or child; they forgot that there were other hells.

After his return, Andrey became abruptly aware of the existence of other hells.

2

He had received permission to go to Orel, where Sergey Ivanovich Burintzev had been sentenced to die. He was to be executed on the eighteenth of December. Although Sergey was not a Roman Catholic and had refused the solace of the Church, Andrey was permitted to visit the condemned man in his cell and accompany him on his last walk.

It was snowing; the heavy flakes seemed to hang suspended in mid-air. On the long walk from the cloister to the prison, Andrey breathed deeply. People spoke of the beauties of life—what was beauty but life itself? How could Sergey imagine, when he looked out the narrow window of his cell, that the next day he would be gone, yet life would not be gone? Death lurked, attacked, surprised—all clichés; yet they expressed a benign law of nature. But when death did not lurk, attack, surprise, when one hailed death as if it were a cab driver—what then? Who had the right to say to any man: "You are going to die tomorrow morning at six fifteen"? Thou shalt not kill. Did the law that God had given to Moses on Mount Sinai count only for the murderer, not for the executioner? Were the people taking punishment and justice out of God's hands, and death as well? When would the power of this disempowered God come upon the world?

The prison was a large building, towering above the neighboring houses as in southern countries tombs sometimes towered over homes. The front wing, through which Andrey was led, was noisy and filled with an eerie merriment. Here the petty sinners were housed, whom the scaffold did not threaten, who could therefore afford a macabre kind of humor as they washed floors and cleaned windows. In the section where the political prisoners were being held, the corridors grew stiller; not a sound came from the cells. Perhaps only political prisoners thought of what they had done. Finally, behind a steel door, there were only four cells. In one of them, Sergey Burintzev was awaiting his hour.

He had been told of Andrey's visit. With no surprise, smiling, he stepped forward to greet him.

"So you see, your warnings bore no fruit," he said, offering Andrey a seat on his cot. "Siberia didn't bear fruit, either. When I got home, the revolution was in full swing. It is a little grotesque—or tragic, if you like; they're mostly the same thing—that I really didn't take part in the attempt on the life of the Chief of Police of Bryansk, but of course I might very well have had a hand in it."

Andrey was horrified. "But then there must be a way . . ."

Sergey shook his head. "The victims of a miscarriage of justice are usually those who didn't commit the crime but could have committed it. I wasn't exactly what you would call a sympathetic defendant. I showed little respect for the court; I have little reason to complain. Forms of government differ, but justice remains the same. State justice will remain a tyrant even in the state of the future. I could have appealed, but that would have been ridiculous. The higher courts are just bigger wheels of the same machine. Why should I bother to have confirmed what I know already?"

"You would have gained time."

"The revolution has collapsed. It needs time to gather new strength. My death will help to hasten the process. I am satisfied."

"In Manchuria I saw many die. I didn't see one who wouldn't have given his salvation to live a year longer."

Sergey sat down beside Andrey. "While I was waiting for my sentence, a boy was brought in from one of the other courts. He couldn't have been more than seventeen or eighteen. He was crying bitterly. I spoke to him, and he told me that he had been given a year for stealing. 'Look at me,' I said. 'In an hour I shall be condemned to death, and I am not crying.' I think often of that boy. What deceptive comfort I gave him! It is harder to lose a year of one's life for a poor cause than to sacrifice one's entire life for a good one."

"You know why I am smiling?" said Andrey. "I have to think of

336

Shitomir. I came to save you, and in the end you comforted me. Do you want to comfort me now, Sergey?"

"No. But I am grateful to you for not trying to comfort me."

Andrey shook his head. "Since I walked into your cell, I have been thinking only of myself. Do you know that in all these years, I never found another friend?"

"I didn't, either. Many comrades who would have given their lives for mine, and I for theirs—but no friend. It isn't true that their lives pass before those who are doomed to die. But to separate what is important from what is unimportant—that I think the doomed can do better than the others. During the past days I have thought often of how I sat at your bedside. . . . How old were you then?"

"Fourteen."

"We were practicing Latin prepositions. *Ante apud ad adversus circum circa citra cis* . . . Perhaps that was very important, more important than anything that came afterward." He got up and walked across the cell. Under the narrow window, he stopped. "To be quite honest, when they told me you were coming, I hesitated. If you had come to save my soul, I would have thrown you out."

"I know you don't believe in God. . . ."

"I doubt if anyone believes in Him. For those who are in power, He is an idol they carry on ahead of themselves; for the sick He is a crutch with which they hobble; for the rich, a safe in which they keep their possessions; for children, a horn of plenty full of presents; for the beggar, an almsbox; and for the Church, a signboard. I find this God too material and too simple. He doesn't exist, and He takes the place of something that doesn't exist."

"You can't stop me from praying for you," said Andrey.

"Pray all you like, only don't ever forget that more than one man has died by my hand. I'm afraid you're going to make yourself unpopular with your intercession."

Andrey rose. He wanted to see his friend's face. Death had not marked it. It was a peasant face, like thousands of others; still, without wrinkles, with light, calm eyes, no bitterness about the mouth, the nostrils too large, giving his face a droll expression. Had the martyrs, whose names Jean Bollard had recorded, died as easily? Did the truth make death easy, or did faith suffice?

"You may not believe in the hereafter, Sergey," he said, "but at least believe that you will live on in me. I shall never stop missing you."

"If there were a hereafter," said Sergey, "I would miss you, too." He sat down again beside Andrey. "I think your father liked me. When you and I went out together, he used to call after me, 'Look after my boy, Sergey.' It's silly, I know, but I still have the feeling I should be looking after you."

The tears were choking Andrey. He set his jaw hard and said, "Why do you suppose we two always loved each other?"

"I've asked myself that." Sergey laid one arm across Andrey's shoulders. "I still have to thank you for persuading Prilukov to defend me. In the meantime he too has been caught in the wheels of justice."

"They say he is a common criminal."

"Who knows? When the Athenians wanted to get rid of Alcibiades, they said that he had urinated against the Hermes statues. Do you remember—we studied it together. You and I, we have loved each other as only men can love who are sure of the other man's innocence. Perhaps love is nothing but the readiness to accept the other as he is. I don't know whether you can bend a branch, or a piece of leather, or an iron bar, without hurting them, but I do know that you cannot bend a human being without causing him pain. When we were young, I might have tried to persuade you to join the revolution, and you might have converted me. Do you think that the bowed soul of the one would have loved the forceful love of the other? And what would the forceful love have done with the bowed soul?" He laughed softly. "And now the Dominican comes from a faraway land to accompany the revolutionary on his last mile, and the revolutionary comforts the Dominican. That is what I call love victorious, Andrey."

"If you are right, then we have never loved anyone but each other. You and I have done nothing since our earliest youth but try to bend souls. Shouldn't love give to others what it has recognized as right?"

Darkness fell quickly, as if it wanted to cover up the day like a sick man.

"Don't think that I die without doubt," Sergey said softly. "But I do not doubt our cause any more than you doubt God. Only if both of us had to die today, we would admit that we were sure of our cause, but not so sure of our mission. Do you understand God? Do I understand the revolution? Are you sure of forgiveness? Am I sure I don't need to be forgiven? Let us be thankful that we have said to all the others but never to each other, 'This is the truth.' "

They heard steps outside. "The lifers," said Sergey. "They are being led to supper. Our monarchy is humane. One man has killed his mother, another killed to steal, a third—I don't know. Since they abolished capital punishment, only traitors go to the scaffold. That saves those three out there from death, and me from their company."

"Can I do anything for you, Sergey?"

"My mother is dead; my girl is in prison, too. You can lend me your support tomorrow, in case I weaken."

Andrey put his arm around his friend's shoulders. How many had he helped in the hour of their death and known nothing about them? It seemed to him as if he knew nothing about Sergey Burintzev, his only friend, and as if Sergey didn't need his help. Why? Was it because Sergey was already dead; as calm, as happy, and as powerful as the dead? When Sergey spoke, it seemed strange.

"If you really want to pray tomorrow," he said, "I won't make it too difficult for you."

When the warden unlocked the door, Andrey looked back once more. Sergey seemed to have grown years younger. He looked as he had looked in the corridor of the police station in Shitomir.

3

Andrey went to the Hotel Berlin, where the members of the press had set up their headquarters. They were waiting. After all, there had been cases of pardon in the last minute.

Nine or ten journalists were sitting around an old, white-bearded man, the prison doctor. He had kept on his fur coat, as if he intended to leave right away, but one of the reporters whispered to Andrey that the old man had been telling them stories for hours, instructive stories, the kind Russians liked to tell when they felt uneasy. The doctor was in the middle of a story.

"So our Fyodor grumbled because he was poorer than all the others, and because his seven children were hungry for bread, and because he could never get enough vodka. But in the night of which I told you, an angel appeared to Fyodor, looking just like an angel, except for the fact that he held an empty coalsack in one hand." The doctor paused, looked at Andrey, and said with a wry smile, "You may listen, Father. It's a clean story." Then he went on, "In this sack—the angel said— Fyodor was to pack all his troubles and all his grief. Fyodor had so much trouble and grief, the sack was barely big enough. Then the angel took Fyodor by the hand and led him up to heaven. The sack was heavy, and Fyodor wasn't young any more, so he groaned and moaned and grumbled about the many steps, and because he was accustomed to curse God as an unjust God. He mumbled all sorts of things about the others, too, who were better off than he. But the angel said nothing, because he wasn't a very high-ranking angel, and all he'd been told to do was get Fyodor up there. At last Fyodor arrived in heaven and discovered that he had had a quite different idea of what it would be like. All the clouds, for instance, were sacks; something you couldn't see from below. And an old man sat enthroned on the biggest sack of all. Fyodor recognized him at once from the many pictures he had seen. The old man said he had heard Fyodor's prayers, also his curses—more curses, by the way, than prayers. Fyodor was therefore, please, to put his burden down and pick out another sack—the lightest and best-looking one, if he liked." The doctor glanced again at Andrey, who was sitting in the background, only half listening. "Of course, Fyodor was suspicious. He didn't want to buy a pig in a poke." The doctor laughed at his own whimsey. "The old man told him he needn't do that; he might open all the sacks and examine their contents, but he had to take one with him. Fyodor found many names he knew. He opened one sack after the other, small ones, gold ones, fine-looking and insignificant ones. But he closed all of them up again, because the sack of his rich friend was full of imaginary illnesses; in the sack of his employer was the man's misery over his faithless wife; in the sack of his landlord was the fear that the story of his illegitimate child might leak out; and many sacks that were small but heavy were filled with nothing but boredom. And in the sack of the Czar, oh my friends, he found all of Russia. I know, I know, you have guessed the end." He looked about him as if he wanted to hear the contrary. "In the end, Fyodor meekly took his own sack back again, because at least he knew his own misery, and who could tell if the other sacks didn't weigh a lot more. He carried his old sack on his back as if it had been a beloved child. Suddenly, to his great astonishment, it seemed quite light. At first he thought his burden was so light because this time he was going down, but as you can readily imagine, my dear friends, that wasn't the reason at all."

"But that was your last story, Doctor," said one of the journalists.

"I only wanted to help you pass the time," said the doctor, a little annoyed.

"And we appreciate it," said another reporter. "But now I suggest we draw lots for who is to stand watch during the night. There's no sense in all of us staying up."

A man standing behind Andrey, puffing on a big cigar, tapped the friar on the shoulder. He was gray-haired and wore horn-rimmed glasses. "We can let you know, too, Father, if anything unexpected happens in the night," he said. "I don't think it will, though." He introduced himself. Dr. Hugo Friedlieber, *Neue Freie Presse,* Vienna.

Andrey thanked him.

"Are you the condemned man's confessor?" asked Friedlieber.

"No. His friend."

"A friend of his youth, I imagine."

"A friend."

"You know, I suppose, that it is a miscarriage of justice."

Andrey nodded.

"Not only Burintzev, but this whole country is condemned to death," the man went on without lowering his voice. "The prettiest fairy tales can't cover it up. And nothing that may be undertaken to distract the condemned can, either. One day the Burintzevs will gain the upper hand, and they will erect a monument to your friend. Monuments are the bronze portraits of the guilty conscience of a nation. But the new Burintzevs won't know what to do with their power any more than their judges do now. Those in power abuse their power; the people abuse their freedom."

"If you know it is a miscarriage of justice, why don't you do something about it? I mean, the world press . . ."

"I could ask you why the Church doesn't do anything about it. But I don't. People have been told for such a long time to mind their own business that they are finally doing it. Our newspapers don't get themselves mixed up in foreign affairs. Oh no! For the human race, human affairs are foreign affairs."

He puffed the smoke of his evil-smelling cigar in Andrey's face, but he jotted down the address of his cloister.

"Why do you no longer have hope?" asked Andrey.

Dr. Friedlieber said softly, "Because of Russia, it cannot be said that they hang the little men but let the big ones go free. Here they hang them all!"

4

Andrey couldn't sleep. The candles burned low; he read the whole night through. In Matthew, the Book of Wisdom, the words of the Prophet Jeremiah, and in the Acts. He knew many of the psalms by heart; he spoke the prayer for sorrow and loneliness; the supplication for fulfillment of the Divine Promise; the psalm about the living Messiah, and the nineteenth psalm. It was almost four o'clock when his tired eyes came across the thirty-fourth psalm, after which he read no more. A wonderful stillness filled him, not because he was consoled, but because he thought he had found the passage that could console Sergey. He not only believed it; he was as sure of it as if Sergey had walked into his cell and he, Andrey, had read the psalm to him, with Sergey nodding his affirmation. Now he thought that Sergey must be sleeping, and decided to stay awake and watch over his friend's slumber.

He lay down on his cot and looked up at the ceiling, on which the candlelight drew a restless circle. Sergey was going to die without the comforting belief in a hereafter, only with a meager belief in the future. "My God, why dost Thou let it happen?" The eternal question, and the Master in Sacred Theology could not answer it any more than the young man in the seething city of Shitomir had been able to find the answer. Andrey thought back, and thought he had known all along that it would come to this; had known, and had done nothing about it. Wasn't it his duty now to hurl himself against the executioner? "Not my will but Thine be done." The Son of God had not protested, but who had the strength of the Son? Andrey asked himself why he could not condemn Sergey, who was not only an enemy of the Czar, but of the Church as well; or why he couldn't at least understand those in power who had condemned his friend. But perhaps it was for the best as it was; this way he took a part of the guilt from Sergey's shoulders. Andrey grew calm, although his pain grew no less. But it was not a desperate pain; rather, it was the pain of fidelity—and he begged that Sergey might die faithful, too.

The doctor and the journalists who were permitted to be present at the execution met at five o'clock in the Hotel Berlin. They drove to the courthouse in two sleds. It was still night. The snow was falling peacefully. In a few windows in the suburban houses, oil lamps were already burning. Behind dirty curtains the day to come was stirring.

The inhabitants had slept or begot children, had tossed and turned in lust or suffering, had forgotten their existence or cursed it, had awakened from nightmares or succumbed to the deceptiveness of dreams. Not one of them had known that a man was to die at six fifteen, fifty-five minutes from now. It was inhuman to be able to see ahead fifty-five minutes; superhuman to be able to bear even the briefest glance into the future. The two men in the sled with Andrey spoke about the cold. One of them was complaining about the poor train connections. Andrey was thinking that the only friend he had ever had was about to die. "All alike have gone astray; they have become perverse; there is not one who does good, not even one."

They got out of the sled, entered the building, were led through a corridor; keys rattled; they found themselves in a courtyard. Two gas lanterns spread a venomous light; snow was stuck to their thin glass. The scaffold stood against one of the stone walls. Only a few steps from it, a tree, a lost suburban tree. It wasn't white because its branches were so thin that the snow had fallen off them. There were many people in the courtyard, but Andrey could not tell them apart. They turned up and disappeared again like shadows, and the shadows got lost in each other. A few were knocking the snow off their fur caps; others were brushing it off their coats; some stamped their booted feet; everyone was doing something superfluous. Andrey was cold in his thin coat, and couldn't understand how he could be aware of it. Now the doctor was standing beside him, drying his wet beard with a handkerchief. "Did you ever attend an execution, Father?" he asked. Andrey shook his head. "He slept for a few hours," said the doctor. "It's a strange thing—they all sleep the last night." People were walking up and down. A man was straightening out a table. He did it meticulously; the table had to stand just so. Another was lighting a storm lantern, and cursing because he had to use so many matches. A third busied himself at the scaffold, a stagehand before curtain time. Everybody was busy. Andrey thought that one of them was probably the executioner, and wondered that he didn't recognize him.

Sergey was led into the courtyard. When the wardens reached Andrey, they stepped aside. Sergey was bareheaded. The snow had turned his hair white, but his face still looked young. The water was running down it, but his eyes were dry. He put his hand in his coat pocket, gave Andrey a thin gold chain with a small gold cross hanging from it. Apologetically he said, "I always wore it. It belonged to my mother."

Andrey took the chain and stepped in front of Sergey so that he might not see the scaffold.

"I won't weaken," Sergey said.

They stood facing each other while a man in a high fur cap read the sentence aloud, quickly and unintelligibly.

Andrey was thinking that he had met Sergey when he had been four-teen, twenty-one years ago; yet he had no idea what Sergey was think-ing or feeling. Andrey's feet seemed rooted to the spot; it seemed to him that he would have to remain standing there for the rest of his life, be-tween Sergey and the scaffold. Despair overwhelmed him again. He forgot that he was the Dominican Father Andrey Antonovich Vyru-bov; he wanted to cry out and fall on his knees before the judge, fall upon the executioner and overpower him. But all he did was embrace Sergey and kiss him on both cheeks. Sergey kissed him, passed his hand over Andrey's head, and said, "Be calm, my boy."

Then they took each other by the hand and moved away, hand in hand, as if both of them were condemned, to the three wooden steps that led up the scaffold. At the top stood the executioner. He had on a thick fur coat, a fur cap, and fur-lined gloves. He looked like a cattle dealer in the market of Kiev.

Sergey let go Andrey's hand, turned away, walked up the steps. Andrey was holding his rosary in his hands, and now he said in a loud voice, " 'Do me justice, because you are just, O Lord; my God, let them not rejoice over me. Let them not say in their hearts, "Aha! That is what we wanted!" Let them not say, "We have swallowed him up!" Let all be put to shame and confounded who are glad at my misfortune. Let those be clothed with shame and disgrace who glory over me. But let those shout for joy and be glad who favor my just cause; and may they ever say, "The Lord be glorified; he wills the prosperity of his servant!" ' "

Sergey had turned around and was listening to the words of the psalm as if he could not believe it was a psalm, as if he thought they had to be Andrey's own words. Then Andrey saw a blessed smile pass across Ser-gey's face, and he too had to smile. Behind him, someone said, "Amen."

5

Andrey hesitated for a long time before answering Maria Tarnovska's call. It was the beginning of August, eight months after Sergey's execution. Andrey had been teaching in theological seminaries, and was staying in a monastery in Upper Austria. It was incomprehensible to him how Maria could have found out he was there. He did not answer her letter, which the Prior had handed to him after reading it, but he recalled the help Maria had given him for Sergey. When he arrived in Vienna, on his way to Cracow, and called the Hotel Sacher, he was hoping that Maria would already have left. But the desk connected him with her. She rejected his suggestion that he come to see her that morning. She had reasons, she said, for not wanting to see him until evening.

Although he had much business to attend to during the day, he thought with increasing displeasure of their meeting. He did not think often of Maria any more, but when he did, he could never quite trust his feelings. For him she was still sex personified. He had forgotten the love affairs of his early youth; they had lost all reality for him; he could think of them without shame. He remembered the fleeting episodes as divinely predestined necessity—he who preached against the sins of the flesh, heard confession, and advised those who had gone astray should know what sin was. But he could feel an aversion toward Maria growing in him, and it made him distrustful of himself. Would she tempt him, as she always had done? Was he yearning for temptation? That he was certain of withstanding the temptation of her meant little to a man who took for granted that a priest should be capable of resisting carnal sin. He considered temptation itself a sin, just as lust was sinful without consummation.

These thoughts were on his mind as he walked through the city to the hotel where Maria was staying. It was a humid August evening. One thought calmed him: the memory of his visit to Charkov. In five or ten years, he had promised himself then, his love would be so purified that he would be able to help Maria without mistrusting himself.

When he entered the room, he realized at once that his intentions had been deceptive or vain: vain, because he had thought only of himself and not counted on her; deceptive, because although it was possible for the human will to resist temptation, the devil was empowered—apparently by God—to put this will to the test.

Maria was wearing a light dressing gown, which barely hid the outlines of her body. She was just as beautiful as he remembered her, but small fine lines had settled down in the corners of her mouth, and the expression in her eyes fluctuated between restlessness and apathy. He found it not only in poor taste but stupid of her to receive him so scantily clad. The arrogance of the flesh was too obvious; the Devil was so sure of himself, he evidently thought he needed no disguise.

"I searched for you; I had to find you," she said. "Since I saw you last, things have gone from bad to worse. I am more lost than ever. I don't know what to do. Only you can save me."

"Why only I?"

"Because you are the only man who ever aroused healthy feelings in me."

"If you wish to speak to the priest I am, I shall listen to you."

"You will listen to me anyhow. You cannot let me perish. I have three lovers, and I love none of them. I can free myself of none of them. Two of them want to murder the third."

"I heard that you were engaged to Count Kamarovsky," he said. "I hate him."

"Does he know that?"

"All of them know that I hate them. Every one of them sleeps with death. I hate them because I am their death, but they love me."

He believed that she had three lovers; aside from that, he didn't believe anything she said. "My advice is so simple," he said, "that you don't need it. Instead of talking to me, who can do nothing about it, you must speak to the man you are engaged to."

She laughed. So that was how simply he saw the world. She thought he had studied theology so as to be able to help others—or had it been only his egoistic fear of the world? If he had forgotten the world, how did he think he could help others? She expressed herself like an accuser, but soon her voice became gentle and pleading. For years she had been living as if under a terrible curse, she went on; now, any time, tonight perhaps, it might be fulfilled. A demonic power was forcing her to destroy these men. She had destroyed others before them. There was only one sign in her life that she was not definitely damned—Andrey had stood at all decisive crossroads; he, the friend of her youth, the only man she had ever loved, the only man she had not been able to destroy, had not wanted to destroy, the only one with whom she had had the feeling that evil spirits feared him. She had cried out to him, but he had not heard her. "Have you ever saved a soul? Do you intend to scorn a soul?" Now she sounded aggressive, but almost immediately she was plaintive again:

346

he could not leave her alone; alone she would have to make the wrong choice.

She had sat down on the upholstered bench he was sitting on, beside him, close to him. He had to see her breasts, to feel her breath. Every word she said could have been true; yet none were true. Every word was directed, not at the priest, but at the man. Could he possibly be faced with a woman possessed? Did she believe that she could rid herself of the sinful love of three men by the sinful love of a fourth? Did she want to save herself from ruin by ruining the one man she had not been able to ruin? Was she fleeing from her own power, or was she being driven on by the devilish compulsion to try her strength on one last victim?

She spoke on and on, in confused sentences; she abandoned the present, exorcised the past. "It will be decided tonight," she whispered. "You must stay with me."

He leaned back. "What is to be decided tonight?"

"Whether he must die."

"Who?"

"The toad."

"For heaven's sake, Maria, pull yourself together."

"I have vowed that he shall die. You must drive the Devil out of me."

She moved even closer to him and looked at him as if she had said nothing until now, as if she were seeing him for the first time. "Your love can save me," she said. "You must love me. You must." She threw her arms around his neck, pressed her lips to his mouth.

He pushed her from him and stood up, trembling with rage. For a fleeting moment he tried to love her, tried to tell himself that she was sick and in need of his compassion. Love and compassion could be temptation. Had he believed that the Devil ever appeared undisguised? Of all the Devil's disguises, the most Satanic was the one in which he presented himself as the miserable wretch who wanted to be freed of the Devil.

He walked toward the door. Maria jumped to her feet and barred his way. On her knees, she clung to his. "Think of Mary Magdalene."

That she dared to utter the name of the Biblical sinner caused his rage, which had died down, to flare up again. He stepped forward so brusquely that she fell to the ground. The robe fell from her shoulders; she was naked to the waist. Before he could grasp the door handle, she was on her feet, at the door. With the palm of her hand she pressed three buttons at once, the ones marked waiter, valet, maid. In a few moments, they would be there. She stood in his way, her hair falling down her forehead, her face white, her lips trembling.

"They will come and find you here," she said, and began to laugh so loudly that it would have to be heard in the corridor. She was still laughing when he grasped her by the wrist and pulled her away. A waiter was standing in front of the door. Andrey didn't care if the man could see the laughing, half-naked woman through the crack in the door.

Evening had descended upon the city. Festively dressed people were leaving the hotel. The rubber wheels of fiacres glided across the hot asphalt. It seemed even hotter than it had been during the day. The Dominican turned the corner of the Kärntnerstrasse and walked toward the St. Stephen's Cathedral. He was grateful for his deliverance, but not proud of it. He had encountered a woman possessed, and saved nothing but himself. He had encountered destruction, and only he had remained whole. He had witnessed despair, and had succeeded only in averting his own disaster. That there had been no other way out . . . ? Did only God know the way through the dense entanglements and fires of love that led past the abyss of love, to love?

CHAPTER 17

Maria Tarnovska contemplates suicide. It is too much; only she doesn't know what is too much—the three men from whom she cannot free herself, the fear of life with Pavel or the fear of a life of poverty, her love for Tioka and her inability to devote herself to him? If she can think one thing through to the end, it is the thought of suicide.

Prilukov is in Vienna; Prilukov is everywhere. He is staying at a shabby pension in the Wieden suburb. He calls her up; wherever she goes, he is lurking. He threatens suicide. Laughing, she hands him her revolver. If only all three would kill themselves—Donat and Pavel and Nicholas!

In a small coffeehouse on the periphery of the city, she meets Prilukov. Elevated trains rattle over their heads. Sometimes their noise swallows up what they are saying. Maria hopes that Donat cannot understand her, and that she doesn't understand him. He is developing a plan to kill Kamarovsky. It is to happen on an excursion to the Vienna woods. She is to lure him into a trap. "Leave the rest to me, Mura." He speaks about the insurance money: "Half of it will suffice to pay my debts." He mentions a widow with four children whom he has done out of her savings. "It worries me." Perhaps he even believes what he is saying. She calls him a liar, a thief, a murderer. "For you, Mura." He speaks about Tioka. "Do you want him to die?" She refuses to go on the excursion.

She becomes nevertheless more and more convinced that Pavel has to die. He does not suspect what is going on in her mind. He brings her pornographic pictures of orgies, flagellations. She lashes out at him. He mocks her for her prudishness. Tioka hurts himself while playing, a superficial wound; Elise Perrier can bandage it herself; but that night Maria wakes up screaming. It is a sign from God. She doesn't need any signs from heaven; it doesn't depend on her vow any more. When Donat speaks of the insurance money, she is no longer horrified. She has stolen from the living, why shouldn't she steal from the dead? Like a drowning man she clings to the power that is leaving her. She has no more power over Prilukov; she is his accomplice. She has no more power over Naumov; he evades her. And she has no more power over Pavel. If she tries to be kind to him, he misunderstands her kindness; if she punishes him, he enjoys it. The whole disaster began on the train, when she first met him.

She won't listen to Elise Perrier's entreaties. She tells the maid about Andrey's visit. He eluded her because his conscience was clear. He who is pure does not long for punishment; he who does not long for punishment cannot be shackled by pain. She has no power over anyone to whom she cannot cause pain. The logic of her thoughts doesn't calm her; it succeeds only in horrifying her more, as if she were the prosecutor of her own case and was proving the deliberate intention of her crime to herself. She flees into confusion.

Kamarovsky has to go to Berlin for a few days. He leaves Maria alone with Naumov. Pavel sends long, loving telegrams; in four weeks they are to be married. Naumov won't leave her side. She smokes a great deal. He watches every cigarette she smokes like a dog watching a bone. She puts out her cigarettes on his arm, on his chest. If she throws a cigarette away without burning him, he cries. One morning he brings a basket of flowers to her bedside, removes the tissue paper—under the flowers lies a whip. He implores her to flog him. She laughs, and locks the whip away. Sometimes he is unmanageable, won't do her the smallest service, is impolite, behaves like a spoiled child. She knows he is doing it to be punished; she takes the whip in her hand, doesn't strike him.

Once more under cocaine, she meets Prilukov. Everything comes to her easily, naturally. They go to his pension, make love. She tells him about Naumov. In his jealousy, he smashes glasses, an ash tray. Suddenly he grows quiet. "I'll get rid of them both," he says.

Kamarovsky comes back. She insists that they get married in Kiev. The more he tries to talk her out of it, the more determined she is to become the Countess Kamarovsky in the city of her childhood.

Prilukov is waiting for her. They sit in the Dairy Bar in the Stadtpark. The River Wien is trickling wearily in its dry bed; children are playing with hoops; white baby carriages stand in the shadows of the chestnut trees; nursemaids and soldiers are walking hand in hand. Prilukov is changed again. His self-confidence is restored; the fear is gone from his eyes. Calmly he develops his latest plan. She has to persuade Naumov to kill Kamarovsky. If she wields sufficient power over the youth, he will do it. If he manages to escape punishment, he, Prilukov, will get rid of Naumov for her. "I am not Kamarovsky," he says. If Naumov is caught, all the better—Kamarovsky dead, Naumov in jail. "And my vow?" she asks. "You only swore to get rid of the disgusting animal, not to stain your hands with his blood, nor mine." He justifies the murder, not like a deed planned, but as if it happened long ago.

She hurries back to the hotel. On the way, she stops in front of St. Stephen's Cathedral. She is damned, but divine grace can still save her. She is about to enter the church when she recalls Andrey's visit. Why should she give God a chance when He gave her none?

Her thoughts are dead spots between her actions. She spends the evening with Kamarovsky and Naumov in a summer restaurant. In a light dress and large, airy hat, she looks enchanting. Kamarovsky speaks about the wedding. Naumov is silent, watching Kamarovsky, his eyes filled with hatred. "Do you think I am too old for Mura?" Kamarovsky asks jocosely. "You are not good enough for her," Naumov replies. "You should go home," Kamarovsky says. "Your father is worried about you." Viennese singers are singing sentimental songs. Maria is drinking this year's wine; it goes to her head; suddenly she is in an exuberant mood. Nothing has happened yet; if she can hold this moment fast, nothing will have to happen. "You are my murderer," Pavel could say, but it is not true yet. Not only what happened but what is to happen can be as unreal as a nightmare. "A great many men will still fall in love with Mura," Kamarovsky is saying, and Naumov's eyes are darting to and fro like startled birds. "You shall never possess Mura," he says. When Kamarovsky leaves them for a moment, she says to Naumov, "An hour after we get back. In my room."

She is lying on her bed when he knocks. She behaves as if she never told him to come. When he reminds her, stammering, she calls him a liar, picks up the whip, asks him if he would kill Kamarovsky for her sake. He hesitates.

"You promised you would, on our first evening."

"I was speaking about a duel."

"An idiotic farce."

"I am too weak."

"Then someone else will do it." She lets him wring from her the fact that her former lover, Prilukov, is in Vienna. "You may meet him tomorrow; he will tell you that it is true. You are always in second place. I detest cowards."

Three days later a telegram summons Naumov to his father's bedside. His father is ill. Now she is at the mercy of Kamarovsky. That evening he talks about how different Granya and Tioka are. Tioka, he says, needs more severity, a more orderly life, regular school hours. "Perhaps a tutor," she says, and tells him how she deceived Prilukov with the student, Zolotariev. "My mother wants to be reconciled with you," Kamarovsky says. "We shall marry in Kiev, but then we shall move to the castle. In the clean atmosphere of my home, under the kindly eyes of my mother, you shall forget everything, Mura." She looks at him as if he were a dying man speaking of the future.

On the day Kamarovsky sets the wedding date for September 18, she receives a telegram from Naumov. "I am resolved." He implores her to meet him in Kiev. Prilukov advises her to tell Kamarovsky that she wants to be reconciled to her father and ask his blessing. Pavel is touched. In the meantime he will go to Venice, where he has bought a house. "Our house, Mura." She wires Naumov that he can expect her in Kiev. When she wants to take her jewelry, Pavel says, "It is safer in my care." He takes her, Tioka, and Elise Perrier to the station. When he is buying something for her to read, he is given a false coin, and bickers with the man over it. In her compartment, she finds roses. Through the open window she gives him her hand once more. She looks down at his bald head, with the thin hair combed meticulously over it. The thought that he is condemned to death without knowing it fills her with such irresistible merriment, she has to hold her handkerchief to her mouth. "Don't you feel well, Countess?" Elise Perrier asks. Tioka is looking at her fearfully, worried about his mother. The urge to laugh is replaced by the irresistible compulsion to tell Pavel the truth. "Pavel, Pavel . . . I must tell you something." Steam, pouring out from under the car. Kamarovsky coughs. Coughing, he begins to walk alongside the train, which has started to move. "Pavel—take care!" He points to his ears, indicating that he cannot hear what she is saying. She leans farther out the window. She recalls that in her childhood—God only knows why—the signs in railway compartments amused her: Don't lean out of the window. *Nicht hinausbeugen. Ne pas se pencher en dehors. E pericolosi sporgersi.* As if flagging beside the constantly accelerating train, the little dark figure falls back into the night.

When she gets to Kiev, Naumov has not yet arrived. She is lying on the divan in her hotel room, dozing. Pavel thinks she is in Otrada. What if she really went to Otrada? Terrible O'Rourke is seventy-three. Perhaps he is not terrible any more. She can see his blue eyes staring at her; it is her sixteenth birthday; her mother is combing her hair high. The carriage with the two aunts rolls out of the courtyard; her father lifts his hand and waves. He knew best. Tomorrow she will go to the cemetery. She can trust only the dead.

She asks herself why Pavel has to die. Because of her vow? Her love for Donat? Her horror of life with a toad? No. For freedom's sake. She doesn't know the meaning of freedom. Again she cries out in her sleep. At once Elise Perrier is there, dressed in black. "Nicholas will arrive tomorrow," she tells her maid, "and he will murder Count Kamarovsky." "The journey has tired you, Countess," says Elise. Maria tells the maid that Prilukov is in Vienna. "Didn't you call him our Lohengrin?" Elise Perrier nods. Perhaps Prilukov is her savior; at any rate, he knows what he wants. Once he took her life out of her hands; now he is taking death out of her hands.

For days she struggles with Naumov. He regrets his decision. She explains that she came to Kiev under a pretext and cannot go back to Kamarovsky. If Naumov doesn't do it, she tells him again, then Prilukov will. "My savior is the man who kills Kamarovsky." She will belong to him forever. "Such a plan can come only from a mind gone mad," Naumov whispers. Again he speaks about the possibility of a duel. She shakes her head. "Bertha is hesitating," she telegraphs Donat. Bertha is the name they agreed upon for Naumov. Prilukov replies, "Letter on the way show it to Bertha." She puts her shoes out and locks the door to Naumov. He rattles the door handle; she thinks of the night in St. Petersburg when she locked Vassily out. "Bertha is undecided—what do I do?" "Bertha is ready." "Bertha refuses." She sends off half a dozen telegrams.

On a hot August night, she stays at the Château des Fleurs with Naumov until three in the morning. She drinks champagne with vodka. It is as if thirteen years ago a magician waved a magic wand and turned all of them to stone—guests, gypsies, women's orchestra, waiters. Now they have awakened; the same people, no older, only yellowed, dusty, waxen. Mademoiselle Larue, Vassily, the French diplomat, the singers from Paris are sitting at her table. She is seized with a hopeless yearning for her youth. Like someone blind, on all fours, groping for something lost, she feels for the milestone where she chose the wrong way. Nobody wanted her to see; how could she possibly have become seeing? She realizes that she lost something. What? What did she have in those days, in the Château des Fleurs, that she has meanwhile lost? Not her youth—her power. And when did she lose it? When Vassily fought the duel with Yuri Tolstoy? When Andrey left her with her hairless head? When Vladimir Stahl was able to take her like the landlord his maid? When she surrendered to Donat? When she slept with Adele, Olga's toad? She wanted to see all of them suffer, but she had suffered more than all of them. She thought she was powerful, but she has subjugated no one. Her gaze falls on Naumov. This one, she thinks, this one! He could restore her lost power, or destroy her.

She sees it all clearly. If this beautiful weakling can oppose her will, then he can destroy her. If he is ready to murder for her sake, her power is regained; then she is wrong, and it was never lost. The figures of Kamarovsky and Donat sink away in a mist. Pavel does not have to die; it is Naumov who has to murder. All she can see is Nicholas Naumov, her executioner or savior.

Back at the hotel, she opens her door to him. She kisses him, draws him down to her bed. "I love you, love you." He kisses her, buries his face between her breasts, weeps. Shame over his failure shakes his young body. She fears his defeat more than he does. His chaste kisses disgust her. He stammers explanations, excuses, lies. If he goes from her unloved, she is lost. "Bring the whip," she tells him. "No, on all fours." He finds the whip. "No, in your mouth." He obeys. "Undress. No, on the floor." She flogs him until the blood streams down his back. No more thoughts, no plans, no hope—all goes under in a deadly ecstasy.

In the morning she asks him if he is still too much of a coward to kill Kamarovsky. "I shall kill Kamarovsky if you swear never to see Prilukov again." "I am yours, Nicholas, forever." That afternoon she drives with him to the cemetery where her mother and Vladimir Stahl are buried. Once more—or so it seems to her—he tries to withdraw from her power. That night she removes all marks of identification from his clothing. Trembling, he watches her. "If I do not succeed, I shall kill myself." "You swear?" "I swear." She gives him a little gold cross. He weeps, kisses it. On the evening of the following day, he intends to leave for Venice.

She takes sleeping pills, sleeps until noon, gropes her way back into reality, hopes that she has been dreaming, calls Elise. "I must speak to Naumov at once." "He has left, Countess." The day bursts in on her with angry rays. "What is today?" "Monday, Countess." "What was yesterday?" Elise Perrier looks startled. "Sunday, Countess." Maria falls back on her cushions.

For three days and nights she lies in bed with a high fever. The doctor comes. She thinks it is Dr. Orlov, the eye specialist. She thinks it is Pavel. On September 5, she receives a telegram. "Am badly wounded, but if my *dushka* hurries to me, I shall soon recover." The telegram comes from the Hospital San Giovanni e Paolo in Venice. It is signed "Kamarovsky." The quickest train connection is via Vienna. She leaves two hours later. It is a hot day, the fifth of September, 1907.

BOOK III

THE TRIAL

CHAPTER 1

I

The trial of Maria Nikolaevna Tarnovska, Dr. Donat Dmitrievich Prilukov, Nicholas Gregorievich Naumov, and Elise Perrier began on the fourth of March, 1910, with President of the Assize Court, Commendatore Antonio Tusitano, presiding. Naumov stood accused of murder with express malice prepense; the Countess and Prilukov of conspiracy and incitement to murder; Elise Perrier of abetting and failing to report the crime. Each of the accused was represented by three lawyers; the Countess by Italy's most famous defense lawyer, young Cavaliere Francesco Vecchini. The court consisted, besides the presiding magistrate, of a jury of twelve and two appellate court judges. Over two hundred and fifty witnesses, nine psychiatrists, and thirteen doctors were summoned to appear. All the accused had learned how to speak Italian while under detention; the witnesses were permitted to avail themselves of the services of a translator. The trial was expected to last three months.

On the eve of the trial, Dr. Hugo Friedlieber, *Neue Freie Presse,* Vienna, wrote the following article, in his usual florid style:

As I write these lines, sensation-seeking spectators are already gathering in the squares around the courthouse, where they will presumably spend the night. Hundreds of requests for tickets had to be turned down. Over fifty correspondents from every corner of the globe have arrived in the city of the lagoons; even Madame Nicolle, of the *Matin*—considered by many to be the most famous female reporter in the world—is expected to be present. The populace is greedy for a show.

Countess Maria Tarnovska—who is of royal blood, and presumed to be a descendant of Maria Stuart—as well as those on trial with her, have been under arrest for two and a half years. The sensational newspapers have done more than their share to highlight the scandalous circumstances under which Public Prosecutor Garzoni was relieved of his post and Lawyer Calzini resigned from the defense of the Countess. Less well known is the fact that, originally, Assize Court Judges Angioletti and Svanascani, respectively, had been selected to preside. Angioletti died suddenly under rather mysterious circumstances, and Svanascani declared himself unable to take the case because of prejudice and was transferred to Pisa. Assize Court Judge Tusitano is a man of about seventy-five, a legal expert of world renown, who has been honored with the highest decorations of the monarchy and is famous for his clement yet circumspect handling of a case. He was retired, but apparently it was felt that only this venerable old man could resist the wiles of the beautiful Russian countess.

The defense of the Countess in the case can best be described as crafty. She has confessed—after having first denied it—to knowing about the plan to murder Count Pavel Ergrafovich Kamarovsky; but she still denies stubbornly that she incited the student and translator of Baudelaire, Naumov, to kill the Count. No wonder, since the Russian Lorelei may very well receive life imprisonment for her part in the crime.

The student Nicholas Naumov, son of the former Governor of Orel and a relative of Turgenev—as already mentioned, we are moving in high society—has made a complete and abject confession. It remains unclear, however, whether he was influenced to the deed by the beautiful Russian, or by the forceful lawyer, Prilukov. Naumov's confession does not even state clearly from which one of the two he received the weapon with which he killed the Count on September 3, 1907.

The thirty-three-year-old defendant doesn't seem to have lost any of her beauty, which has been the undoing of quite a few men. As is often the case with those who have lived licentiously, life behind prison walls seems to have had the effect of a rest cure on Madame de Tarnovska. At first, so they say, her behavior was quite hysterical—for instance, she had to be moved to the Inquisition Hospital when a slight earth tremor shook Venice—but the prison authorities now attest to her best behavior.

The serious observer, however, will find all this of minor interest when compared with the social and moral aspects of this "sensational" case. The trials of the ladies Steinheil and Borovska in Paris, of Count Pfeil in Thorn, of Frau von Schönbeck in Allenstein, are still fresh in the memory of a populace that unfortunately seems scarcely aware of the profound connection between all these cases.

In Russia, the third duma is in session; the leader of the revolutionaries, Vladimir Ilyich Ulyanov, called Lenin, has fled; a train robbery by Joseph Djungashvili, called Stalin by his fellow travelers, is making headlines; the New York Stock Exchange is being rocked by uncertainty; the affair

Rasputin at the court of the Czar of all Russias is on everyone's tongue; Czar Nicholas II is in Potsdam; the Triple Entente threatens our allies; half the Russian press has been silenced, but a certain coterie of society seems to have inscribed Madame Pompadour's words on its flag: *"Après nous le déluge!"*

It should therefore hardly come as a surprise to see members of Russian society in the prisoner's dock. Wasn't Bismark supposed to have said, *"Grattez le Russe, et vous trouverez le Tartare"*? Who can therefore be astonished that, in the former building of the Fabbriche Nuove di Rialto in Venice, just that society is on trial that is suppressing Russia's fight for freedom, encouraging Jewish pogroms, and displaying an arrogance that is absolutely unjustified? Presiding Magistrate Tusitano's warning to keep private life and the question of guilt carefully separate in our minds therefore seems all the more justified. The *vox populi* has already given its verdict, certainly in as far as the seductive Countess is concerned. Is the voice of the people deceptive? Be that as it may, from tomorrow on, we can expect a morality play of unparalleled hideousness to unfold before our astonished eyes in the courtroom on the Canale Grande.

2

Punctually at seven, the door of Maria Tarnovska's cell is opened. A female warden steps into the room. Sister Rosa, her wart flattened on her nose like a leech. Or Sister Sofia, who suffers from the sins of the prisoners as if they were her own. Or Sister Lucia, a young, plump peasant girl—why had she taken the veil? Maria Tarnovska knows that the nuns are quarreling among themselves as to who should accompany her. The trip in the gondola with the *carabinieri;* the crowds in the courtroom—a welcome change from their humdrum existence in the Istituti Penali Femminili.

A few people are standing at the gates of the prison: canal workers, women on their way to the vegetable market, employees of the spaghetti factory, children. The thought that they are not being led from the prison themselves makes them shiver pleasantly. They are poor but honest; now they feel richer and more honest. The *carabinieri* are always the same ones, not unfriendly any more. He who has dealings with sin long enough finds it quite human. A second gondola. Elise Perrier steps into it with her wardens, male and female. Dressed in black silk, her hair brushed back neatly. In a moment she will ask, "Is there anything I can do for you, Countess?" The Countess smiles; Elise Perrier smiles back gratefully. A few of the women going to market shout obscenities at Elise Perrier. Her kind they will never forgive.

The gondola is draped in black. The Countess cannot be seen, but she can see. A sunny March day; the water white as an opal, like glass from Murano; Venice spread out before her as proper as a postcard; people standing in front of a canvas backdrop at the photographer's. In the harbor of La Giudecca, warships, freighters, ocean liners; fishermen returning home; vegetable barges approaching the city slowly, as if they have all the time in the world; a farewell whistle from the funnel of a departing steamer. Bellboys from the hotels are helping honeymooners into their gondolas. The gondolas from La Giudecca are two black spots; yet to Maria Tarnovska it seems as if the life going on around her is standing still. Venice is lying in a Sleeping Beauty sleep, waiting for a kiss. Every morning she has the feeling that what is happening to her cannot be happening, not here; but since it is happening, the place where it takes place has to be unreal.

The gondolas turn into the Canale Grande. The Countess thinks of Tioka, how she told him about Lord Byron. The Rialto Bridge comes closer; the air begins to smell more strongly of vegetables, salad greens, fruit. The courthouse is over the vegetable market. Full crates are being dragged along; empty crates are being stacked; dirty water washes rotten greens into the canal; an orange rolls down the steps. Men and women with bloody aprons come from the fish and meat market. A guide is saying, "Would you like to see the Countess Tarnovska?" A tourist attraction, like the pigeons in St. Mark's Square, the lions in front of the Campanile, Shylock's booth. Then there is the crowd that has come only to vent their indignation. Public opinion. The bookkeeper who can say afterward, " 'Murderess!' That's what I cried out to her. 'Murderess!' " The housewife who can say, "I showed her my fist—the adulteress!" Or the street urchins, who know every lewd song about her by heart. During the first days she hurried past them, head lowered. Now Dr. Vecchini comes down the steps to fetch her. Her "defense counsel"—she experiences the words literally. She walks upright in her black dress, big black hat, black veil. From the first she chose to wear mourning because it seemed the only fitting dress. Whom is she mourning? Simply mourning. Already on the second day, they had a lampoon for the "widow" who was mourning her victim. Let them have their lampoons.

She throws back her veil. In Otrada, at the funeral of her mother, she threw back her veil.

The large Assize Court room is situated on the second floor. On the first, plaintiffs, defendants, lawyers stand around; she thinks they are ridiculous. She enters the courtroom from the rear, past a big cold stove. The spectators turn their heads, like the audience at a vaudeville show when a clown has the original idea of making his entry from the rear. A select audience: many women, flowered hats, lorgnettes. The prisoner's dock is on the right; a narrow, wooden cage. She thinks of Vassily's parrot, Andrey's finch. *Carabinieri* sit between the four defendants—the Countess and Elise Perrier and Naumov and Prilukov. Now and then she turns around to see if Kamarovsky isn't there, to make it a portrait gallery of the actors, as in the Royal Theater in Moscow. In the center, in front of the spectator benches, stands the black leather bench where the lawyers sit. All in profile. The Roman profile of Dr. Vecchini calms her. The members of the press sit opposite her in a more airy cage—Russians, Italians, French, Austrians, even Americans. The world wants to know the details. The keyhole of her bedroom, big as a tunnel. The courtroom, her salon. The public drinks with her, chats with her, makes love with her. Outrage puts indignation to sleep. The journalists nod at the Countess: the French one, wrinkled as a dachshund, from *Le Temps;* the massive German one, hair bristling from his forehead, from the *Münchner Neueste Nachrichten;* the one with the horn-rimmed spectacles, Dr. Hugo Friedlieber, from the *Neue Freie Presse,* Vienna.

Then comes the Public Prosecutor, Commendatore Randi. He gets into his black robe between door and table. He rubs his chin, fiddles with his earlobes, shrugs, and his robe slips off his shoulders. The Countess does not hate him; he simply enters what is owing in a ledger, like debts. The Presiding Magistrate appears through the archway of the center door. Commendatore Tusitano looks like the fruit of a cactus, red-yellow, thorny, sweet-sour; the fruit of a tree from which you expect no fruit. He probably wishes he was at home grafting roses. Of what concern is it to him that thirty-three years ago, in Otrada, near Kiev, a daughter was born to Knight Marshal Nikolay Vladimirovich O'Rourke and his wife, Katharina, née Seletzka? The Countess hates only the two lawyers, Feder and Carnuletti, sitting beside the Public Prosecutor. They represent the

Countess Kamarovskaya; they urge justice on like a limping nag. From the first day, she has divided the jury into friend and enemy. The professor from the academy, who never stops drawing her; the veterinarian, with the faithful head of a St. Bernard; the writer, with his glowing, hungry eyes; the deputy, who looks at himself in a mirror and is startled when the sun is suddenly refracted in it; the schoolmaster, wrinkling his nose as if there were a bad smell; the nervous apothecary, who succeeds in irritating even the Presiding Magistrate.

The walls are yellow, white, pink marble. In a wooden oval over the door the judges use, the words, *"La legge è eguale per tutti."* Sometimes the judge has the windows opened. Smell of vegetables, smell of canals, smell of fish. Pigeons settle on the sills, cooing, fluttering; noisily, they fly off; they don't think much of the law. The bells of Santi Apostoli are ringing. When the Countess rises, she can see the bell tower. If she turns around, she faces the Canale Grande, the Palazzo da Mosta, the Palazzo Michiel dalle Colonne. Commendatore Tusitano orders the curtains drawn; his eyes are weak. The curtains are a nondescript color, perhaps silk, once perhaps pink; their effect is feminine, like that of a boudoir. Maria Tarnovska lets her gaze wander across the drapes. They move, wave at her, seem to be dancing for her.

In the morning, one of the clerks draws the curtains closed, as if he has been told to put a stop to their frivolity. Fully aware of the importance of his duty, he walks up to the rostrum, bows in front of the crucifix, and does what he does daily at this hour. He tears a leaf off the calendar.

3

Maria Tarnovska looks at Naumov. She is conscious of every one of her own moves. Every gesture speaks for or against her, as if her motions are giving testimony, unwilling witnesses. She is being watched; is her mouth twitching; is she breathing more heavily; is her chest rising or falling; are her fingers restless?

Naumov is describing the crime. He has gained weight. His complexion is yellow; his eyes are lifeless. With his bloated cheeks, blue tearbags under his eyes, with his soft chin, he looks like a pretty young man who has committed suicide and been fished out of the water. A fat dreamer, Maria Tarnovska thinks.

Yes, before his departure for Orel, he had met Prilukov. Signora di Tarnovska introduced them. Did all three of them discuss the murder plan? They only agreed that Kamarovsky had to be removed from the life of Signora di Tarnovska. "Signora di Tarnovska stroked Prilukov's hand all the time." Laughter. Dr. Luzzatti, one of Prilukov's lawyers, makes a witty remark. He is the jokester among the defense lawyers. "She wanted to make me jealous," says Naumov. "Under those circumstances, what did you hope for by the removal of Count Kamarovsky?" "I wanted to prove that Prilukov was a coward and unworthy of her." Did he meet Prilukov later, alone, and discuss the murder with him? "Yes. But I wasn't serious about it at the time." So it was Signora di Tarnovska who finally persuaded him in Kiev? Yes, that is right.

The weapon. Did he receive it from Prilukov or from Signora di Tarnovska? Naumov cannot remember. His jaw is set hard. Sometimes all you can hear is his teeth grinding. Maria Tarnovska knows that she did not give Naumov the weapon, but it was her revolver. She gave it to Prilukov when he threatened to commit suicide. If Donat had killed himself, she thinks, Pavel would not have had to die. Prilukov's death would have been an adequate tribute to her power —the last. "Signor Naumov seems to remember everything else," cries one of the Countess' lawyers, Dr. Diena. "He does not remember the days when he was under the influence of the defendant Tarnovska," replies Dr. Marigonda, for Naumov. Both men were too cowardly for suicide. Murder requires no courage. She wonders why Naumov wants to incriminate her. He does not hate Prilukov. He loved her; therefore he hates her. A fat, wicked child. *"Oh Satan, prends pitié de ma longue misère!"* Baudelaire. Fat, wicked dreamer.

"Why did you leave Kiev so soon after going to the cemetery?" the judge asks.

"I was afraid to see Signora di Tarnovska again."

"Why? You had already promised to kill the Count."

"I couldn't stand the sight of her."

The Countess senses that the old man cannot understand this. He knows nothing of the sick love that flees from the object of its sick love.

The day of the murder, September 3. At six in the morning Naumov went to the Campo Santa Maria del Giglio in a closed gondola.

"You found Count Kamarovsky sleeping?"

"He opened to me in his nightgown."

Laughter threatens to choke Maria Tarnovska. Pavel never showed himself to her in a nightgown. He had been in the habit of laying his clothes down on a chair, trousers folded under his chin. She, already naked in bed, had watched him. Perhaps he had to die because he had folded his trousers so neatly.

"Kamarovsky led me into his bedroom," says Naumov. "He was surprised to see me. I said nothing. I drew the revolver. When the first shot hit him, he cried out, 'My dear young man, why? What harm have I ever done you?'" Naumov sobs uncontrollably, like a child that has hurt itself and has no handkerchief.

The Countess feels only disgust. He did not have to repeat Kamarovsky's words. Nicholas wants to incriminate himself. A man who likes to be flogged is an ideal defendant.

Is it true that he tried to shoot himself in the mouth, the judge asks.

Naumov nods eagerly.

"Did you promise Signora di Tarnovska to kill yourself?"

"Only if I was arrested." Naumov describes how, his mind a vacuum, he sat for half an hour opposite Kamarovsky, who was covered with blood. "I thought he was dead."

The Countess isn't listening. Well-behaved defendants have motives. They show their dirty hands like children in school. Nicholas and Donat know everything; they don't have to be told why they had behaved as they had. Why had she behaved as she had? The psychiatrists told her, but she still doesn't know. She hopes to find out in the courtroom. Too late. She is a bad defendant. "K. is an animal and should be exterminated," she had written to Donat. They found the letter. So she had been the first one to formulate the idea. Had it been a plan or a thought? When Donat had written to her about the insurance, she didn't know what he meant. So he had that idea first. Is no one going to help her find out the truth? Commendatore Tusitano raises roses; the veterinarian married his childhood sweetheart; the deputy hopes to be re-elected. They drag out to the light what ceases to exist as soon as it is dragged out to the light. They touch upon the truth, and gold turns to coal. Only the three men know the truth. Pavel also knew, an accomplice.

One of Prilukov's lawyers, Dr. Ronchetti, a hunchback with the

364

face of a camel, cross-examines Naumov. Most people bear a resemblance to plants or animals; after all, they had been there first.

"You called the defendant Tarnovska a cruel person. What do you mean by that?"

Naumov stammers as he replies that she refused to make her feelings clear to him, and goaded his jealousy and made fun of him.

"Is it true that the defendant inflicted corporeal punishment on you?"

Not a sound in the courtroom. The March wind moves the curtains. As in a bedroom at night, all that can be heard is Naumov grinding his teeth. A woman wearing a large pink hat is sitting in the first row. Her hatpin is a big black pearl, like a third eye. Maria Tarnovska can feel everyone looking at her. Had she been mistaken? Were Vassily, Pavel, Stahl, Donat, Naumov not the only ones who wanted to be punished? Does everyone want to be punished and whipped; to punish and whip; to hear about expiation and chastisement?

At last Naumov replies. Yes, the Countess had beaten him. With a whip? Yes, with a whip. With a switch? Yes, also with a switch. Had she engraved his initials in his flesh with a dagger? Yes, that too. Washed the wound with eau de cologne? Yes. And the cigarette burns? Yes. And did she ride on him as on a horse? Yes. And make him bark and retrieve like a dog? Yes, yes, yes.

Maria Tarnovska wants to jump up and cry that Naumov is lying. She knows that he is not lying; he is only concealing the truth. She did not beat him because she was cruel, but because he had begged to be beaten; she had been cruel as long as she had not beaten him. She had not beaten him because he was disobedient, but as a reward for his obedience. She had not beaten him to cause him pain, but because their lust, his and hers, had mated. The psychiatrists call it a sickness. What do they know about it? Isn't sickness dirtier than sin?

And Maria Tarnovska becomes aware of the fact that she can defend herself only by sullying herself, that the trial will expose only half truths—worse than lies. And she realizes that her choice lies only between lifelong imprisonment and lifelong shame.

A cold March rain is falling over Venice. It drums importunately against the panes. The windows have not been cleaned for a long time, as in all courtrooms, everywhere. The rain is dirty water coursing across them.

Prilukov is cross-examined all morning. The plan to murder Kamarovsky was the Countess' invention. Letters and telegrams corroborate this. "She destroys men, then does with them what she wills." The idea of the insurance? Kamarovsky was a miserly man. He, Prilukov, wanted to prove to the Countess that her fiancé would never take out insurance in her name. "I am not even sure that he intended to marry her."

Commendatore Tusitano counters with the declaration of a private detective, who testified that he had been hired by Prilukov to find Naumov in Venice.

"I wanted to have him arrested," says Prilukov, "so that Signora di Tarnovska should be mine alone. I was obsessed."

"But Signora di Tarnovska telegraphed you in Vienna on the day of the murder. Wasn't the purpose of her telegram that you warn Count Kamarovsky or stop Naumov?"

"On the contrary, your Excellency, I was supposed to denounce Naumov."

She must destroy him, Maria Tarnovska thinks. Destroy him! An old idea, but a new sensation. She feels no sweetness of lust at the thought. Have the psychiatrists healed her? Or is she only worn out by her long incarceration? She is no longer a child who tortures animals. She is a huntress after her prey. She wants to live. "Preferable 'tis to live/ A lowly slave in upper regions . . ." Alexis. If she is free, they will not take Tioka from her. One day she will explain everything to him. She doesn't know how; outside they speak a language she has forgotten. But there are countries that never heard the name Tarnovska. Summer, a sun-baked beach; winter, the snow glittering from below; Christmas, shimmering shop windows; the south, the smell of hay on a night in August. Perhaps even people. No one ever loved her; why should she ever have loved anyone? Not all who were unloved become murderers. Not all who were unloved need love.

In the afternoon, Prilukov asks to be permitted to explain his relationship to the defendant Tarnovska in a prepared speech. A *carabiniere,* Elise Perrier, a *carabiniere,* Naumov, a *carabiniere* separate her from Prilukov. She has seen so many of his faces. Now he again looks like the man she first met in his imposing office. "Leave everything to me, Countess!" The courtroom is to Donat what his acres are to a peasant. His ability to lie to himself is limitless. He thinks he is defense counsel for Donat Prilukov, not Donat Prilukov.

His background was modest, he begins, the proletarian appealing to the proletarians. "My grandfather was a serf on the estate of Prince Trubetzkoy. The grandson of a serf and a Countess O'Rourke—who in my place could have resisted it if this woman of royal blood had thrown herself at him?" The Countess loses control. "Liar!" Then a witty remark from Dr. Luzzati. "She offered me no fee," Prilukov goes on. "She didn't have a ruble. She offered herself." The Countess jumps to her feet, screams, "Liar!" Commendatore Tusitano looks at her sadly, as if she is grieving him personally; a man who retired long ago and wants nothing now but to raise roses.

Prilukov speaks of his unfortunate fatherland. "I was close to the revolutionary movement. I was not the only one who confused freedom from political oppression with license, the freedom to love with free love." Prilukov has to raise his voice; the rain punctuates his words with periods in the wrong places. Kamarovsky was a symbol of the arrogant aristocrat. "I couldn't bear the thought that little Tioka, whom I loved as if he had been my own, should grow up with such a heartless, arrogant stepfather." The Countess faces the plaintiff furiously. "Leave my child out of this!" she cries. "How sensitive she is!" comments Luzzati the jokester. Somebody applauds, probably the young man in the last row, who looks like a starving student.

"I accuse myself," Prilukov declaims. She knows his plea. Hotel rooms in Orel, Paris, Nice. A defendant who accuses himself—the darling of the courtroom. He accuses himself of vanity. "It flattered me to be the lover of a woman whose paramours bore Russia's most illustrious names. I had no other ambition than to imitate Tarnovsky's extravagance, Bozevsky's bravado, Kamarovsky's elegance." He accuses himself of betraying his class. "I let her convince me that there was nothing so contemptible as the common citizen who loved his wife, his home, his work."

Maria Tarnovska turns away. The jury lower their eyes, as if they hope they might not be seen if they cannot see. Only the second man from the right looks at her, the poor lovesick writer. She doesn't dare to smile at him. Everyone fears her smile; she is afraid of it herself.

Prilukov speaks on and on, and she has to agree with him. It was an unequal battle between them, the proletarian and the aristocrat. Vassily, beloved Vassily. He had shot Alexis. The snow in front of the Eremitage had been dyed red. She could have incited Vassily to murder; he would have killed Pavel for her; but in the end, he would have taken all the blame upon himself. In her world there were laws that no proletarian would ever understand. The apothecary doesn't understand her either, nor the hotel manager, nor the teacher. The lady with the big pink hat leans forward. Later, in the rain, the hat will get wet. The pink lady is asking herself how the two looked in bed, the proletarian and the aristocrat. Maria Tarnovska is asking herself if it really happened. If only those mated whom one could picture as a pair, mankind would have died out long ago. Through the noise of the rain, she can hear Donat: "I thought that I, the grandson of a serf, was subjugating the world as symbolized in the kin of the kings of Connaught. Instead, I subjugated myself." He is speaking the truth. Perhaps he was thinking of the kings of Connaught when he overflowed inside her. A motive, as justice calls it. Dr. Vecchini is wrong. "You don't have a motive," he has told her consolingly. Motives excuse everything. Only those who have no motive are condemned.

Commendatore Tusitano, either with the patience of an angel or just sleepy, certainly sad, admonishes Prilukov to finish. Immediately, Prilukov complies. She called him her muzhik, he says. She thinks how once in Franzensbad she said it in anger; then he wanted to hear it again and again; a hundred times she had to repeat it. "What am I?" "My muzhik." The hideous word drove him to revitalized passion. A word for him, a whip for Naumov.

"She called me her muzhik," Prilukov concludes, "and she abused my devotion as the lords of our estates have been abusing the devotion of their muzhiks for centuries. Gentlemen, I have kept nothing from you. What Murasov in Gogol's *Dead Souls* said to Tshitshikov I say to myself now: 'The sad thing is not that they have sinned against others; the sad thing is that they have sinned against themselves, against their rich potentialities and talents. . . . It was you fate to become a great man, but you wasted and destroyed yourself.' "

Commendatore Tusitano looks at the clock and calls a short recess. Maria Tarnovska shudders. The announcement strikes harder than Prilukov's speech. During the recess, she will be taken to the hole in the wall behind the courtroom, a barred cell with no window and a single bench. There they will sit side by side: Naumov, Elise Perrier, Prilukov, and she. They will not speak; they will not look at each other. But for half an hour they will be accomplices again, and she will be once more what she was for thirty long years.

5

The representatives of the coplaintiff inform the court that Countess Anna Fyodorovna Kamarovskaya has arrived in Venice. She is immediately given a hearing.

The Countess approaches the auditorium via a door at the side of the main entrance to the court. In deep mourning, one hand on her cane, the other on the arm of her servant. The servant is old, too; they seem to be an old married couple, helping each other along. Maria Tarnovska cannot see the face behind the veil. Pavel showed her pictures of his mother. At the time she hadn't been able to say how much she hated the old woman.

The servant steps aside; a chair is brought for the Countess. She is a tall, bony woman with prominently big feet. It would not surprise Maria Tarnovska to find a man hidden underneath the veil. The Countess raises her veil. Maria Tarnovska sees her from the side. All she sees is a large hooked nose.

Commendatore Tusitano thanks the Countess for appearing. He nods his head at her, one aged person greeting another: Wonderful to think that both of us have managed to grow so old.

How did the Countess receive the news of the attack on her son, he wants to know. The telegram, she replies, did not go into any details. She traveled three days and three nights, but on her arrival, her child was already dead. They did not allow her to see the body. Firm, without any effort to arouse sympathy, is the voice of Kamarovsky's mother.

"You found out only in Venice that Nicholas Naumov had committed the murder?"

Only in Venice. And it had seemed incredible. Her child and Nicholas' father had been friends. Her "child," not her son. She speaks only of her child. "Young Naumov was often a guest at our palace. We knew and loved him from the day he was born."

Maria Tarnovska hears Naumov sob. Thank heaven, he has stopped grinding his teeth. He has become a child again, as he was at the Kamarovsky palace; an ungrateful child who murdered Pavel Kamarovsky. The ungrateful child who came to her engagement to offer to free her from Pavel Kamarovsky. The ungrateful child who liked to play with whips.

"Did you find any explanation for the deed later?" the judge asks.

"Not until I heard the name Tarnovska."

Commotion in the courtroom—that was how it would read the next day in the papers.

Had she known about her son's marriage plans? And how had she reacted when Kamarovsky told her about them?

"I refused to receive the woman."

And her reasons?

"I don't think I have to state them. Pavel was my only child." Yes, she had enjoyed an excellent relationship with her deceased daughter-in-law. "She was a lady."

Could she explain her son's relationship to the Countess Tarnovska?

"At this point, your Excellency, I don't understand anything."

The ladies in the audience have to blow their noses. The mother of the victim, thinks Maria Tarnovska, a good role; any dilettante can play it. A clever director told the actress to play the role with an original twist—no tears. Perhaps he should also have left out the black veil, the cane, and the old servant.

"Did your son's relationship to you change after he met the Countess Tarnovska?" the judge asks.

"He only visited me once after that."

"I don't know if you understood the question, Countess."

"I understood perfectly, your Excellency. After my child made the acquaintance of the lady in question, he was lost to me."

"Did you notice any personality changes?"

"He became very extravagant."

"Did he speak to you about the insurance he had taken out, naming the Countess Tarnovska as beneficiary?"

"He didn't speak to me any more."

Now it is the Public Prosecutor's turn. He scratches his chin by rub bing his right shoulder against it. Commendatore Randi is like the doctors who can't bear to see blood; they start off as surgeons and end up as biologists. You have to fight the nausea, he had probably been told, and he does his best, but he would rather collect stamps or beetles.

Does the witness think it is possible that the defendant Naumov committed the murder of his own volition?

"I am sure that the unfortunate boy was just as much under the influence of this woman as my child," the Countess replies.

In the silence, you can hear Naumov's sobs. In a moment they will fall into each other's arms, the murderer and the mother of the murdered man. Everyone understands the murderers, but not the instigators. Doesn't everyone, at some time or other in his life, wish that someone else might kill for him? Isn't everyone at some time or other an instigator? An instigator—not a murderer. The surveyor is looking at his fingertips. There are tears in his eyes. The hotel manager is also deeply moved. He is moved easily.

The Countess Kamarovskaya describes the murdered man's character. A flawless child, loved by everyone. Does she really believe what she is saying, Maria Tarnovska wonders. Are parents blind? Terrible O'Rourke was never blind. Pavel had traveled with obscene pictures; a few were found in her trunk. Flawless, beloved by all, a child.

Vecchini asks for permission to interrogate the Countess Kamarovskaya.

The judge: "Is that indispensable, Dr. Vecchini?"

"I am sorry, your Excellency, it is indispensable."

The judge asks the witness to face the lawyer. She stands up. Will the eyes of the two women meet? The Countess Kamarovskaya succeeds in evading Maria Tarnovska's eyes.

Dr. Vecchini asks why the witness has become coplaintiff in the case. Commendatore Tusitano objects to the question.

The Countess Kamarovskaya gave her blessing to her son's engagement—why, Vecchini wants to know.

"I did not want to cut off all hope for the lady in question."

Didn't she rather hope to win her son back with this step?

"Does that seem so strange to you, Dr. Vecchini?"

The journalists nod; the journalists write.

"Strange?" Vecchini replies. "On the contrary, I think that—who can tell?—you might have prevented the disaster if at that time, in Orel, you had taken your future daughter-in-law to your heart."

The Countess Kamarovskaya's lips are so thin that the wrinkles between chin and lower lip, between nose and upper lip, seem to merge. "I gave my child my blessing. It was not necessary for me to compromise myself by having anything to do with his fiancée."

A good answer. Honest injustice. Terrible O'Rourke would have said the same thing.

"Do you know anything about the relationship of the Countess Tarnovska to your little grandson, Granya?"

"He was fond of her."

"More than to be expected?"

"He adored her. He forgot his own mother and could speak of nothing but his new one, who kissed and hugged him while she was thinking of a way to murder his father."

Cries of shame. "Unbelievable!" cries the lady in the pink hat. Tioka and Granya. Every word true, yet only half true. With his small, liver-spotted hands, Commendatore Tusitano gropes for the bell.

"When Granya heard what had happened," says the Countess Kamarovskaya, "he took all the toys that this woman had given him, made a heap of them, and set fire to it. He has never mentioned her name since. The child is under medical care."

Tioka. Who is thinking of Tioka? Will he open the papers tomorrow in his Geneva boarding school and read the testimony of the Countess Kamarovskaya? Where is Andrey? Is he with her child? Why hasn't she heard from him in weeks? Did she do the right thing in entrusting her child to Andrey? To whom else could she entrust him? Will Tioka also never mention her name again, make a bonfire of her gifts?

"I regret," said Vecchini, "that I must show the witness a letter that a friend of the dead Count, Corvette Captain Alberto Rossi, put at the disposition of the defense only yesterday. Is the name familiar to you, Countess?"

"He was a friend. . . ."

"Alive with the desire to see justice done, yesterday Corvette Captain Rossi handed me this letter, dated Vienna, the twentieth of December, 1906. It reads: 'You cannot imagine, my dear Alberto, how

372

happy I am. I can hardly wait to introduce you to this angelic, this ethereal creature. I think you are the only one who knows what a detestable sinner I am. How I have suffered since I had to deceive my poor sick Emilia in the arms of girls of highly dubious reputation! I am not exaggerating when I say that Mura has redeemed me from the agonies of hell. After the talk you and I had that night in Rome, I am sure you are not surprised to hear that I would be willing to commit murder for this angel who is my salvation.' "

Vecchini walks past the witness and puts the letter down on the table in front of the judge. "I have changed my mind," he says. "I don't think the witness should be asked to comment on this letter."

The bells of Santi Apostoli chime four, then eleven. The old servant moves the Countess Kamarovskaya's chair, but she remains standing. She is leaning heavily on her cane, as if she would like to dig a hole in the floor with it. She looks like a very sick old man, and as the tears roll down her cheeks, it is as if an old man is crying.

As Vecchini walks past Maria Tarnovska, he gives her a look of triumph. What does he know, her counsel? What does he know of a soul that is damned to murder the dead?

6

On the day of her cross-examination, she wanted to be beautiful, although she knew that even her beauty would speak against her. She wanted to sleep, but she could not sleep.

Her judges. Her lawyers had told her who the jurymen were—but what did professions mean, and what did the lawyers know? How was she to make herself clear to these strangers? The hotel manager. He recognized a man who was not traveling with his wife; in the night he let the dead disappear through the back entrance, because the dead were not fitting customers for an elegant hotel; he could look through fine material and see an empty wallet. Or the surveyor. He had a habit of sitting back and putting fingertips to fingertips so that they looked like two cards in a card castle touching; he could tell the length of a street without measuring it, and evaluate the dimensions of a forest. Or the writer. He had fallen in love with her. She knew the eyes of a man in love, trying to make themselves understood like deaf-mutes; lalling, stupid, guttural eyes. Or the veterinarian. When he pressed on a dog's jaw in a certain way, the animal opened its mouth; he

bandaged a cat's paw; and when an animal's day was done, he put it
to sleep. Sometimes he put animals to sleep that were suffering too
much. Veterinarians felt sorry for animals. Or the retired colonel.
Since the reading of the indictment, he had sat as if paralyzed. He had
heard nothing like the Tarnovska case in the officers' casino or in the
mess hall, and such matters weren't dealt with at court-martials, either.
He sat there stunned, as if his honor as an officer had been insulted,
an honor that was different from all other honors because it had a
gold collar. Or the schoolmaster. He looked like a ripe plum that
despised those that were not ripe. He taught history and knew all
about bloody heroes; about bloody heroines, he knew nothing. Or the
Crown Prosecutor. With a face that one forgot immediately, he
looked like a bookkeeper entering twenty-kopek murders and fifteen-
ruble robberies in a ledger. He looked as consternated as if he had
just discovered the embezzlement of a junior partner in his firm,
and didn't know whether he should report it to one of the directors
or not. And Commendatore Tusitano. He was sad, and that was all
he was—sad. He let everyone speak, rarely interrupted them; he waited
for them to betray themselves—the defendants, their counsels, the
plaintiffs. But when they betrayed themselves, he was sad, too. If
someone exaggerated, his aged face became mournful. He considered
exaggeration a sin; but he also considered truth sinful, if it was
exaggeratedly true. All of them would listen to her; then they would
go home and show hotel rooms, operate on cats, measure streets, graft
roses. And only the Appellate Court judges would return to the court
and seek the truth, because that was their profession and because they
had been told that the courtroom was the place to find the truth.

In front of these people, therefore, and in front of the ladies with
their lorgnettes and the journalists with their pencils sharpened, she
would bare her soul tomorrow, as the whores in bordellos let their
clothing drop to the floor, piece by piece. Was she well prepared,
Vecchini had wanted to know. She had to laugh. Yes, she was well
prepared. She would convince the surveyor that there was nothing unusual about a Count Kamarovsky hidden behind a screen and watching
his fiancée burning a young man's chest with her cigarette. And she
would impress the schoolmaster with the fact that the mistresses of a
seventeen-year-old girl's husband had stood around her bedside, and
that she had unfortunately bled for the first time on her wedding night.
And how could the veterinarian fail to understand that, although she

hated Prilukov, she had longed for him like the parched earth for rain—just as aridly, just as greedily, and just as lifelessly? And since she was so well prepared, why shouldn't all of them understand that there were men who couldn't be men unless one tortured them like animals, beat them like dogs, and stepped on them like vermin? Why shouldn't her judges grasp all this? And the nuns, and the *carabinieri,* and the ladies, and the protectors of public opinion?

Of course she didn't have to say a word about all this. She thought of Andrey, and was angry with him, as she was always when he was not with her. If she had not weakened that day, she would not have confessed. From her confession that she had known of the plan to murder Kamarovsky, it had been only one short step to the conclusion that she had conceived it. But she was prepared. She could explain easily how all her life she had wanted only to test her power; that she had had a sensual liaison with death; that she knew no other proof of love but death; that she had wanted to know if Vladimir Stahl would die for her and Nicholas Naumov commit murder. That she had not desired Pavel's death; that she had wanted to see his murderer on his way to, but not arriving at, the scene of the crime. It was perfectly simple for anyone to grasp that she wanted to punish Prilukov for the death of Alexis, whom Prilukov had never known; that she had believed she could not break the vow she had made by the life of her child without being punished by the God against whom she had blasphemed with the vow; that Pavel would be alive today if Vassily had not fought a duel for Olga Kralberg.

She was well prepared, but tomorrow she might forget everything. For two long years, psychiatrists had been reminding her of things she had wanted to forget. Just as Andrey has pretended to be her friend, they had pretended to be her friends. Memory was compulsion; because she had remembered, she now had to speak. The psychiatrists ought to know—the presiding judge, the schoolteacher, the nuns, and the officer would believe her—how simple it was to play three men against each other; to cheat a man into giving ten thousand rubles with the help of an empty envelope; to make love next to a dying man, under the influence of morphine, and still not be a murderess.

She lay awake until dawn. She prayed, although she feared that she was insulting God by addressing him, although she was certain that He did not hear her. She shook the bars of her cell, not because she wanted to free herself, but because she thought someone was waiting outside whom they would not let in to see her. She cursed herself, her fate; she laughed, cried, screamed, buried her head in her hands. But in the morning, when Sister Sofia entered her cell, Maria Tarnovska was smiling, dressed, rested, ready to leave. She was convinced that she was prepared, and that she would not be defeated.

7

"Un grand jour du procès Tarnovska"—that was how Madame Nicolle, whom Dr. Friedlieber had called "the most famous woman reporter in the world," headlined her report in *Matin* of Maria Tarnovska's cross-examination.

Madame Nicolle did not have anything friendly to say about the atmosphere in Venice. An oppressive scent of Houbigant and Guerlain had pervaded the courtroom; the ladies had shown off the newest creations of Drecoll, had sized each other up, had fixed their lorgnettes, not only on the four accused—"especially on handsome young Naumov"—but also on judge and counsels. "Is it really true that one condemns most harshly those whom one envies most?" She had met Madame Réjane. The famous tragedienne was considering playing the Countess Tarnovska on the stage. Dégas had been present, and was thinking of painting a portrait of Maria Tarnovska.

L'appetit vient en mangeant. Every sensation gives rise to new sensations. In the Hotel Danieli, I was told that an English lord would like to marry the Countess; in the Quadri, that the Countess was carrying on a flirtation with one of her lawyers; in the Bauer-Grünwald, that she intends to take the veil; and everywhere they are saying that the judge intends to bar women spectators from the courtroom. Then they will probably declare the proceedings unfit for sensitive ears. I think the old man is less afraid of shame than of shamelessness.

Madame Nicolle began by describing superficial events:

Madame de Tarnovska, wearing a black dress and a big black hat that cast a shadow over her unnaturally large blue eyes, was captivatingly beautiful. There was nothing to remind one of the former drug addict. Although she was constantly being besieged by questions, she held her head high and seemed never to lose the thread.

Her defense had been brilliant. She had declared that since she met Prilukov, she had lived completely under the influence of this *advocat*

376

du diable. If the jury would accept this interpretation, then all incriminating evidence would shrink to the proportions of a confession made by a hypnotized medium.

Madame Nicolle continued:

To describe the afternoon session is one of the most difficult assignments of my entire career. After the noon recess, all interest centered around two men recently arrived from Russia—Governor Gregory Ivanovich Naumov and Knight Marshal Count Nikolay Vladimirovich O'Rourke, father of the accused Countess Tarnovska. The Governor resigned his post before the beginning of the trial. A man of barely sixty, he gave the impression of a very old man. I have been told that he was one of the most cruel Governors in Czarist Russia, who put dozens of rebels in the prisoner's dock, and is responsible for many deaths among the revolutionaries. His son's tragedy seems to have struck him therefore all the harder. He went up to Nicholas Naumov, embraced him, and the two men cried so bitterly that Commendatore Tusitano was unable to proceed. Understandable as the conduct of the Governor may be—he sat during the entire afternoon session with his head in his hands—it is impossible to admire it. Count O'Rourke's behavior was quite different. This Irish-Russian nobleman, nearly eighty years old, who, with his long white beard, looks like a venerable patriarch, never for a moment betrayed his feelings. He also walked up to his weeping child and embraced her, after which he stroked her hand lightly and soothingly for a moment, then walked back to his seat, erect, with firm steps. For the rest of the afternoon Count O'Rourke sat motionless beside Naumov's father, except for two or three times when he seemed to be whispering a few words of encouragement to the Governor. During the entire scandalous events of the afternoon, Count O'Rourke's face never betrayed the slightest emotion, so that I took for granted that he did not understand Italian; but I know now that he understood every word that was being said. As their children's ruined lives were enacted before the eyes of these two old men in the auditorium, they sat like memorials: the one, a monument; the other, a tomb.

Madame Nicolle went on to describe in detail how Maria Tarnovska spread out her entire life before the court for an hour and a quarter; then Madame Nicolle drew her conclusions.

It would be simple to look upon the Tarnovska case as an individual one, but it is much more than that. It is historic; it is a history of our times. The requisites for this modern drama may have been taken from a musty storehouse, but experimental plays are nearly always produced with old requisites. Wings and backdrop of the old actors are still standing, but the players are young. I don't want anyone to think that I would like to see La Tarnovska as a suffragette beside Emmeline Pankhurst. The woman of today has other weapons beside dagger, poison, and revolver for achieving a position that is worthy of her, but Madame de Tarnovska's greed for power—with which she herself justifies her actions—can be understood only as the result and manifestation of a centuries-old patriarchal system. The "slave driver Tarnovska," as Naumov's lawyer called her, is possible only in an era in which the guilty conscience of the male thirsts for punishment. For Madame de Tarnovska, the male sex was *le sexe hostile:* she did not hate one man; she hated all men. If you want to believe Naumov, he wished to remove both his rivals, Kamarovsky and Prilukov. Prilukov persuaded Naumov to commit the crime in order to rid himself of murdered man and murderer at the same time; that he also had one eye on the insurance money does not seem crucial to me. La Tarnovska, on the other hand, wanted to rid herself of all three men: Kamarovsky, who revolted her physically; Naumov, whom she despised; and also of Prilukov, on whom she was physically dependent, but who had taught her to abominate herself and to despise her own soul. She had to torture, and suffered the tortures of the damned herself. These—who knows?—may be *les métamorphoses du vampire,* of which Naumov's poet, Baudelaire, spoke.

But what touched me most was Madame de Tarnovska's ruthless honesty. As she stood before us, penetrating and laying bare the most intimate recesses of her past, some of which were unknown even to the court, she gave me the impression of a creature who had lost her soul and was rummaging desperately in the most secret chambers of her personality to find it. And she did all this in the presence of her father, in front of a hostile and indignant audience. Two women fainted; a few cried; some held their perfumed handkerchiefs to their noses; there were cries of "Shame!" The courtroom had to be cleared. La Tarnovska was still speaking. Twice she broke down and wept. The beads of perspiration stood on her brow. Once she laughed and could not stop laughing. In the end she shriveled and became old before our eyes. But she raised her voice only once; only once did she cry out so loudly that those waiting along the Canale Grande or on the *marchés* could hear her. That was when one of Donat Prilukov's lawyers asked her if she had not also seduced the Dominican friar, Andrey Vyrubov. Then she let flow such a flood of abuse that the lawyer had to withdraw his question.

Why this frankness? Frankness and shamelessness are twins. Does La Tarnovska see the courtroom as a bedroom in which to undress? Does she think she has to turn on lights because she has looked for her soul in vain in the dark? Has she become so insensible that world opinion no longer means anything to her? Did she really want to test her power, or was she so hopelessly caught in her own web that she could think of nothing any more but destruction? All of us—judges, journalists, nuns, and *carabinieri* —know all about Maria Tarnovska's past, up to her arrest. Is it not possible, though, that some things may have happened since then about which we know nothing? The past of a human being does not end arbitrarily with his arrest. Since these two and a half years—although never mentioned— are still a part of Maria Tarnovska's life, I can only feel again, as I have done so often, that judge as well as criminal find themselves constantly in conflict with justice. We are never farther from the truth than in the moment when we think we recognize it fully.

8

The bells of Il Redentore had already struck eleven when they brought Maria Tarnovska back to La Giudecca in the shrouded gondola. Now it is two. The gaslight creeps along the wall like a satiated snake. She does not have to put out the light—privilege of a prisoner during trial. She paces up and down, sits down, lies down, paces up and down again.

The last hour after the proceedings, alone with her father. The visiting room of the courthouse. The lights from the Canale Grande were quite different from the lights in the courthouse; lights shining in freedom. The cries of the *gondolieri,* voices from the outside world. How far away was Otrada? "Did you hear everything, Father?" He nodded. "Why did you come?" "So you know that I have not abandoned you." Hadn't he abandoned her the day she was born? He said, "I am going to Geneva to see Tioka." What had happened to her father? She wanted to ask him, but he said, "It is my fault. It is also my fault." Tears in her eyes. He was over seventy, and had never taken the guilt of others upon himself, never acknowledged his own. He sat opposite her, stiff, stern, as assured as ever. "You must not lose courage," he said. "They will acquit you." "I am guilty," she said. "You have suffered enough, Mura." He spoke of Tioka. Years ago, he had taken the care of the boy off Andrey's hands. Maria Tarnovska nodded; Andrey had written to tell her about it. "Thank you," she said. She had never thanked him for anything before. "He will bring you nothing but joy," said her father. She smiled. "Whom does he resemble?" she asked. "Not me or Vassily, I am sure." "You were not bad, Mura." Why did he tell her that today, after this afternoon, when she had rid herself of everything, all the blood, the dirt, the pus? Why

379

today, why so late, why too late? "It is lonely in Otrada," her father said. "What about Olga's children?" she asked. Yes, they came sometimes. "Then it is as it used to be," said her father. She looked at him, and suddenly it seemed to her that it wasn't she who had been blind; he had been blind, the old man. As it used to be! He had no idea that it was this "used to be" that had driven her from Otrada. His visits to the cemetery, the departure of the aunts, his beating Ivan; her mother fading away—as it used to be! In his loneliness he heard only the laughter of the children, their practicing on the piano, sounds from the kitchen. He believed, he really believed, that it had been a good home. Otrada. He knew nothing; he was the one who had been blind. "You shall come to Otrada with Tioka," he said. Otrada—the answer to everything. He still knew everything better. "And if I am convicted?" "They will acquit you," he said. "The shame of it—what do they know about it in Otrada?" she asked. "I don't care what they know about it," he said. He really didn't care—she could feel it. She asked how Zoa was, and Alexander. Alexander was in St. Petersburg, married, two children. "He is a very fine engineer." Zoa was in Davos, some trouble with his lungs. "Nikolay," said her father—she hadn't dared to ask—"is carrying on with the revolutionaries in Switzerland. He has taken another name. Most of them are doing that. It's better that way."

In the palace opposite, on the Canale Grande, a party had been going on. You could hear the music, see the crystal chandeliers, the fluttering shadows of people. "I may visit you once a week," her father said. "Are you going to stay?" she asked. "To the end," he told her. "Naumov's father is going home tomorrow. I can't stand cowards." He never could stand cowards. "You are not Terrible O'Rourke any more," she said, smiling behind her tears. "People don't know very much about us," he said. "They are not important. We can live without them." He looked at his watch. He was allowed to visit with her for an hour, and he was not going to overstep his allotted time by a minute. She got up, went over to him, wanted to tell him that she loved him. "And I hated you," she said. "I know," he said, "and it was my fault." He held out his hands to her. As usual, he held them palms down, but this time she could feel their blessing. He kissed her on both cheeks. Then he walked over to the door and ordered the warden to come as if he had been one of his servants.

Maria Tarnovska paces up and down in her cell, sits down, lies down, paces up and down again. She doesn't dare close her eyes, for at once she sees herself in the courtroom. The dead eyes of the judge, the lovesick eyes of the writer, the mousy eyes of the surveyor, the astonished eyes of the French woman journalist, the greedy eyes of the spectators, male and female. Everything she said today Tioka will read in the papers tomorrow. It would be better for him to change his name, like Nikolay. She looks for his last letter, reads it again, for the hundredth time. "When we are together again . . ." She must release him from his love for her, as if it were a vow; all the more so if she is to leave prison in a few weeks or months. It makes no difference any longer whether she is a murderess or not. Her father's words make no difference, either. What would Andrey say? Would he not say that the sufferings of one man liberated others of their sins? Her suffering had liberated Terrible O'Rourke, as his had freed her. Does she really believe that? Can she believe it? Who believes her? Did anyone believe her today? Is the guilt of one man the sum of the guilt of all the others? If Vassily had not abandoned her on her wedding night in Charkov . . . if he had stayed to hold her hand when Tioka was born . . . if she had not fled to Alexis . . . if she had torn the hypodermic needle out of Stahl's hand . . . if she had not wanted to destroy Donat . . . if, if, if . . . The guilt of others and her own.

Maria Tarnovska paces up and down, sits down, lies down, paces up and down again. Why had she said all the things she said? Not because of a sinful passion to hurt others with her confession. She hasn't felt that sinful passion for a long time. Professor Ceresa. He has taught her healing through truth. She spoke the truth, but it did not heal her. Running the gantlet, hatred and distrust. Shouldn't she have entrusted Ceresa with the telling of her case history? She hadn't thought of it before. Life imprisonment or a life of shame. Truth is the only salvation—is that why she had spoken the truth? Compassion for the sick? There is no such thing. She had stripped herself as naked as if she had been at the doctor's, but there were no doctors in the courtroom. Her body naked, her soul naked, her past and present naked. And the old man in the first row. When she had seen him, she had hesitated for a moment, but then she had spoken after all. Could it be that she had spoken, not in spite of the old man sitting in the front, but because of him? Had he been the doctor, Terrible O'Rourke?

Maria Tarnovska closes her eyes. In the men's prison, Nicholas Naumov is sleeping and dreaming of the governess who had whipped him because he was afraid of a thunderstorm. In the men's prison, Donat Prilukov is sleeping and dreaming that the jury is hoisting him on their shoulders. In the Hotel Danieli, old Nikolay O'Rourke is sleeping and dreaming that his children are playing in the park, as it used to be. In a hotel room, former Governor Naumov is sleeping and dreaming that he is the judge. In a Geneva boarding school, Tioka is sleeping and dreaming that he is on the train to Venice with his mother, counting the tunnels. In his cell, Andrey is sleeping and dreaming that he has conquered the Devil. In her cell, in the women's penitentiary on the island La Giudecca, Maria Tarnovska is sleeping.

CHAPTER 2

I

Under the trees it was cool, but on the shores of the Lake of Geneva, for which Jean Jacques Rousseau had found the word "romantic," the sun shone hot on the green grass. It was a season that stands between the seasons; one foot still in the shadows, the other already in the sun; one foot still in the grave, the other among the living. The friar and the straw-blond boy who had grown tall so suddenly sat on a bench, talking and watching the gulls sailing out across the lake as if they were bringing the cold water a message of greening meadows.

"No, Andrey," Tioka said, "the boys are really taking it very well. Most of them have known me for years. For them I am Tioka Tarnovsky, for better or for worse. That's why I'd like to stay here as long as I can."

Andrey knew it was a courageous lie. Children and childish people delighted in finding hidden flaws in others, hereditary flaws. Tioka had been able to bear the ridicule and insults, the cruelty and shame, because the powers of life were not yet used up in him. What would happen when he left the security of his childhood prison?

"Sooner or later you are going to have to leave school," said Andrey. "You mustn't be afraid."

"The trial may be forgotten by then. It's not that I am ashamed of my mother . . ."

"Have you ever given a thought to what you want to study?"

"At first I thought of becoming a priest, like you. But that was only as long as I wanted to hide. I don't think I would be a good priest. I read a lot. What I'd really like to do is write."

"Monsieur de Vauthier tells me that your compositions are excellent."

"My grandfather wrote and said that I could study whatever I liked. Anyway, as soon as I am through here, I want to go back to Russia."

Andrey was surprised. "You don't know Russia very well."

Tioka was watching the gulls. "You see, in Russia I would be something more than the son of my mother. I don't mean just because of Grandfather. There must be people in Russia who knew Mother before all this happened. Here they only know what's in the papers."

Andrey's heart ached. During the past years, whenever they had had a chance to talk like this, no time at all would pass but Tioka's thoughts would revert to his mother. Wherever he wanted to live or whatever he wanted to be, his inclinations and disinclinations, his piety and his ambition, his childishness and maturity—all in one way or another had been determined by "the Tarnovska case."

"It isn't impossible that your mother may be acquitted," said Andrey.

He knew that he would not be seeing Tioka again for a long time, perhaps never. His unavoidable talk with the Master General weighed heavily on his mind. He could not predict Tioka's future or guide it. The least he could do was give the boy some good advice to take with him.

Tioka was shaking his head. "I don't think she will be. I pray for it every day, Andrey, truly I do. But I don't think she will be."

"Would you go with her if she was acquitted?"

Tioka turned to face him. "That's something I wanted to ask you. What would you do if you were in my place?"

From the day he had rescued Tioka in Vienna, the boy had always asked him embarrassing questions. And if one evaded them, one was lying.

383

"I would stand at the prison gates if I were you," said Andrey, "and spend some time with her, but I would not remain with her forever."

Almost provocatively, Tioka asked, "Are you afraid she will harm my soul?"

"No. But I think one often confuses the soul with the heart. The soul is more. It is not a sin to believe that our souls think. If you were to remain with your mother, you would make her happy for a while; but since she loves you, she would soon realize that it is not the right thing for you."

"Why do you say that it would not be the right thing for me?"

"Because the things that have happened are going to determine your mother's life in the future. They would therefore also influence yours."

"Are you asking me to betray Mama?"

Andrey reflected. How many souls had he advised in the past years? How difficult it was to advise those one loved.

"I am not asking you to do anything, Tioka," he said. "You will make your own decisions. Try to understand me. I have told you a lot about the war with Japan, and that we Russians should not be proud of it. Still I was often tempted to pick up the flag a wounded man had dropped and carry it on with me. It would have been heroic, but it would have been love misplaced, bad advice from the heart. You must never stop loving your mother, who loves you more than anything else in the world. You must never condemn her, for she was either sick or wounded. But that doesn't mean you must hate those who condemn her. It doesn't mean that they are evil, or even unjust. Nor does it mean that they hate you, although some may be stupid enough to give that impression. You don't have to prove that you are like your mother or better than she."

"During my first year here, you told me just the opposite."

Andrey looked at the boy, puzzled, although he felt sure Tioka had good reason for his doubts.

"You told me," Tioka explained, "that I must believe in Mama's innocence even if no one else did."

"You were barely twelve then, and you would not have understood me. I couldn't tell you that you must love her even if, before the court and mankind, she is declared guilty."

He could sense how the thoughts were crowding in upon each other behind the boy's high, sensitive forehead. At this moment it was not easy for Andrey to think of Maria without anger. She had not mentioned her vow by the life of her child during the trial, but she had permitted her counsel to mention it. Could her longing for freedom be so great that she was ready to risk her child's respect for it? Why hadn't she denied it? And he himself? Had he not been wrong to urge her to confess? Wasn't heartless truth worse than lies? How could he demand that Tioka love the guilty woman, who had not loved her guiltless child enough? Had anyone—he or Maria—the right to burden this child's soul with the terrible questions of guilt and atonement?

"You know, Andrey," Tioka said, "I find it hardest not to be angry all the time. As a matter of fact, I am constantly angry. I read the newspapers and am angry at Mama and, at the same time, angry at those who condemn her. I am angry because she didn't think of me; but if people reproach her for not having thought of me, I get just as angry."

"And that is why I advised you as I did," said Andrey. "It is not good to live in anger. I have always expected a great deal of you." He was smiling. "And things haven't turned out so badly, have they? What I want you to do now is to stop thinking like a lawyer, and to start thinking like a doctor. Don't defend your mother, but do something to help her to get well."

The boy looked him in the eye, and Andrey was seized with such happiness, he forgot what was waiting for him in Rome. Tioka had understood him. He would often forget what his friend had told him, but he would remember it just as often. He had come to erect a dam between Tioka and a flood of filth; he had not succeeded in erecting a dam, but he had channeled the flood.

They got up and walked along the lake, back to the school. "Do you really think she may be acquitted?" Tioka asked hesitantly.

"It is not impossible."

Tioka shrugged. He still held one shoulder a little higher than the other. "Why did she have to say all that, Andrey? Didn't she think of me at all?"

"You ask something that I can't explain to myself. I am going to talk to you as if you were grown up, or as if I were talking to myself. You know what a psychiatrist is. He calls himself a doctor of the soul, because he believes he can heal the soul as if it were a broken bone. Psychiatrists not only examined your mother; they advised her.

These doctors feel that frankness can heal a sick soul. I believe in frankness, but I expect no miracles from it. Without faith in God, science can save no souls. But all that is meaningless now, since what we have to do is fight your anger. Your mother is trying to save her soul. However she chooses to do it, it remains a noble effort. And that is why she is also doing it for you. Let us pray that she succeeds."

He wasn't sure any more if Tioka understood him, but he believed he had been able to help Maria Tarnovska's son bear the monstrous thing that had happened to him, and the monstrousness that still awaited him. Not without suffering, but not in anger. And for him it had grown lighter, too, to take the hard way he had to go.

2

Only a large crucifix and a picture of Saint Catherine of Siena hung on the walls of the anteroom. Andrey was alone. The windows were open. You could hear church bells—those that were close, like a song; those far away, like an orchestra. The April sun was beginning to dry the damp leaves and petals of trees and blossoms, but fresh rain clouds were already gathering in the west. You couldn't tell if the gray was blue, or the blue gray; resentful weather. A friar was walking through the garden, past the walled-up door that had once led to the Inquisition. Compassionately, he looked down at the flowers hanging their heads.

Sixteen years ago, Andrey had entered this room for the first time. Could it be that he would never enter it again? What he had done fell, in the language of Saint Basil, under the heading of "sacrilege," and among the three groups of transgressions, it belonged to the *culpae gravissimae*. He could expect, if not expulsion from the Order, then a long period of disgrace, and certainly banishment from Santa Maria sopra Minerva. He loved Santa Maria sopra Minerva, and he loved the old man who was waiting for him behind the heavy oak door. Andrey had not seen him often and, in the past three years, not at all, but he had felt the small old hands being held protectively over his head. The Master General was in his late eighties. He appeared in public only rarely; he reached all his decisions alone. No one doubted him. A much, much older man spoke through the mouth of the Master General. No one worried about his years or his health. A much, much older man was looking after the years and health of the Master General. For a moment Andrey did not think of himself, only of the sorrow he was going to cause the Master General. If only he could feel remorse! It was strange that he could not understand now how he could ever have transgressed against the Order; yet he was not filled with the remorse that alone could have granted him salvation. His thoughts flew over the walls of Santa Maria sopra Minerva, across the wine hills of Tuscany, northward, to the lagoons of Venice. Maria was being tried; now he was about to stand trial.

The oak door was opened. The secretary of the Master General asked him to come in. As in the case of all secretaries, his master's mood was reflected on his features, and it was not a good mood. The door closed behind Andrey.

The Master General seemed to have grown no older, only smaller. Spectacles were perched on his tiny nose; two more pairs lay in front of him. Sometimes he took off the ones he was wearing and put on another pair, but he did it as if it were a game; he didn't seem to need any of them.

"Come closer, my son," he said, "and speak up. They tell me my hearing is not what it used to be, although I still hear everything I want to hear."

That, too, thought Andrey. He would have to say in a loud voice what would have been difficult enough to formulate in a whisper.

"I asked for an audience, most Reverend Master General," he began, "because I have sinned, and confession has brought me no relief. I have been confessing my sin for three years, but without the suitable punishment, the sacrament of penance must remain without absolution."

The Master General looked at him disbelievingly, as old people looked at young ones from whom they expected exaggerations.

Then, in a loud voice, Andrey began to confess that he had misappropriated funds of the Order in that he had used an opportunity that had offered itself, to transfer a part of his revenue from his father's estate to a bank, to pay for the education of young Count Tioka Tarnovsky. And as if that were not enough, he had done the same thing a second time, and would probably have done so again if the boy's grandfather, Count O'Rourke, had not intervened.

Andrey was finished. He did not want to substantiate what he had done, and did so only when the Master General asked him to. He began by explaining his earlier relationship to Maria Tarnovska. The

Master General interrupted him. "I know all that." Andrey went on to describe Maria's arrest, her anxiety for her child, his conversation with Olga Katerinovich in Venice. At the time, he had been convinced that in such a hostile atmosphere, the child would be ruined, and his mother irrevocably banished into darkness. "Maria Tarnovska hung over the abyss by the thin threat of her love for her child."

The Master General put on another pair of spectacles, but continued to shake his head as if he couldn't believe his eyes, as if he saw a Father Andrey before him whom he did not know. "You speak like a layman," he said at last. "The Rule of Saint Augustine . . . but that is not all. Haven't you read the Rule of Saint Basil on the laying aside of all worldly goods? 'Those who do not recognize this are guilty of the sin of sacrilege.' I don't have to explain this to you; you know it. I didn't send you out into the world so that you might take the world unto you, but to bring the word of God to the world."

"I was not worthy of your trust in me, most Reverend Master General."

"It isn't a question of my trust. Sit down."

He looked at Andrey without anger, with scarcely a trace of disapproval, but rather uncomprehendingly. "Three years ago," he said—he seemed to recall every detail precisely—"Prior Johann Redlich in Cracow sent me a report in which he mentioned that he had given you permission to travel to Vienna. You are supposed to have said at the time that you recognized the Devil in Maria Tarnovska. What did you mean by that?"

For this question, Andrey was not prepared. He had expected to be asked about the funds he had misappropriated, whether he had used any of the money for himself, why he hadn't confessed before, if he felt remorse and was ready to do penance. He had admired, yet underestimated, the old man. Now he gave him a report on his encounters with Maria—in Charkov, in Vienna, and once more in Vienna—and he spoke of the murder of Count Kamarovsky and the trial.

"So you took it upon yourself to drive out the Devil," said the Master General. "Don't you know the rules of exorcism? '*Imprimis ne facile credat aliquem a daemonis obsessum esse.*' That is valid even for those who have been charged by the Holy Father. You were not."

"I didn't mean that Maria Tarnovska was possessed literally."

"Of course you didn't! What do you young priests take literally?

Hell is a condition; our happiness is heaven; God is a principle; the Savior a philosopher. I wish you could tell me what sense dogma is still supposed to have. An interpretation of Christianity that continues to develop, develops away from Christ. Abstraction is created by substraction. Nibble long enough at the proof of God—eudaemonically, teleologically ontologically, cosmologically, or morally—and all you have left is a skeleton. Must we keep step with skepticism? Must we look upon evolution as a negative proof of God, instead of recognizing in evolution the confirmation of the *Summa Theologica* of Saint Thomas Aquinas? Skepticism has not progressed. It was in flower when Paul had to write to the Corinthians: 'But if there is no resurrection of the dead, neither has Christ risen.' If you had meant that this woman was possessed literally, you would have had to hand her over to the Church. You did not mean it literally; yet you wanted to exorcise the Devil in her. So what am I to believe?"

"I have traveled through the world now for many years, Reverend Master General. Never have I believed I recognized the Devil so clearly as in Maria Tarnovska. I wanted to save her soul before the Devil could take possession of it wholly."

"Don't shout," said the Master General. "I am not deaf. Don't you know that the Devil shows himself without his mask only when he is sure of being followed? You did not discover the Devil in Maria Tarnovska; he showed himself to you. He appeared before you again and again so that you should follow him. And three years ago he finally made this rotten bargain with you. He behaved as if he were freeing this woman's soul; instead, you sold him yours."

Andrey's fingers were clenched around the arms of his chair. "No. That is not what I did!" he cried. He thought of the walled-up door of Santa Maria sopra Minerva, and behind the old man, who had sunk down in his armchair, he thought he could see the picture of the Grand Inquisitor.

"None of your motives were selfless," said the Master General. "You wanted a child from this woman, and because you could not sire it, you usurped the child she already had. What is more, you created an unbreakable bond between yourself and this woman. That you cheated the Order of money is beside the point. The Order has gotten over greater losses than that. But that you did yourself out of salvation, and the Order out of a priest, that pains me." Again he quoted Saint Basil: " 'For he who has dedicated himself to God but then goes over to another way of life, has committed sacrilege, for he has stolen himself and robbed the blessed sacrifice of God.' "

Andrey lowered his eyes and was silent. A sudden April shower was falling outside, as if a housewife were spilling a pail of water onto the street. "Close the window," said the Master General.

Andrey rose, relieved. The everyday request seemed like a good omen.

"Why did you come to me?" asked the Master General. "I have nothing to do with your punishment. You will have to answer to the Provincial Council. Did you think I might protect you?"

"I have enjoyed your confidence, Reverend Master General," said Andrey. "Since I abused it, I had to come to you."

The Master General took off his spectacles. This time he did not put on another pair. He stroked the bridge of his nose with his tiny fingers and sat for a while with his eyes closed.

"That isn't the only reason you came to me," he said. "Only you don't dare to say any more of what you intended to tell me. I see very few people, because too many of them say yes. I loved you my son, because you were brave. You have nothing to lose. Speak."

What did the Master General mean when he said Andrey had nothing to lose? Had the old man already broken his staff over him?

"For years," Andrey said, "I have fought for the soul of Maria Tarnovska. Now I shall not be able to do so any more."

"Do you mean by that that you regret nothing but your inability to complete this alleged mission?"

"I regret my transgression against the Church before everything else, but I also regret the fact that my mission failed just because of this transgression. And still I believe that now—at this very moment— her soul could be saved. Send one of the fathers to Venice, most Reverend Master General."

"Why at this very moment?"

Andrey forgot that he stood accused before his judge. The old fever seized him and made off with him. Maria Tarnovska, he explained, had confessed; had confessed far more than was to her worldly advantage. She was stretching out her arms to be saved; she was seeking her soul, and stood in danger of taking the wrong way irrevocably. Did the Master General know that in this new century, all over the world, a new doctrine was being spread? Its name was psychoanalysis; it was a science of the soul, a dangerous, fascinating science. Christianity without love, based on confession without *attritio*. It worshiped only happiness on earth, and simulated a paradise on earth that had to end in eternal damnation. It freed mankind not from vice but from a feeling for vice. It taught man how to live with his wicked ego so that he no longer needed to live with God. This science took man along the right road, but only up to the last fork, which led to the abyss; it was logical to the last consequence but one; an economics of healing with the greatest economy, yet dispensing with healing; egoistic to excess because it preached not the duties but the tolerability of communal living. It was atheism's last declaration of war; no longer ashamed of shamelessness, but making a postulate of it; dangerous and tempting above all because its disciples and followers meant well, so that they deceived themselves, and the deception therefore became unrecognizable.

The Master General had listened to Andrey with no sign of impatience. For the first time a smile played on his features, such an ironic smile that Andrey stopped, too surprised to go on. Since the Master General's desk was large and his arm short, he had to raise himself a little to reach the end of the table. He took a book from it and pushed it in Andrey's direction. It had been published in 1901, and the title was *Psychopathology in Everyday Life,* by Dr. Sigmund Freud.

"If I understand you correctly," said the Master General, "the Devil, whom you think you know so well, handed the soul of Maria Tarnovska over to the disciples of this new science for execution. And I am to send a man from our Order to Venice, to dispute with these scholars, as the Dominican Johann Tetzel disputed with Martin Luther? A very strange idea . . ."

He put on his glasses again, as if he wished to bring the audience to a close with the gesture. He let Andrey go—without a word of reproof or comfort.

3

One year of complete seclusion, far from Santa Maria sopra Minerva; twice a week fasting on bread and water—the sentence passed by the Provincial Council.

The train is taking Andrey south, to Naples, where he is to board a ship for North Africa. He does not rebel. It was a mild sentence, so mild that he was sure the Master General had held a protective hand over him. The argument for the sentence had sounded almost like a *laudatio;* all Father Andrey's honors had had to serve as a recommendation for the Council's leniency.

Meanwhile, it is not easy for Andrey to suppress the thoughts he had to conceal from his judges. In vain does he accuse himself of arrogance. Although he had been sentenced before a worldly sentence was passed on Maria, he is not ready yet to grant the Devil a victory. Tioka is well in body and soul, a miracle and a sign. Count O'Rourke, according to Tioka, is on his way to Venice; perhaps he is already with his daughter. Maria may have acted under the influence of her psychiatrists, or she may have felt that fruit might grow out of the ground of self-recognition even without God's blessing; but the ground is ready. God's sunshine and rain will make it fruitful. Man's ability to do good is not proof of the Almighty; his ability to do better is. In spite of everything those versed in jurisprudence and the science of the soul think they have proved so definitely, Maria could have taken another direction; and who could say that she still might not take it? There is only one homesickness that is of equal value to the home-coming, and that is the homesickness for love. And he? He had come a long way from the hour when he had been unable to comfort the sick woman in Charkov because he had feared the temptation of the flesh, to the day when he dared bring Maria's child to Geneva. A victory of Agape over Eros? That, too, but not that alone. When the longing for pain ceases, love ceases to be impure. He who comes to an understanding with his conscience stops wishing to receive or give pain. The Devil is temptation, but since the love that tortures is also temptation, the Devil sits in that torture. And Andrey begins to under-stand, sixteen years after crossing the threshold of the monastery, what love is—that in order to be itself, love has to free itself from its demonic twin brother, pain. The disciples of the new science have found a word for the love that has to give or receive pain to find fulfillment, but they have no idea that only the love that frees itself from pain is love. Pain is the supreme matchmaker of Eros, and Agape's greatest enemy. Today he knows more about love than he had ever known before. The Devil did not get the best of the bargain.

In Naples, Andrey leaves the train and walks slowly toward the harbor. Here the April sun is almost summery. Andrey looks up into the blue sky. Perhaps he is taking his punishment too blithely; per-haps he no longer knows how to mistrust himself.

CHAPTER 3

I

Witnesses, witnesses, witnesses . . .

Maria Tarnovska hears them as if through a glass wall. Figures rise up, sink down again; faces look alike, are different, look alike. The woman is fat and has dark hair—no, that is a man; perhaps both are fat and have dark hair. Most of the witnesses are people she never saw before. They come, raise their hands, swear to speak the truth, say nothing, disappear. Their testimony is unimportant; the witnesses feel important. The judge is the director of a theater; the witnesses are auditioning for him. Every one of them has studied a part—comedians, ingénues, society ladies, fathers, character parts—and secretly each one is hoping to get the lead.

The past of Maria Tarnovska, the pasts of Prilukov and Naumov and of Elise Perrier, have nothing in common. Their pasts are like boxes that were put away in the attic long ago, full of yellowed bills, old clothes, diaries from boarding school, pictures of forgotten relatives. Now the boxes are being opened; the dust flies high, papers flutter, specters appear wearing clothes, books have legs, pictures come to life. The witnesses are probably telling the truth, but nothing so long past is true.

Witnesses for Prilukov take the stand. Semstvo President Vladimir Pisarev, a schoolmate of Prilukov's. He looks at least sixty; yet Maria Tarnovska wonders why he isn't wearing a sailor suit with short trousers. A schoolmate. Prilukov had been an excellent student, the best in his class. Now they will let Donat solve a few logarithms; if he gets them right, he will be acquitted. A Dalmatian journalist, Taburno, formerly from Moscow, now an émigré, testifies that in

1905, Prilukov had handed over every cent of the money the rebels had given him for safekeeping. The witness and Donat shake hands. Thank you very much, Dr. Prilukov, you only squandered the money of the rich in Nice, at l'Hirondelle. Astonishing that the jury isn't moved to tears—there, they are weeping. A statement by Prilukov's wife is read aloud: she has forgiven her husband; his two children are praying for him. Prilukov weeps. Maria Tarnovska turns to look. No doubt about it, this time it is not Naumov—Donat is sobbing. Franzensbad—the gray mouse, his career, he loves Tioka more than his own children. But his gray mouse has forgiven him. Gray mice bear no grudges. Dr. Kaiser, lawyer from Moscow. He had warned Prilukov about Maria Tarnovska. A prophet with hindsight, not the only one. Has he come all the way from Moscow to say that in 1903 he had warned Prilukov? Back into his carton and up to the attic with him. General Rhil. Distinguished, a white beard, his civilian clothes a masquerade like the uniforms the students had worn on Tatiana Day. Twenty-five thousand five hundred rubles of the sum embezzled by Prilukov had belonged to the General, but he does not want Prilukov incriminated by it, because in a certain inheritance case, Prilukov had expended himself on the General's behalf far above the call of duty. The General makes a dignified exit; the only thing missing is applause. Josephine Haselmann, who runs a pension in Vienna. Her hat, made for the occasion, is so large, the judge has to ask her to remove it. A short juggling act with hairpins; laughter; comic relief. It is necessary that she be visible; her testimony is important. One afternoon, the defendant Countess Tarnovska had visited her lodger, Herr Prilukov, after which the bed had been disarranged. That anything like that should have happened in her respectable house . . . Dr. Mankovsky, lawyer from Moscow. Maria Tarnovska remembers him. He was the first person to tell her that Donat did not have a fortune. He is talking about a mad dog that had bitten Tioka and her. Seven years ago. Dr. Mankovsky has total recall. He doesn't want to hurt anyone. The Countess had been very unhappy in Moscow; society had boycotted her; the mad dog . . . A room full of roses, all of them withered. Back into your carton, Dr. Mankovsky.

Her own attic. A statement by the nurse, Matilda Skopin: the Countess Tarnovska had been a good lady, friendly and generous. Her husband had abandoned her when she had typhoid. "The darling of the servants!" cries Dr. Luzzatti the jokester. "Be quiet!" cries Elise

Perrier, the first sound she has uttered since the beginning of the trial. Italo Eulampio, former valet of Count O'Rourke, testifies that the young Countess had been the friendliest of the Count's four children. Dr. Luzzatti: "What did I tell you?" A little old woman comes pattering through the archway. The dead come to life—Maria Tarnovska's childhood resurrected, Anna Dobroyubova. No, she had never noticed anything peculiar about little Mura. She weeps as if it were very sad that there had been nothing peculiar about little Mura. "The only thing—she always liked to go to the cemetery." Maria Tarnovska grasps her forehead. Has she too grown so old? Anna Dobroyubova patters out again; Maria Tarnovska will never see her again. Perhaps the little governess will now tell other children lovely horror stories about little Mura, who became a murderess. A letter from Countess Maria Alexandrovna Bozevska. Her son had been the victim of his love for the Countess Tarnovska, but the Countess had nursed her son devotedly and unselfishly. Tears in the eyes of the accused; she wipes them away as if she were wiping perspiration from her face. Alexander Gabrilovich Polovtzov, journalist from St. Petersburg. He is in Venice by chance, and considers it his duty to report to the prosecution. Count Tarnovsky, after his arrest in the Bozevsky shooting, told Polovtzov in an interview that the Countess Tarnovska had incited him to shoot Bozevsky with the ulterior motive that he survive, and Tarnovsky be sent to Siberia, whereupon she could live riotously with Bozevsky. Dr. Vecchini protests. The witness declares he is only doing his duty.

There are many zealous witnesses. Count Yuri Tolstoy is not zealous. He is big-game hunting in Africa. Prince Ivan Trubetzkoy is zealous. Slender, blond, elegant in a pearl-gray suit—lorgnettes glitter. Commendatore Tusitano has the court cleared. The Countess stares fixedly at her former lover. Why had he been her lover; how had it happened; how long had it lasted; why hadn't he remained her lover? He had used a certain toothpaste—Botot—that is all she can remember. He testifies about her insane extravagance, her drug addiction; all very friendly, very polite, a gentlemanly witness. Why was the court cleared? The strangest thing about people out of the past is that their lives haven't changed. Then a brief statement by a certainly not very zealous witness. The court listens tensely. Count Vassily Vassilyevich Tarnovsky, in a statement to the police on his estate near Gomel: "I refuse to answer the questions." To all questions: "I refuse the answer." Maria Tarnovska laughs. Her laughter startles the *carabiniere* sitting at her side. He touches her arm. Yuri Tolstoy's *dacha,* the night in Charkov, the Grand Duke's palace, Tioka's birth, the scandal at Stahl's house, the shots outside the Eremitage. "I refuse to answer the questions."

Witnesses, witnesses, witnesses . . .

The blood runs cold in her veins. The former student and teacher Zolotariev. Why has she turned to ice? What does it matter? One more. Zolotariev looks like a muzhik; he looks like Ivan, the groom. In Paris, she hadn't noticed it. Perhaps Ivan will appear, too. She had been a good employer, Zolotariev says, and an unparalleled mother. The judge nods. One of Prilukov's lawyers asks, "Did you have intimate relations with the defendant?" "No," Zolotariev answers, "never." Maria Tarnovska bites her lip. Had she heard right? Is the former student and tutor ready to commit perjury for her? The Prosecutor is already waving a letter, dated from Vienna, from the Countess Tarnovska to Prilukov in Strasbourg. "Perjury!" the Prosecutor cries. The former student and tutor says nothing, only shakes his head. The judge turns to Maria Tarnovska. "I lied," she says. "I wanted to make Donat Prilukov jealous." Prosecutor Randi fiddles with his robe. "One of the hotel employees has stated that you had an affair with the maid, Perrier," he says to Zolotariev. A *carabiniere* pushes Elise Perrier back onto her seat. "The employee lied," says Zolotariev.

The best days for the spectators—testimony that concerns Nicholas Naumov. The actress Olga Ivanovna Asmanova, an imposing woman of about fifty, looking more like forty, behaving as if she were thirty. She whispers her age. Yes, she actually let Naumov run naked behind her sleigh, just as another lady had done before her. "He wanted to so badly." Loud laughter. Then the fairy tales begin to take shape. In a moment Snow White will appear with the seven dwarfs. "A poor sick boy, but he did recite such lovely poetry," says Olga Asmanova. Loud laughter. Naumov grinds his teeth. Someone should make him stop it, Maria Tarnovska thinks. An ancient little woman with a bandana around her head, a Russian peasant doll. She is hard of hearing and goes up close to the rostrum where the judges are sitting. Yes, she is ready to testify that she had let little Nicholas fall into the Oka River, and he had hurt himself. The back of his head. But it hadn't been her fault. She explains why it hadn't been; perhaps she is afraid they might still arrest her now because of the child she had let fall. All the nurses have to come marching up, all the servants, all

the teachers. Why not the midwives? The next to appear is the poet
Mishkin. A friend of Nicholas Naumov had told Mishkin that Nicholas
could love only "severe women." A seventeen-year-old cousin had
stuck pins into Nicholas. Mishkin tosses back his long blond hair.
"There's nothing unusual about it, your Excellency. A lot of poets
love only severe women." The judge shakes his head; the red-yellow
fruit threatens to fall off the cactus. He knows nothing about poets.
  Witnesses speak about Kamarovsky as if he were still alive. The
bank director Krivoshkin from Orel. After the beginning of his
relationship with the Countess Tarnovska, it had been low tide in the
Count's checking account. Flood, low tide—the bank director likes
maritime expressions. The Knight Marshal of the province of Orel
made the following statement to the police: the whole province had
been proud of Kamarovsky. Maria Tarnovska can see Pavel standing
in front of her in his black suit. "I know every bordello in Europe,
Mura." Administrator and servants: "The best master far and wide."
Friends from Orel, Moscow, St. Petersburg. *Chevalier sans peur et
sans reproche.* When will the midwife appear to testify that Pavel
Ergrafovich Kamarovsky had behaved extraordinarily well at his birth?
  Next morning the spectators are disappointed. Commendatore Tusitano has the court cleared for two days while the letters and telegrams
of Maria Tarnovska, Prilukov, Naumov, and Count Kamarovsky are
read aloud.

2

On the second of May, 1910, Dr. Hugo Friedlieber, *Neue Freie
Presse,* Vienna, wrote:

  The Tarnovska trial has now lasted almost two months, yet one can say
that not a day passes without some sensational event. The last three days especially were fraught with testimony that may very well influence the outcome of the trial. No less than thirteen medical advisers came forward to
cast light upon the actual cause of Count Kamarovsky's death, in the
course of which it became only too clear how little we know about the
human body even in this century of progress, in which we believe we have
stalemated death; and how little cause we have to be proud of that progress.
  The defense had mobilized Dr. Italo Menini, from the San Giovanni e
Paolo Hospital, who operated on the victim. Dr. Menini, a young man who
made an excellent impression, told the jury that of the four bullets, one penetrated a loop of the intestine, and therefore punctured it eight times. On the

397

other hand, this had resulted in a part of the intestine being hit only tangentially. Dr. Menini, who found the bullet in a muscle, made a three-layer closure of the abdominal wall and, to be on the safe side, inserted a drain. The operation had to take place without a complete narcosis. The patient was extremely courageous, and conversed during the operation with the magistrate and the Russian consul. On the fourth day, chief surgeon Professor Enrico Cavazzini had appeared on the scene. When the drain was removed, there was discharge, and since the patient was complaining of nausea, it was feared there might be intestinal obstruction. Professor Cavazzini therefore ordered the patient's stomach pumped. Dr. Menini carried out the order, after which Kamarovsky's condition worsened considerably, and he became delirious.

Dr. Menini's testimony, however, did not remain unchallenged. Dr. Facta supported it unconditionally, but court physician Professor Trevisan accused Dr. Menini of giving only a superficial account of what had taken place. Another opinion was expressed by the present head doctor of the Venice hospital, Professor Giordano, a surgeon of international repute, who declared that the operation should never have been performed in the first place. According to Professor Giordano, operations on the stomach were nearly always fatal, whereas medical experience in the Russo-Japanese War had demonstrated that if the patient was kept absolutely still in such a case, Mother Nature usually attended to the healing. In the Boer War, laparotomy performed on the lower intestine had "killed"—as he called it—hundreds of soldiers. "Not a surgeon's unsure hands but his unsure head is responsible for most medical failures," said Professor Giordano. He also declared that Count Kamarovsky had not died as a direct result of Naumov's attack on him. This opinion was supported by Dr. Coccon, another surgeon of repute, who expressed the suspicion that inadequately sterilized hands during the operation might have brought about the fatal outcome. So many doctors, so many opinions!

But the highlight of the case's medical aspects was provided by the aged Professor Cavazzini, who had ordered the patient's stomach pumped. Rarely has human frailty been so crassly displayed. The professor, recently retired, declared that he was not only unable to remember any orders he might have given, but he couldn't remember a patient named Kamarovsky at all! During some operation or other, he, Professor Cavazzini, had contracted an ailment, and since then his memory has been failing. But the defense wouldn't let it go at that, and the court communicated by telephone with the hospital. This resulted in a flooding of the court by assistant doctors, nurses, and orderlies—not one of these witnesses had ever noticed a loss of memory in Professor Cavazzini before! For hours it was as if not the Countess, her maid, and her lovers were in the dock, but this pitiful old man. Be that as it may, this "fainting spell" of the medical profession served at the same time to demonstrate the frailty of justice, and quite a few of the spectators must have been reminded of the words of the *Iliad:* "Our knowledge is naught; all we go by is rumor."

If the Countess was forced into the background during these days, she was thrown all the more clearly into the limelight this morning. Alert followers of the case could notice a new face among the jurors. Reluctantly, the presiding judge explained that juryman Luigi Santelli had declared himself prejudiced; the court would therefore swear in a substitute juryman, Giuseppe Barbera, ship's captain from Murano. Commendatore Tusitano gave no further details as to the reason for Santelli's resignation, but the far-too-numerous representatives of the more sensational press immediately left the courtroom to hunt up the thirty-nine-year-old not very successful writer. They succeeded, as they always do, in ferreting him out in a tavern, where—already drunk at this early morning hour—he told them that he had fallen in love with the defendant Tarnovska. He protested that Signora di Tarnovska was in no way to blame; according to him, she had not cast any seductive glances in his direction. He could not explain the fascination of "this marvelous woman," but it was his intention to write a play about her. He would of course have voted for her acquittal.

The testimony of the Countess' maid, Elise Perrier, is worthy of note, rich as it was in comic detail. The Swiss woman defended Madame de Tarnovska, and described her as "a very kindhearted lady." This in spite of the fact that the Countess had occasionally beaten her, and burnt her with cigarettes! When defense lawyer Luzzatti asked her if it hadn't hurt, she answered, "I should say so!"—which everyone seemed to find highly amusing. The witnesses testifying on her behalf did much to exonerate her; on the other hand, this was not very favorable for Madame de Tarnovska. The witnesses stated that Elise Perrier had grown so accustomed to her mistress' tantrums that she couldn't possibly have taken the Countess' intention to have young Naumov "dispose of Kamarovsky" any more seriously than her declaration that she had vowed by the health of her little son that Kamarovsky had to die.

That the *vox populi* is demanding the most severe punishment for the beautiful aristocrat goes without saying; still, the outcome of the trial is by no means certain. The confusion caused by the medical testimony could have favorable results for the defendants. The trial has now lasted two months, yet the people of Venice are still snatching the papers out of each others' hands, and seem to have forgotten all about such important events as the visit of Czar Nicholas II in Potsdam, the abdication of Manuel II of Portugal and the proclamation of a republic in that country, the latest Moroccan crisis, and the annexation of Korea by the Japanese. The world is seething. But only a few seem to see any connection between the enjoyment of the populace over the moral degeneracy that is being clearly demonstrated in the Venetian courtroom on the one hand, and, on the other hand, the lack of interest of the same populace in the thunder clouds forming overhead.

3

A long bench had been placed in front of the rostrum. When Maria Tarnovska is brought in, nine men are already seated on it. All nine are dressed in black. The oldest is over seventy; the youngest, not yet forty. They have come from Venice, Padua, Rome, Naples. To Maria Tarnovska they seem to be facing an enemy like a battle row of Greek soldiers. On the extreme right, nearest her, sits Professor Ceresa, lean, with deep-set eyes that glow like the faraway exit of a tunnel.

As their names are called, the psychiatrists rise. Professor Bossi from Genoa, Professor Tanzi from Florence, Professor Morselli from Rome, Professor Belmondo from Padua, Professors Cappeletti, Angelo, and Ceresa from Venice, Professor Franconi and former Minister of Education, Professor Bianchi, from Naples.

When Professor Bianchi speaks, Maria Tarnovska is reminded of the big, clumsy county policeman in Otrada, who had always seemed to her a symbol of security. The experts have decided, he explains, to give their individual opinions only when they do not coincide with those of the other psychiatrists or augment their findings. The summing up is to be given by Professor Ceresa. Commendatore Tusitano asks His Excellency Professor Bianchi if he considers it necessary to clear the court. The professor turns to face the press. "The findings of this new science of healing," he says, "have been accessible only to the privileged few for far too long." A naked woman lying on the operating table, thinks Maria Tarnovska. The doors of the operating room wide open. Come, see, marvel at the findings of the new science!

Professor Bianchi makes a wide gesture in the direction of the open windows. Warmly, May sunshine is streaming into the courtroom. You can hear the wing beat of doves, like the rustling of paper. In this Venetian spring, says the professor, it is hard to transport oneself into the rugged climate of Russia. If he were to say that Russia was a hundred years behind Western civilization, he would not be exaggerating. People should not let themselves be confused by the great men of Russian literature. "Geniuses thrive on the opposition of their people." The Countess Maria Tarnovska's apparent intelligence doesn't prove anything, either. "A knowledge of languages is often the expression of an inarticulate soul." The greater the gap between the populace and the privileged class, the more uninhibitedly that class believes it can behave. On the other hand, this very Russian society feels that the end is near, and is therefore in the grip of a disaster psychosis. "We are dealing here with orgies on a sinking ship. The more decadent a society, the more confused its ideas on love. And, paradoxically enough, the more strongly it identifies love and sex, the more ready it is to accept sexual love without the love of the soul. Only yesterday, we could read in the papers about a wave of suicides in Russian aristocratic circles. The defendants Naumov and Prilukov, and, in all probability, the murdered man, Count Kamarovsky, were typical suicide candidates. But just as many a conquered field marshal in the days of ancient Rome did not kill himself but chose to fall on the sword of a slave or a friend, men like Naumov, Prilukov, and Kamarovsky seek their murderer."

Maria Tarnovska thinks of Andrey, who said something similar when she had been scarcely sixteen years old. Is Professor Bianchi recommending Article Forty-seven—substantial negative responsibility for the offense—because he is insinuating that she grew up in a madhouse? She looks at her father, who has started up several times.

Professor Morselli concerns himself primarily with Prilukov. He is an old man and speaks so softly that the judge has to hold his hand to his ear. Prilukov's is the case of the tragedy of a parvenu. "The parvenu's behavior is an unconscious caricature of the society in which he lives." Prilukov admired what he hated and hated what he admired. "A parvenu," says the professor, "is like a child who first and above all copies the mischief the other children do." With Kamarovsky, Prilukov wanted to do away with the society that had never accepted him.

Is the psychiatrist accusing or defending Prilukov, Maria Tarnovska wonders. She had called Donat "muzhik." If the experts prove that he is a muzhik, then she, his master, is responsible.

Professor Morselli goes on, "Prilukov is, moreover, an amoral man. The amoral man—unlike the immoral man—is unpredictable. One might say his skin is insensitive. He is a gambler who does not always cheat, but is perfectly capable of cheating. For instance, when Dr. Prilukov embezzled the funds of his clients and handed all their money over to the revolutionaries, he was convinced that he was not only behaving morally but heroically. An immoral man thinks before he acts, however falsely; the amoral man acts without thinking. Millions of amoral humans are living among us as highly respected citizens, and in the end receive beautiful eulogies. It is wrong to bring up the question of whether the Countess Tarnovska seduced Signor Prilukov, or vice versa. Amoral people speak the same language, which is all the clearer to them because no outsider can understand it. I would consider the application of Article Forty-seven justified in the case of Donat Prilukov."

The jury is staring uncomprehendingly straight ahead; a few ladies in the auditorium yawn. The lady with the big hat—today it is a light blue cloud—is sucking a sweet. The spectators' lack of interest is a consolation to Maria Tarnovska. Then Professor Bossi rises. The man from Genoa, with his Mongolian face, visited her many times in the hospital.

His honorable colleagues, he says, seem to underestimate the physiological aspects in their evaluation of the Countess Tarnovska. Volumes could be written about the medical history of the accused. Almost totally blind after a case of the measles; no menstruation until she was sixteen; typhoid fever—a severe case; blood poisoning after the birth of her second child; bitten by a rabid dog—all of which would suffice to give a pathological picture even if there were no tendency toward epilepsy, and the health of the defendant had not been undermined by morphine and cocaine. "Whoever sniffs thirty centigrams of cocaine daily is not capable of sound reasoning."

Maria Tarnovska knows that no defense counsel could plead more convincingly for her than Professor Bossi is doing; still, she has to cling to the bench in order not to jump up and scream, "Enough! Enough!" Pavel was operated on without narcosis; now she is experiencing her operation wide-awake. Professor Bossi speaks about the mother of the accused. Maria Tarnovska feels a closeness with her father. Together they had stood at Katharina O'Rourke's grave. At the time she had hated her father. Her mother will be a sad, withered flower no longer; they are tearing off her petals. Forgive me, Mother, she thinks. Aunt Anna, Aunt Sonya. And a great-grandfather who had ended his days in an asylum, a fact she hadn't known. And an O'Rourke who had died at the age of ten, feeble-minded— Otto Gustave Gerhard, 1821. Forgive me, Father. The proud O'Rourkes; the regal O'Rourkes! A courtroom in Venice, an operating table, Professor Bossi from Genoa—midwife and gravedigger.

Dr. Eugenio Tanzi, professor at the university and director of the clinic for the mentally ill in Florence, is a tiny man with a thick crown of hair around his bald head. He is dressed meticulously, yet wears a Lavallière cravat. He looks like a violinist in a night club. As he talks, he leaves the bench and walks up and down around jury and spectators. He is lecturing to students.

The case has to be understood medically and historically. Two terms with which they are here concerned have not been mentioned yet. "We are dealing with the love relationship between sadists and masochists," says the professor. He proceeds to read aloud Dr. Eugene Dührens' definition of sadism in his definitive work, *The Marquis de Sade and His Times;* reads a no-less-appropriate definition of masochism, by Krafft-Ebing, who had coined the word "masochism" from the heroes of the Austrian romancer, Sacher Masoch. In a splendid work, the professor goes on, the French Doctor E. Laurent said, "Generally speaking, masochism is the opposite of sadism; the latter being the sensual pleasure of the hangman, the former the lust of the martyr." Meanwhile, the new science of the soul is moving forward in such a revolutionary manner that what was hailed as a great discovery yesterday may be considered antiquated today. Not long ago, Dr. Schaefer, in the *Yearbook of Psychology,* described pugnacity and the urge to kill, in all animal species, as "attributes of the male," but today it can be proved that sadistic elements are to be found more frequently in the female, masochistic ones more often in the male. "For instance," the professor says, "men who frequent bordellos rarely ask to whip the prostitutes; whereas many prostitutes are equipped with a whole arsenal of torture instruments."

Maria Tarnovska's brain feels empty. She is the prostitute of whom the professor is speaking. Now all eyes are wide open. It is 1910; she is in a courtroom, black robes, black lawyers. Actually, though, she is the adulteress of the Middle Ages that they had chased through villages with a shorn head. Physically sick, a prostitute, an adulteress, insane, sadistic—she can't be all these things and still be alive? Who is right, and who is she?

This, says the professor, eyes downcast, is where the medical-historical connection begins. In their book *Woman in the Eighteenth Century*, the Brothers Goncourt had written that "one had played too much with the sufferings of a woman's heart not to have acquired the desire to really see her suffer." That had been in the era of the Marquis de Sade. The Marquis had been of the opinion that God had made an "error of construction" when he created woman, and had made her "the worst of all creatures, physically absolutely repulsive!" In the nineteenth century, Dr. Tanzi goes on, all this was changed; woman's emancipation released all her latent sadistic impulses. That these had existed goes without saying. "Pain and lust," he declares, "are simply different degrees of the same manifestation." The emancipated woman is like a woman in a harem who, at the first opportunity, murders the eunuch, not only out of revenge, but because she has become conscious of the fact that she had to endure the abuse of power of an inferior creature. "The equal evaluation or the equal rights of women," says Professor Tanzi, "are monstrous conceptions, not because woman is inferior to man, but because there can be no such thing as equality of the sexes. The natural sex instinct demands that one sex, male or female, dominate the other. Emancipation, therefore, is nothing but a struggle for supremacy under the cloak of a struggle for equality. Instead of the Marquis de Sade, we today have the Marquise de Sade."

And now—the little man speaks as if to himself—how about male masochism? The emancipation of women is a male invention. The origins of masochism are nearly always rooted in a feeling of guilt. For centuries the male was responsible for everything under the sun—and what didn't happen under the sun? After the expulsion from Paradise—for which a completely emancipated Eve had borne the main burden of responsibility—guilt, and with it all responsibility, was placed upon the shoulders of Adam. "Adam thirsts for punishment." It is therefore no coincidence that in the century that has just come to a close, one finds no male illustration of sadism, but in Sacher Masoch, an illustration of male masochism. The professor goes on to recite from the proverbs of Solomon: " 'Let not your heart turn to her ways, go not astray in her paths, for many are those she has struck down dead, numerous those she has slain. Her house is made up of ways to the nether world, leading down into the chambers of death.' "

For the first time in years, Maria Tarnovska feels the desire to torture a man. One hour with this violinist from a night club, and he would be groveling at her feet. The woman with the big hat; the old lady sitting at the window, trying to get a breath of fresh air; the lady journalist; the tragedienne—they are not her enemies. Cactus-face, the Prosecutor, even Dr. Vecchini, who conjured up all these hangmen dressed up as saviors—they are the enemy.

Suddenly Professor Tanzi takes a provocative stand in front of the judges, as if only now does it occur to him why they have listened to him all this time. Suddenly he begins to talk about the murder on September 3. With the defendants Naumov and Prilukov, they are dealing with masochists. Naumov is a clear-cut case of algophilia—the urge not only to suffer emotionally but also physically. "Like Sacher Masoch, the author of *Venus in Pelz,* Naumov is an aristocrat, a poet, and lives in a country that is undergoing cruel changes. In Signora di Tarnovska, he found his Wanda Donayev, also a Slav." Prilukov, he goes on to explain, is a masked masochist. "It is not only possible, but happens often, that the masochist finds his satisfaction in a brutal, apparently sadistic, manner."

While the psychiatrist continues to talk about her, Maria Tarnovska feels that she is no longer able to control her nausea. So they had lived in a madhouse, she and Naumov and Kamarovsky and Prilukov; Vassily, too, and Alexis; and the doctors had not prevented their copulating; she and Prilukov, she and Naumov, she, over and over again. They had watched, these doctors for the insane, watched the mad creatures copulating, and now they are spreading out their findings for everyone to see. Professor Tanzi walks slowly back to his seat, saying, as if in an aside, "I do not consider the application of Article Forty-seven sufficient; I ask for the acquittal of the accused, and her temporary commitment to a mental institution." Judges, furnishings, curtains, and spectators suddenly begin to swim before Maria Tarnovska's eyes, and she collapses in the dock.

She doesn't come to her senses again until she hears a voice saying, "Pulse one fifty, absolutely insensitive." Cold water is running down her forehead. She can feel herself being lifted. All she can see is the ceiling: the frescoes of the courthouse, Justice with her eyes bound, the scale in her hand. Better Justice than the violinist from the night club. Trumpeting angels, blue clouds, a woman wearing a flowing garment, all above her head. "Make room! Make room!" the crowd is yelling. "Humbug! Don't believe her," the crowd is yelling. It smells of salad and fruit and rotten vegetables. A *carabiniere* is speaking to the *gondoliere*. Sister Lucia is holding Maria Tarnovska's head and shoulders in her lap; between the gaps in the black curtains, the lights of Venice are gliding by.

4

Saturday, Sunday. On Monday morning it is the turn of the psychiatrists Angelo, Belmondo, Cappeletti, and Franconi. In the afternoon, Professor Ceresa rises for the summing up.

He has known the Countess Tarnovska for over two years, he says. Jurisprudence undoubtedly left no stone unturned to interpret the Countess' motives from the facts of her life. Jurisprudence, however, never forgets that the court is dealing with a sinner. The indictment is the tower from which jurisprudence looks down into the valley of human suffering. Medicine . . .

Commendatore Tusitano interrupts the professor. With all due respect for the experts, he feels he has to beg Professor Ceresa to reserve his aversion for jurisprudence for his work, *Justice and Psychiatry*. Those listening grin knowingly; the judge looks at them with disapproval.

Since the theories of Sigmund Freud, Professor Ceresa goes on, the science of psychology has taken full cognizance of the importance of youthful experiences, especially those of childhood. He tries to explain the Oedipus complex to the judges. "Terrible O'Rourke" is what they called the father of the accused. "We hate those who are terrible," he says, "but, gentlemen, we also want to be like them. To be more terrible than Terrible O'Rourke was the major impulse of the little Countess O'Rourke. The discipline of her father's household was her first experience with sadistic and masochistic elements. The discipline that we deify," he explains, "is a recognized composite of sadism and masochism; but it functions only when the dependent is a masochist. This was not so in the case of the young Countess."

Maria Tarnovska looks down at her folded hands. Ceresa is trying to save her. If she raises her eyes, she will see Terrible O'Rourke, for whom she now feels nothing but tenderness. Can they not save her without crucifying her father?

Professor Ceresa speaks of the magical attraction the Countess exerted over masochistic men. With the instincts of a masochist, the roué Vassily Tarnovsky gave up his freedom. Masochists always want to be robbed of their freedom.

"Are you calling marriage a deprivation?" cries Prosecutor Randi. For once he has the laughter on his side.

Professor Ceresa pays no attention to him. "My purpose is to make the accused comprehensible to you, not sympathetic," he says. "The self-sacrificial care, for instance, that the accused bestowed on Count Bozevsky undoubtedly included sadistic elements."

"No! No!" cries Maria Tarnovska. Dr. Luzzatti makes a short, succinct remark.

The relationship of the Countess to Baron Vladimir Stahl offers no riddles, Ceresa goes on to explain. Drug addicts are often masochists. They flee from pain, only to inflict much greater pain upon themselves. For most of them, the lust of masochism begins when they plunge the needle into themselves.

A feeling of gratitude overwhelms Maria Tarnovska when she realizes that Professor Ceresa is not going to mention the night in Baden-Baden, although she has confessed to him what happened then.

"You may have asked yourselves," says the professor, "why the Countess Tarnovska led the accused, Naumov, to the grave of the despised Baron. It was because, among all her slaves, this man, who wrote her over three hundred unanswered letters, was the most obedient. For her he was the incarnation of the absolute slave. When she told Naumov at Stahl's grave that the Baron would have freed her from Kamarovsky, she was behaving like a teacher who holds up to a student the unconditional discipline of a model pupil. It is no coincidence that Naumov felt drawn to Baudelaire. Baudelaire describes several friends discussing the term 'love' as follows: 'The only and supreme ecstasy of love is the certainty of doing evil. And man and woman have known since time began that all ecstasy lies in evil.'" From these and similar utterances, people have come to the conclusion that the poet who wrote *Les Fleurs du Mal* was a sadist, but the reading of one verse of *"Une Charogne"* would suffice to unmask him as a masochist. *"Les jambes en l'air, comme une femme lubrique/ Brulante et suante les poisons,/ Ouvrait d'une façon non-chalante et cynique/ Son ventre plein d'exhalaisons."* Baudelaire, who had intimate relations with dwarfs and giantesses—"One of the dwarfs was only seventy-two centimeters high; you can't have everything in this world"—certainly hated and despised women, yet he wanted nothing more than to submit to the hated, despised female.

"What do you know about Baudelaire?" cries Naumov, his first protest since the beginning of the trial. It arouses merriment; even the jury smiles.

"But I must warn you," Professor Ceresa continues, "against keeping sadism and masochism strictly apart in your minds. All sadists have masochistic, all masochists have sadistic, impulses."

"And there are no healthy people?" the Prosecutor interrupts him.

"No, Commendatore Randi," Ceresa replies. "There are no healthy people."

"Then why do we go on with the trial?" Randi protests. "Let us move the proceedings to an asylum. Don't you realize, Professor Ceresa, that there isn't a soul in the hall at this point whom you have not insulted?"

Maria Tarnovska sees nothing but insulted faces. The lady with the hat as big as a cart wheel—insulted; the veterinarian with the head of a St. Bernard—insulted; the reporter with the horn-rimmed spectacles—insulted. Even the defense lawyers are insulted.

"In that case," says the professor, "the ladies and gentlemen may be discovering the Naumovs and Tarnovskas within themselves."

Men in the courtroom jump to their feet; ladies drum on the floor with their umbrellas; the pale student in the back row whistles. "Another demonstration like that," says the judge, "and I clear the court."

"I am ready with my concluding statement," says Professor Ceresa. "In the dock you see a sadist and two masochists. The third, Count Kamarovsky, is dead. Although sadist and masochist attract each other with a sure instinct, that does not say that every sadist has to love every masochist. The accused undoubtedly hated Count Kamarovsky; but at the moment of the crime, she hated Prilukov—the man she had once loved—just as much, so that there can be no question of her having incited Naumov to the deed in Prilukov's interest. And it would be just as wrong for us to acquit the masochist of responsibility, and place it upon the sadist because we believe the latter, erroneously, to be a masterful personality. The desire to be ruled is no less strong than the desire to rule, but since our entire civilization is based on admiration of the masterful personality—that is to say, on the sadist—it is more difficult to unmask him. We admire the sadist up to the point when his acts of violence end in a social, political, or personal catastrophe. In that moment we about-face, and identify with the masochist, without whose desire for subjugation, punishment, or pain, the catastrophe brought on by the sadist could never have taken place. The role of the masochist in society is static; he is always the slave, abused and pitied. But the role of the sadist is subject to constant change: admiration when he is successful, condemnation when he fails. The masochistic world in which she lived admired the Countess Tarnovska; since the September day in the year nineteen hundred and seven, when she was arrested in Vienna, she has been the object of condemnation. When you retire for your decision of guilty or not guilty, I beg you to keep in mind the coresponsibility of those who let themselves be dominated. I speak on behalf of my colleagues when I say that in the tragic case you are judging here, we are faced with neither seducer nor seduced; that the assurances of the Countess Tarnovska that she wished only to test her power—and this not for the first time—are absolutely credible; that on the other hand, the slaves, Naumov and Prilukov, did not consider the final consequence of what they were doing but had only one thing on their minds—to serve their mistress, just as the dead man wanted to and did serve her; that we cannot separate the deed from the milieu in which it took place; that, although no one is free of sadistic and masochistic impulses, we are dealing here with three sick people who are not going to get well behind prison walls. Not one of the doctors assembled here can promise you a complete recovery of the accused. We believe we are on the right path, but as long as the two great human emotions, love and pain, are not only inseparably bound together, but, in the co-life of the sexes, seem to be identical, we are still far from a final answer. I beg you not to demand of three sick people the answer that nine doctors are barely able to give you, and I warn you against believing that you have the answer. In the name of my colleagues and myself, I recommend the recognition of extenuating circumstances, as covered by Article Forty-seven, for the three chief defendants."

Maria Tarnovska experiences what is happening as if from far away. The Public Prosecutor demands that Professor Ceresa's lecture—which was no "expertise," but a speech for the defense—be struck from the record. The presiding judge asks the jury to come to their own conclusions, and not to forget that the passionate adherence to a new science might well have dimmed the objectivity of the experts.

The faces of the whispering defense lawyers betray their disappointment over the role taken from them by the professor, mingled with their satisfaction over his verdict. The excitement among spectators and press is so great that loud conversations become audible. The two Appellate Court judges turn anxiously to the jury to translate the words of the psychiatrist for them, as if he spoke a foreign language. Count O'Rourke buries his face in his hands for the first time. Maria Tarnovska only sees the nine men in black rise, bow one by one, and leave the courtroom one after the other, without a glance at her, as if she were an inanimate object. The bench is empty; two men carry it away. Maria Tarnovska feels as if they are carrying a coffin. There is no bulwark any more between her and her judges.

5

Three long days: pleas, counterpleas, more pleas.

Maria Tarnovska does not pay much attention. It is as if they are speaking about a stranger whom she knew once but no longer recognizes. She has seen those eyes somewhere, that mouth—an acquaintance. No, perhaps not. In the morgue, they show you the dead and ask you if you recognize them; they don't just show you an arm, a leg, the ears, the shoulders.

Public Prosecutor Randi is mainly concerned with attacking the psychiatrists. According to them, the accused is nothing but a series of examples to elucidate their theories. See illustration so and so. . . . The Slavic soul as an excuse? "Don't forget, gentlemen, that a Slavic woman sits on the Italian throne." Excellent effect. Maria Tarnovska knows nothing about the Slavic soul. Do souls have passports? The Countess Tarnovska's illnesses? They have to be counted again. She read once about a perverse swindler who, posing as a doctor, examined hundreds of women. Commendatore Randi says, "If every woman who consulted a gynecologist committed murder, we would have more murders than births." She cannot tell whether he is convincing the jury or not; but he is convincing her. The bridges that Professor Bossi built between body and soul probably hang in the air. "Are we to understand that Franzensbad is a breeding spot for murderers?" Laughter. Public Prosecutor Randi toys with his earlobe. A shy man, Maria Tarnovska decides. He gets his effects conscientiously, but would rather address his remarks only to the judge. Negative responsibility? "She developed enough will power to play three men against each other." No, this stranger doesn't know her. It doesn't take any will power to play three men against each other; it is weakness to cling to three men one doesn't love. Her financial ruination? "The accused can afford three lawyers. She is paying for the defense of her maid. She deposited twenty thousand francs for the traveling expenses of her witnesses. Why didn't she ask her father for help before?" Maria Tarnovska looks at her father. He could ask the same question if he were the Prosecutor; her defense lawyer could ask it. Randi has gone on to other subject matter while she is still wondering why she hadn't turned to her father before. Because he didn't say a word when they had put up her hair? No one will understand it. And all this talk about an unhappy childhood, the Prosecutor is saying, about complexes, sadism, masochism, or whatever the *termini technici* of the psychiatric experts might be. "The gentlemen have found a new toy." Sadism is simply a fancy word for cruelty; masochism for weakness. "Criminals are cruel and seduce the weak." Maria Tarnovska could explain that to him. Signor Randi would understand it; Prosecutor Randi, never. If she believes the Prosecutor, she is a criminal; if she believes the lawyers, a mad woman. She always feared madness. Is madness to be her sanctuary now? She is afraid to think clearly, because if she thinks clearly, she is a criminal. She is afraid of becoming confused, because then she is mad. It could be that courtroom, pigeons, market noises, the Public Prosecutor's twitching face are only figments of a mad woman's imagination. In a moment the doctors would be there, orderlies; they would do something to calm her and put her in a strait jacket.

Dr. Feder is speaking for the mother of Count Kamarovsky. "The accused has been presented to us as a fascinating demon. We have been looking at her for three months, and have felt nothing but disgust." She had not intended to enchant anyone; disgust is something to which she has grown accustomed. They should stick to the facts, cries Dr. Feder. He is going far beyond his duty; he is excited, his face is red, his veins are bulging. The Public Prosecutor mentioned Donat and Nicholas now and then; Dr. Feder speaks only about her. "When Count Kamarovsky took out the life insurance, he signed his death warrant." The Countess—no one else—persuaded him to sign it. The Prilukov collection of letters? "A vain man is a poor keeper of secrets." Maria Tarnovska thinks she knows why all are sworn against her. Vengeance of the opposite sex. She tries to find the eyes of her sisters, finds them closed. In the decisive battle, women desert to the men. Or is she suffering from a persecution complex? She sees enemies everywhere; but if she is mad, they are imaginary enemies. He who suffers from a persecution complex does not believe in a friend. She sees Andrey. So she does not have a persecution complex. Is that better? According to Dr. Feder, she ruined Prilukov, but she intended to live with him. An insurance murder—that's all.

The lawyers are pleading for Elise Perrier. Maria Tarnovska forces herself to be attentive. Why should the accused have told her maid about the murder plan? God be thanked, it sounds convincing. The jury knows nothing of lonely women speaking only for the sake of speaking. And why should Elise Perrier have believed her mistress? "The accused Tarnovska is a pathological liar." Well put! What connection could the maid possibly have had with an insurance murder? Maria Tarnovska nods. The judges seem to be believing the lawyers. In a Shakespearean play, the simple people speak in prose. The judges take it for granted that the souls of simple people are prosaic.

The defense for Nicholas and Donat.

Naumov: a spineless tool, sick, young, by love possessed. Remorseful from the first moment, pleading guilty, crushed. A healthy home atmosphere is ready to receive him—his father's house. Should he be punished for his remorse, and the Countess Tarnovska rewarded for her tenaciousness? That would be carte blanche for all hardened criminals. Maria Tarnovska's gaze wanders across to the fat dreamer, listening with tears in his eyes. A little girl who has broken her doll and says another child did it. A healthy home atmosphere? She thinks of the Governor's palace in Orel. She knows what healthy homes are worth. That Prilukov might have led the weakling astray is a theory Naumov's lawyers don't want to accept. He would not have let Prilukov influence him; he loved the Countess Tarnovska. Maria Tarnovska knows that he didn't love her. Naumov's lawyers cite letters; Prilukov's testimony. "Signora di Tarnovska would not persuade Prilukov to commit the crime because she feared she could not love a murderer." Love, love, love—what do they know about it? Before God all is confusion; before the judges, all simplicity. There has to be order. One's emotions have to be orderly. In Otrada, too, everything had been orderly.

And Prilukov. They were, please, to compare Prilukov's snow-white past with the past of the defendant Countess Tarnovska, his lawyers demand. Did anyone ever commit suicide because of him? Did his wife shoot her rival? Was he ever a drug addict? The affair with the detective only demonstrates his obsession with love. It is not to be considered culpable. Maria Tarnovska knows that Donat never had any dealings with a detective; but if she were to prove it, she would get lost in a labyrinth of proof and counterproof. You cannot add apples and pears: elementary school, first grade. The letters? A criminal would not carefully keep incriminating material, certainly not a former lawyer. Vladimir Stahl had written over three hundred unanswered letters to the defendant. Why? Why does anyone do what he does? Women make their own decisions, Dr. Luzzatti declares, but when they make mistakes, the man stands accused. Prilukov's lawyers tear to shreds the evidence that points to his instigation of an insurance murder. In whose name was the policy? And could Prilukov have depended on the rich "widow" remaining with him? With whom had she ever remained? "The accused has spoken lovingly of only two men: one is dead, the other is in a monastery." They are right, these fine lawyers. She had not thought of Pavel's money, but she would not have stayed with Donat, either. Or would she? They don't know the past; how can they predict the future?

Her own lawyers speak about a stranger. Vecchini makes every attempt to save her. She is reminded of Donat's pleas. More than once, Vecchini is interrupted by applause. When it happens, Maria Tarnovska looks up as if in a dream. What did he say? That such a subtle murder plan could never have originated in the mind of a woman. Why not? That Naumov and Prilukov are being treated like witnesses, when actually their own lives depend on the destruction of the Countess. But doesn't her life depend on Donat's destruction? That Naumov can recall everything, but not who had given him the revolver. That the Countess Tarnovska could have become a wealthy woman; besides Kamarovsky, she could have kept lovers— even Prilukov! Prophets! That the Public Prosecutor had availed himself of psychiatric reports in innumerable cases before; only here, because they exonerate the defendant, does he speak of "a new toy." Maria Tarnovska listens with downcast eyes. You can hear the splashing of paddle-boat wheels in the water. Street urchins whistling. A voice singing. She does not want to hear what Vecchini is saying. They are agreed, all of them—the prosecution, the witnesses, the defense. From various sides they see something that doesn't exist. If the jury believe the plaintiffs, she will end behind prison walls; if they believe the defense, she will end in shame.

The judge has to speak to her twice before she rises. Does she have anything further to say? She shakes her head. No, nothing. Not one of them knows who she is or what has happened. She doesn't know herself.

6

Maria Tarnovska hated nothing so much in the past years as the walks in the prison courtyard, around and around in a circle like a circus horse, five steps apart. The prisoners in detention had changed: a woman who had murdered her husband ahead of her, a jewel thief behind her. Bent backs, fat rumps, bony shoulders, bowlegs. Elise Perrier was never allowed to walk before or behind her, but they always saw each other, nodded at each other; and the other prisoners stared at them—there they were, mistress and maid, walking the same mile. Hundreds of times, the same walk. Even in the rain, they had to trot around, one behind the other; the sky above them a rectangular tin roof. And in the sun; the sky a blazing mirror. Always a nun sat in the prison doorway. Always the nun was knitting, looking up every now and then with watchful eyes. Always the heads of other nuns popped up at windows: were the little horses trotting? Were they being good?

Now it was Sunday again; the walk lasted a half hour longer. Later the prisoners were allowed to converse with each other for fifteen minutes, unless there were any misgivings about it, as in the case of the Countess Tarnovska and Elise Perrier.

In front of Maria Tarnovska, a thief's enormous rear end was swaying. She was here for the sixth time. Behind her, Maria Tarnovska could hear a young woman coughing. She had strangled her newborn baby in a toilet. Whenever Maria Tarnovska looked to the left, she could see Elise Perrier in her black Sunday dress, walking as briskly as if she were bringing her mistress something. Every now and then Elise had to stop because the distance between her and the woman ahead had become too short.

And there they are, Maria Tarnovska thought, sitting down to the

Sunday roast—the veterinarian, the surveyor, the deputy, the school-master. They have tied their napkins around their necks; they are drinking a Grignolino; the corners of their mouths glisten with grease; soon they will be taking their after-dinner naps. Every one of them knows how he will vote tomorrow. In a way they are sorry that it will be all over then. When one has been so important for three months . . . They will tell their grandchildren about it. "When I was on the jury of the Tarnovska trial . . ."

What had they decided, her judges? The ship's captain, the painter, the colonel? She should have spoken when the judge asked her if she had anything further to say. She should at least have spoken about the future. Not of her remorse, because remorse would have been an admission of guilt. But that she intended to live differently, and that this was impossible behind prison walls. Behind prison walls you could have no qualities, good or bad. That she knew something was waiting for her in freedom, something that would save her. What? The judge would have asked that, and she would not have been able to answer. Yet this "something" existed. Now she walked more erectly, five steps behind the swaying buttocks, five steps in front of the coughing murderess. The verdict had not yet fallen, and Maria Tarnovska believed she could still influence it, if only she could convey her thoughts to her judges—the certainty that in freedom something was waiting for her that was far safer than Naumov's father's home, warmer than the arms of a forgiving Signora Prilukov.

The nun in the doorway put her knitting away. Elise Perrier and two other prisoners were led off. Maria Tarnovska wanted to leave, too, but it was Sunday. It was more difficult to avoid the prison's blessings than its punishments.

The woman with the fat buttocks walked up to Maria Tarnovska. She limped a little, like many women who were slight above the waist and shapeless below it. She had a smart, crafty face—the smart thievish face of a man.

"So tomorrow is your big day," she said.

Maria Tarnovska nodded.

"What do you think?" the woman asked.

"I don't know."

"I think you'll be acquitted."

"Why?" Maria Tarnovska asked gratefully.

"I have a feeling about it. There are people who fit into prison, and others who don't. To most people the things happen that go with them."

She is right, thought Maria Tarnovska, and remembered the teacher in the Vienna prison. With how many women she had spoken since then! With murderesses, thieves, burglars, and with a few who had been innocent. She had learned something from every one.

"If you take any pretty trips," said the woman, "send me a postcard. My son collects stamps."

"I'll send you a postcard wherever I go," said Maria Tarnovska. "I promise you."

The woman laughed. "I believe you. You're not bad."

Maria Tarnovska could feel her eyes fill with tears. She cried easily now, quite different than in the past, when she had cried only with rage or joy.

"It isn't at all certain that you will be convicted," she told the woman.

"Oh yes, it is. First of all, it's the sixth time. Here it's just the opposite from outside; the better they know you in the courtroom, the less they like you. And secondly, I fit in here." She looked up at the windows of the prison, behind which the black-ruched hoods of the sisters of Maria Bambina bobbed up and down.

"You must write to me, too," said Maria Tarnovska.

Suddenly she also was sure that they would acquit her. She would never walk in a circle again. Andrey would come and bring Tioka. She would explain to him what she couldn't understand herself, and he would understand it. They would go to Otrada. Otrada would heal the wounds it had inflicted. The smell of the steppes, grass, dust; the sun dial decorated with flowers; the neighing of horses; the jingling of the harness. Kamarovsky, Naumov, Prilukov, Stahl, Tarnovsky—names in a book her father had forbidden her to read.

The nun clapped her hands.

"I'll be thinking of you tomorrow," said the thief.

7

The jury withdraws to confer. At ten, two hours later, they are still out.

Maria Tarnovska, Naumov, and Elise Perrier are sitting together, each separated by a *carabiniere*. Only Prilukov is standing; smiling,

416

chatting with one of his lawyers. He radiates optimism. A little optimism is to be found in every criminal, Maria Tarnovska thinks. Sometimes he looks at her, without hatred, as if he were wooing her. It is all a farce. On the stage we are enemies. Let's meet in the theater café; afterward we'll go up to your bedroom. . . . Maria Tarnovska shivers. If it is going to start all over again, then preferably prison. Everyone in the courtroom can imagine how she has lain in Prilukov's arms, has imagined it a thousand times; only she cannot imagine it.

The jury is still out. Vecchini comes up to her: "A good omen, Countess." He goes away again. At the buffet they are eating sandwiches and drinking red wine. If she is convicted, the lawyers will go home to their wives, or they will dine at a restaurant on the Rialto, *bon appetit!*

The windows are open, as if they want to air the court of the Tarnovska case forever. The clerk has torn off a leaf of the calendar. May 20. The frivolous flies are humming as if it were summer. You can hear the voices of market women bargaining. The cost of a head of lettuce, so important. Maria Tarnovska stands up. Through the window behind her she can see the Canale Grande. Two gondolas almost collide. How interesting, that *gondolieri* should be so adroit. Her stomach seems to shrivel; her heart is pounding in her throat.

At eleven thirty, the court reconvenes. The foreman of the jury— the owner of a shipping line, whom she has never noticed before— gives the verdict. Nicholas Gregorievich Naumov, guilty of murder with express malice prepense; allowing for rational function impaired: unanimous. Elise Perrier, not guilty—nine to five. Countess Maria Nikolaevna Tarnovska, guilty—thirteen to one; allowing for rational function impaired: no—nine to five. Donat Dmitrievich Prilukov, guilty—thirteen to one; allowing for rational function impaired: no— thirteen to one. The answer to the additional question, as to whether his clinical treatment had anything to do with Kamarovsky's death, is yes, unanimously.

The judge pronounces the sentence. Naumov: two and a half years' penitentiary, less the time already served. Elise Perrier, acquitted. Maria Nikolaevna Tarnovska, eight and a half years' penitentiary, less the time already served.

She hears Prilukov's sentence—ten years' penitentiary, less the time already served—as in a dream. As if in a dream, she listens to the argument for the sentence, which follows it. Although the jury rejected Article Forty-seven in the case of Prilukov and the Countess Tarnovska, premeditation of the incitement to murder could not be accepted as proved in either case. Naumov had undoubtedly been influenced to the crime from two sides, but the court decided that it had been originally conceived by Prilukov.

The Countess Tarnovska has sunk down on the bench. Her hat has fallen from her head. It lies in front of her in the narrow aisle between dock and defense lawyers. No one picks it up. Everyone is heading for the exit, walking around the hat. At last Vecchini picks it up and puts it down on the bench. "My child, try to be calm." The voice of her father. She looks up, then sinks down again on the bench, sobbing. The *carabinieri* are waiting. "I shall never forget you, Countess." Elise Perrier. Maria Tarnovska rises, embraces her maid; Elise Perrier strokes her mistress' head. Her smile is like the light music that in the south accompanies the burial of a child. The Countess Tarnovska is crying so vehemently that somebody calls for a doctor. When the doctor approaches, she pulls herself together and straightens up. She picks up her black hat. It is dusty from the floor of the courtroom; now it sits askew on her head. Prilukov holds out his hand to her. She doesn't recognize him, turns away. Naumov bows. She gives him her hand. A deafening roar from outside. "The fire brigade!" someone cries. Is it burning somewhere? A chorus of voices. The crowd cheers. Maria Tarnovska is thinking that Tioka is in Venice, waiting for her. Eight and a half years have eight and a half times three hundred and sixty-five days. Thirty-three and eight made forty-one. As Vecchini leads her from the courtroom, she is wishing that the trial could have lasted forever. Her illusions forever. Only now does she realize that she never doubted her acquittal.

In the doorway of the courthouse, Vecchini stops abruptly. The *carabiniere* hesitate, too. Thousands are waiting outside. They are singing a jeering song, in chorus. A woman screams: "Hang her! Hang her!" The arcades under the courthouse are black with people. They are sitting on the steps, on empty orange crates; they are watching from the windows of *palazzi;* they are waiting in gondolas. "Throw her in the water," the thin voice of a child cries. Hundreds shout "Bravo!" A *vaporetta* sails by slowly, hundreds of people at its railing. Oranges are flying through the air; the fruit splashes against gates and walls. Maria Tarnovska recognizes a few faces.

She has seen them every day for three months. They have not become more human. "Look out, Countess, be careful," somebody at her side says. It is the journalist with the horn-rimmed spectacles. She remembers the day she saw him for the first time in the hotel lobby in Baden-Baden. Alexis was dying. Her mouth twists in a suppressed smile. She will not laugh. She will not cry. She will not be careful.

She tears herself free of Vecchini. Before the *carabiniere* can stop her, she is on the narrow gangplank between courthouse and gondola. Someone close by screeches. A woman laughs. From a motorboat firemen turn a hose on the crowd. Some stand firm, some fall back spluttering, others flee laughing. The water falls on Maria Tarnovska. She doesn't move. It falls on her hat, runs down her hair, her face. Her black dress is wet. A *carabiniere* takes hold of her on the right, Sister Sofia on the left. Soaking wet, she gets into the gondola. She takes off her hat, throws it in the water. For a moment it floats on the surface, a black wreath, as if cast on the wet grave of someone who died at sea. Sister Sofia wipes Maria Tarnovska's face with her handkerchief. It is only water. Maria Tarnovska is not crying.

8

Summer was at its height when they moved Maria Tarnovska to Trani.

She sat at the window, as she had done when they had taken her from Vienna to Venice. Sister Rosa and two *carabinieri* accompanied her. The curtains over the corridor window were drawn. The local train puffed through the summer afternoon.

Trani. She had never heard the name before. A little town between Barletta and Bari, not far from the canal of Otranto. She had never been farther south than Rome. You went to Italy because the beach at the Lido was tempting, or because you wanted to admire the paintings at the Uffizzi Gallery, or because it was the thing to do on your honeymoon.

The train followed the Adriatic coast. The sea was as blue as the blue on maps, as monotonous and as dead. On maps, the water was always light blue, the mountains were green, the rivers dark blue, the railway lines black. Italy or Russia—the same colors. On maps everything was also very near. You could put your thumb on Trani and your little finger on Kiev. But the maps lied. It was a good thing that at least Otrada wasn't on any map, one lie less. Otrada did not exist. The swing had never swung; the stony boy had never collected snow apples in his basket; the chestnut trees had never rustled in the breeze. Nothing that was so far away had ever existed.

What she saw didn't exist either. Ravenna, Rimini, Riccione. It was the height of the season. Women dressed in white, hotel clerks wearing green aprons, wicker-canopied beach chairs, sunshades, bathing suits. A spark flew in the window and went out on her dress. She brushed off the ash, and it occurred to her that this was a superfluous gesture. She wouldn't be wearing her dresses any more six years from now. They would be wearing different dresses, different hats. Only her prison garb would remain unchanged. Prisons didn't follow the fashions.

Like someone who wanted to hurt himself in order to find out if he was still alive, Maria Tarnovska tried to recall Tioka, her father, Andrey. It didn't hurt. You comforted the dying with the thought that they would live on in the living. But who lived on in the dead?

Pescara, Termoli. The train moved inland as if running away from the tide. It got hotter and hotter. Maria Tarnovska thought of past summers. Lost summers were lost years. The olive groves on either side of the tracks gave no shade. Olive-tree woods were ridiculous woods. Sad, leathern leaves, with the dust thick upon them; the earth was a dusty green, as if covered with olive leaves. The fields were scorched, but the sun was up to burn them again: the sun was killing dead ground. Not a breath of air came in through the half-open window. Maria Tarnovska did not hate the sun, and she didn't hate the stupid houses or the dead earth, either. You couldn't hate anything so strange. Trani. T-r-a-n-i. She would try to remain a stranger, and not hate.

Prayerbook and rosary lay in Sister Rosa's lap. Her snores were competing with the locomotive. The *carabinieri* had opened their collars. It smelled of sweat, sour male sweat. Maria Tarnovska fought her nausea.

In the night, the light remained on. Maria Tarnovska leaned her head against the wood. She slept, sat awake, slept. She was fighting sleep, because she feared the awakening. "Tomorrow morning you'll scream, because the worst thing is to wake up to misery," the teacher in the Vienna prison had said. They were wise, the women in prison. With every waking hour you grew more accustomed to death; with every sleeping hour you came closer to life.

420

In the morning, the train stopped in Trani. In front of the station stood a small nun in black and white, like a penguin. Maria Tarnovska looked for a carriage. The nun pointed straight ahead. There, by the monument. They began to walk, the two nuns, the two *carabinieri,* the prisoner.

The street was empty. An avenue of oleanders, straight as a die, led to the sea, where the prison stood. The oleander trees looked as if they were planted in pots; their pointed leaves hung limp, their pink blossoms had fallen. Trani. T-r-a-n-i. Maria Tarnovska could think of only one color. White. Trani was white. The houses were painted white and the Via Cavour was white with dust and the statue was white and the oleander trees were white, and the sky was white, too. Not a breath of morning air. In the night the sun had besieged Trani, now it took the city. Its inhabitants had fled. Or they were dead. A smell of fish hung over the town, a cadaverous odor.

They came to a big white square. The nun from Trani touched Maria Tarnovska's arm. To the right she saw a large building, one story high, sprawling, white. The windows were barred, but over the bars, blinds had been pulled down. Even the convicts had to be protected from the sun; perhaps the sun was not a part of their punishment.

"You may enter the church," said the nun.

The church was adjacent to the prison. Chiesa di S. Domenico e della Madonna del Rosario. The nuns and the *carabinieri* remained standing beside the holy water font. Slowly, Maria Tarnovska walked up to the altar.

It was like a poor village church. The saints stood in glass cases. They were made of the same material as dolls. They were as pink, as gay, as expressionless as dolls. They were childish and eerie. The Madonna under glass had on a blue-white dress embroidered in gold. A small plaque said that prisoners had sewn it. The prisoners sewed bridal dresses for holy dolls. Under glass, Saint Dominic; in his hands, the book of the preacher, the white lily; at his feet, a dog with a burning torch in its mouth; just as the saint had appeared to his mother in a dream. The lily looked like a withered swamp plant; the dog seemed to be gnawing on a meager bone. Heavy locks were attached to the glass cases. They seemed to be afraid here that the saints might escape, or that the prisoners might steal them. In front of the imprisoned saint, she knelt, because she knew her wardens were expecting it of her. She couldn't think of any prayer but the Lord's Prayer. "And forgive us our trespasses as we forgive those who trespass against us." But as she prayed, she thought that she was no longer guilty, for the people had taken justice out of God's hands. She didn't have to ask forgiveness of anyone, nor forgive anyone. As she walked back through the church, she had the feeling that the dolls behind glass were laughing at her; the prisoners behind glass, the woman behind bars.

"*Istituto de Pena per Donne Trani*" stood over the door. Maria Tarnovska leaned against the wall. Recalcitrant criminals are ridiculous, she thought, yet she was overwhelmed by an angry despair, a thousand despairs, pressing in upon her from all sides. She was standing at the gates of hell and was not dead. She wanted to scream, protest, run away. The *carabinieri* would draw their little pistols and fire. She would lie on the white asphalt, and her blood would dye it red, as Alexis' blood had dyed the snow red in front of the Eremitage. Suddenly it was all there again—the music coming from the restaurant, Yuri's *dacha,* Mademoiselle Larue, the room in the pension in Vienna. And Russia and the snow and the clear air of Kiev. But she didn't cry; she didn't protest; she didn't run away.

Four or five nuns received her. A fat nun, wearing thick glasses, put something down in a fat ledger. Countess Maria Nikolaevna Tarnovska, née Countess O'Rourke. She should not have said the name, because of the old man. Born June 19, 1877, in Otrada, near Kiev, Province of Poltava. It was a lie—her birth, and Otrada. Married. Marriage annulled. Two children. Whom was she talking about?

A nun led her to a bathroom. The window was barred, the blind down. She let her clothes fall onto the wet, wooden floor; her silk petticoat, her silk drawers. The nun looked out the window. She didn't pick up Maria's clothes; Maria did not pick them up, either. When she got out of the bath, the nun handed her something that looked like a white-and-brown striped sack.

CHAPTER 4

A year later, on the twelfth of August, 1911, Father Andrey walked away from the station of Trani.

He had returned from North Africa in April. The Church knew the meaning of punishment, but did not hold previous punishment against the repentant. The Order had taken him in again, as if it knew nothing of his transgression.

A few weeks later, the Master General had ordered Andrey to appear before him. The Master General had been ill; death had held him by the hand; soon the Council would choose a new Master General. He had been thinking a great deal, he said, more perhaps than Father Andrey. And because he had thought a great deal and consequently had discarded much of what he had thought before; and because fanaticism was strange material, out of which not only sinners were made; and because you could read in John: "To this end the Son of God appeared that he might destroy the works of the devil"; and because punishment would be meaningless if the man punished remained the same as before; and because no one should depart this life without at least having freed one of those who "throughout their life were kept in servitude"—therefore, then, Father Andrey should proceed to Trani to see if he could complete the work he had begun, and had had to interrupt through his transgression. Not until he saw Andrey hesitate did the Master General say more. Ten months ago, the Countess Tarnovska had begun to write letters to the Order, one every month. Six months ago, the Master General had told a traveling friar to visit the prisoner. The Prior's report had moved the Master General to send Andrey to Trani. More the Master General did not say, and he had not seemed to hear any further questions put to him by Andrey.

Andrey was expected at the women's penitentiary at noon. It was still early. He walked along the oleander avenue, through the scorched town that was like an island of the damned. Because of the heat, most shades were down, and the few tradespeople, sitting in the shade, looked like convicts during a recess. A carriage, closed, as if even strangers were reluctant to show their faces, rolled across the soft asphalt. A convict, handcuffed, was being led from the station, down the Via Cavour. No one paid any attention to him. Andrey followed the man. The squares were so wide, it was as if the houses had moved back, seeking coolness in their own shade. A square of smooth stone looked like a ballroom. It was empty. Someone had cried "Plague!" and the dancers had fled. Fishing nets hung like withered grapevines along the shore; not a fisherman in sight. The men's prison was a fortress with wall and moat, towering into the present from the Middle Ages. Like the women's prison, it was situated on a promontory; from here you could see the women's prison. They thought they could see each other, the men and the women. Everything was white. In some places in the south, white was the color of grief. Andrey turned around.

Next to the women's prison, a large park with fountains, terra-cotta vases, statues, a bandstand, its chairs and music stands leaning against each other. On Sunday the inhabitants of Trani went for walks under the windows of the prison. The grass in the sun was singed; the grass in the shadows of the pines was black. The walls of the park fell down sheerly to the sea. Angrily, the waves pounded against them. Andrey looked up at the prison and thought that Maria must hear the pounding of the waves day and night. He thought of Russia, of the snow, the chestnut trees of Otrada. The wind was playing in the stubborn leaves of the palms like a child that had undertaken a too-difficult task. Andrey would have liked to cry out to fate, "Enough! Enough!"

He was told to wait in the cool stone hall. A glass case stood next to the door of the waiting room, with all sorts of primitive objects in it, things made by the prisoners: Venetian gondolas of braided straw; Madonnas embroidered in blue; a circus horse made of silk cord, with a violet saddle and glittering hooves.

He was led into a small waiting room. The windows were not barred; the green shutters stood half open. Andrey looked down at the endless, bleak stone shore. Why had the Master General sent him here? The thought that Maria might be planning to take the veil after serving her sentence made him feel uneasy. But the Master General could not have sent him because of that: he was the last to guide her hand. So why? To complete his work? What work? He had been punished because he thought he had recognized the Devil in Maria Tarnovska. Under his very eyes, the Devil had completed his work. Had the Master General sent him to comfort Maria? Any stranger could do it better. It was hard not to doubt the old man's decision.

Maria entered the room. She was wearing a wide convict's uniform, brown and white striped. She looked younger and thinner than Andrey remembered her. Her dark blond hair fell in one long braid down her back; that was what made her look so young.

She thanked him for coming. "When did you see Tioka last?" she asked.

"Immediately upon my return. He was in Rome with your father."

They spoke about Tioka. She had very little to say and seemed absent-minded, as if she were thinking about something she wanted to say. When he asked her about her life, she smiled. "In the old days, at the beginning of every year, I used to make up my mind to keep a diary. Sometimes I managed to keep it until March, sometimes to April. Then life became too rich. Here I used to count the days. I don't any more."

Finally she interrupted him in the middle of a sentence, sat down, and began to speak.

"Something has happened to me that you must know." The newspapers, so she had been told, had reported her conversion. He should not worry; it was not that. She had not grown more religious than she had been before; at best, she was ashamed now of a piety that had not existed. She had written to the Order because she had not heard from Tioka for a long time. Then, one day, Father Anselm appeared. And he had told her why Andrey had been sent to Africa. "I didn't know whether he had been sent to tell me about your punishment, or whether I drew it out of him."

She wet her lips, passed a hand across her forehead.

She had had much time to think, she went on. Now she was sure someone had ordered Father Anselm to tell her everything. Because when the Father was done, when she knew that Andrey had been punished even before the court had condemned her; that she had corrupted him from behind prison walls; that he had done what he had done in order to drive the Devil out of her, and had had to atone for it—then it was as if the Devil had truly gone out of her. "It did not take place with thunder and lightning, or a pestilential stench, and I didn't writhe like a witch, either. It just suddenly became still around me, Andrey."

Now she spoke excitedly, as if afraid he might not understand her. "It was not my sickness going from me, or whatever you want to call it." His suffering had not filled her with passion. It was the contrary. "For the first time in my life I felt pain because of the pain of another, perhaps more violently than you felt it."

She rose, walked to the window, sat down again. Andrey forgot where they were, that there was little time, that neither of them was innocent any more. The walls of the room widened; a cool sun strode through the blinds; the sea rustled like the chestnut trees in Otrada.

"It isn't the prison," she said. No one could improve here. You could only survive such punishment by playing dead, and the dead knew nothing of good or evil. As far as she was concerned, her punishment had exhausted but not improved her, so that when Father Anselm had appeared, she had been in a condition of absolute apathy. "But then everything changed. Not suddenly, as if by a miracle, but slowly, gradually. The word '*Veritas*' is carved in the stone tiles of the prison church. I thought about it every day. It could have been written anywhere else; I told you—one doesn't become religious here. Now I know when I began to understand it. When you told me that for Tioka you had broken your vow. When you came to see me in Venice for the first time. But mistrust soon concealed my gratitude. I asked myself why you had done it, and gave myself the old answer. Then my father came to Venice, and Terrible O'Rourke was transformed before my eyes. I know what the psychiatrists would say to that, but it did not happen because of the psychiatrists, and not because of the sentence, perhaps not even because of you. Anyway, you knew nothing about it. I found out that someone loved me, and what Father Anselm told me proved it." She went on more quietly. "After my arrest in Vienna, my first thought was, 'Call Andrey!' I had often cried out to you before, and often I hadn't known why. Sometimes you came, more often you didn't. And when you left me, I didn't know that you loved me, because I was looking for a false love. But when you were a thousand miles away—I in prison, you in exile—then I knew that you loved me, and that one day I would be able to say it without meaning anything else but love."

She was trying desperately to make herself understood, although he had understood her long ago. "Since you love me, you must be suffering because of what has happened to me," she said. "That is why I am glad you came. I don't want you to suffer."

An hour later Andrey walked toward the white station. The heat lay over Trani like the hand of a giant. A few convicts were coming back from work. The people looked as if they had guilty consciences, and the station looked as if trains arrived there but never left. Andrey thought of the woman behind the walls of the prison by the sea, and wished he could remember her like this always: standing erect, smiling, the bliss of salvation in her eyes, and so young, as if none of the years had been lost. He thought of Sergey Burintzev, his own youth, Shitomir, the day he had gone to help Sergey, and instead Sergey had pressed him to his heart. He didn't know whether he had driven the Devil out of Maria; he didn't dare to believe it. He didn't know if Maria was free and would remain free. Five years were a long time; the waves broke against the walls of Trani, and prison walls were not safe walls. He did not know if he had had a mission and had fulfilled it, or if the mission had been fulfilled in spite of his mistakes. He did not know what would be waiting for Maria in five years at the gates of Trani: hatred and bitterness; anger and disappointment; revenge and pain, the enemy of love; or remorse and innocence, and, in their wake, the blind singer—hope. He knew only that the Prince of the World had no more power over Maria Tarnovska, and that she had found the crossroad where, beside many signs pointing the wrong way, there is one that points the way.

Epilogue

When a novelist writes the word "End" at the conclusion of a novel, he commits an arbitrary act. Neither life itself nor the lives of his other characters end when the life of his hero or heroine has come to an end.

This is particularly valid for what is called a "true story." Maria Tarnovska's life did not end in the penitentiary. Some of my readers may ask what fate had in store for her when she left the prison walls of Trani. It is, however, a question difficult to answer.

Although the life of the Countess went on after the heavy door of Trani prison opened, she had died long ago for a public interested only in the more outward phenomena of crime and punishment. When she was freed by a royal amnesty in 1915, only a half year before her full sentence would have elapsed, the interest of the public, which had known no greater interest five years before, had faded away. The pages of the newspapers, once filled with the Tarnovska trial, were now occupied with a greater tragedy: World War I had exploded. Once more, personal drama was submerged in the helplessness of common fate. Only a few lines reported the end of an affair.

I have searched in vain for more authentic material about the "future" of the Countess. I can only say with certainty that she did not return to Russia. Her father was dead. Russia was at the doorstep of a revolution, one that Maria Tarnovska had not caused, but to which "the Tarnovskas" had contributed as much as some of the more modern "Tarnovskas" contribute to the crisis of our present society. According to certain sensational newspapers, she went to England, where she became the wife of a nobleman and died many years later as a respected member of society. I am rather inclined to believe other sources, stating that she went from Trani to Brazil, where she died soon afterward. This is supported by the fact that Count Tarnovskys still live in Brazil. They are probably descendants of Maria's son, Tioka. To my inquiries I received no answer.

Naumov, her youthful victim, did not return to Russia, either. He left Venice for Switzerland, where he lived until his early death. Prilukov, on the other hand, died during the time of his sentence. Viennese newspapers reported that he had committed suicide.

From time to time witnesses of this *"cause célèbre"* emerge from the past. When I was lecturing in Berlin in May 1963, a very old man came to me, giving his name as Alexander Andreyevsky. His father, a prominent Russian lawyer, had defended Vassily Tarnovsky when Maria's husband was accused of killing her lover, Alexis. The Tarnovsky case was an unforgettable part of the old man's own childhood.

For reasons that the reader will comprehend, I cannot answer the question of what happened to Father Andrey. For me, he is still alive.

H. H.